MURDER AT
THE SAVOY

By Jim Eldridge

HOTEL MYSTERIES SERIES
Murder at the Ritz
Murder at the Savoy
Murder at Claridge's

MUSEUM MYSTERIES SERIES
Murder at the Fitzwilliam
Murder at the British Museum
Murder at the Ashmolean
Murder at the Manchester Museum
Murder at the Natural History Museum
Murder at Madame Tussauds
Murder at the National Gallery

a&b

MURDER AT
THE SAVOY

JIM ELDRIDGE

Allison & Busby Limited
11 Wardour Mews
London W1F 8AN
allisonandbusby.com

First published in Great Britain by Allison & Busby in 2021.
This paperback edition published by Allison & Busby in 2022.

A CIP catalogue record for this book is available from
the British Library.

10 9 8 7 6 5 4 3 2 1

ISBN 978-0-7490-2716-2

Typeset in 10.5/15.5 pt Sabon LT Pro by
Allison & Busby Ltd.

FSC
www.fsc.org

MIX
Paper from
responsible sources
FSC® C171272

Printed and bound by
CPI Group (UK) Ltd, Croydon, CR0 4YY

For Lynne, and she knows why

CHAPTER ONE

Saturday 14th September 1940, London

The wail of air raid sirens filled the air. On the pavement outside the Savoy hotel an angry crowd of about fifty people shouted, demanding to be let in, but found their way barred by the giant figure of the doorman, Lund Hansen, resplendent in his uniform of deep blue, his long overcoat decorated with brass buttons that shone even in the blackout.

'Let us in!' shouted a small pugnacious man who seemed to be the crowd's self-appointed leader. He waved his arms towards the people behind him. 'Look at us! We are the poor!'

Hansen looked. There were men, most of them shabbily dressed, many women, some of whom looked to be pregnant, and children.

'We are dying!' shouted the man. 'We have nowhere to be safe. While you and that lot in there—' and he jabbed his index finger angrily towards the doors of the Savoy 'stay safe deep underground, on beds with silk sheets and with the best food and wines!' And he produced a page torn from a newspaper, an advert extolling the virtues of the air raid shelter deep beneath the Savoy. 'That's what it says here! But we don't need beds with silk sheets. All we ask is the decent right to safety, because we don't have any shelters in Stepney, just surface shelters. All they do is maybe stop shrapnel tearing you to bits, but they won't protect you if a bomb comes down on top of it, or too near. Eight days we've suffered this, night after night. There's thousands of us dying in the East End while your lot hide in this expensive hole in the ground under this hotel. Well, we want some of that safety. We deserve it! Aren't we human beings, too, the same as them? Or aren't we worth as much because we're poor?'

'Let us in!' some of the crowd shouted, and soon other voices joined in so that it became a chant. 'Let us in! Let us in!'

At the back of the crowd the two police constables who'd been on duty outside the Savoy when the protestors had arrived had now been joined by more uniformed police, some of whom had drawn their truncheons, obviously intending to disperse the protestors by force if necessary.

The door of the Savoy opened and a tall man immaculately dressed in a frock coat, striped trousers and gleaming white shirt and black tie stepped out, and surveyed the crowd with an imperious gaze under which the crowd fell silent, as the majority of people did when confronted with the hard penetrating stare of Willy Hofflin, the Savoy's assistant manager. Hofflin turned to the doorman.

'What is occurring here, Mr Hansen?' he demanded in his clipped Swiss accent.

It was the small man who spoke up, having recovered his voice.

'We are the poor!' he said. 'We've come all the way from Stepney in the East End because we have no shelter to hide in when the bombs come down on us. They won't let us into the Tube stations, where we'd be safe. There's nowhere but surface shelters, which fall down when they're hit by bombs and kill everyone in them. It's been this way for eight days and nights.' Once again he waved the advertisement from the newspaper, this time at the assistant manager. 'Yet you boast of having the strongest underground shelter in London here at the Savoy, with every luxury. We only want one luxury – to stay alive when the bombs fall. And that shouldn't be a luxury! It should be the right of everyone to be able to get shelter, not just the rich.'

And the small man glared at the tall Swiss, challengingly. Hofflin returned his stare, then nodded and turned to the doorman. 'There is no reason why these people should not have the same shelter as the Savoy's guests. Let them in.'

With that, he stepped to one side. Lund Hansen pulled open the main entrance door.

At first, the crowd stared, bewildered; this was not what they had expected. Then suddenly a cheer went up, starting at the back of the crowd and echoing around the rest, and the small man stepped forward, leading the way for his comrades into the pristine, luxurious Savoy hotel.

In Hampstead, the corrugated iron Anderson shelter half-buried in the garden of the small block of flats shuddered but held solid as the bombs fell.

Seven people were crammed into the shelter: Detective Chief Inspector Coburg and his wife, Rosa, Eric and Norma Henderson, Peter and Dorothy Watts, and widower Walter Marsden.

Those bombs were a bit too close, thought Coburg, pulling Rosa close to him in a hug he hoped was reassuring. She nestled into his shoulder.

'It'll be fine,' she whispered. 'The thick layer of earth on top of this thing is doing its job.'

Who's reassuring who, thought Coburg. That was one of the things he loved about Rosa, her apparent fearlessness. Not that she didn't get scared. She'd told him that when she first began appearing in public as a singer she sometimes used to vomit in her dressing room as the result of nerves, before composing herself and walking out to her piano and the waiting audience. Even here in this tiny, cramped air raid shelter, seven days into the Blitz, as the intensive bombing night after night by the Germans was being called, she hid whatever fear she may have felt, doing her best to appear calm.

DCI Coburg – or, to give him his full title, the Hon. Edgar Walter Septimus Saxe-Coburg – and Rosa Weeks, the celebrated jazz singer, had been married just two weeks before at Hampstead Registry Office. A very simple ceremony, no families in attendance, just Coburg's detective sergeant Ted Lampson, as his best man, and Maisie Oxley, a fellow musician friend of Rosa's who played saxophone in Ivy Benson's all-girl big band witnessing for Rosa. Rosa's family were in Edinburgh and both Edgar and Rosa felt it was too dangerous for them to travel to London while the bombing continued, especially as the main railway lines seemed to be a major target for the Luftwaffe, and Edgar had decided against involving his elder brother, Magnus, the Earl of Dawlish, because he was sure that Magnus would insist on the wedding being held at the family's ancestral home, Dawlish Hall, and that would only lead to rows as Edgar and Rosa both wanted a quiet occasion.

The Anderson shelter shook again as another bomb struck nearby and there was the sound of rubble crashing down on the protective earth covering of the corrugated iron roof, causing the occupants of the shelter to exchange nervous looks.

'They should open the Tube stations as shelters,' scowled Eric Henderson. 'We've got the deepest in the whole system here at Hampstead station. What is it? Two hundred and fifty feet deep?'

'One hundred and ninety-two feet,' said Walter Marsden quietly, adding an apologetic smile to take the edge off correcting his neighbour. 'I work for London Underground,' he explained.

'Then why don't you get them to open the stations during air raids?' demanded Henderson.

'It's not my decision,' said Marsden. 'That's down to

the Government, and I get the impression they're worried that if they do, the whole mass of London will disappear down them and remain there.'

'Nonsense!' snorted Henderson.

'Eric's right,' said Norma Henderson, backing her husband up as she usually did. 'It's all right for those in Government; they've got all those places all along Whitehall they can hide in.'

'I've been told that Winston still goes to his country home in Kent, Chartwell, and sits on his roof watching when there's an air raid,' put in Dorothy Watts.

'That's because the Germans aren't bombing Chartwell!' Henderson snorted. 'He knows he's safe there.'

'I hardly think so,' said Peter Watts thoughtfully. 'After all, Chartwell's not far from Biggin Hill, and that whole area is still taking a battering.'

The shelterers fell into thoughtful silence at this reminder of the Battle of Britain that was still taking place. The airfields of Kent and Sussex being bombed during the day; London and the other major cities bombed at night.

'What do you think, Mr Coburg?' asked Dorothy Watts. 'What's the word from inside Scotland Yard? What can we expect?'

'I'm afraid I'm the wrong person to ask, Mrs Watts,' replied Coburg ruefully. 'I'm just a humble detective inspector.'

'Humble?' scoffed Henderson. 'Don't you have a brother who's high up in the War Office or something? Lord Whatsisname?'

'My brother Magnus is the Earl of Dawlish, but he

doesn't work for the Government,' said Coburg. 'It was my other brother, Charles, who used to work for the War Office but he re-enlisted in the army when war broke out. He was taken prisoner at Dunkirk and is currently in a German prisoner-of-war camp.'

'How awful for you,' Dorothy Watts shuddered.

'Rather worse for Charles, I feel,' said Coburg.

Norma Henderson turned towards Rosa and enquired, intrigued: 'Pardon me for asking, Mrs Coburg, but aren't you Rosa Weeks, the singer? I'm sure I recognise you from when Eric and I saw you at the Ritz about a month ago.'

'Yes, that's me,' said Rosa.

'You were wonderful!' beamed Dorothy. 'Wasn't she, Eric?'

'Yes. Very good,' said Henderson, but reluctantly as if it wasn't the done thing to throw compliments around.

Dorothy gestured towards the plaster cast that adorned Rosa's left arm.

'Bomb damage?' she asked.

'Dorothy, really!' her husband rebuked her.

'That's all right,' said Rosa. 'No, an accident, I'm afraid.'

'Difficult to play the piano, though,' said Dorothy sympathetically.

'Dorothy!' repeated her husband, sharper this time.

'Honestly, I'm not offended, Mr Henderson,' said Rosa. 'Your wife is just being caring. The answer's yes, it does make it difficult to play, but I can vamp the bass notes to a degree. And the plaster cast will be coming off very shortly and I hope I'll soon be able to get back to normal.'

Another heavy shower of rubble rained down on the roof of the shelter, this more sustained, and the occupants once again exchanged concerned looks.

'I think it's going to take a long time for any of this to feel normal,' sighed Marsden.

CHAPTER TWO

Sunday 15th September 1940

The all-clear was sounding as dawn broke and the centre of London slowly came back to life. At the Savoy the crowd of people who'd sought shelter there the previous night were making their way out, most of them still stunned at the opulence of the basement shelter, and their talk was of the beds and the sheets and the tea and toast and jams they'd been given for breakfast. Even though they'd been in a separate area curtained off from the night quarters of the Savoy's paying guests, none of them had ever experienced such surroundings, except those few who'd worked as maids in some of London's grand houses in Belgravia or Kensington. But even they had to admit they'd never known such luxury.

The short man who'd led the crowd the night before stopped beside the same tall doorman who'd been on duty the previous evening, Lund Hansen, and asked: 'Excuse me, but who was that gentleman who allowed us in last night?'

'That was Mr Hofflin, the assistant manager,' responded Hansen.

'Would you tell him how much we appreciated what he did for us? Treating us like proper people.'

'I will,' said Hansen.

'And can you tell him that Tom Huxton – that's me – said if he's ever Stepney way, there'll be a drink or two for him behind the bar at the Bull and Bush, on me.'

'I'll tell him that as well,' said Hansen.

'Thank you,' said Huxton. He turned to the young woman waiting for him, his 18-year-old daughter, who was standing with a young man of about the same age. 'Come on, Jenny. Time to go home.'

Inside the Savoy, Willy Hofflin stood at the entrance to the restaurant and, with mixed feelings, watched the last of the crowd leave. On one hand, he felt he'd done a good thing by allowing them to stay the night in the Savoy's shelter, especially the children and the women who were pregnant. But he was apprehensive of what Mr D'Oyly Carte would say when he discovered what he'd done, especially without consulting the general manager, Charles Tillesley. But Mr Tillesley had been at home, where there was no telephone, and Hofflin, as his deputy, had been in charge. As far as Hofflin had been concerned, the reputation of the Savoy had been at stake. If the visitors had turned violent and there had been a riot, children and pregnant women would certainly have been injured when the police moved in wielding their truncheons.

'Excuse me, Mr Hofflin.'

Hofflin turned and found one of the waiters from the basement shelter standing behind him.

'Yes, Sando,' he said.

'I'm afraid there's been a tragedy in the shelter.'

'What sort of tragedy?'

The man swallowed nervously, before whispering: 'The Earl of Lancaster has been stabbed. Murdered.'

In Hampstead, Coburg and Rosa, along with the other residents of the block, left the damp, dark confines of the Anderson shelter and returned to their flat. The phone was ringing as they opened the door.

'I bet that's my parents checking to make sure we're OK,' said Rosa. She picked up the phone. 'Mrs Rosa Coburg,' she said with a smile at Coburg. Then the smile vanished and she said, rather more formally: 'Yes, certainly. He's here.' She held out the phone to Coburg. 'It's a Mr Rupert D'Oyly Carte from the Savoy Hotel.'

Coburg took the phone from her.

'Edgar Coburg,' he said.

'Chief Inspector Coburg,' said D'Oyly Carte, 'I apologise for troubling you so early on a Sunday morning. I got your telephone number from your brother, Magnus. He's often been a guest here at the Savoy.'

'How can I help you?' asked Coburg.

'I'm afraid there's been a murder in the hotel's air raid shelter in the basement. The Earl of Lancaster appears to have been stabbed to death. It's a very delicate situation and I'd be most grateful if you would come.'

'Certainly,' said Coburg. 'I'll be with you shortly.'

He hung up and looked at Rosa. 'There's been a murder at the Savoy.'

'Yes, I heard,' said Rosa. 'D'Oyly Carte? As in the Gilbert and Sullivan operas?'

'That was his father, Richard,' said Coburg. 'But the answer's yes, because Rupert inherited the Savoy Hotel from his stepmother.'

'Your family knows some very rich people,' observed Rosa.

'Magnus moves in different social circles from me,' said Coburg. 'I'm afraid I have to go. I'll have breakfast when I get back, but don't wait for me. You must be hungry.'

'I am,' said Rosa. 'I'll do some toast to keep me going until you return. Are you going to pick up Sergeant Lampson?'

'No. It's Sunday and he doesn't get to spend much time with his son. I'll just go to the Savoy and see what the situation is, and I'll bring Ted in if I need to.' He pulled her to him and kissed her. 'I'm sorry about this,' he apologised. 'It's one of the drawbacks of being married to a police officer.'

'I forgive you,' she said. 'In your case, the benefits outweigh any drawbacks. I wouldn't have it any other way.'

When Coburg walked through the main entrance of the Savoy, the first person he saw was Inspector Arnold Lomax from the Strand police station, standing by the reception desk. So, I've been pre-empted, he thought ruefully. And by someone who hates my guts.

There was no mistaking the undisguised anger in Lomax as he saw Coburg. The inspector was a short, thin man in his early fifties with a sallow complexion, whose well-worn clothes – the faded, pale grey suits he habitually wore – always looked as if they were made for someone larger. His thinning hair was stuck down with grease, and Coburg was fairly sure he greased his thin moustache as well. Lomax's face twisted into a snarl as he saw Coburg.

'What the hell are you doing here, Coburg?' he demanded angrily.

'I had a telephone call from Rupert D'Oyly Carte, the owner, asking me to come,' said Coburg.

'If it's about the murder, you can go again,' snapped Lomax curtly. 'We received the call at the Strand, so it's my shout.'

Coburg shrugged. 'That suits me,' he said.

He turned to go, and Lomax called after him: 'What, no clever response? No calling for your high and mighty aristocratic pals?'

'It's your shout,' said Coburg. 'I didn't know that. I received a telephone call asking me to come, which I did. I assumed it was all above board, official.'

'Well, it wasn't,' snapped Lomax. 'And just to let you know, the case is as good as wrapped up. We're pretty sure who did it: the Earl of Lancaster's estranged son, William, who was part of the invasion the previous night. I've sent my sergeant to have him picked up and brought in.'

'What invasion?' asked Coburg, puzzled.

'See?' Lomax smiled smugly. 'You don't know everything.'

'What invasion?' repeated Coburg.

'It doesn't matter,' said Lomax. 'You'll find out in due course. In the meantime, I'm in charge of this case and at this moment in time you're just a member of the public. So I'll ask you to leave so I can get on.'

'In that case I'll go home and have some breakfast,' said Coburg.

Lomax walked off, a smug expression on his face, and Coburg headed for the exit, but before he reached it the figure of Charles Tillesley, the Savoy's general manager, came hurrying to block his path.

'Mr Coburg,' he said. 'I'm so sorry. I heard the scene between you and Inspector Lomax just now . . .'

'There was no scene,' said Coburg. 'I just told him that Mr D'Oyly Carte telephoned me and asked me to call . . .'

'That was my doing,' said Tillesley. 'I'm sorry. I hadn't realised that someone had also informed the hall porter and told him to telephone the local police station.'

'It doesn't matter,' said Coburg. 'The police are on the scene and that's all that matters. And, according to Inspector Lomax, he has the case well under control. He told me he has a suspect who's about to be taken into custody, so I doubt if there's anything I can do to assist. And, as you will have heard, he would prefer it if I wasn't involved. So please pass on my thanks to Mr D'Oyly Carte for his telephone call, but tell him that it seems my services are not required.'

'But they are!' burst out Tillesley. He looked anxiously towards the door through which Lomax had disappeared, then turned back to Coburg, lowering his voice as he hissed urgently: 'The person he accuses.'

'The son of the dead man, the Earl of Lancaster,' said Coburg.

'Lady Lancaster is convinced the inspector's wrong.'

'That's something she'll have to take up with Inspector Lomax,' said Coburg. 'It's his case, not mine.'

'She's attempted to talk to him, but he refuses to listen to her.'

'I'm very sorry, but—' began Coburg.

'Please, Mr Coburg, even if not in your official role, won't you talk to her? Hear what she has to say?'

'Please, Mr Coburg,' said a woman's voice, and Coburg turned to see a tall, elegant woman in her fifties looking at him in appeal, and recognised her from an evening at his brother Magnus's a year or so earlier.

'Lady Lancaster,' said Coburg, with a polite bow of his head.

'I know what you say is correct, that protocol demands that Inspector Lomax is in charge of the case. So be it. I appeal to you not as a police officer, but as a man who I know to be capable of listening and understanding why my son could not have killed my husband.'

Coburg hesitated. I should not even be considering this, he thought to himself. It's not my case. Inspector Lomax is in charge.

The problem for Coburg was that he knew Lomax, and had no respect for him. In Coburg's view, Lomax was lazy, someone who took the easiest and simplest route when carrying out an investigation dismissing nuances or anomalies that didn't fit with his view of a case. The situation was made worse because he and Lomax had a history: on at least two occasions, Coburg had cause to intervene in a case of Lomax's when he knew the inspector to be so dramatically wrong that it could well result in an innocent person going to the gallows. For his part, Lomax made it very clear that he resented Coburg's background of privilege: the son of an earl, and the rumours that, with a name like Saxe-Coburg, he was related to the royal family. As far as Lomax was concerned, those were the reasons that Coburg had advanced in the police force to the position of chief inspector, while Lomax remained just an inspector: the social elite taking care of one of their own, and nothing that Coburg could say in his defence would alter Lomax's view of him.

'Please, Mr Coburg, if you could just spare me five minutes of your time and hear what I have to say.'

'You can use my office,' offered Tillesley, adding his voice to the appeal.

'Very well,' said Coburg. 'But unfortunately, Lady Lancaster, I doubt if it will change the situation. As a police officer, I'm bound by the rules. I can listen to you, but I cannot intervene.'

'Just to talk to you will ease my heart,' she said.

Edgar, Coburg mentally chastised himself as he followed Lady Lancaster and Tillesley towards the general manager's office, *you're too soft for your own good.*

CHAPTER THREE

'Inspector Lomax mentioned an invasion last night,' said Coburg as they mounted the carpeted stairs to the first floor where the general manager's office was situated.

'Yes. About forty people from Stepney, I believe,' said Tillesley. 'They'd seen our advertisement about the air raid shelter in our basement. The board had suggested putting it in the newspapers. So many people are fleeing London with this dreadful Blitz that it was felt it would be a good idea to reassure our patrons that if they stayed at the Savoy they would be able to do so in complete safety.'

'Yes, I saw the advert in *The Times*,' said Coburg. 'It also emphasised the luxurious aspect of the shelter, which might have aroused strong feelings in some sections of society.'

'That does seem to be the case,' said Tillesley, a tone of regret in his voice. 'That wasn't the intention, of course; the last thing we wanted was to stir up social antipathy towards the hotel. It was just to reassure prospective guests that they would receive the same standard of service and hospitality they've been used to at the Savoy, that there would be no lowering of standards just because of the bombing. Sadly, it seemed to anger the people who arrived last night.'

'You weren't here?'

'No, I was at home. My assistant manager, Willy Hofflin, was in charge, and he took the decision to allow them in. A decision which I endorse, especially after he explained his reasons to me. To protect the Savoy's reputation.'

'And was your son one of these invaders, Lady Lancaster?' asked Coburg.

'Yes, he has been living in Stepney for the past six months, ever since he left home. He said he wanted to live with the ordinary people. It angered his father very much. On reflection, I feel that may have been why William did it.'

'Here we are. This is my office,' said Tillesley. 'I'll leave you to talk.' And he pushed open the door for them.

'Thank you, Mr Tillesley,' said Lady Lancaster. 'You've been very kind.'

Coburg followed her into the general manager's office. He had been here once before, a couple of years previously, when there'd been a problem with a member of some foreign royal family – Coburg couldn't remember which – who'd woken up to find the prostitute he'd hired for the night had died in the bed next to him. Suspicions had been aroused by a number of livid bruises on her body. As it turned out the foreign royal was innocent of any brutality, the bruises had been inflicted by an earlier client, and the prostitute had died as the result of an accidental drug overdose. But

24

the fact that the case had been dealt with, without any publicity, had earned Coburg the gratitude of Mr D'Oyly Carte and the board of the hotel, with the offer of a room any time he wanted it. It was an offer he had never taken up, feeling that it was a step on the path to accepting other gifts and bribes. I'm too much of a puritan, he'd decided somewhat ruefully at the time. And he still was.

Lady Lancaster and he sat down in two of the comfortable leather armchairs that furnished the room, along with Tillesley's desk and high-backed chair.

'I haven't offered my condolences for the loss of your husband,' apologised Coburg.

'To be honest, Chief Inspector, he was no loss to me, or to William. He was a brute, crude, and if you ask around I'm sure you'll find gossips eager to tell you about his affairs with all classes of women, most of whom he treated badly.'

'I'm still sorry,' said Coburg. 'In this case, for the situation you now find yourself in. As I said, I have no jurisdiction in this case; that's being overseen by Inspector Lomax . . .'

'Who is an arrogant oaf with the intelligence of a gnat,' said Lady Lancaster calmly.

Too true, thought Coburg. Aloud he said: 'He is in charge of this case . . .'

'He thinks William killed Hector based solely on the fact that William was here last night in the shelter, and that he was estranged from his father. I get the impression he refuses to consider any other possibility.'

'The investigation has only just started. As far as I know, your son has not yet been taken into custody. I'm sure that when Inspector Lomax looks further into the case he will be open to other options.'

'I'm afraid I don't share your confidence, Chief Inspector . . .'

'Please, Lady Lancaster, as I'm not supposed to be taking part in the enquiry, perhaps we'd better drop my official title for this conversation. Mr Coburg will be more appropriate, if that's all right by you.'

'Mr Coburg.' She nodded. 'I need to tell you about William, in case things go badly once he's taken into custody.'

'Why should they go badly?'

'Unfortunately, because of his poor relationship with his father, William has developed a rather antagonistic relationship with authority.'

'And this will not go down well with Inspector Lomax,' said Coburg.

'No. The inspector will not be sympathetic to him. I'm afraid it will only make him even more determined to find a case against him. But the truth is, Mr Coburg, that beneath William's rather hostile attitude towards authority figures, he is a gentle soul. He is incapable of violence. That's why he registered as a conscientious objector, refusing to be called up. And he's a vegetarian, opposed to all forms of blood sports. It's unthinkable that he would do something like this to anyone, let alone his father.' She leant forward towards him, her expression urgent and imploring. 'He needs someone on the inside to speak for him. Won't you at least ask Inspector Lomax if he will let you talk to William? I'm sure William will talk openly and honestly to you, whereas with Inspector Lomax he will be . . .'

She struggled for words, and Coburg suggested: 'Defensive, aggressive, and possibly insulting?'

She nodded. 'Yes. You see, already you understand.'

'I do, and I sympathise, but the situation is still the same. I have no power in this case.'

'But you are a chief inspector, while Mr Lomax is merely an inspector.'

'I would strongly advise against using words like "merely" when talking about Mr Lomax. It would only antagonise him further.'

'You mean he's already antagonised? Prejudiced against William?'

'Inspector Lomax has his own views of the upper ranks of society.'

'He doesn't like us. That's why he refused to talk to me.'

'I doubt if it was an actual refusal. I expect he was preoccupied with acting on the initial information he had. He will talk to you.'

'But will he listen sympathetically to what I have to say?'

'I believe him to be sincere, despite his rather abrupt manner. I'm sure he will do his best to look into this case dispassionately, regardless of how your son acts towards him. After all, he is an inspector with a long experience in the police force.' He stood up and added earnestly: 'Your son will not be charged on prejudice, only if there is real hard evidence against him. If there is none, he will be freed.'

But inside, he thought unhappily: If only that were true.

* * *

'You're back quicker than I expected,' said Rosa as Coburg entered their flat.

'It turns out that my presence wasn't required after all,' said Coburg. 'The local police station had also been informed and they've taken it on.'

'They took long enough to tell you,' commented Rosa.

'It wasn't that straightforward. The inspector who's in charge is not someone I'm fond of, nor him of me, so we had a bit of a discussion.'

'A row?'

'Not from my perspective. I told him I was happy to leave everything to him. But then, as I was leaving I was collared by the dead man's widow, Lady Lancaster, along with the manager of the Savoy, asking me to take over the investigation. I made the point that I couldn't, that protocol was laid down: the case belongs to the first officer on the scene in an official capacity. And as I'd been asked to call in as a favour by Rupert D'Oyly Carte, my presence wasn't officially sanctioned.'

'Why did they want you to be in charge of it and not this other inspector?'

'Because Inspector Lomax, the man in charge, has arrested Lady Lancaster's son and she insists he's innocent.'

'Is he?'

'I have no idea, and it's not my case. So I suggest we head off somewhere, out of London. If the Germans mount another daylight raid, I don't fancy spending the whole day stuck in that Anderson shelter.'

'Me neither,' said Rosa. 'I mean, our neighbours are nice enough people . . .'

'Now you're just being polite,' said Coburg. 'Eric Henderson is one of the most boring and irritating people I've ever met. The idea of having to endure hour after hour of him . . .'

Rosa laughed. 'So where shall we go? Where isn't being bombed?'

'I suggest we head northwest. Buckinghamshire. In particular, Chesham Bois. It's in the Chilterns, and there's no reason for the Germans to bomb it. There's nothing there except a lovely little village, halfway between Amersham and Chesham. It's far enough out of London, but not too far for me to be accused of excessive use of petrol.'

As they set off in the police car that Coburg had been forced to accept in place of his Bentley, which had been compulsorily garaged as part of Government restrictions on private travel, they saw that the skies above them were filled with German bombers. Harrying them were the British Spitfires and Hurricanes, who also had to contend with the German Messerschmidts protecting the German bomber fleet. More bombers were incoming, and the smaller British fighters buzzed around them like mosquitoes, tracers of bullets from the fighter planes hammering into the giant German bombers, the larger planes returning fire, and as they looked up they saw one of the British planes take a hit and spiral downwards, black smoke pouring from its fuselage. The next second something white appeared, growing larger like a flower suddenly blossoming, and they realised the pilot had parachuted out of his burning aircraft.

'You don't mind us running away?' asked Coburg as he headed for the main road.

'I don't think of it as running away,' said Rosa. 'It's us doing what we can to survive.'

They drove north, and the more distance they put between themselves and London, the clearer the skies became. The roads were almost completely free of traffic, most drivers restricted by petrol rationing, and many people deciding to seek shelter rather than drive. Once they'd left Harrow, Coburg took a route that avoided most of the built-up areas, making first for Rickmansworth and Chorleywood, then rolling down the hill from Amersham into the small, picturesque village of Chesham Bois.

'We're getting some curious looks,' said Rosa.

'It's the car,' said Coburg. 'The sight of a police car always evokes interest, especially in a small place like Chesham Bois. I keep expecting to be stopped by the local constabulary and asked what we're doing here.'

'What will you say if that happens?'

'I'll produce my Metropolitan police warrant card and say we've come to talk to someone who has some information relating to a case we're investigating.'

'And my presence in the car?'

'You're a witness who knows the person we're looking for.'

'It's a lie.'

'Yes, it is, but I'm Detective Chief Inspector at Scotland Yard, so I doubt very much if that will be challenged.'

'And if it is?'

'I'll say we discovered that the person we were looking for is no longer here, but I'm taking the opportunity to remind myself of what a wonderful village Chesham Bois is, and how I spent many happy days here as a child. There's nothing like flattery to disarm people.'

'You can be very devious.'

'It's not a lie. I did spend many happy days here as a child. My brothers and I used to come here as children with our father,' said Coburg. 'An old comrade of our father's lived in the village and we used to listen to them swap stories.'

'A comrade?'

'They served together in the Boer War.' He gave a weary sigh. 'It seems that in recent times the Coburg men have spent a great deal of their time fighting, usually overseas. My father and other relatives during the Boer War. Magnus, myself and Charles during the First War, and now Charles is in a German PoW camp. It would be nice to think we'll be the last having to do this.'

Coburg drove to a spot he remembered from his childhood visits, a wooded area.

'Maybe we should move here,' said Rosa wistfully. 'It's beautiful, and so peaceful.' Then she corrected herself as they looked at the aerial battle still raging, but now many miles away from where they were: 'Relatively peaceful.'

'We have a duty to carry out,' said Coburg. 'Me, keeping the streets safe from crime. You, keeping people's spirits up and – when your arm comes out of plaster – driving an ambulance and saving lives.'

'Yes,' she said with a sigh. She looked around at the pastoral scene. 'It was worth coming out here just to remind ourselves of what we're fighting to preserve.'

They spent the day savouring their surroundings, very

31

aware of what a luxury this time was for them, and how different life was here, not so many miles from London. There were still the signs of war, road signs and fingerposts taken down to hamper the enemy in the event of an invasion – which was expected any time – and sandbags stacked up ready for use if needed. They had lunch at a pub, and Rosa commented that – with rationing – it was a pleasure to see real meat on the menu.

'You're in the country now,' said Coburg. 'There's a lot of meat out there walking around.'

Finally, as the hours ticked past all too quickly, Coburg announced it was time to head home. 'We need to get back before it gets dark and the blackout kicks in,' he said.

The air battles were still going on as they neared the outskirts of London, although there seemed to be fewer German bombers in the sky. As they drove through Neasden they saw that the sky directly ahead of them was thick with black smoke pouring up from the ground, the smoke getting denser and bigger as they drew near to their home.

'Something's been hit,' said Coburg.

'Here in Hampstead?' asked Rosa, bewildered. 'There's no military targets here.'

'The Germans are just bombing everywhere to try to get the civilian population to demand the Government surrender,' said Coburg. 'They even hit Buckingham Palace again on Friday just to show that no one is safe.'

'Yes, I heard it on the news,' said Rosa. 'They said it was the third time the palace had been hit.'

'After the first strike the Government urged the royal

family to leave the country, go to Canada, but they refused.'

'"The children will not leave unless I do",' recited Rosa, recalling the Queen's words in answer. '"I shall not leave unless their father does. And the King will not leave the country in any circumstances whatever." Pretty stirring stuff.'

'It was indeed,' said Coburg. 'Less demonstrative than Churchill's style, but just as powerful.'

They turned the corner into their road, then stopped. Ahead of them, their block of flats had been half-demolished and was burning, the road filled with fire engines, hordes of firemen pouring water on the burning remains of the building from their hoses.

Coburg pulled the car to the side of the road and he and Rosa ran towards the blaze, but were stopped by a civil defence warden who said: 'Sorry, you can't get through.'

'But that's our home,' said Rosa.

Coburg produced his warrant card and held it out to the warden. 'I'm Detective Chief Inspector Coburg from Scotland Yard . . .'

'I'm sorry, sir. I don't care who you are, but no one's allowed through.'

Suddenly a section of the upper part of the wall fell away and crashed to the ground in a cloud of dust and smoke, shaking the pavement beneath them, and then more of the building collapsed, forcing the firemen to retreat, but still keeping the jets of water from their hoses aimed at the ruined remains.

'Did anyone get out?' asked Coburg.

'We don't know yet, but it's unlikely.'

'What about the shelter?'

'The Anderson shelter?' The warden shook his head. 'It took a direct hit. We can't get to it until the fire brigade say it's safe, but it looks like everyone who was in it's dead.'

CHAPTER FOUR

Coburg put his arm round Rosa and led her back to the car. She was shaking.

'All of them, dead,' she said hoarsely, stunned. 'And only last night we were with them.'

'And we'd have been with them today if we hadn't decided to take a break from that damned shelter,' said Coburg grimly.

'What are we going to do?' asked Rosa. 'Where are we going to stay tonight? Where are we going to stay, full stop?'

Suddenly she began to cry, her body shaking, and Coburg hugged her close to him.

'It'll be all right,' he said, his tone gentle, but at the same time fiercely urgent. 'We'll get through this.'

'I'm sorry,' she apologised, straightening up and looking at him. 'I didn't mean to come over all "the little woman".'

'I know you didn't,' said Coburg. 'And if I hadn't seen all the things I did during the First War, I'd be in tears right now. Everything we had, gone. The people we shared the shelter with, all gone. But right now we take care of us tonight, and then tomorrow we start rebuilding.'

'How?' asked Rosa.

'We'll ask Magnus if we can stay at his London flat.'

'Won't he mind?'

'He's rarely there, and even less so since the Blitz began. And it'll only be a short-term thing, a few days while we fix up somewhere else to live.'

'So is that where we're going tonight?'

'No. I don't have a key, and it's unlikely Magnus will haul all the way from Dawlish Hall at this hour. Tonight, Mrs Coburg, I have something else in mind.'

Charles Tillesley, having been advised that Mr and Mrs Coburg had arrived at reception, came down from his office to greet them with a welcoming smile.

'Mr and Mrs Coburg! This is a pleasure!'

'We've come to take you up on your offer of a room for the night, if you have one spare,' said Coburg. 'Unfortunately our flat in Hampstead has just been struck by a German bomb.'

Tillesley stared at them, shocked. 'How awful! But you are safe and uninjured?'

'We weren't there at the time. We returned home to find everything in ruins and the fire brigade doing their best to save the block, although we feel they'll be unsuccessful. It was a direct hit.'

'We do have a room, but it's one we keep in reserve for staff who may have to stay overnight,' said Tillesley apologetically.

'Providing it has a bed and a bathroom, that's all we need,' said Coburg.

'Please don't misunderstand me,' added Tillesley hastily. 'It has all the necessary requirements we feel are important for a room at the Savoy. It is more than comfortable. I have stayed in it myself when the occasion arose. It is just not a suite of rooms, as many of our guests expect.'

'Thank you, Charles,' said Coburg.

'And there is no need for you to vacate tomorrow,' continued Tillesley. 'How long will you need it for, do you think?'

'Just the one night,' repeated Coburg. 'I'll be telephoning my brother Magnus shortly to see if he will let us stay at his London flat.'

'I assume you'll be dining here this evening?'

Coburg nodded. 'After our recent bad experience, I believe we deserve to treat ourselves.'

'On the Savoy, as I said before, Mr Coburg,' stressed Tillesley.

'Thank you, Charles, but the rules for police officers on accepting gifts are quite strict, and I don't want to be seen breaking them. But we do appreciate the offer.'

Tillesley called for one of the porters to escort them to the room on the second floor. Once they were in, Rosa stood and looked in awe at the luxurious furnishings and decor.

'This is a spare room for the staff?' she said, incredulous.

'It is the Savoy,' Coburg reminded her. 'Now I must

phone Magnus.' He picked up the receiver and gave the switchboard operator the number for Dawlish Hall. The telephone at the other end was picked up almost immediately, and an elderly and rather prim Scottish voice announced: 'Dawlish Hall.'

'This is the Savoy hotel,' said the operator. 'We have a telephone call for you.' Then, to Coburg: 'You're connected, caller.'

'Good evening, Malcolm,' said Coburg.

'Master Edgar?' said Malcolm, and Coburg could picture the smile on the elderly butler's face.

'Indeed it is,' said Coburg. 'Is my brother there?'

'He is,' replied Malcolm. 'I'll bring him to the telephone.'

There was a pause and Coburg heard muttering in the background, then the voice of his brother, Magnus, was heard.

'Edgar. I hope you didn't mind my giving Rupert your number. He was most distressed. A guest murdered, he said. The Earl of Lancaster, I believe.'

'Indeed, but as it turned out my presence as a police officer wasn't required. The nearest police station were also informed and a local inspector has taken charge.'

'But you're still at the Savoy, according to Malcolm.'

'Alas, nothing to do with the investigation. Our flat took a direct hit in today's air raids. The whole block was completely destroyed, so we've taken a room at the Savoy for the night.'

'My poor dears. But you're both all right, are you? Not injured?'

'No, we were away from the area at the time. We only

38

discovered the damage when we returned late this afternoon. We're obviously having to find alternative accommodation, but it may take a few days, so I was wondering . . .'

'The London flat,' finished Magnus. 'Absolutely. It's yours for as long as you want it. You don't have keys, do you?'

'No.'

'In that case I'll travel up to town tomorrow and let you in. What time would suit you?'

'Actually, I have things to do in the morning, report to Scotland Yard and then make the rounds of letting agents, so I wondered if you'd mind if you met with Rosa.'

'Not at all,' said Magnus, but now there was a note of reserve in his voice, the reason for it becoming clear with his next statement. 'I'm looking forward to meeting my new sister-in-law. I had hoped to meet her at your wedding, or even before it.'

He's annoyed because we didn't invite him to the wedding, thought Coburg. Correction, because I didn't invite him.

'Where was it?' continued Magnus, his tone still icy. 'Registry office, I presume. You could have had it here, you know. The church is still part of the estate and Reverend Barnes would have been delighted to see a Coburg wedding take place there. And holding a reception here at the Hall would have cheered people up no end, especially at a time when they could do with cheering up.'

'I know, Magnus, but we – I – wanted it low-key.'

'Well you certainly got what you wanted,' said Magnus, still disapproving. 'But I'll be delighted to meet your new wife tomorrow at the flat and give her the keys and show her where everything is. I can be there for ten thirty. Will that be all right for her?'

'Will a bit later be all right? We need to go back to the flat and see if we can salvage anything from the wreckage. Personal items and such.'

'What time, then?'

Coburg looked at Rosa questioningly.

'If we go to the flat first thing, I should still be able to make ten-thirty,' said Rosa.

'Let's say eleven,' suggested Coburg. 'Just in case things turn up.'

She nodded.

'Rosa says—' began Coburg.

But Magnus interrupted. 'I heard. Eleven it is. I'll see her there.'

'I'll give her the address,' said Coburg. 'And so you know what she looks like—'

'I already know,' Magnus interrupted again. 'Malcolm saw a piece about the wedding in a newspaper. Not The Times or The Telegraph, one of the lesser ones. It had a photograph of the pair of you on the steps of the registry office with the caption: Jazz star weds aristocrat cop.'

'Nothing to do with us,' said Coburg. 'I think these photographers hang around there in case someone turns up who they think might be interesting.'

'In the photo it looked like she had an arm in plaster.'

'Yes,' said Coburg. 'She got shot.'

'She must be finding life with you to be dangerous,' commented Magnus. 'Tell her I'll see her in the morning.'

Coburg hung up and looked at Rosa, who said: 'So, he

40

saw the piece about our wedding in the Daily Mirror.'

'His butler, Malcolm, reads it.' He gave a thoughtful frown. 'I'm still not convinced that Ted didn't leak it to someone and they passed it on. Ted's parents, for example. They were very proud of him being best man.'

'It sounds like your brother hasn't forgiven us for not inviting him,' said Rosa with a sigh.

'Magnus has very traditional views about how things ought to be done,' Coburg shrugged. 'But he'll be fine with you tomorrow. He's an old-fashioned gentleman with perfect manners. And he's nice, when you get to know him.'

'But you're not coming with me.'

'I need to make arrangements for another flat for us.'

'I heard Magnus tell you we can stay at his flat as long as we like.'

'I'm sure we can, but I'd prefer to have our own place rather than be beholden to Magnus.'

'You don't get on with him?'

'Oh, we get on well enough,' said Coburg airily. 'But sooner or later Magnus will be round all the time, poking his nose in, telling us what we can and can't do in his place. It's the way he is. And if I came with you tomorrow I'd lose the whole day, because once Magnus gets talking he goes on and on, and I need to get to work. I'll see him later, when we've got things sorted out.

'Right now, I suggest we have a bath to get rid of the stress of the day, and then go down to the restaurant.'

'Mr Coburg!' The woman's voice stopped Coburg and Rosa as they were about to enter the restaurant. They turned and saw Lady Lancaster making for them.

'The murdered man's widow,' Coburg whispered to Rosa. Aloud, he said: 'Good evening, Lady Lancaster. This is my wife, Rosa.'

'You're staying here?'

'Just for the one night. Unfortunately, our block of flats was bombed, so we're officially homeless.'

'How awful!' She looked at them, puzzled. 'But you're here. And undamaged.' She looked at Rosa's plastered left arm and gave an embarrassed smile. 'Well, not damaged today.'

'No,' said Rosa. 'This happened just over a month ago.'

'Luckily for us, we weren't at home when the bombs struck,' said Coburg.

'I've learnt that William is now in custody at the Strand police station,' said Lady Lancaster, her strained voice showing her deep unhappiness. 'I've tried to get him released on bail, but Inspector Lomax refuses to allow it. He says he has questions to ask.'

'I'm afraid the inspector has to stick to the rules,' said Coburg.

'There really is nothing you can do?' appealed Lady Lancaster.

'I'm afraid not,' said Coburg. 'But, as I said before, I'm sure William will be treated fairly. And now, please excuse us, but I believe our table is ready.'

'Of course, my apologies.' She turned to Rosa and said: 'It's lovely to meet you, Mrs Coburg.'

They watched her walk off, making for the stairs.

'That is a very stressed woman,' murmured Rosa.

'She's got a lot to be stressed about. Her husband stabbed to death in the bed next to hers in the Savoy air raid shelter. Her son arrested on suspicion of the murder. To be honest, it's one case I'm glad I didn't get. It has all the hallmarks of a tangle with lots of important people watching very closely.'

After their meal Coburg and Rosa made their way downstairs along with the rest of the Savoy's guests to the air raid shelter deep below ground.

'Wow!' exclaimed Rosa in an awed whisper.

'Wow is right,' muttered Coburg.

The shelter was worthy of the Savoy: a vast open space turned into a dormitory with curtained and separate sleeping quarters for single men, single women and couples. The beds had matching sheets and pillows in green and pink and blue. Sandbags painted in the colours of the Union Jack were stacked against the scaffolding poles that supported the curtain rails.

Separate from the curtained sleeping quarters was a dance floor with a stage ready for a small combo, along with a bar that Coburg noted was exceedingly well stocked with every form of alcohol one could want.

'I can't help but think about Hampstead, and our Anderson shelter,' whispered Rosa, doing her best not to show the distress she was obviously feeling. 'They're all dead, and we're here, surrounded by this luxury.'

'No wonder the people from Stepney invaded this place,' muttered Coburg. 'I'm surprised they didn't come back again tonight, and every night while the bombing continues.'

They were shown the way to their cubicle by one of the porters, where they settled themselves into the double bed.

'Is there bombing going on tonight?' asked Rosa.

'If there is, I can't hear it,' said Coburg.

'Nor can I, that's why I asked. All I heard was the air raid siren.'

There was a sudden dull thud from somewhere outside that sent a slight vibration through the basement, followed by another, then another. Rosa reached out and clutched Coburg's hand nervously.

'There's the answer,' said Coburg. 'But we'll be all right. Unlike our block of flats, the Savoy's built around a steel framework. It may shake, but it won't fall down.'

Gratefully, she released her tight grip on his hand but still kept hold of it.

'We'll get through this, won't we?' she asked.

'Yes we will,' said Coburg, pulling her to him and hugging her close. 'I promise.'

CHAPTER FIVE

Monday 16th September

Next morning Coburg telephoned Scotland Yard and left the same message twice, once for Superintendent Allison, and also for his sergeant, Ted Lampson: 'Please tell them my home was destroyed in yesterday's air raid and I need to arrange alternative accommodation this morning and also inspect the damage. I'll be in around lunchtime.'

That done, they had breakfast, then checked out and drove to Hampstead. There were barriers around the site of their block of flats and a police constable on duty. The fires were out, but the whole building had collapsed and was now just a huge mass of rubble. Where the Anderson shelter had stood was a deep crater.

'My God,' muttered Rosa.

As Coburg and Rosa approached the barrier the policeman on duty stopped them. 'Sorry, sir, madam, you can't go in.'

Coburg produced his warrant card and showed it to the constable.

'DCI Coburg, Scotland Yard,' he said.

The constable frowned. 'There's nothing to investigate here, sir. It was a bomb. Two bombs, according to the fire brigade, one hit the building and the other the shelter. I'm here to stop any looters.'

'We're not looters, Constable. This was our home. Fortunately for us, we were out yesterday when the bombs struck. We're here to see if we can salvage any personal items.'

The constable nodded. 'Of course, sir. But there's not much of the place left, and what there is was on fire, so anything that survived it would have got damaged from when the fire brigade put their hoses on it.'

'I understand, Constable, but we still need to take a look.'

'All right, sir. But be careful. It's all unstable.'

Coburg and Rosa pushed their way through the barrier and walked towards the pile of wreckage, then stopped. The heap of broken bricks, rafters and roof tiles was about ten feet high and covered an area roughly the size of half a football pitch. Here and there, caught between the wreckage, bits of broken furniture and crockery could be seen, but just fragments barely observable beneath the rubble.

'We can't do this,' said Rosa. 'Not on our own. We don't even know where to start to look for our things. All four flats have just collapsed in on one another, and everything is just broken bricks and roof tiles, with our stuff maybe somewhere beneath it all.'

'I know,' agreed Coburg. 'I was hoping that some things

might have been easy to spot, but you're right. I think we have to say that everything's gone. We'll have to start from scratch.'

'We can do that,' said Rosa. 'We're lucky, we still have each other.'

Coburg checked his watch. 'It's ten o'clock. I suggest we head off for Belgravia.'

'Is that where the flat is?'

'It is,' said Coburg. 'Eaton Square.'

'Very upmarket,' commented Rosa.

'Magnus is a very upmarket kind of person.'

'In that case I'm not sure he'll approve of me.'

'Oh, he will,' Coburg smiled. 'He may look all stiff and starchy, but inside he's an old softie, really.'

Despite the lack of private cars on the road due to petrol rationing, their journey across London took them almost an hour, mainly because the previous night's bombing had resulted in some of the buildings on their route falling into the road, leading to traffic diversions as the wardens and fire brigade worked to clear the debris.

'Is this what life is going to be like for us now?' asked Rosa unhappily as they passed yet another building whose frontage had fallen away leaving a pile of rubble in the street. It looked like a doll's house with the front removed. Downstairs there was a table laid for a meal, with food still on the plates. Upstairs, the bath was hanging over a large hole in the wooden floor, held in place by the pipe to the taps.

'We'll survive,' said Coburg.

'Wishful thinking?' asked Rosa.

'No, determination,' said Coburg. 'And because we've got each other.'

He pulled up outside the tall, white terraced Regency house in Eaton Square where Magnus's flat was located and let Rosa out.

'Flat three,' he said.

'I'll phone you later and let you know how I got on,' she told him.

'He'll love you,' he said. 'How could he not?'

He watched her mount the steps to the front door, then put the car into gear and headed for Scotland Yard.

Sergeant Lampson was in the office at his desk when he arrived and he looked up at Coburg as he walked in.

'You're all right, then?' he asked anxiously.

'We're alive, which is the main thing,' said Coburg. 'Tragically, everyone else in our block of flats was killed. And we'd have suffered the same fate if we hadn't decided to escape from London for the day. How about you? Being as close to Euston and St Pancras as you are, Somers Town is right in the path of the bombs trying to destroy the main railway lines.'

'I don't think the Germans are that accurate, to be honest. Why did they hit you up at Hampstead? What's there? Nothing. The Heath.'

'I think you're right. They get to London and then just drop their bombs so they can get away from the RAF fighters as quick as they can.'

'The RAF did a really good job yesterday,' said Lampson. 'I don't know if you heard it on the wireless?'

'No,' said Coburg. 'What with one thing and another, I

48

haven't heard any news today.'

'No, of course not,' said Lampson apologetically. 'They reckon it was the worst day of the Blitz so far. The biggest number of German planes ever launched against London in daylight. Five hundred bombers, they reckon. I don't know how they missed us in Somers Town. I don't know why they don't open the Tube stations for people to shelter. They're deep underground.'

'I think sooner or later they'll have to,' said Coburg. 'The official reason is they think that people will just hide down there for ever and never come up and the economy will crumble.'

'There won't be any economy if people keep dying at the rate they are,' said Lampson. 'The only good thing is the Germans seem to be laying off attacking the airfields now they're concentrating on London.'

'To be honest, Ted, it's hard to think of any aspect of what we're going through as a good thing.'

'Yes, but it gives our fighter pilots more chance to attack the German bombers.'

'In daylight hours, maybe. But not at night.'

'I'm just trying to think of something positive, guv,' said Lampson defensively. 'There's too much defeatist talk in my opinion. People only saying bad things about what's happening. We need to lift morale, think the Churchill way.'

'Yes, I suppose you're right,' said Coburg with a sigh. 'Oh, I was called to the Savoy hotel yesterday morning. There'd been a murder on Saturday night. The Earl of Lancaster stabbed to death.'

'So that's one for us, then?'

Coburg shook his head. 'I was sent on my way with a flea in my ear by Inspector Lomax.'

'That arsehole!' snorted Lampson.

'That may be, but he's in charge of the case. He picked up the shout.'

Lampson frowned thoughtfully. 'Wasn't there an invasion of the Savoy on Saturday night? I saw about it in the papers.' He gave a snort of disapproval. 'Bloody communists.'

'I didn't know they were communists,' said Coburg. 'I was told it was a party of about fifty people from Stepney who were seeking shelter because they had no proper shelters of their own.'

'They were communists,' said Lampson firmly. 'My dad told me, and he knows people who know things. Shoot the lot of them, that's what I say.'

'The women and children who were there?' asked Coburg, amused.

'Well all right, not them, obviously, but the ringleaders. I mean, they're our enemy, signing that treaty with Hitler and the Nazis. They all ought to be locked up for treason. After all, we locked up Oswald Mosley and his fascist lot because they were siding with Hitler. How's that different from the Russians doing a deal with Hitler?'

'The Russians aren't actually involved in the war. Not as far as fighting us,' said Coburg. 'As far as I can make out this deal is to stop Germany attacking them.'

'I don't trust 'em,' said Lampson. 'Not the Nazis nor the Russians. And I don't trust people who support them, whether it's the British Fascist lot or the so-called British

50

Communist Party. Traitors all, that's what they are.'

They were interrupted by the phone ringing, and Lampson picked it up.

'Chief Inspector Coburg's office.' He straightened to attention as he listened to the voice at the other end, then said: 'Yes, sir. He's here. I'll tell him.'

He put the phone back on the hook then said: 'That was Superintendent Allison. He wants you to report to him.'

Rosa shook the hand of the tall, elegant man who welcomed her to the apartment. Magnus Hildebrand Peregrine Saxe-Coburg, the Earl of Dawlish, was in his late fifties. There was a distinct family resemblance to Edgar, although Magnus was plumper and his neatly cut hair was white, as was his moustache. Rosa had to admit that Edgar dressed smartly, but plainly. Magnus dressed fashionably and the tailored dark suit, along with his tie matching the tip of the handkerchief poking up from the breast pocket of his elegant jacket, reinforced his aristocratic heritage.

'How wonderful to meet you at last,' said Magnus.

'The pleasure's mutual,' replied Rosa. 'What do I call you? My Lord? Your Grace?'

Magnus smiled.

'I think we can dispense with that,' he said. 'We are family now, after all. And I have heard you sing. You were on the wireless before the war. The Henry Hall Show.'

'I was,' said Rosa. 'I'm surprised you caught it. I'd have thought the Home Service or the Third Programme to be more your taste.'

'Please, I'm not a complete fuddy-duddy,' said Magnus.

'Although I have to admit in that case my butler, Malcolm, was listening to you in the kitchen when I came in, but I stayed. You did two Hoagy Carmichael songs, I recall.'

'"Stardust" and "Georgia on my Mind",' Rosa nodded. 'Wonderful songs.'

'And beautifully sung.' Magnus looked at Rosa with a smile of regret. 'I do so wish you and Edgar could have tied the knot at Dawlish. We have a lovely old medieval church, and the hall would have been ideal for the reception.'

'I know,' she said with an apologetic smile. 'But, what with the war on, and the fact that my parents wouldn't have been able to get down from Scotland . . .'

'I understand,' said Magnus. 'But you must come down to Dawlish Hall and see it.'

'We will,' Rosa promised him.

'Malcolm!' called Magnus, and a man in his early sixties appeared. 'Put the kettle on.' He looked at Rosa. 'Coffee or tea?'

'I'm fine with whichever,' said Rosa.

'In that case, coffee, please, Edward. With some biscuits.'

'Yes, sir,' said Edward, and disappeared.

'Malcolm is my factotum,' explained Magnus. 'Since my chauffeur, Carlo, was interned, Malcolm acts as my driver. He also looks after me when I'm in town. But don't worry, he won't be staying here, he'll be coming back to Dawlish Hall with me.' He smiled affectionately as he added: 'Excellent fellow. He was my batman in the army.' Then, still keeping a light tone to his voice, he said: 'You realise what this means, you marrying Edgar?'

'That I love him?'

Magnus laughed. 'Yes, that of course. No, I meant the demesne.'

'The demesne?' asked Rosa, uncertain what the word meant.

'Well, as Edgar may have told you, my wife passed away a few years ago. Same for Charles, who's currently languishing in a German prisoner-of-war camp somewhere. So, as it's unlikely either Charles or I will marry again and sire heirs, it could be down to you and Edgar. If Edgar does outlive Charles and I, how do you feel about becoming Lady Dawlish?'

CHAPTER SIX

Superintendent Allison was sitting behind his desk as Coburg pushed open his office door at the superintendent's call of 'Come in!'

'Ah, Chief Inspector,' said Allison. 'A bad business, losing your home like that. You and your wife weren't injured?'

'No, sir. Fortunately we weren't there when the bombs struck.'

'If you need time off to make arrangements for new accommodation, do take it.'

'Thank you, sir. I was planning to do that this morning, if that's all right with you. It should only take an hour.'

'That's fine. Go ahead.'

'Thank you, sir.'

Coburg was on the point of leaving, when a subtle cough stopped him.

'That wasn't all I wanted to see you about.'

'Sir?'

'This Savoy business is a mess,' said Allison with a heartfelt sigh. 'Rupert D'Oyly Carte and other influential people have been on to the commissioner and Home Secretary demanding that you be put in charge. I've told them that the protocol is it's Inspector Lomax's case, but with this much pressure coming from the top, the commissioner himself insists you take it over.'

Coburg looked at the superintendent unhappily. 'This won't be good for morale, sir. Nor relations between local districts and Scotland Yard. There'll be a great deal of resentment, not just from Inspector Lomax but from his colleagues, and when that happens there's often discreet obstruction. This is putting me in a no-win situation, frankly.'

'I appreciate that, Chief Inspector, but my hands are tied. This has come from the very highest authority.'

Coburg nodded, still unhappy. 'There'll be trouble, sir. I'll need to move the investigation to Scotland Yard, but that will depend on Inspector Lomax handing over his notes and everything about the case to us. He also has a suspect in custody at the Strand station, William Lancaster, the son of the murdered man. I'll need to transfer him to the custody cells here at Scotland Yard. There may be some resistance about that from Inspector Lomax. To avoid a difficult confrontation, I'm going to need a letter of authority from the commissioner, or the Home Secretary, at the very least.'

'Very well,' said Allison. 'I'll arrange for that to be delivered here as a matter of urgency.'

Coburg returned to his office, where he told Lampson the news.

'Great!' Lampson grinned. 'That'll be one in the eye for Lomax.'

'Which is something I'd rather not happen,' said Coburg. 'Lomax has never liked me, claiming I get unfair privileges because of my family name. This will only compound that.'

'Who cares? What can he do about it except moan?'

'He can sow discord amongst other officers so it'll be local forces against the Yard. This job is hard enough, but it's even harder when we're working against one another instead of working together.'

'It's always been that way, whatever job you're in,' said Lampson sagely. 'Rivalry, jealousy, whatever. It's the way people are. I'd have thought you learnt that when you were in the army and when you were coming up through the ranks in the police.'

'Yes, you're right,' sighed Coburg.

'Your trouble, guv, is you're an idealist,' said Lampson. 'It don't work in the real world.'

'Yes, all right. Thanks for the lecture. I shall do my best to be a cynic like you.'

'I'm no cynic,' Lampson defended himself firmly. 'I just get on with life as it is.'

'Which is what I'm about to do right now,' said Coburg. 'I've got permission to go and arrange a flat for us. It shouldn't take me long. And when I get back I'm hoping we'll have our letter of authority from the commissioner or the Home Secretary authorising us to take over the case, and we'll start by collecting William Lancaster from the Strand.'

Lampson grinned.

'The Home Secretary,' he chuckled. 'Sounds like important people pulling strings to me. Preferential treatment.'

Coburg gave him a look of mock reproof. 'I hear that Inspector Willikins is looking for a new sergeant,' he said pointedly, naming one of Scotland Yard's most notoriously snobbish and mean-spirited officers.

'Point taken, guv,' said Lampson. 'All the best with the flat hunting.'

Coburg made his way to Raglan and Hall, a property rental agency he'd used in the past and been impressed by, and learnt that they had a property which would be available in two weeks' time.

'The current tenants have decided to leave London,' the agent, Gerald Tubbs, informed him. 'They're just the latest to take that decision. The Blitz, you know. Everyone seems to be after properties in the country.' He handed Coburg a brochure with details of the flat, including photographs of both the exterior and interior. 'It'll be available unfurnished. The present tenants have decided to take all their belongings with them. Furniture, curtains, everything. They believe this bombing of London is going to go on for some time. Will that be a problem for you?'

'The bombing or the fact it's unfurnished?' asked Coburg. When he saw the man's concerned look, he smiled. 'I'm just joking. The fact that it's unfurnished won't cause us any difficulty. Of course, we'll need to make arrangements for furniture and everything before we move in.'

'Absolutely,' said Tubbs. 'You can go in to look at the flat at any time. If the tenants aren't available, one of our staff will accompany you.'

'It'll be my wife who'll be handling things,' said Coburg. 'May I use your telephone to tell her what's happening?'

'Certainly,' said Tubbs, and he pushed the phone to Coburg, who put a call through to Magnus's flat.

'The Earl of Dawlish's apartment,' announced the sombre tones of Magnus's factotum.

'Malcolm, it's Edgar. Is my wife there?'

'She is indeed, Mr Edgar. I'll get her for you.'

There was a pause, and then he heard Rosa's voice saying, 'Edgar?'

'How are you getting on with Magnus?' he asked.

'Very well indeed.' She lowered her voice to a whisper. 'He's a sweetie.'

'I told you it would be all right,' said Coburg. 'I'm calling because I'm at Raglan and Hall, the property agents. I've found us a flat. It's in a very safe block in Piccadilly, not far from the Ritz. It's steel framed, so it shouldn't fall down on us like the last one. There's also a shelter in the basement. Nothing as grand as at the Savoy, but safe.'

'Sounds great. When's it free?'

'In two weeks' time. The thing is, it's unfurnished. What I was wondering if you'd mind arranging for furniture and things for us. I've got accounts at Heal's and Selfridges, so just order what you like.'

'I'll need to look at the place first and work out what we need and what will fit.'

'No problem. The agents say you can go in at any time. If the tenants aren't there, the agents will accompany you.'

'Have you seen it?'

'No,' admitted Coburg. 'I haven't had time. I've been landed with the murder at the Savoy after all, so I've got to concentrate on that.'

'You trust me to handle the decor?'

'With absolute confidence,' said Coburg.

'In other words, you can't be bothered what it looks like.'

'I can be bothered . . .' began Coburg, but stopped when he heard her laugh.

'I'm just teasing,' she said. 'Give me the details, the person I'm to talk to at the agents, the address of the flat, and I'll deal with it this afternoon. But right now, Magnus is about to take me to lunch.'

'Lucky you,' said Coburg. 'We'll talk later.'

He replaced the receiver and took his cheque book from his inner pocket. 'Now that's arranged, shall we do the paperwork?'

Coburg returned to the Yard to find the letter signed by the Home Secretary waiting for him, giving him the authority to take charge of the murder investigation at the Savoy.

'Right,' he said, putting the letter into his pocket.

'We'll go to the Strand and bring William Lancaster back here. Then while I question him, I want you to head for the Savoy and talk to the staff who were on duty in the shelter that night. I'll phone Charles Tillesley, the Savoy's general manager, ahead of you going, and ask him to give you a list of the main people to talk to: the head chef, the chief porter, the key ones who'll be able to point you to the staff who might be able to help best.'

'I can start doing that while you pick William up from the Strand,' suggested Lampson.

'I'd rather have you with me when I do that. I've got a good idea that Inspector Lomax will do everything he can to disrupt us taking over, so I'll need you as a witness in case he starts levelling charges against me.'

'What sort of charges?'

'Anything. Lomax is capable of twisting all sorts of things, and he's not going to be happy when we turn up with this letter. When I've finished with William, I'll join you at the Savoy. I thought that while you talk to the staff, I'll talk to the guests.' He gave a wry smile. 'I'm hoping that each group sees it as talking to one of their own. Upstairs and downstairs.'

'And I'm downstairs,' grinned Lampson.

'If you prefer we could always share them out. I have some of the staff, you take some of the guests.'

'No thanks, guv,' said Lampson in firm tones. 'Some will be nice, but some will treat me like some jumped-up bus conductor, and that'll only get up my nose and I'll end up upsetting them. They see you as one of their own so they'll know it's no use trying to pull the wool over your eyes. Same with me with the staff. At least, the ordinary ones: cleaners, waiters, that sort of thing. The top ones, the head chefs and that, they'll still look down on me.'

'In that case, I'll take them,' said Coburg.

CHAPTER SEVEN

As Coburg had anticipated, the duty sergeant at the Strand police station wasn't keen to co-operate and hand William Lancaster over to Coburg and Lampson, in spite of being shown the letter of authority signed by the Home Secretary.

'I'll need to confirm it with Inspector Lomax,' he said sourly. He began to walk towards the inspector's office, but Coburg stopped him, saying: 'I'll hang on to that letter.'

'Inspector Lomax will need to see it,' said the sergeant.

'And he will,' said Coburg. 'I'll show it to him when he comes out here.'

The sergeant hesitated, then unwillingly handed it back to Coburg and stomped off with a scowl.

'You don't really think that they'd do something to that letter, guv?' muttered Lampson.

'I've had dealings with Inspector Lomax before,' responded Coburg darkly. 'I wouldn't trust him in any way.'

They were kept waiting for a further ten minutes before the sergeant reappeared, accompanied by Inspector Lomax.

'What's this about you taking over the Savoy murder?' demanded Lomax.

Coburg produced the letter and held it out towards Lomax.

'This is from the Home Secretary giving me the authority. I've come to take William Lancaster to Scotland Yard.'

Lomax shook his head. 'You want to talk to him, you do it here. This is where he was brought on remand. That's the rules.'

Once more, Coburg pushed the letter towards the inspector. 'You'll see this letter gives me the authority to transfer him, and everything else related to the case, all your notes and interviews, to Scotland Yard.'

This time Lomax took the letter, read it, then glared at Coburg, almost shaking with anger. 'I knew you'd go over my head to your cronies at the top. You rich bastards are all the same.'

'I did not go over your head,' said Coburg taking the letter back. 'As far as I'm concerned, I was very happy for you to keep this investigation. I didn't want it. But as I've been forced into it, I'm going to do it by the book, and that means everything goes through my office at Scotland Yard. If you don't like it, you can take it up with the Home Secretary and the commissioner.'

Coburg and Lampson walked out of the Strand police station on either side of the handcuffed William Lancaster and steered him towards their waiting car. Coburg carried a bag containing reports, notes and transcripts of interviews relating to the case, that Lomax had very reluctantly surrendered.

'Where are you taking me?' demanded William. 'Who are you?'

'I'm Detective Chief Inspector Coburg and this is Sergeant Lampson. We've taken over the investigation of the murder of your father, which will now be conducted from Scotland Yard.' They reached the car and put William in the back, sitting next to Lampson, while Coburg slid behind the steering wheel.

'I didn't do it,' said William.

'We'll talk when we get back to the Yard,' said Coburg.

On their arrival at Scotland Yard, Coburg put William in charge of the custody sergeant. 'Put him in the custody suite until I'm ready to talk to him,' he said.

Coburg and Lampson then went up to their office, where Coburg put a call through to Charles Tillesley at the Savoy.

'Mr Tillesley. it's DCI Coburg. I'm now in charge of the investigation into the death of the Earl of Lancaster. William Lancaster is now in custody at Scotland Yard. I'm sending my sergeant, Sergeant Lampson, to the Savoy to begin questioning the members of staff who were on duty the night of the murder.'

'I look forward to his arrival, Chief Inspector,' said Tillesley. 'Is there anything I can do to assist?'

'Indeed there is. He'll need a list of the staff members who were on duty. I'll be arriving later to talk to your guests, so I'll need a list of the guests who were in your shelter that night.'

'Of course,' said Tillesley.

Coburg hung up and said: 'Right, Sergeant. I suggest you take the car. It'll make your arrival more official if you turn up in a police car.'

'Right, guv.' nodded Lampson. 'When will you be there?'

'As soon as I've finished with William. I'm hoping he'll be able to provide us with the names of the invaders from Stepney.'

'They might be in Inspector Lomax's notes, guv.'

'They might be, but I prefer to get our own information. See if the Savoy got any of their names.'

'You don't trust Inspector Lomax?'

'Between us, Ted, no I don't. But if we're asked, we say we're double-checking.'

Once Lampson had departed, Coburg turned his attention to the notes he'd taken from Lomax. First, he checked the report from the medical examiner. He wasn't familiar with the doctor who'd written the report, a Dr Welbourne from University College Hospital. It was well-written, lucid and easy to understand, avoiding the medical jargon which so many MEs loved including in order to show off.

According to Welbourne, the Earl had been lying on his side in the single bed. The knife had been plunged into his back, the blade entering his heart. According to the report, the blanket had been pulled down to expose the Earl's back before he had been stabbed, the blanket being drawn up over him again afterwards. Death had occurred some time between two and four a.m. Dr Welbourne said that from the evidence of the wound, the weapon had been an ordinary steak knife, the sort found in a restaurant.

The heavy blanket being pulled up had meant that no blood was visible, which was why the murder hadn't been noticed until someone came to wake the Earl at 7 o'clock.

Coburg checked and learnt that members of the Savoy's staff had been appointed to gently rouse those guests who were not yet awake and up. The waiters, bar staff, porters and maids on night duty had been given the roles of 'waker-uppers'. A porter called Wilfred Barnes and a maid called Agnes Smith had been allocated the task of gently waking the male and female guests. When they'd entered the cubicle where the Earl and Lady Lancaster slept, Lady Lancaster's bed was empty. It had been Wilfred Barnes who'd discovered that the Earl was dead. Barnes had informed the Savoy's assistant manager, Mr Hofflin. According to Lomax's notes, Hofflin had found Lady Lancaster at breakfast and informed her.

Why hadn't Lady Lancaster tried to wake her husband, Coburg wondered. Was it just because she had – as she'd already told Coburg – a far from perfect marriage? She'd told Coburg the Earl was a brute and a womaniser. Could she have been the one who'd stabbed her husband? Was she the sort of person who could do that, and then calmly return to her bed and sleep?

Coburg turned to Lomax's notes on William Lancaster. There was no interview detailed; according to Lomax, William had refused to answer any questions. Additionally, according to Lomax, William was one of the instigators of the invasion, 'which was part of a communist plot aimed at the ruling classes, including the victim, his own father.'

So, Ted's communists again, he mused.

Could William's reluctance to talk be because he believed his mother had killed his father, and as his sympathies were with her and he loathed his father, he didn't want to say anything that might implicate her?

Coburg lifted his phone and called the custody suite.

'This is DCI Coburg. Take William Lancaster to one of the interview rooms. Let me know when he's there.'

He then looked through the rest of Inspector Lomax's notes, but they offered little information. There had been no interviews with the night staff on duty, apart from Wilfred Barnes and Agnes Smith. There had been a brief conversation with Willy Hofflin confirming the discovery of the Earl's body, and him advising Lady Lancaster. There were no interviews with any of the other guests. The only person from Stepney mentioned, other than William Lancaster, was Tom Huxton, who the doorman and Willy Hofflin had said seemed to be the leader of the invasion. There was no interview with Huxton in the notes. But then, giving Lomax the benefit of the doubt, Lomax had devoted his time to trying to get a confession from William Lancaster. But it was still a lax investigation, in Coburg's view. Why had he not interviewed Lady Lancaster? She had told Coburg she'd tried to talk to the inspector, but he refused to talk to her. Was it because Lomax was sure she'd be trying to cover up for her son? But the best way to get to the truth would be to talk to her, see if she was lying, and if she was, press her.

His phone rang.

'William Lancaster is ready for you in Interview Room One, sir.'

'Thank you,' said Coburg.

William was sitting at a table when Coburg walked in. A sergeant and a constable stood to one side, keeping guard. Coburg settled himself in the chair opposite William, who looked at him, a surly scowl on his face. He was about nineteen, sallow-faced, his long dark brown hair dirty, as were his clothes. A cultivated image, decided Coburg. I am rubbing the fact that I am the son and heir of the Earl of Lancaster in my father's face by deliberately looking as anti-social as I can.

'Is this where you beat me with a rubber truncheon?' sneered William.

'Actually I thought we'd talk,' said Coburg casually.

'About what?'

'About the fact that your father was murdered at some time during the night in the air raid shelter at the Savoy hotel. Inspector Lomax seems to think you were the one who killed him.'

'Inspector Lomax is an idiot,' grunted William.

'How did you get on with your father?'

'I didn't.'

'Did you know he and your mother were staying at the Savoy?'

'Yes.'

'How? Had they been in touch with you, or you with them?'

'My mother left a message telling me they were there.'

'Why did she do that?'

'In case I needed help of any sort, I could contact her there.' He scowled. 'She thinks I'm still a helpless child.'

'Did you see your father that night?'

'No.'

'Did you talk to your mother?'

'Briefly.'

'What time did you talk to her?'

'It must have been about midnight. I don't have a watch.'

'Where did you talk to her?'

'I was with the rest of the crowd from Stepney in the area they'd curtained off for us, to keep us away from the great and the good,' William said with a sneer. 'A porter came through and told me my mother wished to talk to me. She was waiting for me in the general area the great and the good had been given. It was all curtains, the whole place was full of curtains. I walked through the curtain and there she was. We talked.'

'About what?'

'She wanted to know if I was all right.'

'And what did you say?'

'I told her I was.'

'And that was it.'

'Yes. There wasn't much else to say, especially in those surroundings. And there were other people around, watching us, and giving me decidedly disapproving looks.'

'Did you recognise any of them?'

'Only one. Lord Winship. And I only recognised him because I'd seen him once with my father. They were a pair of brutes together. Peas in a pod. He went off, but his wife stayed to watch us, looking sneeringly at us. I didn't want to give her a chance to make a thing of it with my mother afterwards, so I told Mother I was all right and left.'

'And you didn't go through the curtain later that night, into the area where the "great and the good", in your words, were sleeping.'

'No. I stayed with my own crowd. The real people.'

'The other invaders.'

'Invaders!' scoffed William scornfully. 'You make us sound like a sub-species. The serfs rising up.'

'How would you describe what happened that night? The arrival at the Savoy demanding entrance.'

'The people demanding equality. Equal protection from the bombing.'

'I've been told the people who arrived were communists.'

William shrugged and said: 'So?'

'Are you a communist?'

'Absolutely not!' responded William hotly. 'Communism is just another form of dominating and enslaving people, just the same as my father's class has done in this country for centuries. I reject all political groups. If I were to describe myself in political terms, I suppose the closest would be as an anarchist.'

Coburg pushed a sheet of paper and a pencil across the table to William, and said: 'I need the names and addresses of your companions from Stepney who were with you that night.'

William looked at the sheet of paper and pencil with a sneer. 'Well you're not going to get that information from me! I don't care what you do to me, beat me, you won't get it.'

'You seem to have an obsession with being beaten,' commented Coburg. 'Did your father beat you as a child?'

William glared angrily at Coburg.

'What is this, playing at the psychologist? You think it'll win me over?'

Coburg shrugged. 'No, just interested. I'll get the names from elsewhere.'

'They won't give them to you,' said William firmly. 'No matter what you do to them. They're used to being ground down underfoot by people like you.'

'The police?' asked Coburg.

'You know what I mean. I hear the way you speak. Do you put on that upper-class accent to try and impress?' He shook his head. 'No, it's ingrained. Where did you go to school? Harrow?'

'Why is my school so important?' asked Coburg.

Suddenly William's mouth opened and he looked at Coburg with startled eyes. 'Coburg!' he burst out.

'Detective Chief Inspector Coburg,' the DCI corrected him.

'No, I know who you are!' said William. 'Your name's on the board of honour at Eton. Saxe-Coburg.'

'I think you're referring to one of my brothers,' said Coburg. 'Magnus and Charles.'

'No, you're all there. All three of you were in the First War.' William sat back and looked at Coburg, a smirk of triumph on his face. 'So that's why you were brought in. The old school tie. Was this my mother's doing?'

Quite likely, thought Coburg with an inward sigh.

Aloud, he said: 'It's protocol. I'm a chief inspector.'

'Well I'm not saying anything more to you. You can tell my mother this ruse has failed. I will not rat out my comrades from the working class.'

CHAPTER EIGHT

The phone in Coburg's office was ringing when he returned, after having had William Lancaster taken back to the custody cells. It was Rosa.

'I'm glad I was here,' Coburg told her. 'As I said, I've been put back on the murder at the Savoy, so I've been in and out all day. How was lunch with Magnus?'

'He was lovely. You were quite right, beneath that starchy, slightly old-fashioned exterior, he's a dear. I like him a lot. You should have been here.'

'I will get to see him, I promise.'

'Make sure you do. He wants to see you, and he deserves to. He's letting us have his flat, and he even said he'd leave it to us and he'd only call if he was invited. Of course, I told him he had a permanent invitation.'

'Which he'll take full advantage of,' said Coburg ruefully.

'Don't be such an old grouch,' said Rosa. 'I'm looking forward to getting to know him. Anyway, I thought I'd let you know I'm visiting the property agents this afternoon to make arrangements to inspect the flat so I can order the furniture and things.'

'Excellent,' said Coburg.

'So, tell me about this murder.'

'I'll tell you when I see you,' said Coburg. 'Right now I'm due at the Savoy to question witnesses.'

'In that case I'll let you go. Say hello to Sergeant Lampson from me.'

Coburg hung up and headed down to the reception area. He was just walking across it towards the double doors to the street when he was hailed by the duty desk sergeant.

'Sorry to trouble you, sir, but there's a young lady arrived who wants to see you. I was just about to ring you.'

'What's it about?' asked Coburg.

'She says it's about William Lancaster.' He pointed to where a girl of about eighteen, tall and thin with long dark hair pulled back from her pale face, was standing beside one of the pillars. 'That's her over there, sir. She said her name's Huxton.'

Huxton. Coburg remembered the name from Lomax's notes. Apparently, Tom Huxton had been the leader of the invasion. He guessed this girl was a relative, possibly Huxton's daughter. She looked about the right age. He walked over to her.

'Miss Huxton?'

'Chief Inspector Coburg?' she asked.

Coburg nodded.

'I'm Jenny Huxton. I've come about William. William Lancaster, that is. I went to the police station at the Strand to try to see him, but they told me he'd been brought here and you were now in charge of the investigation.'

'That's right,' said Coburg.

'He didn't do it,' she said fervently.

She's in love with him, Coburg realised. And people in love can be notoriously blind to the truth.

'Let's go to my office and talk,' he said.

She didn't wait for them to get to Coburg's office but made her appeal on behalf of William all the way up the stairs. Much of it he'd heard before from Lady Lancaster: William's vegetarianism, his opposition to blood sports, his registering as a conscientious objector.

'But that doesn't mean he's a coward,' she added hastily. 'He's prepared to put himself in danger, standing up for people's rights.'

'I have talked to him,' said Coburg. They reached his office and he pushed open the door and gestured her to a chair.

'Then you can see how genuine he is,' she said.

'On the night in question . . .'

'At the Savoy in the air raid shelter,' she nodded.

'Did you spend much time with William?'

'All of it,' she said. 'Except when one of us went to the toilet. But apart from that, I saw him the whole time. We were in a separate area, like a big hospital ward with lots of single beds. William and I had beds near one another. And my dad was near us as well, so he can tell you.'

'William told me he left your area to go and see his mother.'

'That's right,' said Jenny. 'I saw him go through the curtain. He came back after just a few minutes.'

'Did you see William's father at any time? The Earl of Lancaster?'

She shook her head. 'Not as far as I know. I don't know what he looks like, so I may have done.'

'What did William talk about after he came back from seeing his mother?'

'Just that she was worried about him, and he'd told her he was all right.'

'He didn't mention seeing his father?'

'No.'

Coburg made notes of this on a pad, then said: 'I'll need to talk to the other people you were with, the ones from Stepney, just to get their versions of events. After all, the more people there are who confirm that William didn't see his father or go through the curtain except that one time, to see his mother, the sooner we can let him go.'

'You will let him go?' she said, her face lighting up with happiness. 'That other inspector said he'd be staying in jail.'

'That other inspector hadn't had time to look at all the evidence when he said that. But the sooner I talk to the people who were with you, and the staff and guests at the Savoy, the better. Can you let me know where I can get hold of them?'

'I don't know all of them. But most of them were locals.'

'The doorman told us that when you left on Sunday morning, the man who seemed to be the leader told the doorman his name was Tom Huxton. Is that your father?'

She nodded.

'Where can I get hold of him?'

'He's usually at home.' She wrote down the address and passed it to him. 'When will you call?' she asked.

'I've got to be somewhere now,' he said. 'If I get done what I have to do, I'll try and call this afternoon. If not, it'll be tomorrow.'

He stood up, and so did she. 'He didn't do it,' she said again, looking at him pleadingly.

'You're the second person who's told me that,' he said. 'What I now need is firm evidence that he didn't.'

When Coburg arrived at the Savoy he was directed to a room off the kitchens where Sergeant Lampson was quizzing the staff. Lampson had one of the waiters sitting opposite him when Coburg opened the door and looked in.

'Just letting you know I'm here, Sergeant,' Coburg said. 'Everything all right?'

Lampson pointed to his notepad where page after page had already been covered in his notes in pencil. 'Slow, sir,' he said. 'But we're getting there.'

'I'm going to see Mr Tillesley, the hotel manager. After that I'll be talking to the hotel guests. If you want me, send a message to Mr Tillesley.'

Charles Tillesley was waiting for Coburg in his office with a list of names all ready.

'These are the hotel guests who were registered as being in the shelter that night,' he said.

'Thank you,' said Coburg, taking the four sheets of paper. 'From what you know, who among them do you think could be described as friends with the Earl of Lancaster.'

Tillesley frowned thoughtfully. 'None that I can think of, particularly,' he said. 'Possibly Winship. Lord Eric Winship. He's married to Lady Julia. Although I'm not sure if you could call Winship and Lancaster particularly close. Acquaintances rather than friends. To be honest, the Earl didn't have many what I would call close male friends.'

'Close female friends?' enquired Coburg. 'I'm remembering what Lady Lancaster said to me about her late husband.'

'I wouldn't really describe them as friends,' said Tillesley carefully. 'More as conquests. Which is why most of our male guests who knew him treated him with suspicion.'

'Being protective of their wives and daughters?' suggested Coburg. 'Except for Lord Winship?'

'You'll need to take that up with Lord Eric and Lady Julia,' said Tillesley. Then he added, 'although I'd prefer it if you didn't.'

'I think I'll start with them, as they at least had some kind of acquaintance with the Earl. Do you have a room where I could talk to the guests?'

'You may use my office,' offered Tillesley. 'I'll tell switchboard to put any calls for me through to the concierge's desk.'

'Thank you,' said Coburg. 'What can you tell me about the Winships?'

'He's in his late fifties. She's mid-forties. They have a place in Kent, but they elected to move into the Savoy ever since the Luftwaffe started bombing the airfields there and some houses near them were destroyed.' He pointed at the telephone on his desk. 'If you like I'll have them paged and

78

ask them to come to the office.'

'Thank you. I'd appreciate that.'

'And after you've seen them, perhaps you'd seek out Lady Lancaster. After you called I told her you were now taking charge of the case, and she asked to see you when you arrived.'

'Please tell Lady Lancaster I'll be happy to see her once I've talked to the Winships.'

'Thank you.' He picked up the phone and gave instructions to the switchboard operator to have Lord and Lady Winship paged, and for his calls to be diverted.

'And now I'll leave you,' he said. 'But I would like to say how relieved we are at the Savoy that you are in charge.'

Rather wearily, Sergeant Lampson added the evidence given by the maid sitting opposite him, Ella Kemble, to his notes. Not that she had much to say that was relevant. Like almost everyone else he'd spoken to on the staff, she hadn't seen anything out of the ordinary. She hadn't seen the Earl. Yes, she knew what he looked like so she would have recognised him, but she hadn't seen him during that night in the shelter. The first she knew about it was when someone told her he'd been stabbed.

'Thank you, Miss Kemble,' he said. 'If we want any more information from you, we know where to find you.'

Instead of getting up and leaving, as Lampson expected her to do, she leant forward and said: 'According to the papers, your boss is someone important.'

'He is. He's a detective chief inspector.'

'I mean in addition to him being that. That's what it

said in the paper. I saw that picture of him getting married to that jazz singer and it said he was an aristocrat. He's royalty, or something.'

'He might be,' said Lampson guardedly, wondering where this was leading.

'Only there's been a terrible injustice done, and the Earl of Lancaster was the cause of it; and now he's dead, maybe your boss can get Giovanni out.'

'Out of where? And who is he?'

'Giovanni Piranesi. He's one of the waiters. He got into a row with the Earl, and the Earl had him sent to an internment camp.'

'What was the row about?'

Ella looked uncomfortable. 'That's not for me to say,' she said. 'The point is he had Giovanni locked up.'

'I assume Giovanni is Italian,' said Lampson.

She nodded.

'Then him being locked up is nothing to do with the Earl. Once Mussolini declared war on Britain, all the Italians over here were locked up. "Enemy aliens", they called it. It happened to a pal of mine who's Italian. He's a waiter as well.'

'But Giovanni got taken away the next day after he had the row with the Earl, and before the other Italians who worked here got taken. It was deliberate.' She looked at him with a look of desperate appeal. 'Can't you have a word with your boss? If he's royalty like the paper says, he'll know important people.'

'I'll tell him, but I doubt if he can do anything,' said Lampson. 'It's the Government rules. They did it with the

Germans over here when war was first declared, and now it's the Italians. They're all being locked up.'

'Not all of them,' insisted Ella. 'There's still some out. Giovanni Piranesi, that's his name. He's in the camp at Ascot in Berkshire. The place Bertram Mills Circus use as their winter quarters. They've turned it into an internment camp. It's horrible. Barbed wire and everything. And he shouldn't be there!'

'As I said, I'll mention it to my guv'nor,' Lampson told her. 'That's all I can do.'

CHAPTER NINE

There was a knock at the office door.

'Please come in!' called Coburg.

The door opened and Charles Tillesley entered and announced: 'Lord and Lady Winship, Chief Inspector.'

Coburg rose to his feet.

'Thank you, Mr Tillesley. And thank you for joining me, Lord and Lady Winship.'

'Bad business,' grunted Winship, seating himself down in one of the two chairs Coburg had placed on the other side of the desk, his wife taking the other. 'Bloody communists. I said they should never have let them in!'

'We're not a hundred per cent sure that the Earl was killed by one of the invaders,' said Coburg carefully.

'Who else could have done it?' demanded Winship. 'A guest!'

'It could have been a member of staff,' said Coburg. 'At

this moment we're keeping an open mind, which is why we're talking to everyone who was here at the Savoy on that night.'

Winship shook his head. 'You won't be able to lay hands on those communists. They'll have scuttled back to their rat holes in the East End.'

'Really, Eric,' Lady Winship reprimanded him gently. 'Language and attitudes. The chief inspector is quite right to keep an open mind.'

'And I can reassure you that we already have the names of some of those from the East End who were here that night, and are close to identifying the others,' said Coburg.

'See, Eric, I told you the chief inspector was the right man for the job,' said Lady Winship with a smile. To Coburg, she said: 'We know your brother. Actually, we know both your brothers, but I'm referring to Magnus. He told us that poor Charles is in a German PoW camp. Taken prisoner at Dunkirk.'

'Yes,' said Coburg.

'Bloody fool,' grunted Winship. 'You'd think he'd have had enough of it first time round. You didn't volunteer this time, then?'

'I did, actually,' said Coburg. 'I was turned down. Reserved occupation as Detective Chief Inspector. Plus, they said I wouldn't pass the physical.'

'Oh yes. Magnus told us. You lost a lung in the first one. At Sambre-Oise, wasn't it?'

'Indeed,' said Coburg, thinking to himself: Magnus talks too much.

'I copped it at the Somme,' said Winship. He half-raised

his right arm. 'A machine gun burst in the shoulder. Ruined me for golf. I can only putt now. If you ask me, we shouldn't have got involved again. Learnt our lesson the first time.'

'Eric!' Lady Winship's tone was sharper this time. 'You'll give the chief inspector the wrong impression.'

'Yes, sorry,' said Winship gruffly. 'It's just that . . . this seems more of a mess than the first time. We never had the same on the Home Front first time round. Yes, there was some bombing, but not like this.' He looked at Coburg. 'We hear you lost your flat.'

'Yes.'

'Dreadful,' said Winship.

'I think we're rather getting off the point,' cut in Lady Winship. 'The chief inspector is here to find out what happened to the Earl of Lancaster.'

'Indeed.' nodded Coburg. 'Did you see the Earl on the night in question?'

'Only at the start,' said Lady Winship. 'And then those people from the East End turned up. Invading.'

'Bloody communists!' snorted Lord Winship.

'Though I thought Mr Hofflin, the assistant manager, handled it very well,' continued Lady Winship. 'It could have turned into a riot, which would have been very unpleasant. But he calmed them down . . .'

'By letting them in!' burst out Winship, outraged.

'And put them in separate quarters, shielded from the regular guests by a series of curtains, so that there was no interaction.'

'Except for William Lancaster and his mother, I believe,' said Coburg.

'Yes, that's true,' said Lady Winship. 'I saw her step through the curtains and then reappear a short while later accompanied by William.' She shuddered. 'I must say, he looked dreadful. Like a tramp.'

'Was the Earl around at this time?'

The Winships exchanged thoughtful looks. 'I don't believe so,' said Lady Winship. 'Eric?'

'Not that I was aware of,' said Winship. 'I was ready to go to bed, and all the guests' beds had their own curtains around them for privacy. So I didn't see any more.'

'I stayed a few moments longer,' said Lady Winship. 'I was curious to see how Lady Lancaster and her son might be together.'

'And how were they?' asked Coburg.

She thought it over, then said: 'Affectionate. Not over-affectionate. I don't mean hugging and that kind of stuff. But they were more than just cordial. They were . . . like mother and son.'

'How long were they talking to one another?'

'Five minutes or so. Not long. Then he left, walked through the curtain.'

'Did they still seem to be on good terms when he left?'

'Oh yes. She put her hand on his shoulder and smiled, quite affectionate. He smiled back. Then he left. And I went through our curtain and joined Eric.'

'What time was this?' asked Coburg.

'Just after midnight,' said Lady Winship.

'And you didn't see them again?'

'No. Not until the morning. Well, we didn't see William, he and his cronies had departed by the time we came through our curtain. But then we saw all the hullabaloo going on around the curtains where Hermione was. Lady Lancaster. And that's when we heard that Hector was dead. Stabbed. Dreadful!'

'Indeed,' said Coburg. He gave them a polite smile. 'Thank you for all that. You've been most helpful.'

'I hope you catch whoever did it,' said Winship. 'Can't have this sort of thing happening at the Savoy, otherwise none of us will be safe.'

As the three of them got to their feet, Lady Winship said: 'By the way, I understand congratulations are in order. I hear that you recently married Rosa Weeks, the singer.'

'Yes, that's true,' said Coburg.

'We saw her at the Ritz last month. She's a wonderful talent. You're a lucky man.'

'I am indeed,' agreed Coburg.

'There's a rumour that she was going to give it all up and become an ambulance driver,' said Lord Winship.

'That was her intention, but she had an accident recently which has put her out of action for ambulance driving and playing the piano.'

'That's a pity,' said Winship. 'The piano bit, that is. Not the ambulance driving. Someone with a talent like that doesn't want to put themselves in harm's way.'

'She feels that everyone is putting themselves in harm's way at this moment, and the sooner we can bring it to a conclusion the better.'

'Amen to that.' nodded Winship. 'My feelings as well. Wise woman.'

Coburg walked them to the door and showed them

out, then returned to the desk, their conversation running around in his head. They'd given him information, but no real clues as to when Lancaster had last been seen alive. And with all the Savoy's guests hidden behind their own particular curtains in the air raid shelter, he guessed he'd be getting the same when he talked to the others. The staff would be the ones who'd know. He needed to find out what Ted Lampson had learnt from talking to them. When had Lancaster last been seen alive?

But first, he ought to meet with Lady Lancaster.

Lord and Lady Winship walked away from the manager's office, making for the bar.

'You have to be careful,' said Lady Winship.

'I didn't say anything,' protested Winship.

'You said enough to cause doubt,' Lady Winship rebuked him. 'Which we might need to nip in the bud.' Then she said thoughtfully: 'Or we might be able to use it. Remember what he said: "She feels that everyone is putting themselves in harm's way at this moment, and the sooner we can bring it to a conclusion the better." Maybe she might be worth cultivating?'

'Who?'

'Rosa Weeks. Or Rosa Coburg, as she is now.

'You think so?'

'She's a celebrity.'

'A minor one,' said Winship dubiously.

'But with the potential to be bigger, and therefore more influential. And I'm pretty sure she has influence over her husband.' She smiled. 'A two-pronged attack from people close to him: his wife and his brother. Now wouldn't that be a coup if we could bring him in to the fold.'

'I have my doubts about that,' said Winship.

'Let's find out,' said his wife. 'I think it's time to host a little soirée. Nothing grand, just a small thing, tea and chat.'

'But how will you get her in?'

'She's an entertainer, isn't she? I think a word with Tillesley is in order.'

CHAPTER TEN

Coburg had been joined by Lady Lancaster, who sat looking at him with an expression of undisguised gratitude almost bordering on intimacy, which made Coburg feel uncomfortable.

'I telephoned the Strand police station to enquire after William, and they informed me that you were now in charge of him, and that you'd taken him to Scotland Yard.'

'That is correct.' Coburg nodded.

'And I hear from Mr Tillesley that you are now in charge of the case.'

'Again, correct,' said Coburg.

'I was so relieved when I heard.'

'My job is still the same as Inspector Lomax's, to find out who killed your husband, and your son is still deemed a suspect.'

'On the flimsiest of grounds and no actual evidence,' said Lady Lancaster.

Coburg hesitated before saying carefully: 'At first sight that would appear to be the case, but I need to talk to everyone who was here on the night.'

'Of course.'

'When did you last see your husband alive during that night?'

'To be honest, Chief Inspector, I didn't see much of him at all. He went off somewhere almost as soon as we went down into the shelter. And then I didn't see him again until he was discovered dead the following morning.'

'So, as far as you know, he wasn't in the air raid shelter?'

'Not for a good part of the night, I assume. We had a curtained-off compartment, but it had two single beds in it. I retired on my own at half past midnight. When I woke I saw that Hector was in his bed, but not moving. I assumed he was either asleep, or feigning sleep to avoid a conversation.'

'What time was that?'

'A quarter to seven in the morning.'

'You didn't try to wake him?'

'No. I rose and dressed and went to the bathrooms. I then went to the restaurant for breakfast. I was there when Mr Hofflin, the assistant manager, came to me and told me that Hector was dead and that he'd been stabbed.'

'You didn't see him come to bed?'

'No.'

Coburg weighed up his next question carefully before asking: 'Was your reluctance to attempt to wake him because you suspected he had been with someone else?'

'Yes. He was notorious. Frankly, I didn't want to know

who. Although, I did really. I thought it might be one of the maids, but if it had been a guest, someone I knew, I wanted to know how to deal with it when I met her.'

'Did this happen often?'

'All the time.'

'Why didn't you divorce him?' asked Coburg.

'One doesn't do that,' said Lady Lancaster. 'Not at our level of society, showing our dirty laundry in public for people to gawp at. Although some do.'

'Did he want a divorce?'

'God, no! As far as he was concerned, he had the perfect life.' She looked at him earnestly, once more with such open passion that Coburg again felt very uncomfortable as she said: 'You will be able to release William soon, I hope, Chief Inspector?

'As soon as I have the evidence to clear him,' said Coburg. 'But there are still many people to talk to.'

'Thank you.' They stood up and she was about to head for the door, when she suddenly turned and said: 'As your flat was destroyed in Sunday's air raid, if you need somewhere to stay, you're welcome to take Hector's. It's in Fitzroy Square. No one else will be using it.'

'Thank you,' said Coburg. 'That's very kind of you. But my wife and I have already made arrangements.'

She nodded and smiled. 'Of course. But, if you change your mind, it's there for you.'

After Lady Lancaster, Coburg talked to the other guests who'd spent the night at the air raid shelter and got the same answers from them. No, they hadn't seen the Earl of

Lancaster. Yes, they'd noticed Lady Lancaster in the shelter. All of which suggested to Coburg that the Earl had been elsewhere in the hotel until he'd gone to bed in the early hours of the morning, and whoever he'd been with hadn't been one of the guests. As it was doubtful he'd been with the Stepney invaders, that left the hotel staff.

Coburg made his way down to the kitchens and the room that Lampson had commandeered for his interviews.

'How did you get on with the staff?' he asked.

'Three wise monkeys: no one saw anything or heard anything out of the ordinary. I think mostly they're worried about their jobs. You know, getting the sack if they speak out of turn.'

'Did you find anyone who saw the Earl during the night? Going to his bed, for example.'

Lampson flicked through the pages of his notebook. 'Yes, one of the maids. She said she saw the Earl going through the curtain to where he and Lady Lancaster were sleeping at about two in the morning.'

'Which fits with what the medical examiner said; he was killed between two and four in the morning. Did any of the staff report William Lancaster leaving the area where the Stepney invaders were stationed and going into his parents' quarters during that time?'

Lampson shook his head. 'No. The only report I've got on him is he went into the curtained cubicle where his mother was at about midnight. He stayed for about five minutes and then came out again and returned to the crowd from Stepney. And, by all accounts, that's where he stayed until everyone got up in the morning.'

'What time?'

'Six o'clock. The manager wanted the Stepney lot fed and watered and out before the regular guests were ready for breakfast. They gave 'em toast and tea and they left about seven.'

'If that's all true then it looks like William Lancaster's off the hook. We'll double-check. We'll have another go at them, with me joining in this time. I'll do my best to persuade them that Mr Tillesley assures me that anything they say won't affect their jobs.'

'There was one thing that came up,' said Lampson. 'One of the maids, an Ella Kemble, said about a waiter called Giovanni Piranesi. Apparently he had a row with the Earl.'

'Have you spoken to this waiter?'

'Not much chance of that, guv. He's been interned, along with most of the other Italians from here. He's at an internment camp that's been set up in the grounds of the Bertram Mills Circus winter quarters at Ascot in Berkshire.'

'When was he interned?'

'A couple of weeks ago.'

'So we can rule him out of killing the Earl.'

'It depends on what the row was about,' said Lampson. 'If it was about something serious and he feels he got the wrong end of something, maybe he got a friend of his to stick the Earl in revenge.'

'What was the row about?' asked Coburg.

'She didn't say,' said Lampson. 'I got the impression she didn't want to talk about it. All she was interested in was getting this Giovanni released. She claims it was the Earl who had him locked up.'

'I hope you told her that it was to do with the fact he's Italian, and they've been locking up all Italians over here.'

'I did, but she said that this Giovanni was locked up the day after he had the row with the Earl, and before all the rest of them were taken away.'

'Interesting,' said Coburg thoughtfully. 'It might be worth looking into. I'll have a word with Mr Tillesley. If there was a row here, he must know about it. Have you got many more of the staff to see?'

'No, that's about it.' He looked unhappily at his notes. 'Like I say, they didn't give me much. Shall we have another go at them tomorrow?'

'No, I think tomorrow we head for Stepney and talk to the invaders.'

'Bloody communists,' grumbled Lampson.

'Maybe, but we need to build up the picture of what happened that night. So, for now, I suggest we call it a day here. You get off home and see how Terry is. I'll go and check with Mr Tillesley about this row between the waiter and the Earl. And we'll meet at the Yard tomorrow.'

'Providing the Germans don't blow us up tonight.'

'Thanks, Ted,' said Coburg wryly.

'Sorry, guv,' said Lampson. 'I forgot about your flat.'

'At least we have somewhere to stay. I'll see you in the morning.'

Lady Winship had tracked Charles Tillesley to the cubbyhole behind the concierge's desk, and beckoned him to her with an imperious wave, tempered with a smile.

'Mr Tillesley,' she said, 'I understand that Chief Inspector Coburg has recently got married. To Rosa Weeks, the jazz singer, I believe.'

'That's right,' nodded Tillesley, relieved that Lady Winship wasn't here to complain about the staff, something she often did, accusing them of not being respectful enough to her. 'Such a delightful couple. They stayed here a couple of nights ago.' He lowered his voice as he added unhappily: 'Their flat in Hampstead was bombed, so we put them up while they made arrangements.'

'No! How awful!' said Lady Winship. 'Not staying here, I mean, obviously, but losing their home. Actually, Eric and I saw her at the Ritz. She was wonderful. You should invite her to do a session here. One teatime, perhaps.'

'I understand she's damaged her arm,' said Tillesley. 'It's in plaster.'

'I'm sure that won't prevent her singing,' said Lady Winship. 'We can always arrange an accompanist for her. Eric knows some wonderful musicians.' She smiled again. 'I just thought I'd mention it. It would be wonderful publicity for the Savoy to have her perform here.'

Coburg had been heading for the concierge's desk and Tillesley when he saw that Lady Winship was in discussion with the hotel manager, and he kept a discreet distance while he waited for her to leave. Once he was sure she had finished and had departed, he made for Tillesley.

'Thank you for the use of your office today, Mr Tillesley,' he said.

'No problem at all,' said Tillesley. 'Will you require it again tomorrow? If so . . .'

'No, tomorrow Sergeant Lampson and I will be in Stepney, talking to the invaders. I wanted to check something with you I'd been told about a row between the Earl of Lancaster and one of your waiters, a Giovanni Piranesi.'

Tillesley looked unhappy.

'It was a bit more than a row, to be frank,' he said uncomfortably.

'Oh?'

'Giovanni threatened to kill the Earl,' said Tillesley.

Coburg stared at him.

'Kill him? Seriously?'

'Yes. Giovanni discovered that the Earl had either seduced his fiancée, Maria, or raped her, which is what she claimed.'

'Raped her?'

'The Earl denied it. According to the Earl, she was willing and he paid her for sex. And one of the other maids, Ella Kemble, said that was the true version.'

'Ella Kemble was the woman who told my sergeant about it, but she didn't say anything about a rape, or even this other maid being seduced.'

'Yes, well, there are doubts about how reliable Ella's evidence was, because she – in her turn – was in love with Giovanni and would have been happy for Giovanni to break off his relationship with Maria.'

'Is Maria still working here?'

'No.' Tillesley hesitated, looking unhappily, before adding: 'She killed herself. She drank bleach.'

'Giving credence to her version of events, that she was raped. Her life destroyed, she decides to end it.'

'Yes. Sadly, that does seem very plausible.'

'And the Earl got off scot-free.'

'With Maria dead, and the Earl's story backed up by Ella, there didn't seem much sense in pursuing the case. And, Giovanni was taken away for internment as an enemy alien the day after the – ah – row.'

'But before the other Italians here were taken?'

'Yes,' said Tillesley.

'That suggests the Earl used his influence to get Giovanni taken away rather quickly.'

'Yes, it does,' agreed Tillesley.

'Do you have details for Maria? Her full name, her address, any details of family in this country?'

'Yes, certainly, I'll get those from our records and let you have them.' Then, eager to change from the difficult subject, he said: 'By the way, I just received a visit from Lady Winship.'

'Yes, I saw her.'

'She asked me if we'd consider asking your wife if she'd appear at the Savoy. As Rosa Weeks. An afternoon tea session, not an evening, so it wouldn't be too demanding one hoped. But it would depend on her. They've offered to provide a pianist for her if she can't play herself. What do you think? Might she consider it?'

Coburg smiled. 'I think she might, but the best person

to ask about it is her. I've learnt never to make decisions on her behalf.'

'Thank you, I will. Where is the best place to get hold of her?'

'At the moment we're staying at my brother Magnus's flat in Eaton Square. Do you have the phone number there?'

'I believe we do. Thank you, Mr Coburg.'

CHAPTER ELEVEN

The phone was ringing as Rosa returned to the flat from her visit to the property rental agents. Edgar, she guessed, but when she picked up the receiver, she found it was Charles Tillesley calling.

'I know this is a bit of a check, Mrs Coburg, but I wondered how you would feel about appearing at the Savoy tea room during Sunday afternoon tea?' he asked.

'Appearing?' asked Rosa, puzzled.

'I know there's a situation with your left arm in plaster, but we wondered if we arranged for an accompanist for you . . .'

'You mean appear as a performer?'

'Yes. We'd be very grateful. Paid, of course. You are a professional, and for us to advertise Rosa Weeks – you still do use that as your stage name, do you?'

'Yes, although I haven't appeared on stage since I got married.'

'I understand,' said Tillesley sympathetically. 'The injury. The plaster cast. But it would be a major coup for us. There were so many wonderful reports of your two weeks at the Ritz.'

'Well . . .' responded Rosa, warily.

'If you're worried about the accompanist, I can assure you we'd find the very best for you.'

'Actually, I was wondering if I could perhaps see if I can perform, even with the plaster. My right hand is fine, and I think I may be able to vamp the bass notes with the left. Maybe even try the odd trill. My fingers feel fine, and if I can cope with the plaster . . .'

'That would be wonderful!' exclaimed Tillesley. 'Can we say this coming Sunday, twenty-second. We normally start at one o'clock, with a half hour break at a quarter to two, and then resuming at, say, quarter past two and running up to three o'clock. If that wouldn't be too much for you.'

'Not at all. Though I'd quite like to get the feel of your piano first.'

'Of course. It's a Steinway.'

'Yes, I noticed. It looks a lovely instrument. I'm keen to hear how it sounds.'

'Would tomorrow be too soon for you?'

'Tomorrow would be fine, thank you. It's just so I can feel the keys and get used to the instrument. I haven't played for a month, and I don't know how it will work with my arm.'

'I'm sure it will be excellent. But there's no pressure. If, after you've tried the piano, you feel you'd prefer to leave it a bit longer, that will be fine.'

'Thank you, Mr Tillesley. We'll see how it goes. I'll see you tomorrow.'

Inspector Lomax was just packing up to go home, when his detective sergeant, Joe Potteridge, appeared in his office.

'Sorry to trouble you, sir, but something I thought might be interesting has popped up.'

'Oh?'

'Yes, sir. I was at the Savoy just now, making sure that our team hadn't left anything behind. You know what a thieving load of bastards they are at Scotland Yard and if we had left anything they'd soon collar it.'

'And had we?'

'No, sir. But I heard something interesting. My cousin Effie works there as a maid, and she told me that DCI Coburg and his wife stayed at the hotel on Sunday night.'

'What?' said Lomax sharply, suddenly alert.

'Yes. It seems their own flat was bombed on Sunday, so they needed somewhere to stay . . .'

'And they chose the Savoy,' muttered Lomax darkly. 'And the very next day we get kicked off the case and Coburg takes it over.' He looked interrogatively at his sergeant. 'Did they pay?'

'Pay, sir?'

'For the room they had. Meals and drinks and whatever else they had that night.'

'I don't know, sir,' admitted Potteridge. 'I didn't ask. I'm just reporting back what Effie told me because I thought it was interesting. Do you want me to find out?'

'No, I'll do it,' said Lomax. 'I know how to ask without arousing suspicion.'

'Suspicion, sir?'

'You don't think it's a bit more than interesting, Sergeant? A bit more than a coincidence?'

'I don't know, sir. He stays there because he knows them. Effie says his brother stays there sometimes. The Earl of Dawlish, that's his brother.'

'I bet it is,' scowled Lomax. 'We're talking about the old boy's network, Potteridge. All taking care of one another's interests. Doing each other favours. This case would have been a feather in my cap, an Earl getting murdered at the Savoy, a high-profile murder. But it gets taken away from me the next day after Coburg stays at the same hotel.' He scowled again. 'There's something fishy here, Sergeant. And I'm going to find out what.' He got up and put his overcoat on. 'In the meantime, ask your cousin to keep an eye on Coburg while he's at the Savoy. Any hints of him getting favours there, I want to know.'

That evening, Coburg and Rosa elected to eat out at a small restaurant not far from the flat.

'But tomorrow I'll prepare dinner for us,' promised Rosa.

'With one arm in plaster?' queried Coburg.

'It didn't stop me doing it in Hampstead,' Rosa pointed out.

'Yes, but you were familiar with the kitchen there.'

'And I'll get familiar with this one,' said Rosa.

'Or I can prepare something,' said Coburg. 'I used to cook for myself.'

'That worked when there was only you,' said Rosa. 'You'd often arrive about eight, or even later, because of an issue with a job you were on. Until I'm able to get to driving an ambulance and working, I'll have meals for a reasonable hour.'

'And I'll make sure I get home for them,' promised Coburg.

'How did you get on at the Savoy today?' she asked.

Coburg gave a small groan. 'Not well,' he said. 'No one seems to have seen anything. We'll need to talk to the invaders from Stepney and see what they can tell us. Ted and I will head there tomorrow.'

'I had a call from the Savoy today. From Mr Tillesley.'

'Oh?'

'He's offered me a spot performing for their afternoon tea, this coming Sunday.'

Coburg looked at her doubtfully over his tomato soup. 'How will that work, with your arm still in plaster?'

'Mr Tillesley had thought of that, and he offered to provide me with an accompanist, but I thought I'd give it a try. I've arranged to go to the Savoy tomorrow and try out the piano. It might help my recovery, get me driving those ambulances sooner rather than later. And it's for their afternoon tea sessions, so it will be quite low key. Not like the evening spot I did at the Ritz. Just a handful of people, I expect.'

'Not once word spreads,' smiled Coburg. 'I bet the Savoy will be packed when people hear.'

Inspector Lomax walked up to the reception desk at the Savoy and produced his warrant card, which he showed to the receptionist.

'DI Lomax,' he announced. 'I understand DCI Coburg and his wife stayed here on Sunday night.'

'Yes, sir, that's correct,' said the receptionist.

'I just want to make sure the room's been paid for,' said Lomax. 'I'm not sure whether it was coming out of the police budget, in which case I need to make sure it's dealt with, or whether DCI Coburg was paying it direct.'

'If you'll hold on one moment, I'll check,' said the receptionist. He flicked back through the pages of the reservations book, muttering: 'Coburg. Coburg . . . Ah yes, here it is. One night stay, arrival, Sunday fifteenth September, checking out on the morning of Monday the sixteenth.' He looked at the entry, then added: 'Gratis.'

'Gratis?' repeated Lomax.

'Yes. Complimentary.'

'So he didn't pay?'

'No, sir. The room and board were courtesy of the hotel.'

'Thank you,' said Lomax.

He turned away and headed for the exit, a look of deep satisfaction on his face. 'Got you, you bastard!' he muttered triumphantly.

CHAPTER TWELVE

Tuesday 17th September

Coburg drove while Lampson acted as navigator. They were on the way to Stepney, to the address Jenny Huxton had given Coburg for her father. It was the first time either of them had been to the East End since the Blitz began, and even though they'd heard the area had been badly damaged, they were stunned to be driving through areas where street after street seemed to have disappeared, leaving piles of rubble. Amazingly, people were still going about their business, picking their way over the piles of smashed bricks, or wheeling prams along the crater-ridden roadways.

'I thought we had it bad in Hampstead when our flats were demolished, but this is far worse,' commented Coburg.

'It's because it's near the docks,' said Lampson. 'The Germans trying to put our shipping out of action. No ships means no food coming in. They're trying to starve us out.'

'If this is how they suffered it's no wonder they tried to get into the Savoy shelter,' said Coburg. 'In their place, I'd have done the same.'

'Why don't they open up the Tube stations?' asked Lampson angrily. 'That's what they ought to do in places like this.'

'The Government say they're worried they'll interfere with the running of the trains.'

'So let 'em in once the trains stop, at least people'd be safe after ten o'clock at night, and that's when most of the bombing happens.' He fell silent for a moment, taking in the wreckage on either side of them, then said: 'I hear some of the Tube stations have started to let people in already. Not officially, but let's face it, if a woman turns up with four kids and wants to come in and the bombs are falling outside, who's going to turn them away?'

'It's happened,' said Coburg. 'There was a riot the other day at Liverpool Street.'

'Yeh, I heard about it,' said Lampson. 'The station manager had the doors shut to stop people coming in, and the crowd went to work on them and tore the doors open. They should have strung him up.' Then, calming down, he asked: 'So, guv, what do you reckon? Is this William Lancaster in the frame?'

'Perhaps, but what's his motive? He'd broken away from his father and gone off to make a life of his own in Stepney. Why choose to kill him now, and in such difficult circumstances? If we're looking for motives I think revenge for the rape and death of Giovanni Piranesi's fiancée, Maria di Capa, holds more possibilities.'

'She was Italian as well?'

'Yes. I got her details from Charles Tillesley. She was

originally from Sicily, as was Giovanni Piranesi, and the Sicilians have a very long history of revenge.'

'It can't have been Piranesi who bumped off the Earl; he was locked up at Ascot.'

'But he will have had friends. And Maria will also have had friends and possibly relatives over here. I think we need to look into them, and we'll start with a visit to Mr Piranesi at Ascot tomorrow. And you can drive.'

'Thanks, guv,' beamed Lampson. Suddenly he said: 'Here we are. On the right. Cavendish Street.'

Coburg turned into the side street, pulled the car into the kerb and parked.

'It looks like this street's still standing, anyway,' he said.

Number 23 was in the middle of a row of terraced houses which surprisingly stood intact amongst the ruination that surrounded them. Coburg knocked at the door, which was opened by a short, thin belligerent-looking man.

'Mr Tom Huxton?' asked Coburg.

'Who wants to know?' demanded the man.

'Detective Chief Inspector Coburg from Scotland Yard. This is Sergeant Lampson. Your daughter, Jenny, gave us your address.'

'Yes, she said,' grunted Huxton. 'You're looking into the toff who got done at the Savoy.'

'That's correct. May we come in?'

'Why?'

'To talk.'

'I've got nothing to say.'

'Very well,' said Coburg politely. 'It's up to you. We can either have this conversation here, in your house, or you can come with us to Scotland Yard and talk there.'

'What is this?' said Huxton aggressively. 'Gestapo tactics?'

'No,' said Lampson sharply. 'It's the sort of tactics Joe Stalin uses to keep the Russian people under, which he does to keep in with his Nazi mate, Hitler.'

Huxton glared angrily at Lampson. 'You're a traitor to your class you are, mate,' he snapped. 'Siding with the enemy.'

'The enemy is Hitler,' said Coburg. 'Now, may we come in?'

Reluctantly, Huxton stood aside and let Coburg and Lampson walk in, then he led them down a narrow passageway to a kitchen at the far end. The kitchen was quite bare: an iron range, currently unlit, a wooden table and four chairs, and a kitchen dresser, bare of any adornments or crockery.

'Is your daughter here today?' asked Coburg.

'No,' said Huxton. 'She's out.' He gestured for them to sit.

'Mr Huxton, I've been told you led the invasion of the Savoy last Saturday night,' said Coburg.

'Yes, I did, and I'm proud of it!' said Huxton. 'We're sick and tired of being bombed with no proper shelter, while the rich elite have everything. It made me sick when I saw in the paper about the shelter at the Savoy, them boasting about how it had every luxury they could want, if they had the money to stay there.'

'You stayed there.'

'On sufferance!' Then, awkwardly, he added: 'That Swiss bloke who let us in was decent, I'll say that for him. But that one night don't alter the fact that the rich and aristocrats make sure they're safe, while we ordinary people suffer.'

'Five high explosive bombs were dropped on Buckingham Palace last Friday morning, while the King and Queen were there,' countered Coburg. 'The royal chapel, the inner quadrangle, the palace gates and the Victoria Memorial were all either destroyed or badly damaged, and quite a few of the palace staff were seriously injured. But just a few hours later, the King and Queen went to the East End to inspect the bomb damage there. That's hardly staying safe. And it wasn't the first time the palace was hit by bombs.' He ticked the dates off on his fingers. 'The 8th Sept, the 9th Sept . . .'

'Yes, all right,' Huxton blustered uncomfortably. 'But they can get away from the bombing if they wanted to. They're rich.'

'They can, but they've said they won't,' said Coburg. 'Are you saying they're lying?'

'No,' said Huxton grudgingly. 'They're different. Special. They're not like most of that bunch.' He looked at Coburg quizzically. 'Are you related to them?'

'To whom?'

'To whom,' mimicked Huxton. 'Yeh, they said you was a toff. Saxe-Coburg, they said your proper name was in the paper. The Hon. So, same as the King and Queen before they changed it to Windsor.'

'They were Saxe-Coburg-Gotha,' Coburg pointed out.

'All right, one hyphen less,' grunted Huxton. 'What are you? A cousin?'

'I'm a detective chief inspector from Scotland Yard,' Coburg told him firmly. 'And I'm trying to find out who killed the Earl of Lancaster.'

'Well it wasn't one of us,' said Huxton defensively. 'We were all together in a separate section from the toffs. None of us had anything to do with 'em.'

'William Lancaster did,' said Coburg. 'He went through the curtain to talk to his mother.'

'And your inspector nicked him!' shouted Huxton.

'He's no longer on the case,' said Coburg. 'I am. In order to move the case forward, I need to talk to everyone who was in the shelter that night. I already have a list of the guests and the hotel staff. I'll need a list of the people who were in your group.'

'You expect me to grass them up!' jeered Huxton.

'No, I expect a list of their names so I can talk to them, the same as I'm talking to everyone else.'

'Are you going to release William?' demanded Huxton. 'He didn't do it. He was only arrested because it was his old man who got killed.'

'If things add up,' said Coburg. 'There are one or two things about his statement I have to check first. And to corroborate that I need evidence from those people in your group who were with him in the shelter that night. And the only way to get that is by talking to them.' He pushed a sheet of paper and a pencil across the desk towards Huxton. 'You say he's innocent and you want him to be set free. So give me the names of people I can talk to, to clear him.'

Huxton hesitated, then said. 'I think you're being straight, so I'll come round with you. People are more likely to talk to you if they know I'm with you. It'll mean it's OK.'

'That's fair enough.' nodded Coburg. 'According to the Savoy there were about forty people, so that's a lot of houses to call on.'

'Not so much,' said Huxton. 'Some of the houses have got eight people in and they all came. Families round here stay together.'

'We'll still need their names for the record,' said Coburg.

Huxton pushed the piece of paper back to Coburg. 'You can write 'em up as we go round.'

CHAPTER THIRTEEN

Huxton took them to seven houses. Two had just three people living there, the other five were filled to overflowing with parents, grandparents and children of all ages. At each house Lampson wrote the name of the family on the sheet of paper, while Coburg asked the questions. As they went from house to house, Coburg reflected that it was a good thing that Tom Huxton had offered to accompany them. As soon as Coburg opened his mouth and they heard his upper-class accent they became suspicious. It was Huxton's presence, and occasionally nodding to the families that it was all right to talk, that prevented the street doors from being shut in their faces.

The end result confirmed what Huxton had already told Coburg: no one from their group had gone through the curtain to where the Savoy's regular guests were sleeping, except for William Lancaster. And he'd only gone through for about five minutes around midnight.

After the last house, Coburg thanked Huxton for his time and his co-operation, and held out his hand. Huxton looked at it in surprise, then shook it.

'You're all right,' he said. Then he looked at Lampson and added sourly: 'You, I'm not sure about.' He turned back to Coburg and asked: 'Are you going to release William?'

'With what we've heard, I can't see any reason to keep him in jail,' replied Coburg.

They returned to the car.

'Do you want to do the drive back to the Yard?' asked Coburg.

Lampson's smile lit up his face.

'Thanks, guv,' he said.

Driving was one of Lampson's pleasures, but lacking a car of his own, meant his only real opportunity was acting as chauffeur for Coburg. As they drove through the ruined streets, Coburg mused: 'Strange that Huxton was fine with me, but suspicious of you. I'd have thought it would be the other way round.'

'No, guv, that's not the way it works with Commies like Huxton. They expect people like you to be the enemy and hostile to them, so they're pleasantly surprised when you turn out to be a decent bloke. A bloke who talks like me, the same way they do, they expect me to be on their side. The fact I challenged him means I'm the enemy. A traitor to the cause of the workers.' He gave a derisive laugh. 'Not that half of 'em have ever done a proper day's work in their life.'

'And how do they view William Lancaster?'

'With deep suspicion. He talks like one of your lot but tries to act like one of them.'

'Tom Huxton's daughter is in love with him.'

'And that's the reason why Huxton came round with us today. He wants to get the boy freed for her sake. If it wasn't for that, he'd have left him to rot.'

Rosa sat at the grand piano in the Savoy's tea room, the fingers of her right hand gently caressing the keys, and every now and then she allowed her plaster-encased left hand to rest on the piano's wooden edge while she ran bass triplets. So far, so good, she thought with relieved satisfaction. She also determined to go and see her orthopaedic surgeon at St Thomas's, Mr Bailey, and make arrangements for the heavy plaster to be removed and replaced with a lighter support, perhaps an elastic bandage, something she could hide beneath a pair of long opera gloves.

She finished her practice and let her hands drop into her lap, then stood, ready to go.

'That was wonderful.'

Rosa looked at the tall, rather thin, elegantly dressed woman smiling at her.

'I stayed outside because I didn't want to put you off,' added the woman. 'But when I realised you'd finished I just had to tell you how exhilarating that was. I feel privileged.'

'That's very kind of you,' said Rosa.

'Just honest appreciation,' said the woman. She held out her hand. 'Julia Winship. Lady Winship to most people, but I'd feel honoured if you'd call me Julia. I know you, of course. Rosa Weeks. Or is it now Rosa Coburg?'

'Professionally, it's still Rosa Weeks,' said Rosa, shaking the woman's hand.

'I believe you were here to try out the piano and see if it will suit you. I do hope it does and you'll agree to appear here.'

'The piano is wonderful,' said Rosa. 'To be honest, I'm just trying out my arm in case the plaster interferes with my playing.'

'I can assure you, it doesn't. How much longer do you have to have it on?'

'Hopefully, not much longer,' said Rosa. 'I'm due to see the surgeon soon.'

'How did you do it, if you don't mind my asking? We met your husband earlier, Inspector Coburg, who interviewed us about this dreadful murder, and he told us you'd had an accident, but he didn't say how. Not the bombing, I hope.'

'No,' said Rosa. 'It was just an unfortunate incident. One of those things.'

'He said you're planning to drive ambulances.'

'Another reason for playing the piano, to help get strength back in my arm.'

'You don't think it could be dangerous?' asked Lady Winship, concerned.

'No more dangerous than what everyone else is experiencing.'

'Yes. Your husband told us you said you hoped the war would come to a speedy conclusion. I say, amen to that. I couldn't agree more. And the same goes for my husband. Why don't you come to tea one afternoon? Eric and I hold occasional soirees in our suite here. There'll be some

115

interesting people there. Many of them have some good ideas about how we can bring this dreadful war to an end, but with honour. Please say you'll come.'

Rosa hesitated, wondering what to say, then gave a smile and a nod. 'Yes,' she said. 'I'll be delighted.'

Coburg returned to the Yard and signed the necessary documents to release William Lancaster from custody. He and Lampson then took him up to their office.

'I'm letting you go,' said Coburg.

'You've found out who did it?' asked William. 'The person who killed my father?'

'No,' said Coburg. 'The investigation is continuing. Because of that, your release is provisional, so I'll need your address in case I have to talk to you again.' And Coburg pushed a piece of paper and a pencil across the desk to him.

'So I'm still under suspicion,' said William sullenly.

'No more so than anyone else, and we also have all their names and addresses. It's still an open case.'

William wrote an address on the paper. 'I lodge with a family,' he said. 'Mr and Mrs Kennet and their son, Walter. They're good people.'

'I'm sure they are,' said Coburg, taking the paper and putting it in the file.

'Am I allowed to go back to the Savoy?' asked William. 'I'd like to let my mother know I've been released.'

'By all means. Let me pave the way for you, just in case there are any difficulties.'

Coburg picked up the phone and asked the switchboard to ring the Savoy hotel. When he got through he asked for

Lady Lancaster. 'Please tell her it's Chief Inspector Coburg calling.'

There were a series of clicks, then the operator said: 'You're through, caller.'

'Inspector Coburg?' came Lady Lancaster's anxious voice.

'Indeed it is, Lady Lancaster. I have someone here who'd like to talk to you.'

He handed the receiver to William, who said: 'Is that you, Mother?' There was a burst of excited speech from the other end that Coburg couldn't make out, then William said: 'Calm down, Mother. I'm fine, and I've been released. Would it be convenient for me to call at the Savoy and see you?'

Again, came the excited words, then William said: 'I'll see you shortly,' and hung up.

'She said she wants to thank you in person,' William told Coburg.

'Tell her there's no need. Sergeant Lampson and I were just doing our job.'

William nodded and left.

'Mother and son reunited,' said Lampson. 'That's our good deed for the day.' He looked at Coburg. 'What's the plan for tomorrow, guv?'

'Ascot,' said Coburg. 'We'll talk to this Giovanni Piranesi and find out just how much he hated Lancaster, and maybe get a hint if he arranged for revenge.'

'Ascot.' nodded Lampson. 'It'll get us out of the city.'

'It will indeed,' agreed Coburg. 'And you can drive.'

*　*　*

117

When he got back to the flat, Coburg discovered Rosa in the act of making a shepherd's pie. 'Or, a sort of shepherd's pie,' she said. 'Blame rationing. It's mostly vegetables, but there's enough meat to give it a taste.'

'And all done with one arm in plaster,' said Coburg, impressed. 'How did the piano go today?'

'Very good,' said Rosa. 'I'll have a few more practices with it before I put myself before the paying customers, but I'm very hopeful. There was one interesting thing. After I'd done my practice, I was approached by a Lady Julia Winship.'

'Ah yes,' nodded Coburg. 'I talked to her and her husband.'

'Yes, she mentioned that. The thing is, she talked to me about the war.'

'Well, it is everyone's major topic of conversation at the moment,' said Coburg.

'Yes, but I got the feeling that this was different.'

'In what way?'

'She said you'd told her I'd said I wished the war could come to a speedy conclusion, and she said she and her husband felt exactly the same. She added that many of her friends were of the same view and she suggested I join them for tea one afternoon. Just an informal get-together, she said, to chat and see what could be done to spread the word.'

'And what word would that be?'

'It sounded to me like appeasement.'

'Surrender?' asked Coburg.

'I may be wrong,' said Rosa.

'But you may not be,' said Coburg thoughtfully. 'I questioned the Winships as part of the murder investigation, and I must admit I didn't like them much. There's something unpleasantly superior about them. And it's nothing to do with them being upper class. No one's more upper class than Magnus, but he doesn't rub it in people's faces.'

Rosa chuckled. 'It's not just Magnus; you're the same.'

'I'm not upper class,' protested Coburg.

'Oh come on!' chuckled Rosa derisively. 'The son of an earl. Educated at Eton. You speak the most perfect English.'

'I am English,' pointed out Coburg.

'You know what I mean. You can't help it, it's who you are because of the family you were born into and the way you were brought up. It gives you an air. But you don't play on it, just like you said about Magnus. Now the Winships, on the other hand . . .'

'Yes, I agree,' nodded Coburg. 'I suggest the best thing is for you to make some polite excuse about why you unfortunately can't make it.'

'I'm thinking the opposite,' said Rosa thoughtfully.

'What? Why?'

'Even before the war began there was talk of a group of influential people who wanted to make peace with Hitler.'

'Yes, and most of them are now under lock and key.'

'Only those who were members of Mosley's crowd, the British Union of Fascists. But there were others, not so obvious. You told me about them yourself, Edgar. Many of them well-meaning. They supported Halifax over Churchill because Halifax was trying to make a deal with Hitler, using the Italians as intermediaries, one that would keep Britain out of the war.'

'Yes,' said Coburg.

'But there were others who weren't so well-meaning and who positively supported Hitler, but hadn't been spotted as possible traitors because they weren't in the BUF.'

'I don't think they could all be described as traitors.'

'Well what else would you call it?'

'And you think the Winships fit that description?'

'I don't know,' admitted Rosa. 'They may just be disgruntled about things, but if they are some kind of fifth column, don't you think someone should be told?'

'And you plan to go to this soirée of the Winships' to see if there's any evidence of treasonable intent.'

'Yes,' said Rosa. 'And if I feel there is, I'll tell you about it, and you can do whatever needs to be done.'

CHAPTER FOURTEEN

Wednesday 18th September

Coburg was glad of the opportunity to be a passenger and take in the surroundings as Lampson drove them to Ascot. Their journey across Berkshire took them through Virginia Water. Although there were the signs that a war was on – piles of sandbags, Home Guard sentry points protected by barbed wire at intervals – it was still a different feeling in the countryside from being in London. Yes, the odd stray bomb may cause some damage out here as a result of some bomber pilot overshooting his intended target, but it wasn't the same as living under the constant barrage of bombing. Although these last two days, Coburg had noticed a dropping off of the number and length of German attacks. Or it may have been just that he was becoming acclimatised to it, just as had happened to him during the First War when he was in the trenches.

'Bertram Mills Circus,' said Lampson nostalgically. 'I took Terry to see them last year, just before the war. He loved it. Particularly the animals. But he didn't think much of the clowns, which surprised me. I suppose all the animals have been moved.'

'Not just the animals. Once the circus's winter quarters was offered to the Government as an internment camp, everyone had to be moved. Clowns and all.'

Lampson gave a snort. 'Frankly, guv, I think they must've put the clowns in charge of this internment stuff. Take this business of the Italians, for example. There's this neighbour of mine, Antonio, who's Italian. He works as a waiter at an Italian restaurant near St Pancras station. Been here for six years. Married an English girl and they've got three kids. Lovely couple. He told me once he left Italy because of what was happening there with Mussolini, so he's no fan of fascism. But he's been rounded up and interned, just because he's Italian. His wife and kids are still in Somers Town and struggling to make ends meet because they don't have his wages coming in. Fortunately, her family are still around, so they help out. But it don't seem right to me.'

'I agree. Is he at Ascot?'

Lampson shook his head.

'He's on the Isle of Man. Lucky for him he wasn't selected for the Arandora Star.'

'The Arandora Star,' said Coburg thoughtfully. 'Wasn't that the ship that took a load of interned aliens to Canada?'

'Except it only got as far as the west coast of Ireland before a German U-boat sank it,' said Lampson. 'When it happened it was the talk of Somers Town, everyone wondering if Antonio was on the boat. His missus was in a right state. It took ages before they confirmed that he was

122

still on the Isle of Man.' He gave a snort of disgust. 'Run a war? Sometimes I think this lot couldn't run a whelk stall.'

Coburg remembered the event now. The authorities had been concerned at the large number of Germans, Austrians and Italians being interned, and having to be guarded, so arrangements had been made to send a number to Canada, where the Canadians would inter them. Early in July the SS Arandora had set sail from Liverpool with 800 Italians and 500 Germans, 200 military to guard them and the ship's crew of 200. For some reason it had been decided not to give the ship a naval escort to protect it. A German U-boat lying in wait off the west coasts of Ireland had spotted the ship, and torpedoed it. Reports said that 900 died, most of them internees, but also the captain, and many of his crew and the military guards. It was said that bodies from the sinking were still being washed ashore on the Irish coast.

Very few of the newspapers had carried reports of the sinking at the time. The main headlines had been about the Royal Navy's attack on the French fleet in Algeria, when a large number of French naval ships had been sunk to prevent the Germans using them. And then, of course, had come the Blitz. Once that began, mass deaths had to be enormous in order to be memorable.

'It looks like we're here, guv,' said Lampson.

On the outskirts of Ascot they came upon a massive encampment of single-storey brick buildings and enormous bell tents made of canvas. Surrounding it was a high double fence of barbed wire, with machine-gun posts and watchtowers stationed at intervals behind the wire, and huge lights on stands.

'Why have they got those massive lights?' asked Lampson. 'They can't put them on at night because of the blackout.'

'Except for here,' said Coburg. 'I checked and it seems that under international law this camp at Ascot has to be illuminated at night.'

'That's good news for the Luftwaffe,' commented Lampson sourly. 'Helps 'em navigate towards London.'

They parked in the visitors' car park and, after showing their warrant cards, were taken to see the man in charge, John Whitehall.

'Scotland Yard,' mused Whitehall. He was a tall, chubby man in his fifties with a mop of uncontrollable blond fluffy hair. 'I bet you're glad to be out of the smoke for a bit, a bit of a break from being bombed.'

'I'm not sure I'd fancy changing it for being here,' said Coburg. 'All these lights make a perfect target for the Luftwaffe.'

Whitehall grinned and shook his head. 'I get the idea they've been told by Berlin that it marks a camp for internees, German as well as Italians, so not to touch it. Lucky for us. What can I do for you?'

'We'd like a word with one of your internees, Giovanni Piranesi,' said Coburg. 'But, before we do, do you keep records of visitors?'

'Only those who are visiting a prisoner,' said Whitehall.

'In that case, can you let me know who has visited Piranesi since he's been here.'

'I can,' said Whitehall, and he went to a shelf and took down a ledger marked 'Visitors book'. 'Mind, it only

124

includes individual visitors. By that I mean we get all sorts of vicars and priests coming to give spiritual comfort.' He chuckled. 'Frankly, this lot would prefer a good bottle of wine, but it's all part of saving souls, so I'm told.' He opened the ledger and flicked through the pages. 'Here we are,' he said. 'He's had two visits. A pal of his from the Savoy called Hector McMurdie. He brought up some stuff that Giovanni had left in his locker at the Savoy.'

'What sort of stuff?'

'A change of clothes, including a pair of shoes. We check everything that comes in.'

'And the other visitor?'

'A woman called Alessandra di Capa.'

'When did she come to see him?'

'Friday September thirteenth.'

'Did she stay long?'

Whitehall checked the time of entry and time of departure. 'Half an hour.'

'Did she give an address?'

Whitehall nodded. 'Twenty-two Wardour Street, London, W1,' he told them. 'That's in Soho, ain't it. Lots of Italians in Soho.' Then he gave a light laugh. 'Only not so many these days. We've got most of 'em here.'

Whitehall was about to close the book, when he stopped, spotting another name. 'There was another woman who turned up soon after Piranesi was sent here, but I don't suppose she counts because Piranesi refused to see her.' He read the name. 'Ella Kemble.'

'The maid at the Savoy who told me about him,' muttered Lampson.

As they followed Whitehall across the square to the interview room, Coburg murmured, 'So, we have a possible relative of Maria's coming to see Mr Piranesi the day before the Earl was killed.'

'The Sicilians and revenge?' asked Lampson.

'It's certainly worth looking into.'

At the Strand police station, Inspector Lomax sat at his desk and studied the reports that had been coming in during the past twenty-four hours about a team of pickpockets operating in the Covent Garden area. Pickpockets, he cursed silently. I should have been on the Savoy murder, that's where you get noticed. That bastard Coburg cutting him out like that.

'Excuse me, sir.' It was Sergeant Potteridge, peering round the door.

'Yes?' asked Lomax sourly. Whatever it was, it was unlikely to be good news. There was rarely any good news these days.

'You know you asked me to keep an eye on what Coburg was up to at the Savoy. Remember, my cousin Effie?'

Immediately, Lomax was alert. 'Yes,' he said, but his tone was altogether different, keen.

'Well, Effie overheard Lady Lancaster offering Coburg her late husband's London flat to use, because his own got bombed.'

'Did she now! Was this after he got her son released from jail?'

'I don't know, sir. It may have been before.'

'Well find out. Because, whichever it was, it sounds like

a deal to me. She offers him her London flat if he gets her son out of jail. And hey presto, he's out on the streets.' A smirk flickered around his lips. 'What with that and the room at the Savoy he got free, I think we might be able to bring Mr High-and-Mighty Coburg down to earth . . .'

Coburg and Lampson were in a small austere room, the walls of red brick exposed, the windows with boards fixed crosswise over them in an attempt to keep the glass intact in the event of a bombing raid. Giovanni Piranesi sat at the wooden table facing the two Scotland Yard detectives under the baleful, watchful eye of one of the camp's guards. Whether it was called an aliens internment camp or a selection centre, or any other euphemistic label, to Coburg it was a prisoner-of-war camp.

Piranesi was a handsome, slightly arrogant-looking slim man in his mid-twenties with a pencil-moustache, his dark wavy hairs slicked back. Prisoners were allowed to wear their own clothes, and Piranesi was obviously a man who took pride in his appearance. His jacket and trousers were clean and pressed, possibly from being kept under the mattress at night.

'What do the police want with me?' he demanded.

'The Earl of Lancaster is dead,' said Coburg.

Piranesi looked at them warily, then he smiled. 'Good.'

'You're glad?'

'Of course I am. If you're here to talk to me you must know why. He killed my Maria.'

'We understand she committed suicide.'

'Because of what he did to her!' He looked at them

questioningly. 'How did he die?'

'He was stabbed.'

'Good,' said Piranesi again. 'Who stabbed him?'

'That's what we're trying to find out.'

Piranesi gave a mirthless chuckle as he said: 'Well it wasn't me. I haven't been anywhere but here since that bastard had me locked up.'

'Can you think of anyone who might have wanted to kill him?'

'Plenty of people. The husbands of all the women he abused. Everyone who ever met him. He was feccia. Scum.'

'We were told of your situation by Ella Kemble, one of your co-workers at the Savoy,' said Coburg.

Piranesi stared at them in anger, then hissed: 'Do not mention that bitch's name to me. She killed Maria as much as that bastard the Earl. She lied.' He spat on the floor to show his disgust. 'She had the nerve to come and ask to see me here. I told them do not let her in. I never want to see the bitch unless I am holding a knife or a gun.'

'Is there any friend of yours who might want to take revenge on the Earl for what happened to you and Maria?' asked Coburg.

Piranesi stared at him as if he were stupid.

'You think I would tell you?' he demanded angrily. 'If it were so, I would shake that person by the hand!' He shook his head. 'You'll get no names from me.'

'Mr Piranesi, we are police officers. We are sympathetic to you and what happened, but we are investigating a murder. Now it's quite likely that our investigation will require us to dig into the lives of people you know, who were friends of yours, in order to get to the truth. It's quite likely that it was no one who was associated with you, but our questioning will definitely cause their lives to be upset. Innocent people caused distress, and possibly losing their jobs, just because they are friends of yours. You can save most of them pain by telling us if there is anyone you can think of who'd be most likely to kill the Earl to pay him back for what he did to Maria, and for what's happened to you. For example, tell us about Alessandra di Capa. I assume she's a relation of Maria's.'

'Alessandra is nothing to do with what happened to the dead man. Or what he did to Maria.'

'She came to see you.' When Giovanni didn't answer, his mouth remaining firmly shut, Coburg added: 'Her name is in the visitors' book. She came to see you here on Friday Thirteenth September. The day before the Earl was killed.'

'So?'

'Is she a relative of Maria's?'

Piranesi nodded. 'Her older sister.'

'Why did she come to see you?'

'Because she is a good person.'

'She must have been very angry over what happened to Maria.'

'She was – how you say – distraught.'

'She must have wanted revenge for what the Earl of Lancaster did.'

Piranesi glared angrily at Coburg. 'If you are suggesting . . .'

'I'm just asking.'

'Alessandra could not kill.'

129

'With respect, Mr Piranesi, anyone can kill.'

'Not Alessandra. She is in holy orders.'

Coburg frowned, puzzled. 'Are you saying she's a nun?'

Piranesi nodded.

'In Soho?' asked Coburg, still puzzled.

'There is a convent there. The Sisters of St Josephine. The sisters take their message to the sinners they live among. What better place for a church than where sin exists.'

On the drive back to London, Coburg and Lampson discussed what they'd learnt.

'A nun?' said Lampson in disbelief.

'We only have Piranesi's word for that,' said Coburg.

'Easy enough to check,' said Lampson.

'If she's really a nun, why didn't she give her religious name to the staff at Ascot?' mused Coburg. 'Most nuns take on a new name, a new identity, and lose their past one.'

'With luck we'll find out when we talk to her,' said Lampson. 'One thing we can be sure of, it doesn't sound like Ella Kemble is one of his favourite people, so I think we can count her out as his avenging angel. Where to next, guv?'

'Back to the Yard to see if anything new's happened. And then maybe to Soho to check out this alleged convent, the Sisters of Josephine.'

'Alleged?' asked Lampson. 'You don't reckon they're real.'

'They may be real, but whether they're actually a genuine convent or part of holy orders is another matter. When I was on beat duty I knew a brothel where the prostitutes dressed up as nuns, and in Soho anything goes.'

It was late afternoon when they returned to the Yard. They were walking across the marbled-floor reception hall when the desk sergeant hailed them. He was holding the telephone receiver and he held it out towards Coburg.

'It's the Savoy for you, sir,' he said. 'They've just phoned as you walked in.'

Coburg took the receiver from him.

'DCI Coburg,' he said.

'Mr Coburg, it's Charles Tillesley at the Savoy.'

'Yes, Mr Tillesley. What can I do for you?'

'There's been another one,' said Tillesley in a voice filled with anguish.

'Another one?' asked Coburg, puzzled.

'A dead body. This time it's one of the maids. I think she was stabbed, just like the Earl.'

CHAPTER FIFTEEN

Coburg and Lampson stood with Charles Tillesley in the sluice in the Savoy's basement and looked at the dead body of the woman in the maid's uniform lying face down on the floor. Blood had spread across her uniform from the wound in her back. A uniformed police constable stood on guard at the door.

'Daisy Scott,' said Tillesley. 'One of the other maids came in here and opened the cupboard to get a mop and bucket, and she tumbled out.'

Coburg noticed a slight red smear on the rim of one of the row of sinks at one side of the sluice. He examined it closely, then pronounced: 'I'm pretty sure it's blood, but we'll get it checked. If it is, it suggests she was stabbed while working at the sink, then her body was dragged to the cupboard and stuffed into it.' He pointed at some marks on the floor between the sink and the cupboard. 'It looks like someone's mopped the path where she was dragged, but not the rest of the floor.' He looked at Tillesley. 'Does anyone know what time she was in here? Did anyone see her?'

'We haven't asked yet. When she was found, we telephoned you immediately.'

'I'm going to arrange for her body to be removed for the autopsy, so we'll know for certain if she was stabbed, and with what. I'm going to have her body sent to University College Hospital. Dr Welbourne there did the autopsy on the Earl, and I want to see if he spots any similarities. I agree that the blood indicates she was stabbed in the back, the same as the Earl, but I'm puzzled by the fact there's a smear of blood on the rim of the sink. If she was standing up you'd have expected her to fall straight down to the floor. The only way blood would be on the rim from a wound in her back would be if she was slumped over the edge, with her head in the sink.' He looked at Tillesley and asked: 'Have her family been informed?'

'No,' said Tillesley. 'They're not on the telephone, and I thought it best if they were notified officially by the police.'

'I'll do it,' offered Lampson. 'Where did she live?'

'Stepney,' said Tillesley.

'Interesting,' mused Coburg. 'Do you have her address?'

'Indeed. If you come with me to my office, Sergeant, I'll give it to you. And please do tell her family we offer our condolences.'

Lampson nodded in agreement, then turned back to Coburg. 'Anything else while I'm in Stepney, guv? Anyone I should talk to?'

'Not at this stage,' said Coburg. He took the car keys from his pocket and passed them to Lampson. 'Take the car and I'll see you back here. I'll start talking to people once I've arranged for her body to be removed.'

Lampson nodded again, then followed the hotel manager out of the sluice and up the stairs towards his office.

Coburg called to the constable. 'Stay here and keep an eye on things, Constable. Don't let anyone in. I'll get someone to replace you once the body's been taken away.'

Coburg headed up to the reception hall, where he asked to use the concierge's telephone. His first call was to Scotland Yard, requesting a vehicle and officers to come to the Savoy to collect the dead woman's body.

'They're to take it to University College Hospital,' he said. 'I'll give them a note to take with them telling them who to leave it for.'

Next, he phoned the hospital. Dr Welbourne wasn't available, so Coburg left a message telling the mortuary to expect delivery of a recently killed person to be autopsied as a matter of urgency.

He wrote a note to Dr Welbourne telling him that he'd like him to be the one to carry out the medical examination, and wrote his telephone number at Scotland Yard in the note. He put it in an envelope which he took down to the sluice and handed to the constable. 'When they arrive to take the body away, give them this, and tell them to make sure they hand it in and that Dr Welbourne sees it.'

Lampson came down the stairs from Tillesley's office, Daisy Scott's address in Stepney in his pocket, and was heading for the exit to the car park, when he was stopped by a woman's voice calling out: 'Sergeant Lampson!'

Lampson turned and saw Ella Kemble, in her maid's uniform, hurrying towards him, an anxious expression on her face.

'If it's about Daisy Scott . . .' Lampson began, but Ella cut him off.

'No,' she said. 'I mean, it's terrible what happened to her. Everyone's worried about what's happening here. No, it's about Giovanni. I was told you and Inspector Coburg went to Ascot today.'

'Yes,' said Lampson. 'How did you know?'

'Someone told me,' she said. 'How was he? Is he going to be released?'

'He seems well enough,' said Lampson. 'As for being released, that's not for us to say. We don't have any control over that. But my guess is, no.'

'But he's done nothing wrong!' she burst out, almost in tears.

'I'm sorry, but there's nothing we, as the police, can do,' said Lampson.

'It's so unfair!' she raged, glaring angrily at him. 'There are people who know it's unfair! They should be the ones locked up, not him!'

With that, she turned on her heel and stormed away, and Lampson noticed her hand went to her face, wiping tears from her eyes.

Coburg was coming up to the reception area from the basement when he heard a familiar voice calling urgently: 'Inspector Coburg!'

Lady Lancaster hurried towards him and he could see that she was desperately trying not to break down from the way her hands twisted and clenched together.

'Lady Lancaster,' said Coburg.

'You're here because of the . . . the dead woman. The maid?'

'I am,' confirmed Coburg.

'It wasn't William!' she declared passionately, her whole body shaking.

Coburg look at her in surprise. 'No one's suggested it was,' he said.

'Yes they have. It's the way they look at me!' She twisted her hands together, doing her best to calm down as she explained. 'I have to talk to you!'

'And we will,' Coburg reassured her. 'Right now I need to talk to Mr Tillesley, and after that I'll talk to you again and get your statement about William's actions.'

'He didn't do it,' she said again.

'And I hope that the evidence I'll be gathering will prove that,' said Coburg. 'As soon as I've spoken to Mr Tillesley I'll contact you and we can talk.'

'Could you come to my suite?' asked Lady Lancaster. 'I feel so vulnerable outside of it, especially being questioned. I feel like everyone's watching me, accusingly.'

'Very well,' nodded Coburg. 'After I've spoken to Mr Tillesley I'll come to your suite. Give me half an hour.'

Coburg headed up the stairs to Tillesley's office and found the hotel manager on the phone. He hung up as Coburg appeared.

'I was just letting Mr D'Oyly Carte know,' he said. 'He's most unhappy. He said he'd be most grateful if you can clear the situation up as quickly as possible. It's creating a dreadful atmosphere for the hotel.'

'We'll do our very best,' Coburg assured him. 'May I use your telephone? It looks as if I'm going to be here for a while, and I need to let my wife know I'll be late home.'

'Of course,' said Tillesley. 'How is she? She was here the other day trying out our piano.'

'Which she said is excellent, and she's looking forward to appearing here.'

'That is so good,' said Tillesley.

He pushed the telephone towards Coburg, who asked the operator for Magnus's number. Rosa answered.

'Rosa, it's Edgar. I'm at the Savoy. I'm afraid there's been another murder.'

'Oh no! Who?'

'One of the maids. I'll tell you more when I see you, but I'm phoning to let you know I'm going to be stuck here for a while yet.'

'That's all right,' said Rosa.

'I advise you to go ahead and eat without me. I'm not sure when I'll be home.'

'I can wait,' said Rosa. 'By the way, I had a phone call today from Lady Winship inviting me to her soirée in her suite at the Savoy tomorrow.'

Coburg hesitated, then asked: 'You sure you still want to do this?'

'I do,' said Rosa. 'But like you and this latest murder, we can talk about it when you get back. Go on with catching

137

your murderer. I'll see you later.'

Coburg replaced the receiver, then said to Tillesley: 'I understand that William Lancaster stayed here last night.'

'Yes,' said Tillesley.

'Do you know what time he left?'

Tillesley frowned. 'I'm not sure. I know he had lunch with his mother. I think it might have been some time after that.'

'Not to worry; I'll check with the doorman,' said Coburg.

Coburg was heading for the Savoy's main entrance to talk to the doorman, when he changed his mind and headed for Lady Lancaster's suite. If he didn't talk to her soon she'd only come to look for him, such was her state of agitation. He knocked at her door, and immediately the door was flung open and Lady Lancaster ushered him in, her face a picture of grief and worry.

'We can talk frankly,' she said. 'I've sent my maid, Jane, off to give us privacy.' She gestured for Coburg to sit, but she herself paced the room. 'I can't believe it!' she said agitatedly. 'Someone is doing this to implicate William!'

'Why would anyone want to do that?' asked Coburg.

'I don't know! But the fact that my husband and this maid were both killed the same way, and while William was here . . .'

'Tell me about William's visit to you here at the Savoy.'

'He came here yesterday, after you released him, and I let him stay here the night, in our cubicle in the shelter. He dressed properly. He wore some of his father's clothes when

138

we went to have dinner. They're the same build. Like father like son, except in character.'

'How long did he stay?'

'We spent the morning together, then we had lunch, and after that he left. About half past two.'

Coburg looked at his watch. It was four o'clock. Daisy Scott's body had been discovered forty minutes earlier, at twenty past three. But she'd been killed before that and her body hidden in the cupboard in the sluice. From the lack of rigor mortis, Coburg guessed that she'd been killed some time within the last two hours, although that would be confirmed by Dr Welbourne. So, if William had still been at the hotel at half past two, he could have done it. In fact, he could have done it after he'd left his mother and before he actually left the hotel. But why would he? What would be his motive?

'Did you actually see your son leave the hotel at half past two?' asked Coburg.

She stared at him, anguished.

'You doubt him, too!'

'Lady Lancaster, I'm here to investigate this murder. I shall be asking the same sort of questions of everyone. That doesn't mean I suspect him, or anyone else, at this moment. I just need to know where everyone was and at what times, which is why I'm talking to everyone. Later, I shall be talking to William.'

'And arresting him again?' she asked, her voice strained.

'At the moment I have no evidence on which to arrest anyone, and that includes your son,' said Coburg. 'How did he seem when he left you?'

'Relieved. Almost relaxed. It was as if a cloud has been lifted off him.' She went to him and took his hands in hers, holding them tightly. 'Don't arrest him again. He's innocent. Please, give him a chance to prove his innocence.'

Gently, Coburg disentangled his hands from her grip.

'I never arrest anyone unless there is sufficient suspicion that they may be involved,' he told her. 'This crime has just happened. I'm still gathering information. All I can promise is to keep an open mind.'

She hesitated, looking appealingly at him, then swallowed and nodded.

'Thank you, Mr Coburg.'

CHAPTER SIXTEEN

Lampson knocked on the door of the terraced house in Stepney, the address he'd been given for Daisy Scott. It was in the next street on from where the Huxtons lived. Like the Huxtons' house, it had so far escaped bomb damage. The middle-aged woman who opened the door looked out suspiciously at the unfamiliar man standing at her doorstep. When she saw the police car parked at the kerb, her face registered alarm and apprehension.

'What's happened?' she demanded.

'Mrs Scott?' asked Lampson.

'Yes.'

'I'm Detective Sergeant Lampson from Scotland Yard . . .'

At these words, the woman began to show signs of relief.

'Oh. I suppose it's about what happened at the Savoy last Saturday night. We heard you lot were round talking to everyone who was there. Well, we wasn't.'

'I'm afraid it's not about that,' said Lampson. This was the part of his job he hated most, telling people their loved ones had died, usually in violent circumstances. 'Is Mr Scott at home?'

'No. He's away at sea. Him and our boy, Teddy. They're both in the merchant navy, doing their bit.' Then once again she looked at him in alarm. 'You're not here to tell me something's happened to them?' Then she relaxed again with obvious relief and said: 'No, of course not, otherwise you wouldn't have asked me if he was in. Who is it then? What's it about?'

'Can I come in? he asked.

'Why?'

'I have some news that's best said inside.'

Again, she looked at him, worried, but then held the door open so he could enter.

'There's only me and my sister, Ida, who live here, with my daughter, Daisy. But Ida's out at the moment, and Daisy's at work. She works at the Savoy hotel. The posh one.'

'Yes, I know,' said Lampson. He led the way into the nearest room, which was the kitchen. He wanted there to be somewhere for her to sit when she heard the news. Many people collapsed on being told bad news, and quite a few had banged their heads on the wall or floor when they did. He gestured for her to sit, and then took a chair for himself.

'I'm afraid the bad news is about your daughter, Daisy. I'm afraid she was killed today, at work.'

Mrs Scott stared at him, bewildered. 'Killed? In an accident?' And then her head dropped and she burst into tears, moaning: 'No! No!'

Lampson waited until she'd half-recovered, then added, as gently as he could: 'It seems she'd been murdered. It looks like someone stabbed her, but we won't know for sure what happened until after the doctor's examined her.'

She stared at him, and now her expression of pain was mixed with bewilderment.

'Murdered? No, that can't be right. Who'd want to murder our Daisy?'

'We don't know. That's what our job is, to find out. I've just come to tell you.'

'Where is she?' asked Mrs Scott. 'Is she still at the Savoy?' She got up, agitated. 'I've got to go to her.'

'No,' said Lampson gently, gesturing her to sit again. 'They've taken her to University College Hospital. Either I'll come back or I'll send someone from the local force round once we know more.'

'This is that posh kid, William's fault,' she said bitterly.

'William? William Lancaster?'

Mrs Scott nodded. 'He was going out with her. She fell for him and his big talk. I warned her about him. He'll hurt you, I said. I know these posh blokes. And sure enough he did. He dropped her and went off with that Jenny Huxton from round the corner.' She scowled angrily through her tears. 'I rue the day he came to Stepney.'

'Why do you think he's responsible for Daisy's death?' asked Lampson.

'I don't know,' she admitted. 'It's just that it was after he appeared that things started to go wrong for her. After he broke her heart.'

'What sort of things went wrong?'

She shook her head. 'I can't talk any more. I've got to compose meself before Ida comes back. And I'll have to tell people. I don't want people to hear it second-hand and start spreading rumours about my girl. Especially them Huxtons.'

Coburg made his way to the front entrance where the tall muscular figure of Lund Hansen was on duty guarding the main door of the Savoy. Coburg remembered the name from Lomax's report. Not that the inspector had expanded much on that, just named the man as being on duty on the door that night. Coburg introduced himself, then said: 'I believe you were on duty on the night of the invasion last Saturday night.'

'Yes, sir,' said Lund.

'Do you recall William Lancaster?'

'The Earl of Lancaster's son?'

'Yes. He was part of that Stepney crowd.'

'So I was informed later, but I didn't recognise him at that time. He just looked the same as all the rest.'

'He was here yesterday, seeing his mother, Lady Lancaster, and today he had lunch with her here. Did you recognise him?'

'I did, sir. I saw him when he left.'

'And what time was that?'

'It was three o'clock, sir.'

'You're sure?'

'Yes, sir.' He pointed across the Strand to a jewellers and watchmenders on the other side of the road, which had

144

a large clock on display above the shop window. 'As he passed me, my eye caught that clock, which showed three o'clock.'

'Thank you,' said Coburg.

He went back into the hotel and saw four uniformed police officers appear from the rear entrance and make for the reception desk. Noting they were carrying a black body bag, Coburg joined them, telling them: 'DCI Coburg. Are you here to collect the body and take it to UCH?'

'Yes, sir,' said a sergeant, obviously in charge of the party. He gestured to one of the constables. 'Harris here is to take over from the constable guarding the sluice. You said you needed a replacement.'

'I do indeed,' said Coburg. 'Thank you.'

'We've got the van at the back. Tradesmen's entrance,' added the sergeant.

'The body's downstairs. Follow me.'

He led the party downstairs to where the constable was still on duty guarding the sluice. Coburg took his envelope back from the constable and handed it to the sergeant, saying: 'See that this gets to Dr Welbourne.'

The sergeant and two of the constables packed Daisy Scott's body into the body bag, then carried it upstairs. Coburg turned to the constable who'd been on guard duty in the sluice and told him: 'Constable Harris will be taking over from you now, so you can continue with your regular duties.'

'Thank you, sir,' said the constable, and he left.

'What do you want me to do, sir?' asked Harris.

'The same as the constable. Guard the door and keep

people out while I carry out a proper examination of the scene.'

'Yes, sir.'

With Daisy Scott's body taken away, Coburg now had a clear run at examining every aspect of the sluice. It was basically a large laundry room with four big industrial washing machines side by side along one wall; a row of four large white Belfast sinks running along another wall, with sloped, wooden draining boards separating them. Cupboards of different sizes ran the length of the third wall. It had been in one of these cupboards that Daisy Scott's body had been pushed.

The puzzle for Coburg was the smear of blood on the rim of one of the sinks. If Daisy had been standing at that sink when she was stabbed in the back, he would have expected her to either fall backwards, or slide down to the floor. The only way her blood would have made a streak on the rim of the sink would be if she had turned and then tumbled back against the sink, or she'd been already laying over the edge of the sink with her upper body falling down into the sink.

He paced around the sluice, looking for any clues that would tell him exactly what had happened, but when Sergeant Lampson returned half an hour later, he had to confess he was still none the wiser.

'How did you get on in Stepney?' asked Coburg.

Lampson told him about the reaction from Mrs Scott. 'And she also blamed William Lancaster for what happened.'

'Why?' asked Coburg, curious.

'It seems that William was walking out with Daisy until not long ago. Then he dumped her and started going out with Jenny Huxton.'

Coburg stood, thoughtful, then asked: 'Do you think I got it wrong releasing him like that?'

'No, guv. The evidence cleared him.'

'Yes, but he's released and the next day someone else is stabbed at the Savoy, someone William was involved with. It's a bit of a coincidence. Especially as I've learnt that he was here at the time the girl was killed.'

'It doesn't mean he did it.'

'It doesn't mean he didn't. And I think his mother might be concerned that he's guilty of it, too. I think I'll have another word with her and see if she knew that he was going out with Daisy, and why he dumped her.' He looked at his watch. 'I think we've done all we can for today. After I've talked to Lady Lancaster again, I'm calling it a day. I suggest you get off home now, and tomorrow I'd like you to take the car and to go back to Stepney. Talk to Daisy's family again, and anyone else who knew her. That includes William Lancaster, if you can find him, and Jenny Huxton. Talk to William about Daisy. Did he see Daisy while he was at the Savoy? Talk to Jenny Huxton, ask her about Daisy. In short, get as much as you can.'

'Right, guv. You sure you don't want to do it yourself?'

'You're perfectly capable, Ted. More than capable. I've said it before, you deserve to be made up to inspector.'

'No thanks,' said Lampson with a shudder. 'I might turn into someone like Inspector Lomax.'

'I doubt that very much. Lomax would be like he is if he was still an ordinary copper on the beat. He's what I call well-balanced: he has a chip on both shoulders. No, tomorrow I'm hoping to find out from Dr Welbourne about Daisy, and how her death compares with that of the Earl. Were they killed by the same person?'

'It looks likely,' said Lampson. 'They were killed the same way. Stabbed in the back. And in the same hotel.'

'Appearances can be deceptive,' said Coburg.

When Lampson arrived at his parents' house, he noticed immediately the worried expression on his mother's face.

'Sorry I'm late,' he said. 'Something came up at work.' Noticing that this statement did nothing to ease her obvious worry, he asked: 'What's up?' At that point he realised there were no sounds coming from elsewhere in the small terraced house, and a jolt of fear ran through him as he asked: 'Where are Terry and Dad?'

'We don't know where Terry is. Your dad's out looking for him.'

'What do you mean?' asked Lampson.

'Just that,' said Mrs Lampson. 'We expected him in for his tea at four, but he never turned up. Your dad waited till half past four, then he went out looking for him.' She looked at the clock on the mantelpiece. 'That was an hour and a half ago.'

'Where did he go?' asked Lampson, heading for the door.

'I don't know. I think he was going round the houses of Terry's mates.'

There was the sound of a key turning in the lock.

'That'll be them!' said Mrs Lampson in relief.

But it wasn't. It was just Mr Lampson, looking worn out and very worried.

'There's no sign of him,' he said.

Just then they heard the wail of the air raid siren echoing through the streets.

'Come on, Mother,' said Mr Lampson, taking her coat from the peg in the passage and holding it out to her. He turned to Lampson. 'We're going to the Tube station,' he said.

'They won't let you in,' said Lampson.

'They will,' said his father. 'Some of us went down to Mornington Crescent station this morning and had a word with the station master. He's one of us, lives in Crowndale Road. He reckons they're going to open the stations soon, so he's letting us in.' He helped his wife on with her coat, then headed for the outside. 'Come on.'

'No,' said Lampson. 'I'm going to look for Terry.'

'You don't even know where he might be,' said Mr Lampson. 'And the bombers are coming.'

'That's why I need to find him,' said Lampson.

'You getting yourself killed won't help him,' said Mr Lampson. 'And the wardens will kick you off the street.'

'Not me,' said Lampson determinedly. 'I'm a police officer on duty. I'll walk with you to the Tube station and on the way you can tell me where you've looked already.'

'You won't find him,' said Mr Lampson, walking out into the street and pulling the door shut after them.

'I will,' said Lampson grimly. 'So, where have you looked already?'

He listened carefully as his father listed Terry's friends, his gang as he called them, Steve Wilson, Jim Peach, Ned Patterson and Billy Young, making a mental note of their addresses.

'I've been round to all their houses already,' said Mr Lampson. 'Wilson, Peach and Patterson said they last saw Terry with Billy Young, but the Youngs weren't in.'

'I'll try the Youngs now,' said Lampson.

'It's likely they'll be at the shelter,' said Mrs Lampson.

'If they're not in I'll see you at the shelter and we'll talk to them.'

'They won't be able to add anything to what they've already told me,' said Mr Lampson. He shook his head in annoyance. 'That boy of yours is growing up wild, Ted. He's becoming a danger to himself and others. All this business of him hunting for German spies. He's living in some fantasy world.'

'I'll talk to him,' promised Lampson.

'You'll have to find him first,' grunted his father.

'I'll find him,' vowed Lampson. 'If it takes me all night, I'll find him.'

They'd arrived at Mornington Crescent underground station, and Mr Lampson turned to his son, worry etched on his face.

'Be careful out there, son,' he said. 'You shouldn't be out in it.'

'Nor should Terry,' said Lampson.

'It wasn't our fault!' burst out his mother.

Lampson put his arm around his mother and pulled her affectionately to him.

'I know it wasn't, Mum. It's mine for not being firm enough with him.' He released her, then headed off, saying: 'I'll see you later.'

CHAPTER SEVENTEEN

Rosa noticed that Coburg looked tired when he arrived home.

'A hard day?' she asked sympathetically.

'A frustrating one. There's been another murder at the Savoy. One of the maids stabbed in the back, the same as the Earl of Lancaster.'

Rosa stared at him, shocked. 'What do you think? Some mad serial killer haunting the Savoy bumping off people at random?'

'I hope not,' said Coburg. 'They're the worst ones to solve. I'm hoping there'll be a link, but right now I'm not sure what it might be. And we've gathered so much information I'm not sure where to start unscrambling it.'

'Will it help to talk about it?'

'It might,' said Coburg. 'But, before I do, I need to make a phone call.'

'Who to?'

'A pal of mine who works in the vice squad and covers Soho. I need to check on a supposed order of nuns there.'

'Supposed?'

'You know Soho,' said Coburg wryly as he asked the operator to put him through to the home number of DCI Jack Harkness . . .

'Edgar,' boomed Harkness's voice when the call was connected. 'Long time no speak.'

'Indeed it is,' admitted Coburg. 'You know how it is, Jack. I have the best of intentions to get in touch, but . . .'

'Crime keeps getting in the way,' chuckled Harkness. 'By the way, I understand congratulations are in order. I saw in the paper you got married.'

'I did.'

'Rosa Weeks! I saw her perform a couple of years ago at the Blue Angel in Earl's Court. Fabulous! Tell her I'm a fan.'

'I will. In fact, you can tell her yourself. She's right here.' Rosa looked at Coburg, horrified, and shook her head.

'You sure she won't mind?' asked Harkness.

'Not at all,' said Coburg. 'But before I do I want to pick your brains.'

'About what?'

'A supposed order of nuns in Soho. The address I have for them is Wardour Mews.'

'The Order of Josephine,' said Harkness. 'Good people.'

'They're real?' asked Coburg, surprised.

'They are,' said Harkness. 'They're only a small order, but they do good works, mainly among the prossies in the area. They've even got a medical room in their place where they patch up women who've been beaten up, or worse.'

'That's incredible,' said Coburg. 'I've never heard of them.'

'No reason you should have,' said Harkness. 'They don't publicise themselves. It's all word of mouth on the street. What do you want to know for?'

'I'd like to talk to them. Or, at least, one of the nuns.'

'They're not actually nuns, they're sisters,' said Harkness. 'Religious sisters, I mean, not actual sisters.'

'What's the difference?'

'Nuns take a solemn vow; sisters take simple vows.'

'I didn't realise you were an expert on religions,' said Coburg.

'Brought up by the Jesuits,' said Harkness. 'There's nothing like having religion beaten into you by the brothers to gain expertise. The Sisters of Josephine are different, though. Not showy and shouty or threatening hell and damnation if you transgress. They save people, mainly women, but they'll save a man's soul if it needs saving.' He chuckled. 'Are you in need of saving?'

'No, I'm in need of information. Who's the top person there, the one I need to speak to?'

'Mother Agnes. She's the Mother Superior. A tough cookie.'

'Tough?'

'Physically as well as spiritually. A pimp burst in one day looking for his girl who'd sought refuge there after he'd beaten her up. Broken her nose and one of her arms. When the sisters refused to hand her over to him, he pulled a knife and threatened them. Enter Mother Agnes, who smashed him over the head with a chair and then called the police to have him arrested for grievous bodily harm and threatening behaviour. I was part of the crew sent to sort it out, that's how I know about it.'

'A tough cookie indeed.'

'No one's tried anything like that since,' said Harkness. 'When I commented to her that what she'd done technically constituted assault, she just said: "God moves in mysterious ways," and that was that. If you're planning to see her, tell her I gave you her name.'

'I will,' said Coburg. 'Is there any chance you could contact her and let her know I'll be calling and I'm friendly? Just in case she's got another chair handy when I call.'

'No problem. I'll call in there tomorrow.'

'Thanks, Jack. And now, I'll pass you on to my wife and you can tell her how much you like her singing and piano playing.'

He held out the receiver, to Rosa who took it, whispering to him as she did: 'I'll kill you for this afterwards.' Then, into the phone, she said brightly: 'Mr Harkness. This is Rosa, and it's a pleasure to talk to you.'

For the next two hours Lampson visited the addresses his father had given him for the rest of Terry's gang. None of them were in, having headed for the air raid shelters, Lampson guessed.

He returned to his parents' house in case Terry had gone there, then to his own house. Four times as he walked the streets he was stopped by Air Raid Protection wardens and told to get off the streets. Each time he responded with 'I'm

155

a police officer' and showed them his warrant card, adding: 'I'm looking for a boy who's gone missing,' giving them a description of Terry. None of them were able to help.

Finally, realising that his stomach was rumbling with hunger, he went back to his house and made himself a couple of sandwiches, which he put on a plate and took with him into Terry's room. He sat on the bed and started to eat, taking small bites as he looked around the room.

Where was he? Where was Terry? You're supposed to be a detective, he told himself angrily. Work out where he could be.

German spies, that's what his father had said. Where would Terry be looking for German spies in Somers Town? Possibly the railway station, Euston, which was just a short walk away, if he imagined that these spies were going to check out the trains in order to report on them back to their Nazi masters. Although it didn't make sense; why would German spies want to do that? But then, nothing that Terry did lately seemed to make sense.

Could he have gone to Euston station and got stuck somewhere? In a hut, or a signal box?

He finished the sandwiches and then set off for Euston station. He knew there'd be no trains at this time of night, and the station and the railway line itself in and out of London would be a target for the German bombers, but his son was out there somewhere. He needed to find him, and hoped he was alive somewhere.

It was 2 a.m. when Lampson finally walked down the circular staircase at Mornington Crescent to the platforms below. The platforms were packed with people, the more fortunate ones lying on cushions, others having done their best to make temporary beds for themselves out of their roll-up coats. Lampson found his parents halfway along the platform. As he approached, his father put his finger to his lips and pointed to Mrs Lampson, who was asleep.

'She finally went to sleep half an hour ago,' he said. 'Any news?'

Lampson shook his head.

'I talked to Wilson, Peach and Patterson and their families,' said Mr Lampson. 'They're just along the platform. Young Wilson said that Terry was last seen with Billy Young.'

'Where's Billy Young?' asked Lampson.

'Not here,' said Mr Lampson. 'Nor his family. Mrs Wilson said she thought they'd gone to the furniture depository in Pancras Road. That's the shelter they usually go to.'

'Right,' said Lampson. 'That's where I'm off to.'

'You can't,' said his father. 'They're still bombing out there.'

'And Terry's out in it,' said Lampson.

Lampson hurried through the darkened streets, keeping to the roadways rather than the narrow pavements where it was easy to lose footing in the darkness and fall. Although it was a blackout and pitch dark, the occasional distant fire burnt where bombs had fallen, giving an eerie red glow which made parts of his journey easier. Now and then there was an explosion not too far away, which shook the ground beneath his feet, once so near that the effect of the blast nearly blew him over. He passed one burning building which a fire crew were tackling, hoses aimed at the inferno of flames. Even as he watched, the roof collapsed, sending up a shower of sparks and then huge flames reaching up to the dark sky as the roof timbers caught fire.

Lampson reached the furniture depository which doubled as an air raid shelter and made his way downstairs to the large basement area where families had gathered and were lying on makeshift beds of mattresses and rugs. Some had set up small camps with chairs marking their personal space. The majority of people were asleep, though some were awake, unable to relax enough to sleep as the bombs fell outside, shaking the building. He saw that one of those who was awake was Mrs Young, who was with a group of women, children and older men; most of their menfolk being away with the armed services. She looked at him in surprise as he approached her.

'Mr Lampson?' she said, puzzled by his arrival in the depository.

'I'm looking for your son, Billy,' said Lampson.

She looked at him, even more bewildered.

'Billy? But he's with your Terry. Isn't he with you?'

'No,' said Lampson. 'I don't know where Terry is. I heard he was with your Billy, but that was before the air raid warning went off. I've been all over looking for them.'

Mrs Young turned on her youngest son, seven-year-old Paul, who sat huddled up next to her and who Lampson guessed had been too nervous to sleep, and demanded: 'When did you last see Billy and Terry?'

'Yesterday afternoon,' said Paul. 'About five.'

There was something in the small boy's manner, a shiftiness and unhappiness that sent warning signals to Lampson, and he asked: 'Did you know they were going looking for spies?'

Paul lowered his head and mumbled something, but his voice was so low that Lampson couldn't catch what he said.

'Do you know where Billy is?' asked Lampson urgently.

Paul fell silent, his head kept low. Angrily, his mum grabbed him and shook him.

'Yes you do, you little git. I can tell. Where is he, and don't you lie to me.'

'He and Terry went to follow this German bloke.'

'What German bloke?'

'I don't know his name. He's got a shop in Charrington Street that sells second-hand furniture and stuff.'

'Mr Podolski?' said Lampson in realisation.

Paul nodded. 'They wanted to get proof he was a German spy.'

'How?'

'Billy said something about them getting into his house and searching it.'

'Why didn't you stop him!' raged Mrs Young.

'Billy won't listen to me,' said Paul.

'Why didn't you tell me what he was up to instead of letting me think he was safe with Mr Lampson?'

'Cos if I told you he'd have got mad at me and he'd have hit me.'

'You're sure that's where they were going?' asked Lampson.

Again, Paul nodded.

'Right,' said Lampson. 'That's where I'm off to, so if anyone comes looking for me, tell them that's where I've gone.'

'You'll bring my Billy back!' called Mrs Young, her voice choked with fear.

If he's alive, thought Lampson as he made for the exit, but he didn't say it aloud. He was thinking the same thing about Terry.

Lem Podolski's shop was a mainstay for the poor in Somers Town. Everything that people wanted could be had, and for a reasonable price. It might be a saucepan that was bent or battered, or a chair where the paint was a bit chipped, but it did the job. Podolski had arrived in England two years before, driven out of Germany by the Nazis because he was Jewish, but he'd soon made himself at home, taking over a small shop that had been empty for over a year and buying in unwanted furniture and bric-a-brac, and selling it on. He lived over the shop, converting the storerooms upstairs into a flat.

As before, Lampson's way through the darkened streets was helped by fires burning where bombs had fallen, and bombs were still falling, albeit now some distance away. Where was Terry? He hadn't turned up either at the Tube station or the furniture repository. That meant one of two options. Either he'd got trapped somewhere and couldn't get out, or . . .

Lampson left the rest of the second option unsaid, but pain went through him at the thought.

I should have been a better father, he berated himself. Mum and Dad did their best to look after him, but he's grown up wild, and that's my fault because I'm a copper and I'm at work all the time. Please God, he prayed silently, let him be all right. Let him be . . . alive.

Lampson turned into Charrington Street, and the scene in front of him hit him with a force so hard he almost collapsed. Where Podolski's shop had stood was now just a heap of rubble.

CHAPTER EIGHTEEN

Thursday 19th September, 4 a.m.

Lampson rushed towards the heap of broken bricks, roof slates and roof timbers. He shouted 'Terry!' then began lifting the rubble and hurling it into the road, desperately hoping that somewhere beneath the wreckage Terry was caught in a pocket of air. He'd known cases where a building had collapsed and people had been found inside the wreckage days later, having been protected by fallen rafters and doors or furniture that had taken the brunt of the rubble coming down. It depended on where Terry had been hiding when the bomb came down. Did Podolski's shop have a cellar? If so, there was a chance that Terry and his pal Billy may have crept down there, and been there when the house collapsed.

'Oi!' shouted an angry voice. 'What do you think you're doing?'

Lampson turned and saw an ARP warden glaring accusingly at him.

'They stick looters in prison!' shouted the warden.

'I'm not a looter,' said Lampson desperately. 'I'm a police officer and I think my son might be under this lot.'

The warden stared at the pile of wreckage as Lampson returned to hauling bricks and slates out of the pile and throwing them in the road.

'You'll need help,' said the warden. 'I'll send a message, get a fire crew in.'

He put his whistle to his lips and blew a long shrill blast, and a few minutes later a young man in uniform, also wearing a tin helmet, rode up on a bike.

'Take a message to central,' said the warden. 'House collapsed. Possible survivors. Send a crew to help search.'

The young man took out a notebook and jotted the message down, then rode off.

'I hope you find him,' said the warden. With that, he left.

You might have given me a hand, thought Lampson bitterly.

Suddenly the sound of the all-clear echoed through the streets, one continuous note from the sirens, as distinct from the rising and falling sound of the air raid warning.

Lampson carried on throwing rubble aside, stopping every now and then to call out 'Terry! Billy!' and wait for an answering response; but none came. Desperately he renewed his efforts. It seemed to be an impossible task. No matter how many broken bricks and slates he cleared, the pile didn't seem to be getting any lower.

He heard running footsteps and turned to see Mrs Young and Paul hurrying towards him. Others followed behind them: men and women.

'My God!' burst out one man, and Mrs Young let out an agonised cry of 'Billy!'

'They might be alive!' shouted Lampson, and carried on throwing rubble off the pile. He was joined by the recent arrivals, including Mrs Young herself, who began tearing at the rubble with her bare hands.

'Mein Gott!' This time the words were from Lem Podolski, who appeared and looked in horror at the wreckage of his home. 'Someone said my house had been hit!'

'My son, Terry, and his pal Billy Young might have been in it,' said Lampson. 'Is there a cellar?'

'Ja. Yes,' nodded Podolski. He hurried forward and pointed at a spot in the middle of the pile where there was a slight dip in the wreckage. 'There. About there.'

Lampson and the others immediately transferred their efforts to the place Podolski had indicated, working even faster as they lifted broken bricks, slates and roof beams and threw them into the road, Podolski adding his hands to the job.

As the pile shrank, Lampson thought he heard a noise from beneath the wreckage and he held up his hand and shouted: 'Hold it!'

Immediately, everyone stopped and strained their ears, listening. It was Mrs Young who shouted: 'I thought I heard something! A banging!'

'It could be an animal,' said a man.

Lampson looked enquiringly at Podolski, who said: 'I don't have any animals.'

Everyone set to work again, hurtling rubble into the road with even greater fury, and soon part of the wood of the trapdoor to the cellar could be seen. More rubble was lifted and thrown aside until the whole trapdoor was visible. Podolski reached forward and took hold of the metal ring set in the wooden slats and pulled it up, exposing the dark empty space beneath. They could just see the wooden steps leading down.

'Terry! Billy,' shouted Lampson.

For a heart-stopping moment there was just silence, no sound from the cellar. And then a boy's voice quavered: 'Dad?'

'Is Billy with you?' shouted Mrs Young.

There was the sound of scuffling from the cellar, then Terry's head appeared above the edge, with that of Billy close behind. Both boys looked terrified.

Lampson, exhausted, collapsed on a pile of broken bricks and Mrs Young burst into tears.

'Can we come out?' asked Terry.

The ringing of the telephone dragged both Coburg and Rosa out of sleep.

'It's only just gone six,' said Rosa, shooting a glance at the clock. 'It must be urgent.'

'Let's hope it's not another murder,' said Coburg.

He picked up the phone and said: 'Coburg.' Immediately there were clicks, then the sound of coins falling into a coin box at the other end.

'It's a pay phone,' Coburg said to Rosa.

Then Lampson's voice could be heard.

'Guv'nor, it's Ted Lampson.'

'Ted? What's happened.'

'I'm sorry to call you so early, but Terry went missing. I've been out all night looking for him, and I've just found him.'

'Where was he?'

'Him and a mate of his got trapped in some bloke's cellar.'

'Trapped? How?'

'They thought the bloke was a German spy so they got into his house. They must have hidden in the cellar planning to sneak out when it was dark, but a bomb hit the street and demolished the place. The whole building fell down.'

'My God!'

'It's all right, guv. He wasn't hurt, just scared. But I'm gonna need time with him to sort him out. Get him back on the straight and narrow.'

'Don't be too hard on him, Ted. I know you're angry, but he needs to know that what he did terrified you.'

'He needs a clip round the head,' snorted Lampson.

'Maybe, but mainly he needs to know his dad was up all night looking for him because he's the most important person in your life. Right now my guess is he's thinking you hate him for what he did. Tell him you don't.'

'You turning into a psychologist now, guv?'

'No, just remembering what it's like to feel you're a disappointment to your parents. Take all the time you want.'

'But Stepney . . .' began Lampson.

'Don't worry about Stepney. Leave that to me. I'll see

you later at the Yard, or maybe not, depending on how it goes with Terry. He's got to be your priority today.'

Coburg hung up and started to tell Rosa what had happened, but she forestalled him. 'I heard.' She shook her head in amazement. 'Poor Ted. And poor Terry. God, it's a terrible time to be the parent.' She came to Coburg and kissed him. 'You said the right thing. You're a good man and I'm glad I married you.'

CHAPTER NINETEEN

Rosa was still thinking about Lampson's phone call when they sat down to breakfast. 'Poor Ted,' she sighed as she spooned her porridge. 'It must be so hard for him bringing up his son on his own.'

'He's got his parents to help him,' said Coburg.

'I know, but it must be such a strain for him. I was talking to him at the reception after our wedding, and he said he was worried about Terry running wild and getting into trouble.'

'I think this latest incident may put a damper on Terry's activities for a while. There's nothing like having a bomb drop close to you to make you think about being careful.'

Rosa shuddered. 'Don't. I still keep seeing Donna when that bomb hit.'

'Sorry,' apologised Coburg. 'I didn't mean that. I was talking about being in the trenches during the First War.

Forgive me for being thoughtless?'

She reached across the table and took his hand gently in hers. 'I know you didn't mean it. You've got such a lot on your plate at the moment. I was still thinking about what you told me last night, about the murders at the Savoy.' She released his hand and began to count on her fingers the suspects he'd listed to her.' You've got the son of the murdered Earl who went off to live with communists in the East End. You've got the communists themselves. An Italian waiter who's been interned, so he can't have done it, but he could have got someone else to do it. There's a nun.'

'A sister,' Coburg corrected her. 'But after what Jack Harkness told me yesterday, I think she's unlikely, but I need to check.'

'Any number of outraged husbands and abandoned women, if the Earl's reputation is to be believed,' continued Rosa.

'And so far, we're no nearer to working out who,' admitted Coburg. 'I was hoping the maid who was killed might help us narrow our list of suspects, but it might have just confused the situation. I'm hoping I'll find out more when I go to Stepney this morning.' He sighed. 'I rather wish that Inspector Lomax had been able to hold on to this case.'

'You told me you thought he was an idiot. Incompetent.'

'And he is,' said Coburg. 'But at least I wouldn't have this problem.'

Arnold Lomax sat in his favourite wooden armchair by the kitchen range, reading the Daily Mirror. On the other side of the glowing embers in the range his wife, Muriel, sat engrossed in one of her magazines. They used to be glossy, but since the war, due to shortages of paper and ink, they were just printed on ordinary paper, but they were still full of – in Arnold Lomax's opinion – useless gossip about useless people. Lords and ladies, film and singing stars. He scowled as he turned the pages of his newspaper. Ever since the war began and football competitions had been suspended, so no FA Cup, no league matches, there was hardly anything of interest in the paper. He liked reading about football, but with no proper matches being played, just some clubs playing games with scratch teams made up of people he'd never heard of, he wondered why he bothered to buy a paper at all. Most of the good footballers, being young, had volunteered and were now in the services. Like Charlie Clark from his own beloved Queens Park Rangers.

'Here, Arnold, do you know a detective chief inspector called Coburg?' She chuckled as she read out his full name: 'Edgar Walter Septimus Saxe hyphen Coburg. Bit of a mouthful, ain't it.'

'What about him?' Lomax scowled.

'There's a picture of him here getting married. He got married last month to that singer I like, Rosa Weeks. Remember we heard her on the wireless?'

'So?' grunted Lomax sourly.

'Well, I wondered if you knew him, that was all. Him being a detective inspector like you.'

'He's nothing like me!' snapped Lomax angrily. 'I'm a proper copper. I came up through the ranks. I worked for what I've got. That Coburg is just a . . . a . . .' He struggled for words, finally spitting out: 'A toff who got where he is because of his connections. His dad was an earl.'

'Yes,' said Muriel, 'that's what it says here. The Earl of Dawlish.'

'Will you shut up about him,' snapped Lomax. 'I don't want to know about him, or about his singer wife. They're not real people. They've had all the advantages and none of the kicks that ordinary people get.'

'It says here he was a war hero. He lost a lung during the First War.'

Angrily, Lomax threw his newspaper to the floor.

'I don't want to know about him!' he repeated, even angrier this time. 'Detective chief inspector! That's wrong, that is. I should be a chief inspector, not him!'

Muriel, used to sudden outbursts from her husband against his many enemies, most of them – in her opinion – imagined, looked again at the photograph in her magazine. 'She's got her arm in plaster,' she said. 'I wonder what happened?'

As Coburg drove to Stepney, he kept thinking about the phone call from Ted Lampson about his son Terry. Terry had survived, but it could so easily have ended tragically. Ted needs to spend more time with his son, he decided. It was bad enough when the bombing had come mainly at night, but since the Luftwaffe had turned their attention during daylight hours away from the airfields of Kent, Sussex and Essex and concentrated on London there was no time or place of safety for anyone. The RAF were doing their best, but the sheer volume of bombers coming over, accompanied by their own fighter plane escorts, meant the boys fighting them in the Spitfires and Hurricanes had an almost impossible task. The wreckage in the streets of the East End he passed was testament to that.

He found the address for the Scotts, which was immediately recognisable by the black ribbon of mourning that had been tied to the door knocker. When the door opened at his knock, he was faced with a middle-aged woman whose eyes were red-rimmed from crying.

'Mrs Scott,' he said. 'My name's Detective Chief Inspector Coburg and I'm the officer in charge of investigating your daughter, Daisy's, death. My sergeant called on you yesterday to tell you about it, and you have my heartfelt sympathy for your loss. I'm here to see if you can give me any information that may help us track down the person who killed her. May I come in?'

She nodded and moved to one side to let him enter, then showed him to the kitchen.

'William Lancaster,' she said grimly as he sat down at the table. 'Like I told the sergeant yesterday.'

'You believe that William Lancaster killed her?'

'There's no one else who'd do such a thing,' said Mrs Scott. 'She was a good girl until he came along. Never got into any trouble. She was decent because me and her dad brought her up to be decent.'

'Why would William Lancaster want to kill her?' asked Coburg.

'Because he's a nasty piece of work. She doted on him. She'd have done anything for him. And he broke her heart.'

172

'She was killed at the Savoy, at work,' said Coburg. 'Is there anyone at work who might have wanted to cause her harm?'

She shook her head firmly.

'No one. Everyone liked her. She was a good worker. Good-natured.'

'Did she have any particular friends locally?' asked Coburg. 'People she may have talked to? Girl friends?'

Mrs Scott shook her head even more firmly. 'We don't mix with the people around here. We keep to ourselves.'

'Why?'

'Because there are some not very nice people round here.'

'In what way?'

'That's not for me to say,' she said. 'It's enough to say that we never encouraged Daisy to hang around with them. Loose morals, is all I'll say.' She looked at him fixedly, anger seething in her face. 'William Lancaster. That's who you'll find did it.'

Lampson sat at his kitchen table and watched as Terry spread margarine on a slice of toast. By rights, the boy should have been apologetic, ashamed, but he tucked into the toast as if nothing had happened.

'You nearly died!' said Lampson, outraged.

'Yeh, but I didn't,' said Terry.

'But you could have!' persisted his father. 'What on earth did you think you were doing?'

'We were looking for spies. They keep telling us there are spies about and we've got to watch what we say. All those posters saying "Careless talk costs lives". Me and Billy reckoned that Mr Podolski's a spy. We went in to get evidence against him, anything that showed he was working for the Germans.'

'What made you think that?'

'He's German! They're the enemy.'

'Mr Podolski isn't German. He came here from Germany, but in fact he's Russian. And Jewish. He and his family left Russia after the First War when their house in the village they lived in was attacked and burnt down by people who wanted to drive the Jews out. Realising they were at risk wherever they went in Russia, they moved to Germany to be safe. But after they'd been there for some years, Hitler came to power and he got people there riled up against the Jews, blaming them for everything that was wrong in the country. Especially that the country was in an economic mess.

'Two years ago there was a thing called Kristallnacht in Germany. It means "the night of broken glass". The Nazis attacked Jewish shops and houses, smashing them up and killing them. Mr Podolski's wife was killed. Because he was worried about his son, who was the same age as you are now, he brought him to England, intending to settle here where they could be safe. But that winter, his son caught pneumonia and died.

'So there you are. He's not a spy for the Germans. He'd never be a spy for them. They killed his wife and forced him and his son to leave their home, and then his son died.'

Terry looked shamefaced.

'I didn't know,' he said. Then defensively, he added: 'He sounded German.'

'Of course he does, because he'd been living there for twenty years.'

CHAPTER TWENTY

After his call on Mrs Scott, Coburg had to ruefully admit that his visit to Stepney had been a waste of time. William Lancaster hadn't been at the address he had for him.

'He went out,' his landlady, Mrs Mears, told Coburg. 'Did he say where?'

She shook her head. 'He never tells me where he's going.'

He'd also drawn a blank at the Huxtons. Neither Jenny Huxton nor her father were at home, and the neighbours said they had no knowledge of where they were, or when they'd be back.

No one talks to the police, he thought as he drove back to Scotland Yard. There was a message waiting for him on his desk advising him that Dr Welbourne from University College Hospital had telephoned to tell him the autopsy on Daisy Scott had been carried out.

There was a tap at his door, which opened before Coburg could speak and Lampson walked in and announced: 'I'm back, guv, and ready to go.'

'How's Terry?' asked Coburg.

'I gave him a talking to, but not too harsh, just like you said. I think he's all right. My parents will keep an eye on him, that's for sure. I thought it best if I came in rather than hang around, which would only upset him.'

'You could be right,' said Coburg. 'Right, in that case, we've got a call to make. UCH have done the autopsy on Daisy Scott, so that's our next port of call.'

'How did you get on in Stepney.'

He gave a sigh. 'A waste of time.'

Dr Welbourne was in the mortuary, finishing another autopsy, when Coburg and Lampson arrived at University College Hospital. They waited outside for him and after a few minutes he joined them, still wearing his surgical scrubs. He was a short, chubby man in his forties with dark curly hair cut short, his round pink face clean-shaven.

'Chief Inspector Coburg,' he greeted them.

'Dr Welbourne,' nodded Coburg. 'This is my sergeant, Sergeant Lampson.'

'Good to meet you, Sergeant,' said Welbourne.

'I'm sorry I didn't come sooner, something came up which meant I had to go to Stepney,' apologised Coburg.

'Where the victim came from, I believe,' said Welbourne. He looked at them enquiringly. 'I'm curious why you asked for me particularly when you sent the body. I understood

Inspector Lomax was in charge of the first stabbing at the Savoy.'

'Yes, I read your report in his notes, and I was very impressed. I've now been allocated that first murder, and when this one happened, I decided you'd be the best person to look into it. After all, you did the investigation into the first one, so you'd spot if there were similarities.'

'Yes, and there were. The same kind of weapon was used on both occasions.'

'A steak knife.'

'Of which there are many at the Savoy. However, there are two things that make this one different from the first. The first murder was carried out by a right-handed person. In this one, the killer was left-handed.'

'You're sure?'

'There are different pressures on the knife when it enters the body depending on which hand is used. And the other difference is that the victim was already dead when she was stabbed. She'd been poisoned.'

'Poisoned?' echoed Coburg, stunned.

'I have it on the assurance of Mrs Mallowan in our pharmacy department,' said Welbourne. 'And there is no one who knows as much about poisons as she does.' He smiled. 'You may know her better as Agatha Christie.'

'The crime writer?'

Welbourne nodded. 'She's a qualified pharmacist and she wanted to do her bit for the war effort, so she's come to work for us. There was something about this death that puzzled me, so I asked her to take a look, and she confirmed that the woman was indeed poisoned before she was stabbed.'

'But why stab someone who's already dead?'

'That's your puzzle to solve, Chief Inspector. We can only give you the facts. The other fact is that the victim was three months pregnant.'

Coburg and Lampson made their way up the stairs to the pharmacy department.

'Agatha Christie,' said Lampson, impressed. 'We're about to meet a famous author.' He looked at Coburg and added: 'I know you meet famous people all the time, but this is a first for me.'

'Do you read her books?' asked Coburg.

'I do,' said Lampson. 'I think they're great. The way she keeps you guessing who did it right to the end. Though I'm never sure which I prefer: Hercule Poirot or Miss Marple. What about you, guv? Do you read her?'

'I do, when I have time,' said Coburg. 'Although the critics keep urging me in their columns to read what they term quality literature, Virginia Woolf, D H Lawrence and James Joyce and the like, and they studiously avoid drawing attention to Christie's books. The fact is that after a hard day up to my armpits in death and mayhem, the last thing I want is to be tormented by some modern novelist airing their own personal anguish. Give me a good story that I can escape into.'

At the pharmacy department they introduced themselves as detectives from Scotland Yard and asked for Mrs Mallowan. A short while later, a stoutish woman, her hair pulled back and wearing a regulation long white surgical coat, appeared.

She'd just turned fifty this last week, remembered Coburg, from reading a recent profile of her in The Times. If he hadn't known that he would have put her at late thirties or forty at the most, her clear skin and bright eyes giving her a youthful appearance.

'Mrs Mallowan,' said Coburg. 'I'm Detective Chief Inspector Coburg and this is my sergeant, Sergeant Lampson.' He hesitated before asking: 'Forgive me, but do you prefer to be addressed as Mrs Mallowan, or Mrs Christie?'

'While I'm here, I'm Mrs Mallowan,' she replied, adding with a smile: 'And I already know about you, Chief Inspector.'

'From Dr Welbourne?'

'From your brother, Magnus. He invited myself and my husband to one of his social events at Dawlish Hall.'

Another one who's part of Magnus's social circle, groaned Coburg inwardly. Is there anyone on the social register he doesn't know? He looked at Lampson, who smiled at this as if to say: 'Famous people, eh.'

'To be honest, it was my husband, Max, who was the reason for our invitation,' continued Christie. 'Max is an illustrious archaeologist and was the first person to carry out excavations in the Balikh Valley in Syria. Magnus was keen to hear about the excavations from his own lips. Your other brother was there, too, that weekend, Charles. Both of them spoke very proudly of you.'

'I'm sure they were just being kind. I know that Magnus would have preferred it if I'd gone into something more dignified than the police. The civil service, for example, which is where Charles made his mark.'

'Oh no, both were full of praise for the work you do in the police.' She smiled. 'But isn't that often the way with families. They praise one of their own to others, but seem reluctant to do so at a personal level.'

'Dr Welbourne said that the victim had been poisoned.'

'Yes, with thallium sulphate. It's found in some brands of rat poison, and also in treatments to get rid of excess bodily hair, usually used by women.'

'So it's readily available?'

'I'm afraid so.'

She then proceeded to enlarge on the chemical properties of thallium sulphate and the dangers inherent in its use, much of what she said passing over the heads of both Coburg and Lampson, though they both nodded dutifully in pretend understanding.

'Could the poisoning have been accidental?' asked Coburg. 'If she had been using it to remove excess bodily hair, for example.'

'Highly unlikely,' said Mallowan. 'I examined the body with Dr Welbourne, and she did not suffer from excess hair. In fact, her body hair was quite sparse, which is often the case with red-headed people.'

'Thank you,' said Coburg. 'So she was definitely poisoned and then stabbed.'

'Yes,' said Mallowan.

'Why would someone poison someone, and then stab them?' queried Coburg.

'I would suggest to confuse the situation,' said Mallowan.

'But then, I'm not a detective.'

'But you write great detective books,' said Lampson,

'Thank you for saying so, Sergeant,' smiled Mallowan. 'But in those, I am in control of the story. With a real-life murder like this, nothing is in my control.'

CHAPTER TWENTY-ONE

They left UCH and set out again for Stepney, this time Lampson driving.

'After what we've learned from Dr Welbourne about Daisy being pregnant, we need to talk to her mother again,' said Coburg. 'But I suspect she won't be very friendly. So first, we'll see if we can get hold of William Lancaster.'

As they journeyed, Coburg filled Lampson in on his phone conversation with Jack Harkness.

'So, she really is a nun?' said Lampson.

'A sister,' said Coburg.

'What's the difference?'

'The sort of vows they take, according to Jack.'

'But they're genuine religious?'

'Yes, who do very good works among the prostitutes of Soho.'

'It wouldn't stop one of them from killing a bloke.

Especially if he treated her little sister as badly as he did. And this Mother Superior sounds a bit of a tearaway, hitting a bloke with a chair.'

'Only because he threatened them with a knife.'

'Yeh, but all the same, they don't sound very meek and mild, do they?'

This time William was at his lodgings. He suggested they talked at a bombed-out area where a whole street had been demolished. 'It'll be more private,' he told them. 'Anything said in any of the houses will be common knowledge in half an hour.'

They followed him to the ruins of a neighbouring street, where a whole row of terraced houses had been smashed down into piles of broken bricks and roof tiles. Here and there among the wreckage were personal belongings, broken and burnt, crockery, books, pieces of shattered furniture. They sat down on a heap of rubble that had once been someone's home. As he looked around the site, Lampson couldn't help his thoughts going back to when he'd first seen the similar ruin of Podolski's shop in a heap, and the fear that Terry might be somewhere beneath it.

'We'd like to talk to you about Daisy Scott,' said Coburg.

'What about her?'

'She's dead. Murdered.'

'Yes. Jenny told me. Word spreads quickly here.'

'Did she tell you how she died?'

'She said she was stabbed in the back. The same as my father.'

'Did you know she was pregnant?'

William gave Coburg a venomous look.

'Yes, she told me.'

'Did she tell you it was yours?'

'Yes. But she lied.'

'Do you know who the father was?'

'Apparently it could have been anyone.' He gave a mirthless laugh. 'Including my own father.'

'When did you find out it wasn't yours?'

'Once she'd lied about how far gone she was. She told me she was about a month pregnant. That was two months ago. Then I was told that she was actually two months pregnant, and I knew it couldn't have been mine.'

'Who told you she was two months pregnant.'

William hesitated, then said: 'Jenny.'

'Jenny Huxton?'

He nodded.

'How did she find out?'

'She's friends with a cousin of Daisy's. Daisy had told this cousin how far gone she was and she was worried sick, and this cousin told Jenny.' He gave a look of disgust and added: 'There are no secrets here.'

'Is that why you broke it off with her?'

'I broke it off because she'd lied to me. She was pregnant when she threw herself at me and deliberately started a sexual relationship. Her aim was to make me think I was the father of her baby and marry her, and so grab herself a rich husband. Or so she thought.'

'How did she take it when you told her you were finishing it with her?'

'She went berserk. Accused me of using her and then abandoning her, until I told her I knew she was already pregnant when we started. At first she denied it, cried and all that sort of thing, but when she knew that I knew exactly what she'd been up to, she got really nasty. Started sneering, telling me I wasn't a real man. She told me I was a coward because I was a conscientious objector. And then she got worse. Foul-mouthed.'

'Where was this?'

'In the street in Stepney.'

'How long ago?'

'About a month.'

'Did many people see or hear the row?'

'Most of Stepney, I'd have guessed. She was very vocal.'

'Including her mother and aunt.'

'They could have hardly missed it.'

'Did you see her yesterday when you were at the Savoy?'

'No.'

'You're sure?'

'Absolutely. And if you're about to tell me that she was killed during the time I was at the Savoy, I'd worked that out already. Which means someone is trying to frame me.'

'Why do you say that?'

'Look at the victims. The first was my father, and he was killed while I was at the Savoy. The second was Daisy, and – again – she was killed while I was at the Savoy. It seems to me that someone is killing people I've been known to have an association with and doing it at a time when they knew I'd be there.'

'So who do you think would want to frame you?'

'I don't know,' admitted William.

'Why?'

'Again, I don't know. I can't think of anyone I've upset so badly that they'd try to frame me for murder.'

'It might help if you gave us a list of people you have upset,' Coburg told him.

'There isn't anyone,' insisted William. 'The only two are my father and Daisy.'

Rosa found there were about twenty people present when she arrived at the Winships' suite at the Savoy. The majority of them seemed to be middle-aged women, with about five men, including Lord Winship. Also there, to Rosa's surprise, was Magnus.

'Rosa,' smiled Julia Winship, greeting her with an air kiss. 'I'm so glad you could come. There's sherry and other stuff on the table and some nibbles. Do help yourself. I'll introduce you to some people and you can circulate.'

'First, I must say hello to Magnus,' said Rosa. 'He's been so kind, letting us use his flat.'

'Yes, he's such a dear,' said Julia. 'I'll leave you to him.'

Rosa moved towards Magnus, who seemed surprised, and also a little unsettled, to see her.

'Magnus,' she smiled broadly. 'This is a surprise.'

'Yes, it is,' said Magnus. 'I didn't know you knew the Winships.'

'I didn't,' said Rosa. 'Lady Winship – Julia – heard me practising at the piano here at the Savoy and invited me. Do you know them well?'

'Moderately,' said Magnus. 'I've met them a few times in the past. I think they just invited me in the hope I'd meet up with one of the many widows who are here. Matchmaking seems to be one of Julia's hobbies.' He looked at his watch. 'But I'm going to have to disappoint her. I've got a board meeting in half an hour.'

'So you're in London on business?' asked Rosa.

'Yes. I'm on the boards of a couple of companies, and even though there's a war on, commerce has to continue. I've got one today and another two tomorrow, so I'm staying here at the Savoy for a couple of days.'

'You could have stayed at the flat,' said Rosa. 'It is yours, after all.'

Magnus shook his head. 'It's yours and Edgar's while you're there. How are you finding it?'

'It's wonderful,' said Rosa. She looked around and saw Julia Winship heading towards them.

'We're about to be talked to,' she whispered.

'How are you two doing?' asked Julia.

'Excellent. Just catching up,' said Rosa.

'But, alas, I have to go,' said Magnus. He tapped his watch. 'I have a board meeting this afternoon. Do forgive me.'

'Of course,' said Lady Winship.

Magnus gave them both a little bow, then headed for the door.

'Strange,' mused Lady Winship. 'You'd have thought he'd have mentioned it before.'

'I think he's got a lot on his mind,' said Rosa. 'A board meeting today, and then another two tomorrow.'

'Which boards are these, did he say?'

'No,' said Rosa. 'And I must admit, I forgot to ask him.'

'Not to worry,' smiled Julia. 'There's someone who'd like to meet you. Dotty Ravenswood. Do you know her?'

'No,' admitted Rosa. 'In fact the only person I know here is Magnus. And now he's gone.'

'Dotty!' called Lady Winship. 'Come and meet someone new.'

The woman who joined them was short and wide, in her sixties, wearing a tweed skirt and jacket over a white shirt and a floral-patterned tie. Her blonde hair looked suspiciously as if it was dyed to Rosa, and the evidence was there as she got nearer and Rosa saw her black roots.

'Dotty Ravenswood, this is Rosa Coburg. She's married to Magnus's younger brother, Detective Chief Inspector Coburg. You may know her better as Rosa Weeks.'

'The jazz singer!' said Dotty, smiling. She held out her hand and Rosa shook it. Dotty had a firm handshake. 'I heard you on the wireless. Great stuff!'

'I'll leave you two to get acquainted,' said Lady Winship with a smile. 'I promised Greta I'd spend some time with her.' She lowered her voice as she added, 'Her son's got himself in some sort of trouble and she wants to get some things off her chest.'

Lady Winship moved off. Dotty looked at the plaster cast on Rosa's arm and asked: 'What happened? Julia said you'd got bombed out. Is that when it happened?'

'This? Oh no,' said Rosa. 'It was an accident, but it's healing. Hopefully I'll be able to have the plaster off soon.'

'Bad news about your place,' said Dotty sympathetically. 'Where are you staying?'

'Magnus has let us have his flat for a few days, but

we've arranged to take another flat.'

'Wonderful man, Magnus,' said Dotty.

'Indeed,' agreed Rosa.

'What do you think of this war?' asked Dotty suddenly. 'Julia said you hoped it would be over soon.'

'I do,' said Rosa. 'And I'm sure I'm not alone in that wish.'

'I think everyone in this room would agree with you,' said Dotty.

At the other side of the room, Lord Winship looked at Rosa and Dotty with concern and asked: 'Why on earth did you introduce her to Dotty? I thought you said we had to be careful what we say to her.'

'And we will,' smiled Lady Winship. 'Think of it as a test. If Rosa complains about Dotty's views, or tells her husband she's a suspect fifth columnist, we can always deny very firmly that we share Dotty's opinions. We say she was invited because she's an old school friend of mine, but we deplore the views she expresses.

'However, if Miss Weeks agrees to come to our next soirée, it means she's not averse to those opinions. In which case, we can cultivate her.'

Rosa listened as Dotty enlarged on her theme. Rosa had already decided her strategy would be to listen and not argue with any opinions that anyone expressed, but give thoughtful nods that suggested silent agreement. In this way she hoped to draw any possible fifth columnists out. Not that Dotty appeared to need any drawing out, she was only too keen to make her views known.

'The question is, how do we bring this war to a speedy

conclusion without compromising our honour? Not that we should have ever got involved in it in the first place. It's madness. Frankly, we have more in common with the Germans than people realise. We're both from the same stock. The Kaiser was Victoria's grandson, for heaven's sake. It's like family, the British and the Germans. Yet we've tied ourselves to the French! The people we've fought more wars with than any other over the past hundreds of years. Doesn't anyone remember Trafalgar and Waterloo?'

'I guess people think of them as history. Times are different now.'

'Are they? The French couldn't be trusted then, nor could they be trusted during the First War. My husband Eddie says so, and he knows, he was in the trenches.'

'So was Churchill,' said Rosa. 'With the French troops, I believe.'

'Exactly!' said Dotty indignantly. 'What does that tell you about him? Is he really the person to get us out of this mess? Look at this so-called government of his. He's got Labour Party people in! That dreadful man, Attlee. And he's even brought in that awful Bevan, that Welshman. I mean, my dear, he's a communist in all but name!'

'Who do you think should be in charge?' asked Rosa.

'There's only one man who can talk to Hitler sensibly, and who Hitler respects. He's the man who should have been involved in any negotiations. Mosley.'

'Mosley?'

'Sir Oswald. You know that Hitler was at his wedding to Diana?'

'No,' admitted Rosa.

'That shows there is a link between them that could have been the way out of this.' Changing tack, she suddenly asked: 'Do you know Diana?'

'No.'

'Diana Mitford, as was. She and her sister, Unity, were in Germany before all this started. Now she and Oswald are incarcerated in Holloway prison, while poor Unity is ga-ga. She shot herself in the head, you know, when Britain declared war on Germany. Absolutely besotted with Hitler.' She gave a deep sigh of disappointment. 'This war is not the way to go. That's what my Eddie says, and he fought damn bravely in the last one. Decorated for it.' She leant back, nodding firmly to emphasise her words. She hesitated, then said, again, keeping her voice low: 'Ask yourself, why are we fighting this war?'

'For freedom,' said Rosa, but making sure her voice carried no conviction in the words. 'That's what Churchill says.'

'That's what they tell you, but you want to know the real reason?' said Dotty. 'The Jews.'

Rosa looked at her, puzzled.

'The Jews?'

'My dear, the Jews are everywhere around poor Winston, that's what this war is really about. Protecting their interests. I mean, no one respects dear old Winnie more than me, but his own daughter, Sarah, marrying that low Jewish comedian, Vic Oliver? I mean, it's one thing to have them as entertainment, but to marry one . . . Well!' She looked around again, then said: 'And of course, there's always been a hint in the family of it on his mother's side. Jennie Jerome. Her father was a Wall Street banker and speculator. And his father was called Isaac. What does that tell you?'

CHAPTER TWENTY-TWO

After leaving William Lancaster, Coburg and Lampson made their way to Mrs Scott's house.

'This could be an interesting conversation,' commented Coburg as he knocked at the door.

Mrs Scott half-opened the door and peered out at them.

'You again,' she said, her voice and manner showing her displeasure at their return.

'Indeed, Mrs Scott. We're sorry to disturb you again at this time, but there are one or two things we needed to check on. May we come in?'

Silent and unsmiling, she opened the door so they could enter. When they were all sat in the kitchen, she looked at them, almost defiantly, and snapped: 'So, what was it you wanted?'

'Mrs Scott, did you know that Daisy was pregnant?'

Mrs Scott glared at him, anger in her eyes.

'Yes!' she said. 'And it was that bastard William Lancaster who did it, taking advantage of her.'

'You're sure that William Lancaster was the father?'

She stared at him, and now her anger was so great it kept her from speaking for a few moments. But then she spat out at him: 'How dare you! Repeating lies about my daughter, who's not even cold in death! My Daisy was a good girl until she met that William.'

'We've been told that Daisy was pregnant when she first started going with William.'

'That's a lie! Is that what the Huxtons told you?'

'Apparently Daisy told a cousin of hers . . .'

Mrs Scott jerked up out of her chair and pointed at the door. She was shaking with anger.

'Get out of my house!'

'Mrs Scott, I am investigating the murder of your daughter . . .'

'No! You're smearing her name, that's what you're doing! You've been listening to people like the Huxtons who are scum and jealous of us because we live decent lives. Well I'll have no part of it! I want you out of my house!'

Resignedly, Coburg got to his feet. Lampson did the same.

'We'll go, Mrs Scott, but we'll be back,' said Coburg.

'I won't let you in.'

'In that case you'll force me to get a warrant against you and have you brought to Scotland Yard and we'll talk there.'

'Oh no you won't! I'm not being dragged off to Scotland Yard, warrant or no warrant.' Now her anger had turned into an outpouring of grief, and tears bubbled up in her eyes and then began to run down her face. 'My daughter's just dead and you're threatening me with prison! You should be locking up the likes of Huxton and his communist crowd and William Lancaster. Everyone knows he killed his father and now he's killed my Daisy, and you're letting him get away with it! How much are they paying you to cover up for him and let him off the hook?'

'We'll leave you now, Mrs Scott,' said Coburg calmly and politely. 'But we will return, at which time I hope you'll be in a better frame of mind. I know you're grieving for your daughter, and I sympathise deeply with your loss, but I would advise you to think about what you're saying.'

Inspector Lomax was in his office engaged in going through some cold case files, looking for a possible link with a recent spate of shoplifting at some of the more expensive stores along the Strand, when there was a tap at his door and Sergeant Joe Potteridge appeared, looking smug.

'Sorry to trouble you, boss, but I picked up some gossip about Coburg and that Lady Lancaster,' he said with a grin.

'Oh? More about her offering him her husband's flat?'

Potteridge chuckled. 'Better than that. Juicy.'

'Juicy? How?'

'Effie was talking to Lady Lancaster's maid. You know these rich people have their own servants who go everywhere with them. Well Lady Lancaster's got this maid, Jane, who don't seem to care for her much. Jane has her own room in Lady Lancaster's suite at the Savoy so she can call on her when she wants anything, night or day.'

'How the other half live,' commented Lomax sourly.

'Well, the other day, Coburg was back at the Savoy, and Lady Lancaster told Jane she wanted to talk to him privately, so she told her to go off somewhere.'

'And?'

'This Jane reckons her mistress and Coburg were having it off.'

Lomax stared at his sergeant, stunned. 'You're joking!'

'Straight up, boss. According to this Jane, Lady L has got the hots for DCI Coburg, especially since he got her son released. And she knows for a fact that Lady L hasn't had sex with anyone for a very long time. Her husband was a right pig, banging anything that moved . . .'

'Yes, I know about that,' said Lomax irritably. 'Get back to her and Coburg.'

'Well, this Jane told Effie that after she came back to the suite, she went into Lady L's room, and the bedclothes were rumpled. Someone had been on it. And the only two people in that suite during that time were Lady L herself and DCI Coburg.' He grinned. 'What do you reckon, boss?'

'I reckon we need confirmation,' said Lomax carefully. 'If it's true, it'll be the end of his career.'

'But who else could have rumpled the bed?'

'The lady herself. After he left, she might have gone for a lie-down.'

'Jane reckons her and Coburg were doing it.'

'Never take the word of servants, especially those who don't like their masters.' He looked thoughtful. 'No, it's very likely, but we're gonna need proof before I can take this further.' He looked at Potteridge. 'If you can get me proof. Evidence of witnesses, articles of soiled clothing . . .'

'I'll see what Effie can come up with,' smiled Potteridge. 'She's a good girl, is Effie. Very resourceful.' He hesitated, then added: 'Of course, I'd hate for her to think her job might be at risk cos of doing this . . .'

'Reassure her she'll be adequately compensated,' said Lomax. 'And she will be. I'd give half my pension to drop Coburg in it.'

Coburg knocked at the door of the Huxton's house. 'It struck me that as we're in the area, it will be useful to get their take on Daisy Scott and William,' he told Lampson.

The door opened and Tom Huxton scowled at them.

'Oh, it's you,' he grunted sourly.

'It is,' agreed Coburg. 'May we come in?'

'If not, you'll take me to Scotland Yard, I suppose,' scowled Huxton.

'The thought did occur,' said Coburg genially.

'In that case you'd better come in.'

He led them to the kitchen and the three of them sat down at the table.

'Have you heard about Daisy Scott?' asked Coburg.

'Her getting stabbed at the Savoy yesterday?' Huxton nodded. 'Same killer?'

'We're looking into it,' said Coburg. 'What can you tell us about her?'

Huxton shrugged. 'I didn't know her very well.'

'She went out with William before he transferred his affections to your daughter,' said Coburg.

'Well, that was before he knew her properly,' said Huxton.

'What do you mean?' asked Coburg.

Huxton hesitated, then said: 'A little bird told me you two had been to see William before you went to see Mrs Scott.'

'The bush telegraph,' smiled Coburg.

'In that case, you already know why he dumped her. You must know about the shouting match him and her had in the street. And the fact she was pregnant by some other bloke.'

'Her mother says it's all lies,' said Coburg. 'She says that Daisy was a decent girl until William took up with her.'

'Ha!' said Huxton scornfully. 'Of course she says that. She doesn't want to admit that her precious daughter was a chip off the old block. Like mother, like daughter.'

'So, you're saying that Mrs Scott used to put it about.'

'And how! That was before she married Barney, of course. And she only married Barney because she got up the duff.'

'So, her protestations about decency . . .'

'Are rubbish! Giving herself airs and graces. But Daisy was clever with it. She didn't just go with anyone, she was angling for someone with status. One of them rich blokes at the Savoy, that's what she was after. But when she found out she was in the club she latched on to William. Her thinking was that even though he looked like a down-and-out, he was the son of an earl, and she was sure she'd be on easy street once she hooked him. But once he found out the truth, that was it, it was all over.'

'How do you feel about him and Jenny?'

Huxton shifted uneasily on his chair.

'To be honest, I'm not happy about it, him being who he is. Aristocracy, and that.'

'He doesn't act like an aristocrat,' pointed out Coburg.

'That's just posturing,' said Huxton. 'It's cause he's young and he wanted to upset his old man. But nature will out. He'll revert to type, mark my words. Now his dad's dead he's the Earl. It's one thing to knock it when you ain't got it, but now he's up there, let's see what happens.'

'Are you worried he'll upset Jenny?'

'Of course I am. I've been looking out for her ever since her mum died six years ago. All I can say is that at the moment he seems to make her happy, so I just look on and keep an eye open. But the moment he starts messing her about and upsetting her, that's when he'll know what a Stepney dad is capable of.'

'You'd hurt him?'

'Hurt him? I'd kill him.'

'I'd quite like to have a word with Jenny,' said Coburg.

'What about?'

'About her and William, and about Daisy Scott.'

'She's got nothing to add to what I've just told you.'

'That's quite likely, but I'd still like to talk to her. Is she around at the moment?'

Huxton looked at them suspiciously.

'She had nothing to do with it,' he said. 'She was here at home with me yesterday, when Daisy got it. She was doing housework all day.'

'That wasn't my question,' said Coburg. 'I asked if she was around at the moment. At a friend's house, for example. Somewhere nearby where we can call on her.'

'No,' said Huxton. 'She's gone to see my sister, her aunt, who lives over Bethnal Green way. I'll tell her you want to see her when she gets back. I'll ask her to get in touch with you.'

'Thank you, Mr Huxton, I'd appreciate that,' said Coburg.

As he and Lampson walked back to their car, Lampson said: 'You didn't believe all that guff about her being over at Bethnal Green, did you, guv?'

'You have a very suspicious mind, Sergeant,' said Coburg. 'But no, I didn't. Mr Huxton is obviously protecting his daughter for some reason. Which we'll find out about when we get to talk to her. But at least we've learnt more than we knew before about the whole Daisy and William relationship.'

'Does it help us find the killer, though?' asked Lampson.

'At the moment, that's a question to which we don't have an answer,' admitted Coburg.

'Where to now, guv? Back to the Yard?'

'I suggest we call at the Savoy and see if there's anything new there, and then you get home to your boy and make sure he doesn't go off spy hunting again, while I call on the Sisters of Josephine.'

CHAPTER TWENTY-THREE

Charles Tillesley was at the reception desk, engaged in conversation with the concierge, when Coburg and Lampson arrived at the Savoy; and as soon as he saw them he hurried over.

'I'm so glad you came,' he said. 'You got my message?'

'No,' said Coburg. 'We've been out most of the day. We decided to call back and see if there have been any recent developments.'

'Indeed,' said Tillesley. 'Ella Kemble has disappeared.'

'Disappeared?' echoed Coburg.

'She never came in to work today. I sent someone to her address to see if she was all right, there's quite a lot of colds going round, but her landlady said she hadn't seen her since yesterday morning, when she left to come to work.'

'So, she didn't spend the night at home?'

'No.' He looked anguished. 'What's happening? On the same day Daisy Scott is murdered, and another of the maids disappears.'

'Leave it to us, Mr Tillesley. If you give me Ella Kemble's address, I'll call there and see what her landlady has to tell me.'

'Certainly,' said Tillesley gratefully. He handed Coburg a piece of paper. 'I had this ready to give you when you arrived. It's Ella's address in Clerkenwell. Her landlady is a woman called Mrs Sarah Hobbs.'

'Thank you, Mr Tillesley,' said Coburg. 'I can give you a couple of pieces of information about Daisy Scott. She was three months pregnant. And, before she was stabbed, she was poisoned.'

Tillesley stared at him, uncomprehending. 'But why stab her if she was already dead?'

'That's the question I'm also asking,' said Coburg. 'I'll let you know if I have more from Mrs Hobbs about Ella.'

As Coburg and Lampson headed for the car park, Lampson said: 'Suspicious, Ella Kemble just vanishing like that?'

'Very,' agreed Coburg.

'So, we're heading to Clerkenwell?'

'No, I am,' said Coburg firmly. 'You go home and keep an eye on that son of yours. I'll drop you off at St Pancras New Church.'

'That's a bit out of your way, guv,' said Lampson. 'It's more direct to Clerkenwell from here if you head due east . . .'

'If I decide to go a different route, that's my choice,' said Coburg.

'Yes, but under the regulations concerning the economic use of petrol . . .' began Lampson.

'Or you can walk,' said Coburg.

'Point taken,' said Lampson.

After dropping his sergeant off by St Pancras New Church at the edge of Somers Town, Coburg drove to Clerkenwell and the address in Hardwick Street he'd been given for Ella Kemble. For the moment, the Sisters of Josephine would have to wait.

Ella Kemble's landlady, Mrs Hobbs, a pleasant, motherly woman in her fifties, was bewildered.

'I've never had anything like this happen before,' she told Coburg. 'For her to go off without a word.'

'Is her rent paid up to date?' asked Coburg.

'It is,' said Mrs Hobbs. 'She's never been behind with the rent, not like some have been in the past.'

'When did you actually see her last?'

'Yesterday morning, half past seven. The same time she always left for work.'

'How was she dressed? Did she have her maid's uniform on?'

'She did. I saw it beneath her coat,' nodded Mrs Hobbs.

'Did she have anything else with her? A bag, or anything?'

'Yes, she did,' said Mrs Hobbs. 'A big bag, actually. I commented on it. She said she was taking some washing to work to do in the laundry there.'

'And you didn't see her return home yesterday?'

'No. I'm always here from five in case any of my lodgers need something, and all the rest came back. But not Ella. When I didn't see her this morning, I thought she might have spent the night at the Savoy. She did that now and then, especially with the air raids. They've got this extra strong air raid shelter there.'

'Yes, I've seen it,' said Coburg. 'So the first you knew about her not being at work today was when someone came from the Savoy to check on her.'

'Yes. They were worried in case she was ill. But I told the woman who came that Ella hadn't been back since she left to go to work yesterday morning.'

'May I have a look at her room?' asked Coburg. 'I'm just wondering what she might have taken, and it will be interesting to see what she left behind.'

She took him up to Ella's room and stood in the doorway while he made his examination. Two of the hangers in the wardrobe were empty, and it looked to Coburg as if some clothing had been taken from the drawers in the dressing table.

'Can you tell if any of her clothes are gone?' he asked.

'I wouldn't know,' she said. 'I don't nose around in my lodgers' private things. I don't think it's right.'

There was nothing personal on display, no family photographs or small mementoes. There was a week-old magazine on the bedside table, but no books in the room.

'Do you know where her family home was?' he asked.

'No, she never mentioned her family,' said Mrs Hobbs.

'But she had a Midlands accent. You know, Birmingham, Coventry, that way.'

Coburg spent a further fifteen minutes going through the room, but there was very little to examine. It seemed to him that Ella had taken some clothes with her, backed up by Mrs Hobbs saying she'd taken a bag with her when she left, but there was no way of telling what sort of clothes, and how much.

Tomorrow, he decided as he drove home, we'll talk to the maids at the Savoy, see what they can tell us about Ella. But in the meantime, there was one more call he had to make.

Wardour Mews was a small courtyard in the centre of Soho off Wardour Street, with a few tall, shabby, ancient-looking buildings darkened with age and soot crammed into it. Coburg saw the large white cross beside the old oak door of one building in the middle of one side and made for it. Below the cross was a faded sign of blue-painted wood bearing the legend: the Order of the Sisters of Josephine. The name 'Mother Agnes' had been added at some time in the last five years, to judge by the lettering, which was in fresher paint than the original sign.

Coburg reached for the old-fashioned bell pull beside the door and tugged at it. After a while, the door opened and an elderly woman dressed completely in black, including a black headscarf, looked enquiringly out at him.

'Good afternoon,' said Coburg. 'My name is Detective

Chief Inspector Coburg. I'm here to see Mother Agnes, if she's available. I believe Detective Inspector Harkness may have told her I would be calling.'

The woman stepped back, opening the door wider, allowing him to enter. She closed the door, then pointed to a rickety-looking wooden chair in the corridor.

No words, thought Coburg. Let's hope it's not an order with a vow of silence or asking questions is going to be rather difficult.

He sat down on the chair and watched the woman walk away from him and into the house. Fifteen minutes passed without any sign of her returning, or anyone else appearing, and he began to wonder if he'd been forgotten. It was another five minutes before the elderly woman returned. She gestured for Coburg to go with her. Coburg rose and followed her along a series of narrow corridors that had a peculiar smell combining damp with incense, before they arrived at a door on which a sign said 'Mother Agnes'.

The elderly woman tapped gently at the door, then pushed the door open and gestured for Coburg to enter.

Mother Agnes stood up from behind her desk and nodded in a formal way to Coburg, and gestured for him to sit in the chair on the other side of the desk.

'Thank you for seeing me, Mother Agnes,' said Coburg.

'Detective Harkness says you are a good man,' said Agnes, although the formality in her manner suggested that at this moment she was reserving judgement on Detective Harkness's opinion.

'Thank you,' said Coburg. 'He was very complimentary to me about you and the Order of Josephine. Like him, I admire the work you are doing here.'

'Someone has to do it, and it is better it is done in God's name. Our hope is it will bring the women we deal with to Christ.' She hesitated before adding: 'And also the men, although that is a more difficult task.'

'Did Detective Harkness mention why I wished to see you?'

'He did,' she said.

'In that case, may I speak to Alessandra di Capa?' asked Coburg.

'I assume you want to talk to her about what happened to her sister.'

'Yes. I suppose she told you about it.'

'There are no secrets here. And yes, she told me the reason when she asked permission to visit her late sister's fiancé.'

'When she did, she gave her name as Alessandra di Capa. I always thought that when someone entered an order they took on a new name. Sister so-and-so.'

'Alessandra is not yet a sister. At present she is a postulate.'

'I see. Or, rather, I don't. Unlike Jack Harkness, I'm not a Catholic.'

She smiled. 'I won't hold that against you. When someone decides to enter an order, they enter as a postulate. This is to give them time to think about the personal implications of their decision, and can be any period from six months to two years. If, at the end of that time she and the Order agree she has a calling, she becomes a novitiate. She is given a modified version of the habit to wear and remains a novitiate for up to two years. At the end of that period she can take her vows, something that may last up to three years.

'Alessandra first came to us a year ago but she still has a way to go before she becomes a sister. At the moment she is still in postulancy and so she retains her name and ordinary modest dress, with the preferred addition of a headscarf. Why do you wish to speak to her?'

'The man who treated her sister, Maria, so badly, resulting in Maria's death, was murdered recently, stabbed to death in the air raid shelter at the Savoy hotel during an air raid on the night of Saturday September 14th. The killing occurred some time during the early hours of Sunday morning.'

'It was not Alessandra who did it. She was here with us at that time.'

'I never thought of her as responsible,' said Coburg. 'I just wish to ask her if she can think of anyone who might have wanted to kill this man.'

Mother Agnes gave him a firm look. 'Yes you did,' she corrected him. 'You thought her love for her sister would override her being a member of a religious order. That is what any detective would think, and would have to investigate.'

Coburg nodded, shamefacedly. 'Yes, you're right, and I apologise. I did think it was possible at first. But after speaking to Jack Harkness, it was then I dismissed the idea that she may have carried out the deed herself. But I still believe she may be able to help us.'

Mother Agnes studied Coburg, then said: 'Very well. You may talk to Alessandra, but in my presence.'

'I understand,' said Coburg. 'Thank you.'

CHAPTER TWENTY-FOUR

Rosa sat making a prospective playlist for her forthcoming Sunday afternoon session at the Savoy. She'd lost all her sheet music when the Hampstead flat had been bombed, music that she'd collected over many years.

Tomorrow she'd go to Chappells and see what they had in stock. Not that she depended on having the music, she'd played most of the tunes in her repertoire so often that it was like using muscle memory, her fingers automatically went to the correct keys. The problem for her was that, with the plaster cast on her left arm, she had to remember that she couldn't do the bass runs like she wanted to, which meant more work for her right hand.

She really used the sheet music as an aide-memoire for the lyrics. Although she knew most of them in her sleep, like many performers she had the enduring nightmare that one day she'd forget the words to a song while she was in the middle of it. The same fear that some actors suffered when taking on a particular role. She knew that even the greatest had dried on stage, their memory suddenly going blank.

There was also the fact that right at this moment she was thinking about the afternoon soirée at the Winships, and the fact that Magnus had been there. And not just accidentally, or for the first time. Julia Winship had told her that Magnus had been there before. Why? They were so obviously either Fifth Columnists or Nazi sympathisers, or the sort of Moaning Minnies who thought that anyone could do a better job than Churchill, even Oswald Mosley.

She knew she'd have to tell Edgar about it when he came home, but how would he react when he learnt that Magnus was part of the crowd? Or was Magnus really a part of it? It seemed so unlikely to Rosa. She'd only met her brother-in-law a few days before, but she'd liked him a lot. She felt he was honest and straightforward; yet here he was hobnobbing with a bunch of Hitler-lovers.

Yes, there was no doubt about it, she'd have to tell Edgar.

Alessandra di Capa was in her mid-thirties, Coburg guessed. She wore a long plain black dress with a plain white scarf on her head and sat at one side of the desk in Mother Agnes's office, her gaze down. Humility, or just avoiding looking at me so I can't see her eyes when she answers, wondered Coburg.

'I'm sorry to cause you distress, Miss di Capa,' said Coburg. 'I would not be asking to talk to you if the situation did not make it necessary.'

She didn't reply. She kept her gaze looking downwards, but made a slight nod of her head.

'You went to the internment camp at Ascot to see Giovanni di Piranesi.'

Again, the nod. Let's hope she doesn't keep this up for the whole session, thought Coburg ruefully.

'May I ask why?'

Alessandra looked up towards Mother Agnes, who nodded, giving her permission to answer.

'I received a letter from him,' said Alessandra. 'A very angry letter.' She paused, then added: 'He said he wanted to take revenge on the man who had ruined my sister, Maria. I showed it to Reverend Mother.'

Coburg looked at Agnes, who nodded to show it was true.

'I searched my soul,' continued Alessandra, 'and worried that he had lost his faith in God. I talked about it with Reverend Mother, and she said that I could go to see Giovanni and talk to him, to try to divert him from this path of vengeance.'

'He had not discussed this with his own priest?'

'The Catholic priest who visits Acton would perhaps not understand. He is Irish.'

'And this is a Sicilian matter?' asked Coburg.

Alessandra nodded. 'And, as Maria was my sister, it was hoped the words coming from me might have more impact.'

'You went to dissuade him from taking revenge?'

'I went to bring him back to God. I wanted to talk to him about the lessons we learn from Jesus Christ our saviour. About mercy and forgiveness.'

Coburg looked at Mother Agnes, who again nodded in confirmation; and he thought: This is fine coming from a woman who smashed a chair over a man's head when he threatened the sisters. But then, Jesus had used force to throw the moneylenders out of the temple, so Mother Agnes had only been following his example. And killing someone, even for revenge, had no salvation in religion. Except at the time of the Inquisition, he thought. And the burning of Jews and Protestants.

Stop this, he rebuked himself sharply. Stop dragging ancient history into it. This is a murder inquiry.

'How did Giovanni react to you?' he asked.

Her face took on a sad expression. 'He did not argue with me, but I could tell by his manner that he was not easily persuaded. I urged him to think on it, and to consider Maria's memory.'

'Did Giovanni mention anyone he hoped might take revenge, on his behalf. Either in his letter, or when you saw him?'

'No. In his letter, it was just his anger.' She thought it over, then added: 'I doubt if he would have told me if he had anyone in mind in case I interfered.'

Coburg nodded. 'Thank you, Miss di Capa. I know this can't have been easy for you.'

Alessandra looked towards Mother Agnes, who nodded and said gently: 'You may go, Alessandra.'

Alessandra rose, nodded to Coburg and Mother Agnes, then left the room.

'She has a good heart,' said Coburg.

'She has,' agreed Mother Agnes. 'Was what she told you of any help?'

'It was,' said Coburg. 'It means there's one less line of enquiry for me to follow.'

Coburg arrived home as Rosa was finishing preparing a meal.

'Scrambled eggs with mashed potatoes,' she told him. 'Or, at least, one real egg and the rest is dried egg. But hopefully the seasoning will give it some taste.'

'I'm sure it will be wonderful.' As she put the plates on the table, he asked: 'How did you get on at the Winships today?'

'They were an interesting collection. Quite a few media types. Journalists. Broadcasters. Writers. Along with a few titled people. Lord and Lady Winship, another lord whose name I can't remember, a duchess – the Duchess of Fitzwarren, that was it – and some artist. Oh, and a racing driver. Edwin Caldwell.'

'Quite a select gathering,' said Coburg, tucking into the egg and mash. 'And were the views expressed suspect?'

'They certainly were by this one particular woman I spoke to,' said Rosa. 'I got collared and lectured at length by her. Her name's Dotty Ravenswood and in her view the only person who can get us out of this mess is Oswald Mosley. She says he can do a deal with Hitler.'

'A pretty one-sided deal,' observed Coburg. 'Which would have the German flag flying over Whitehall and Buckingham Palace.'

'She also says that the only reason Churchill has got us

involved in this war is because the Jews are behind him. She suggested that Churchill is himself Jewish on his mother's side.'

'That's the sort of rubbish the British Union of Fascists were spouting,' said Coburg. 'What about the rest of them?'

'I didn't really get the chance to circulate much; this Dotty Ravenswood held me captive.'

'The fact that she's there and speaking so openly suggests the Winships approve of her views. I think it might be worth my mentioning this crowd to the security people. They definitely need investigating, and possibly rounding up.'

'Before you do, Magnus was there.'

'Magnus?' said Coburg in surprise. 'That doesn't fit. Magnus is the most patriotic person I know. I can't imagine him supporting Hitler or Mosley. Did you talk to him?'

'I didn't get the chance. He didn't stay long. In fact, he left almost as soon as I arrived. He said he had a business meeting to go to.'

'I expect he left as soon as he realised what sort of crowd they were. I can't imagine him getting involved with those sort of people.'

'It wasn't the first time he'd been,' said Rosa.

'What?' said Coburg, surprised.

'Lady Winship told me he'd been to a couple of her soirées, as she called them. I think he might have left because I turned up.'

'I don't understand it,' said Coburg, bewildered. 'You're sure he'd been there before?'

'Yes,' nodded Rosa. 'Lady Winship said she was

surprised that this time Magnus had to go so soon.'

'I think I need to talk to Magnus,' said Coburg. 'I can't report this crowd to the security people without putting Magnus in question.' He grimaced. 'I'll have to go down to Dawlish Hall.'

'He's not there,' said Rosa. 'He said he was staying at the Savoy for a couple of days because he's got business to do in town.'

'Yes, he's on the boards of a couple of large companies,' said Coburg. 'In that case, I'll see him while he's in town. And, I think, the sooner the better.'

As soon as he'd finished his meal, he picked up the phone and asked the operator for the Savoy hotel, and when they answered he asked for Magnus's suite.

'Magnus Saxe-Coburg,' said Magnus's voice.

'Good evening, Magnus,' said Coburg.

'Edgar,' responded his brother noncommittally.

'I wondered if I could come to see you.'

'When?'

'Are you free now?'

'This sounds urgent.'

'Not really, it's just that I've got a lot on my plate at the moment, what with this second murder at the Savoy.'

'And is your proposed visit to do with that?'

'No. But there's something that I need to talk to you about.'

'Yes,' said Magnus. 'Fine. If it's what I think it is, we'll talk in my suite rather than chat in the bar.'

There was a click as Magnus hung up.

'What did he say?' asked Rosa.

'He sounded . . . annoyed,' said Coburg. He gave a sigh as he added: 'I think he's going to be even more annoyed when I tell him why I want to see him.' He gave an unhappy sigh. 'I'm not looking forward to this.'

CHAPTER TWENTY-FIVE

Coburg was aware that his older brother was edgy and suspicious as Magnus opened the door to him. He stood aside to let Coburg enter.

'Drink?' he asked.

'Yes please,' said Coburg. 'A whisky, if you have it.'

Magnus poured the drinks then handed one to Coburg, and both brothers took their seats.

'To what do I owe the pleasure of this visit?' asked Magnus. 'Or do I know already?'

'Rosa told me you were at the Winships' soirée today,' said Coburg.

'Yes, I was,' said Magnus. 'Just a little social gathering.'

'She was concerned over some of the views expressed there.'

'Ah, the little woman running back to hubby with tittle-tattle. So, is this a visit from my brother, or am I talking to

Detective Chief Inspector Coburg.'

'A bit of both,' admitted Coburg.

'There was nothing treasonous said,' defended Magnus. 'So if you're looking to make an arrest you're going to be disappointed.'

'I'm not looking to make an arrest. I just want to know what's going on.'

'In your official capacity?'

'No, as your brother. I don't want you getting in trouble because you inadvertently had a meeting with the wrong people.'

'Who's to say they're the wrong people?' demanded Magnus.

'From what Rosa said—'

Magnus cut him off with an indignant snort. 'From what Rosa said!'

'She's very good at reading people,' said Coburg. 'If she says there were some . . . signs of dissent from the official line . . .'

'Which is?'

'No surrender.'

'Who said anything about surrendering?'

'There was talk of some kind of peace plan involving Mosley. Adolf isn't going to accept peace without what will be surrender on our part.'

Magnus looked uncomfortable.

'There was no talk of surrender,' he said again. Then, still looking uncomfortable, he added: 'Anyway, you've no need to worry. The majority of people who were in that room are good people. Decent, and honest. And patriots.

It's just that they – like me – remember the last lot. The carnage. And for what? So that we could do it all over again twenty years later? We've barely got another young generation to lose this time around. I was told that some people were looking to find a way to achieve peace, but with honour. No surrendering of our sovereignty. No surrender, full stop. Some kind of truce. An armistice, if you will, and get back to talking.'

'I understand Lord Halifax was trying to set something up like that using the Italians as intermediaries, but it didn't work.'

'No, it didn't,' admitted Magnus. 'But anything's worth trying if we can avoid the kind of slaughter we saw before. For God's sake, Edgar, we were both in that mess, as was Charles. You were nearly killed. Millions died. This time around it won't just be in the fields of France, it'll be over here. It's already happening. London and all the major cities in Britain are being bombed to pieces. The home population is being slaughtered from the air!'

'You said the majority of the people in that room are good people,' said Coburg. 'Who isn't?'

Magnus turned away from Coburg's questioning look.

'It's just a turn of phrase,' he said gruffly. 'A figure of speech.'

'Magnus, I know you. You don't say things idly.'

'So now we have Detective Chief Inspector Coburg coming to the fore,' growled Magnus. 'What is this: interrogation time?'

'If there is treason in the air, if there are fifth columnists, it's our duty to expose them,' said Coburg.

Magnus gave a sarcastic laugh.

'Very moral,' he snorted. 'Very holier-than-thou.'

'I can assure you, Magnus, that people working in Britain for the Nazi cause is a serious threat to this country. Undermining the government will hand victory to Hitler and his brigade of thugs. Is that what you want to happen to the country we both love?'

'I never said they were Nazis!' protested Magnus angrily.

'Well, someone's made you suspicious. As the Winships organised this soirée, as you call it, is it them? Lord Winship working quietly for the opposition?'

'Eric Winship is a political moron.'

'So, it is him.'

'No!' exploded Magnus. 'Winship is a moron, full stop. He couldn't organise anything, covert or otherwise.'

'Lady Winship, then,' probed Coburg. 'Julia.'

Magnus fell silent and looked at his brother, his discomfort and distress apparent.

'So, is she a secret supporter of the Nazis?' asked Coburg.

'Not as far as I know,' grunted Magnus.

'But she's obviously said something to disturb you,' persisted Coburg. He frowned as he cast his mind back to the membership list of the British Union of Fascists he had in his office. 'She wasn't on the list of the BUF,' he said thoughtfully.

'No, she wouldn't be,' said Magnus darkly. 'She's far too clever for that. She hides her opinions very carefully.'

At these words a thought struck Coburg and he turned to his brother and asked: 'Magnus, are you working for MI5?'

'Don't be ridiculous!' said Magnus angrily.

'You are!' said Coburg. 'That's what this was about. You've been asked to keep an eye on these people.'

'What poppycock!' snorted Magnus. 'This is what being a detective's done for you. It leads you down wrong paths.'

Coburg shook his head.

'Magnus, trust me on this. I'm a damned good detective, I've developed a nose for it. Plus, I know you. Godammit, you're the most patriotic person I know. There's no way you'd knowingly hobnob with possible appeasers like the Winships unless you were doing it because someone had asked you to. But the whole thing got blown when Rosa appeared at their 'informal soirée'. She said you left early. Was that why?'

'Yes,' snapped Magnus. 'I didn't dare stay around in case she said something to me that might make the Winships wary.'

'So, who are you working for? MI5?'

'No,' said Magnus. 'If you must know, I was asked by someone high up in government to watch them and report back what goes on.'

'How high?'

'I leave that up to you to work out,' said Magnus curtly. 'You're the detective.'

'If it's a personal request that suggests an old friend. With you that usually means old friends you were at school with.' He saw Magnus's mouth curl into a smile of small triumph, and added quickly: 'but not in this case.' Immediately, Magnus's smile vanished.

'My God!' exclaimed Coburg in realisation. 'It's Winston!'

'Rubbish!' snorted Magnus.

'You smiled when I said it was an old school pal, which means it's someone who wasn't at Eton. Looking at the current Cabinet, that eliminates Halifax who was at Eton. But it wouldn't have been Halifax who asked you, anyway, as he's on the appeasement wing. It won't have been any of the Labour members of the Cabinet, with the possible exception of Attlee, but he's not the type to ask favours of an aristocrat. Most of the other members of the Cabinet are too devious for you to get involved with their plans. You're too clever for that. But Winston . . . he may be devious, but he's honest. He was also at Harrow. And I know you trust him.'

Magnus scowled. 'Are you always this long-winded? You sound like one of those detective fellows in novels when they do their summing up. That Poirot character.'

'Talking of him, I met Agatha Christie today. Or, Mrs Mallowan, as she prefers to be called. She sends her regards to you.'

'You can be so tiresome sometimes, Edgar,' said Magnus. 'So, it is Winston?'

'I refuse to answer on the grounds that you'll go tittle-tattling back to your wife, which is not a good basis for national security.'

'Ironically, she was there on the same mission as you. She told me she suspected the Winships of being appeasers, so she elected to go along with it. That's why she was so shocked when she saw you there.'

'Why did they invite her?' asked Magnus, puzzled. 'They're usually quite careful in who they invite. They sound people out first to see if they might be – as they call it – suitable.'

'So how did you come to be invited?'

'I met Eric Winship casually, and started talking about the carnage we all experienced last time. What was it? Fourteen million dead and God knows how many incapacitated? And I said it would be a disaster for the country if that same tragedy happened again, that it was already a disaster with Dunkirk and now the Blitz, and that it was a pity there wasn't a way to make a deal of some sort. An honourable one, obviously, but one that would stop the mass deaths.

'Next thing, I've got an invite from the Winships to one of their get-togethers. That was ten days ago.' He looked inquisitively again at Coburg. 'So I ask again, why did they invite Rosa?'

'It was my fault,' admitted Coburg. 'When I was talking to them, she asked after Rosa, and I happened to say that Rosa said she wished this war would end soon.'

'Which is something that Julia would pounce on.'

'And she did, and – as with you – Rosa got an invite. I suggested she drop it, but she said she was suspicious of the Winships and thought this would be a good way to find out what they were up to, if they were either part of some appeasement lobby, or pro-Hitler.'

Magnus fell silent, and Coburg could almost see his elder brother's brain working, ticking over with an idea.

'What is it?' asked Coburg.

'Rosa's a tough girl, isn't she,' said Magnus. 'Not easily scared. I mean, that broken arm of hers, getting shot like that. It sounds like she's prepared to take chances.'

'She married me, so she must be,' smiled Coburg.

'I'm talking about protecting the nation,' said Magnus primly. 'We could work together.'

As Coburg stared at him in bewilderment, Magnus enlarged on his proposal.

'Rosa said she wants to do something for the war effort. Until her arm heals she can't drive an ambulance, which is her main ambition. You said yourself, that's why she decided to nose around the Winships and find out what they're up to. Surely it would be better if there were two of us watching each other's backs. She's going to do it anyway, and I'd be there to protect her if things looked like they were going to go wrong.'

'What sort of things? What do you mean, "protect her"?'

'It all looks very polite and refined, just a talking shop of like-minded people, but Winston thinks there are some dangerous people behind them with a serious agenda.'

'And you're suggesting Rosa puts herself in that kind of danger?' said Coburg, outraged.

'We're already in danger,' countered Magnus. 'Wasn't your flat destroyed by bombing?'

'Yes, but . . .' Coburg began to protest, but his brother interrupted him.

'Ask her. Or I will. It might be better coming from me. As I'm in town, why don't I pop over tomorrow.'

'Let me talk to her first,' said Coburg.

'Fine by me,' nodded Magnus.

'What's made Winston suspicious of the Winships?' asked Coburg.

'Julia,' said Magnus. 'She used to run with Wallis's

crowd.'

'Wallis?'

'The Simpson woman,' said Magnus, his voice heavy with disapproval. 'And we know where her sympathies lie. At least, that's what the gossip is. But if you ask me, she'd do a deal with the devil if it got her what she wanted: David getting the Crown back and her beside him on the throne.'

'Did Julia Winship actually say that to you?'

'In so many words. It was at that first soirée of theirs. She said it would be a small price to pay for peace. That we'd have our country back again, just as it was. According to her there are only two obstacles to peace with Germany: Churchill and the King.'

'And what would happen to the present King if David became King again. I assume he'd be Edward VIII once more, with Wallis as his queen.'

'That was the talk. All done as very pleasant chatter, nothing treasonable as such. All for the sake of Britain.'

'Well the woman who spoke to Rosa today, Dotty Ravenswood, was more open in her views. According to her, Oswald Mosley is the best person to negotiate with Hitler.'

'Dotty by name, dotty by nature,' muttered Magnus disparagingly.

'But what would happen to the present King and Queen and the two princesses?' asked Coburg again.

'They'd go to a place of safety. Canada was referred to.'

'And Churchill?'

'I think it goes without saying that he would not be going to Canada.'

'An assassin's bullet,' mused Coburg.

'That wasn't mentioned,' said Magnus. 'Nothing treasonable was raised. But it was the things that weren't said, the bits between the lines. I was hoping to find out more today, but then your wife turned up, so I made my excuses and left.' He looked rueful. 'Pity I didn't know beforehand why she was there.'

'She didn't know you were going to be there,' pointed out Coburg.

'True,' admitted Magnus. 'Do you think she might do it? Pool our resources?'

'Knowing Rosa, I suspect she would,' said Coburg. 'Not that I think it's a good idea; it all sounds highly risky to me. But I'll ask her as soon as I get back.'

'Was Magnus angry with me for telling you he was at the Winships?' asked Rosa on Coburg's return.

'At first, but then he changed his tune when I told him why you were there. It seems he was there on the same mission, but in his case he'd been asked to investigate them by none other than the Prime Minister himself.'

'Magnus knows Churchill?'

'Magnus seems to know everyone. I met Agatha Christie today, and she knows Magnus. She and her husband were guests of his at Dawlish Hall before the war.'

'My God, you move in exalted circles. The Prime Minister and a celebrity author.'

'All of whom are impressed by my celebrity wife, the noted jazz singer . . .'

'And would-be ambulance driver,' she reminded him.

'How does Magnus know Churchill? Well enough to be asked by him to do what is essentially undercover work.'

'Magnus served in the Grenadier Guards during the First War,' said Coburg. 'You remember that Churchill resigned from the Cabinet after the disaster of Gallipoli and went to fight in the trenches. Initially he was with the Grenadier Guards before he was promoted to Lieutenant-Colonel and given command of the Royal Scots Fusiliers. I understand that while he was with the Guards, Magnus saved his life. Not that Magnus has ever said anything about it, but I've heard it from other people who were there. Churchill trusts Magnus, at this difficult time when he's not sure who else to trust.'

'So this is a serious business,' said Rosa. 'The Winships and their crowd, I mean.'

'Yes, which is why I'm having my doubts about you getting involved,' said Coburg.

'It'll be fine,' said Rosa.

'But Magnus is talking about you and he working together.'

'That's a great idea,' exclaimed Rosa. 'He can look out for me and I can do the same for him. And he'll be able to point me in the right direction of who to talk to and get information from.'

'I'm not sure it's such a good idea,' continued Coburg. 'If what Magnus says is true, then you could be up against some very dangerous people.'

'But I'll have two wonderful men keeping watch over me: you and Magnus.'

'I'm not sure that's good enough,' said Coburg.

'Don't dismiss the idea until we've at least talked it over with Magnus.' She smiled. 'I'll phone him in the morning and arrange for him to come round here tomorrow evening.'

Suddenly the penetrating siren of the air raid warning echoed into the flat from outside. Coburg and Rosa looked at one another.

'Time for the shelter,' sighed Rosa.

'It looks like it's going to be another sleepless night,' groaned Coburg as they picked up their coats and gas masks and headed for the door.

CHAPTER TWENTY-SIX

Friday 20th September

Coburg was just a few minutes ahead of Lampson arriving at Scotland Yard the next morning.

'Another night of bloody air raids,' groaned Lampson. 'Thank heavens someone's seeing sense and opening the Tube stations.'

'Everything all right with Terry?' asked Coburg. 'No more spy hunting?'

'No, thank God,' said Lampson with relief. 'After what happened the other night he was scared of getting trapped again. I'm hoping he'll be on his best behaviour from now on.' As he hung up his overcoat, he asked: 'Did you hear about the German invasion barges?'

'No,' said Coburg. 'What about them?'

'It was on the wireless this morning. Hitler had these barges along the French coast all ready to load his troops on to invade us, but yesterday the RAF bombed 'em. Sunk most of the barges, and the ones that didn't get sunk have been moved.'

'Good old RAF,' said Coburg approvingly.

'How did you get on with Ella Kemble yesterday?' asked Lampson. 'Has she done a runner?'

'It would seem so, at first sight,' said Coburg. 'The last her landlady saw of her was half past seven on Wednesday morning, when she set off for work. The landlady, Mrs Hobbs, says she doesn't think she came home on Wednesday night. When she left on Wednesday morning, she was carrying a large bag which she said contained her laundry she was going to do at the Savoy. But it's possible she'd packed some clothes in it.

'The question is, did she intend to disappear when she set off for work on Wednesday morning, or did something happen that led to her vanishing?'

'Something or someone,' said Lampson.

'Exactly. And if it was someone, was it a person she trusted and went off with, or was it someone who abducted her?'

'Whichever it was, the maids at the Savoy are at the heart of this,' said Lampson. 'From Maria, who committed suicide after she was raped by the Earl of Lancaster. Who himself is then murdered. Then Daisy Scott, who's murdered. And now Ella Kemble, who's disappeared.'

'Exactly my thoughts,' agreed Coburg. 'So, our first port of call today is going to be the Savoy where we'll talk to all the maids who are there. They work in shifts, so we'll have to go back this afternoon to talk to the ones we miss this morning, and then any who we don't get to talk to then, we'll see this evening or tomorrow morning.'

'Right, guv,' said Lampson.

'Before we go, I think it'd be a good idea to go through what we know so far. It'll help us identify the gaps in our knowledge that we want to fill in when we talk to the maids.' He pulled a sheet of paper towards him and began to write on it as he spoke. 'Murder one: the Earl of Lancaster. Stabbed in the back with a steak knife from the Savoy. The killer was right-handed, according to Dr Welbourne.

'Murder two: Daisy Scott. Poisoned with thallium sulphate, and then – after she was dead – stabbed in the back, again with a steak knife from the Savoy. This time, according to Dr Welbourne, the killer was left-handed.'

'Or a right-handed person using their left hand to confuse the situation,' posited Lampson.

'In which case, why stab her?' asked Coburg. 'I think it was to make us think the same person who killed Lancaster also killed Daisy. In which case, they wouldn't have deliberately switched hands.'

'Good point,' agreed Lampson. 'So, two different killers. One left-handed, one right-handed.'

'Motive for killing the Earl?' asked Coburg.

'He was knocking off every woman he came into contact with, some willing, some unwilling. So, a jealous husband or boyfriend wanting revenge. Like Giovanni Piranesi, for example. Only one who isn't locked up. Or maybe one of the women, angry at the way he treated her.'

Coburg nodded as he made a note.

'Motive for Daisy Scott?'

'She was pregnant. Any bets it was a guest at the Savoy, someone with money, and she was blackmailing them?'

Again, Coburg made a note on the sheet of paper.

'Or it could be that William Lancaster is the baby's father, despite what he said, and he killed her to shut her up,' offered Lampson. 'Or he isn't the father, and he killed her because he was still in love with her and the idea of her having a baby by someone else drove him mad.'

'What about Ella Kemble? Why did she disappear like that?'

'Maybe she's the one who did it. Or, at least, one of them, and she's done a runner.'

'Why would she kill the Earl?' mused Coburg. 'There's no suggestion she was one of his conquests. And why would she kill Daisy?'

'Maybe Ella's another victim, and her body's been dumped somewhere,' hazarded Lampson.

'It's possible,' said Coburg. He looked at his notes. 'As you say, it's the maids who are the key to this. We need to get absolutely everything from them about Maria, Daisy and Ella, and the Earl. We need every bit of gossip and tittle-tattle. We need to find out who Daisy was having sex with and who might be the father of her baby. We need to find out if Daisy was left- or right-handed. Same for Ella Kemble. We need to find out if any of the maids know if anyone uses thallium sulphate as a remover for excessive hair. We'll go to a chemist on the way and find out what names it goes under when it's sold as a hair remover.'

'It's also used as rat poison,' Lampson reminded him.

'We'll talk to the maintenance people at the Savoy and ask if they use rat poison. And if they do, we'll have a look at the list of components on the tin and see if thallium is included.'

'There's another thought,' said Lampson. 'Thinking about Ella Kemble. Giovanni Piranesi said the next time he saw her he wanted to be holding a knife or a gun. If Piranesi got a pal of his to kill the Earl, maybe he also got him to do for Ella Kemble. He blamed her for Maria's death.'

'If she's dead, that's certainly a possibility,' agreed Coburg. 'And there's another suggestion to consider, one made by young William Lancaster. That his father and Daisy were killed by someone deliberately to implicate him. Who might have a reason to do that? Who hates him so much to frame him for murder?'

'Tom Huxton,' said Lampson.

'Huxton?' Coburg frowned. 'How do you work that out? He's been defending William.'

'He doesn't like him. He doesn't like the fact he's going out with his daughter. Remember what he said when you asked him what he'd do if he hurt Jenny? I'd kill him, he said. And he would. Maybe he's already thinking that William needs to be removed from the equation. Out of his daughter's life. So he sets things up to put him in the frame for two murders.'

'One murder, unless he's ambidextrous,' Coburg reminded him. 'We'll check him out as well and see which hand he favours.' He looked at his sheet of paper and frowned thoughtfully.

'We're none the wiser, are we, guv,' said Lampson wearily.

'Not at the moment,' admitted Coburg. 'But hopefully we will be after we've talked to the maids.' He picked up the phone and asked the switchboard to get him the pharmacy at University College Hospital.

'After some expert advice from our crime novelist?' asked Lampson.

'In her role as an expert on poisons. I want to know how fast-acting thallium sulphate is.'

Fortunately for him, Agatha Christie was working in the pharmacy that morning.

'Almost instant, Chief Inspector,' she told him. 'Especially in its concentrated form as rat poison.'

'And as a hair remover?'

'If ingested, the same, although there could be a few moments' delay.'

'Instant,' Coburg told Lampson as he replaced the receiver. 'So Daisy will have had to be poisoned in the sluice, or nearby so she could be carried there – but carrying her would be too noticeable.'

'The sluice it is,' said Lampson. 'But how could anyone get her to take poison?'

'By forcing her.'

Lampson shook his head. 'That would take two people. One to hold her and her arms, while the other pours the poison down her throat.'

'So, two killers working together. That may be the answer to the business of left hand and right hand.' He got up from his desk and put on his coat. 'Right, Sergeant, let's go to Soho.'

At the Savoy, Sergeant Joe Potteridge had traced his cousin, Effie, to the sluice where she was rinsing ashtrays in one of the big sinks.

'How'd you like to earn some money, Effie?' he asked.

'Doing what?' asked Effie warily.

'You know what you said about Lady Lancaster and DCI Coburg having it off.'

'I was only repeating what her maid, Jane, said.'

'But how likely is it?'

Effie looked at him, puzzled. 'A man and a woman together in a hotel bedroom. I'd say it's likely, wouldn't you?'

'Yes, but my boss needs more to back it up. The thing is, he wants to stitch this Coburg up.'

'Oh no,' said Effie, shaking her head. 'I'm not getting involved if there's that sort of thing going on. I could lose my job.'

'You wouldn't lose your job if it could be proved. And I'd keep you out of it.'

'How?'

'Leave that up to me,' said Potteridge. 'Like I said, there's some money to be made here. My boss hates Coburg and he'd pay good money to get the goods on him. Real or planted.'

'Planted?' said Effie. 'You mean, faked?'

'If it's done properly, it's as good as real,' said Potteridge.

CHAPTER TWENTY-SEVEN

The first thing Coburg and Lampson did when they arrived at the Savoy was to check with their maintenance department on the constituents of the rat poison the hotel used. As Charley, the man responsible for dealing with rodents of any type, told them: 'Most people don't realise it, but in London you're never more than six feet from a rat. Most of 'em underground, in sewers and things, obviously, but you'd be surprised how many of 'em get in through pipes runs. Top places, as well. Downing Street, Buckingham Palace. It's even more likely if you're near a river. Trust me, it's a full-time job keeping on top of 'em.'

He showed them the packet containing the rodenticide they used, and Coburg studied the list of constituents.

'Main constituent, ethyl chloroacetate,' he told Lampson. 'No mention of thallium sulphate.'

'Too risky, in my opinion,' said Charley. 'Always a

danger of someone accidentally getting poisoned.'

As they walked back up the stairs to the reception area, Coburg said: 'Well that rules out rat poison. At least the sort used here.'

'So, it's the hair remover,' said Lampson.

'Seems like it,' agreed Coburg.

There were fourteen maids on duty during daylight hours, with a further six scheduled to come on at 8 p.m. for the night shift.

'I'll come back tonight and talk to the night shift,' said Coburg.

'You want me with you?' asked Lampson.

Coburg shook his head. 'Carry on keeping an eye on Terry at night for the next few days,' he advised. 'Get him back into the habit of not running wild.'

They settled themselves in the basement room where Lampson had previously talked to the staff. Lampson had his notes on those meetings and he was able to give Coburg some background information on seven of the fourteen who he'd talked to previously. The procedure would be the same with each of the maids.

'We'll let them talk,' said Coburg. 'If they clam up we'll throw in questions, but mainly I'm after chatter and gossip, so we'll let them decide what they want to talk about, so long as it concerns the murder victims and Ella Kemble, and anything else that's happened that might throw some light on the case.'

The first maid they talked to was Brenda Witt, a woman in her late forties, and once she realised they were looking for gossip and dirt on Daisy Scott, she was happy to oblige.

'If you ask me, she was little better than a whore,' she said, her face tight with disapproval. 'I told Dolly Wharton, she's the head maid, Daisy was a bad lot, but she didn't want to say anything to Mr Tillesley in case she got into trouble.'

'She had affairs with guests?' asked Coburg.

'If you can call them "affairs",' Brenda sniffed. 'Mostly it was a quick bunk-up and she'd pocket a fiver or a tenner. But some of them she did it more than once with.'

'Any names mentioned?'

'She didn't need to. You could see that smug smile of hers like a cat with the cream, and you knew whose room she'd just been into.'

First from Brenda, then from the other maids, they compiled a list of her frequent customers: the Earl of Lancaster, the Honourable Gavin Pearce MP, Lord Winship, the Duke of Wexford, along with some she only did it with once, reputedly.

There was some disagreement about whether Daisy had been left-handed or right-handed, with the majority who'd noticed being sure she was right-handed.

None of the maids they talked to had liked Ella Kemble.

'She was obsessed with Giovanni, one of the waiters,' one told them. 'She was always talking about him, and she used to go crackers if he so much as smiled at any of us other maids because she thought we were after him. She thought I had eyes for Giovanni and she threatened me, told me she'd have me beaten up if I didn't leave him alone. But I was never after him. I've got my own boyfriend.'

The one thing they all agreed on, and were happy to

pass on to Coburg and Lampson, was that Ella Kemble definitely had an excessive hair problem.

'If she didn't used to shave, or whatever she did, she'd have had a big moustache,' said one gleefully.

'Did you ever see her with a preparation for getting rid of excess hair?' Coburg asked each of them. But none of them had, with one of them telling them: 'I never wanted to be that close to her to find out things like that. People would've thought I was like her if I had, and I didn't want that kind of reputation.'

When it came to Ella Kemble, one told them she was right-handed. None of them, however, could remember having anything to do with Ella on the last day she'd been at work, the Wednesday. Although one of them, Stella Wainwright, thought there'd been a young man waiting for Ella when she finished work.

'I left at five, the same time as Ella,' she said. 'She left just before me, and I saw her go up to a young man who seemed to be waiting for someone. I guess for her.'

'Did they go off together?' asked Coburg.

'I don't know. I was in a rush to catch my bus.'

'Can you describe him?'

She sat there, thinking, trying to recall him, then she gave a sigh and replied sadly: 'Not really. He looked ordinary. Average height. Thin, but not too thin. Hair cut short and neat. No beard or moustache. He looked like he was wearing a suit, but I couldn't be sure because I really didn't take much notice of him. If it was a suit, it wasn't a smart suit, just an everyday one'

'How old do you think he was?'

'In his twenties, I think.'

This information led them to ask each of the maids what they knew about Ella's love life. Did she have a regular boyfriend? Had any of the others seen the young man that Stella Wainwright described with Ella, or waiting for her? None of them had, and none of them had ever heard her mention a boyfriend. 'Only Giovanni,' said one. 'Not that he was her boyfriend, but she wanted him to be.'

Afterwards, after they'd talked to the last of the maids, Coburg and Lampson ran through what they'd learned, especially the young man who Stella had thought had been waiting for Ella.

'In his twenties, but he wasn't in uniform,' mused Coburg.

'Maybe he was home on leave,' suggested Lampson.

'We need to find out why she's disappeared all of a sudden. Was it voluntarily, or did someone make her? Was this young man the reason?'

They looked at what they'd learned about Daisy Scott: that she had thrown herself at guests with money. And, according to the maids, she did quite well out of her efforts financially because she was always showing off the five- and ten-pound notes she earned.

'She made quite a career out of it, by all accounts,' commented Lampson.

'The question is: did she get pregnant by design to force one of them into making an honest woman of her; or, at least, a wealthy single mother. Or was it an accident?' asked Coburg.

'We know William Lancaster dumped her when he

242

found out she was shagging all these other blokes,' pointed out Lampson. 'The question is: did he get so enraged when he found out, he killed her?'

'He's certainly on the suspect list,' nodded Coburg. 'As are all the others we heard about, as they were all in the Savoy at the time she was stabbed.' He frowned. 'But why poison her first? Surely, it would be easier to just stab her. She was knifed in the back, after all. Creep up behind her and . . . thump. All done.'

'Because whoever did it was taking no chances,' said Lampson. 'They were worried she might turn round at the wrong moment and fight back.'

'Which suggests someone not as strong as Daisy was. But most of the men mentioned here are strong enough to overpower a smallish woman like Daisy, I'd have thought. And remember what we said about it needing two people to force her to take poison.'

'Two women working together?' suggested Lampson. 'Poison's often a woman's weapon.'

'It's the fact she was killed in the sluice is the puzzle,' said Coburg.

'Maybe it was two of the maids?' suggested Lampson.

Coburg fell silent, then nodded.

'That would make a lot of sense,' he said thoughtfully. 'Them being in the sluice with her wouldn't be noticeable. None of the maids liked Daisy. Say she'd made herself available to one of the maid's boyfriend or husband. Or even two of them. We need to find out each maid's circumstances. Who's married and who isn't. Who's engaged or got a boyfriend. Any recent upsets. And we need to find out who used the sluice that day between one and three in the afternoon.'

'We won't get the truth by asking the maids themselves,' Lampson pointed out. 'The guilty ones, if it's two of them working together, will cover for each other. And the others all seem loyal to one another, except when it came to Daisy Scott and Ella Kemble.

Coburg flicked back through the notes he'd made during each interview, and found what he was looking for. 'This head maid, Dolly Wharton, she wasn't in today, but she'll be in tonight. I'll have a word with her about the maids' love lives.'

'It's unlikely she'll tell you much,' said Lampson doubtfully. 'Remember what that Brenda said: she was afraid to pass on to Mr Tillesley about what Daisy was up to in case she lost her job.'

'Which is a threat I'll use when I talk to her tonight,' said Coburg.

'That doesn't sound like you, guv, bully a woman,' said Lampson.

'I won't be bullying her, Sergeant. I'll just explain to her nicely the risky position she'll be in if she doesn't spill the beans. Trust me, I'll be a perfect gentleman. In the meantime, I think it would be a good idea to talk to as many of the men who were mentioned as being Daisy's customers as we can. Let's see how many of them are here this afternoon.'

CHAPTER TWENTY-EIGHT

They discovered that Gavin Pearce MP had just finished lunch in the restaurant, and, as he left, they identified themselves and showed him their warrant cards.

'We're investigating the recent death of one of the Savoy's maids,' Coburg told him.

'A tragedy,' said Pearce sombrely, then adding: 'But I'm not sure how I can be of help.'

'We're talking to many people,' said Coburg, 'as we attempt to try and build up a picture of what may have led to her death. May we have a word now?'

'Well, I am due at the House of Commons,' said Pearce regretfully.

'We understand,' said Coburg. 'In that case, if you can tell us when we'll be finished, we'll send a police car to collect you and bring you to Scotland Yard.'

'Scotland Yard!' snapped Pearce in outrage.

'What on earth for?'

'Because you're too busy to talk to us at the moment,' said Coburg. 'However, our enquiries have to continue, so for now we'll talk to other people here, and see everyone else later at Scotland Yard. What time shall we send the police car for you to the House of Commons?'

Pearce stared at him, aghast. 'Do you know how that would look?' he demanded. 'A police car turning up at the House of Commons and driving me away?'

'I'm sure you'll be able to explain it, if anyone asks. Reporters, or such. Or we can explain to them that you are helping us in our enquiries but were unable to talk to us earlier.'

'Are you threatening me?' demanded Pearce. 'Do you know who I am? I am a Member of Parliament, for God's sake.'

'I am very aware of that,' said Coburg smoothly. 'But, as you can't talk to us now . . .'

'Oh, very well,' snapped Pearce with a scowl. 'Anything to avoid the pantomime of being hauled off in a police car.'

'Thank you, sir,' said Coburg. 'Your co-operation is much appreciated. In view of some of the nature of the questions we have, I would suggest we talk somewhere in private.'

'What do you mean, the nature of your questions?' said Pearce suspiciously.

'That would be better discussed somewhere private,' said Coburg. 'Or, if you'd prefer, we could still journey to Scotland Yard.'

'My suite,' hissed Pearce, obviously unhappy. 'That'll be private enough.'

'Is anyone else with you at this moment?' asked Coburg. 'Your wife?'

'No, my wife is at our home. There's just me.'

'Then your suite will be fine,' said Coburg.

They took the lift up to the third floor and Coburg and Lampson followed Pearce to his room. Once inside, he gestured them to two chairs, settling himself down on a settee.

'Right,' he said. 'Let's get this over. What do you want to know?'

'Mr Pearce, we've received information that you had a relationship with the maid who was murdered, Daisy Scott,' said Coburg.

'What do you mean, a relationship?' demanded Pearce angrily.

'Of a sexual nature,' said Coburg.

Pearce stared at them, outraged. 'How dare you!' he said, his lips trembling with anger.

'You deny it?'

'Of course I do. It's a lie. An absolute canard, and if anyone says that, I shall sue them for libel. And that includes you, Inspector.'

'Chief Inspector,' Coburg corrected him. 'You gave her money. And gifts. We have witnesses who will swear to that.'

Pearce sat silent for a moment, then he blustered: 'I did, and I'm proud of it. I felt sorry for the girl. She'd had a hard life and she was having financial difficulties. As a Member of Parliament, my aim is to help those who haven't had the advantages I've had.'

'So the money and gifts you gave her were altruistic.'

'Exactly,' said Pearce. 'She told me her mother needed an operation which the family couldn't afford.'

'What was the operation for?'

'I can't remember,' said Pearce dismissively. 'I just knew that I could help someone in distress.'

Coburg nodded thoughtfully, then said quietly, his eyes on Pearce: 'She kept a diary.'

'What?' said Pearce, suddenly uncomfortable.

'Daisy Scott kept a diary of her . . . adventures. She named names of the men she was involved with.'

Pearce stared at him, momentarily speechless, then he gulped before blurting out: 'I insist on taking possession of it.'

'The diary is police evidence,' said Coburg.

'I am a Member of Parliament,' said Pearce. 'It is likely that diary contains malicious lies naming people of importance. Not just myself, but others in authority. It must be put into the Government's hands to prevent this false information from being leaked out and undermining morale at this time of war.'

'I agree,' said Coburg quietly. 'I have been personally authorised by the Home Secretary to carry out this enquiry. I can show you the letter with his signature giving me that authority, if you wish. So, are you suggesting that I hand this diary to the Home Secretary?'

Pearce looked at Coburg, then at Lampson, then back at Coburg again. He opened his mouth but no words came out.

'There is no reason for this information about you and Daisy Scott to be made public,' said Coburg. 'Or, for it to be passed to any member of the Cabinet. At this moment, no one in the Cabinet knows of the diary's existence. We are trying to build a profile of the murdered girl in order to find out who killed her. There is a possibility that it may have been connected with her sexual adventures.'

'I didn't do it!' blurted out Pearce.

'I'm not suggesting you did,' said Coburg calmly. 'It may have been another of her lovers who was overcome with jealousy. Or someone who decided that she was a risk because of her knowledge about certain prominent people. Or it may not be connected with her activities at all.' He looked at Pearce and asked: 'Did you know she was pregnant?'

Pearce looked shocked. 'Pregnant?' he echoed.

'Two months,' said Coburg.

Immediately, Pearce relaxed. 'It wasn't me,' he said hastily. 'Being the father, I mean. I only started my . . . meetings with her a month ago.'

'You were taking a chance there, guv,' said Lampson as they walked away from Pearce's suite. 'Telling him we had her diary.'

'I didn't say we had it,' said Coburg. 'I said she kept a diary. Which is quite likely to be true. The honourable Member of Parliament made the leap of imagination to us actually having this diary.' He smiled. 'As it seemed to do the trick for us, I think we'll see how it works with another of her alleged conquests, Lord Winship.'

They found Lord Winship in the bar, reading a newspaper. On learning that Lady Winship was resting in their suite, and noting that most of the tables and chairs near them were empty, Coburg opted to quiz His Lordship in the bar. This time, keeping his voice low, he began with the information that Daisy Scott had kept a diary of her amorous relationships while working at the Savoy, and that she named names.

'She wrote things down?' said Winship hoarsely, aghast and casting anxious looks around the bar to make sure that no one was within hearing range.

'She did.' Coburg nodded.

'I've always said we shouldn't have educated the working class,' grunted Winship. 'Not the women, anyway. Why do they need to be able to read and write?'

They asked Winship for his movements for the time span during which Scott had been killed, and noted that during the whole time he seemed to have been accompanied by Lady Winship.

'Not much of an alibi,' commented Lampson afterwards. 'His missus.'

'It's still an alibi unless we can prove that they weren't together the whole time,' said Coburg.

The other men on the list they'd compiled from their interviews with the maids were not in.

'I'll see if I can get hold of them when I come back later this evening to talk to Dolly Wharton,' said Coburg. He looked at his watch and said: 'I think that's time for us to call it a day for now. Tomorrow I suggest we return to Ascot and talk to Piranesi again. Do you fancy doing the drive?'

Lampson's face lit up. 'Thanks, guv,' he said.

CHAPTER TWENTY-NINE

Magnus was already at the flat with Rosa when Coburg arrived home.

'She said yes,' beamed Magnus before Coburg had even taken off his overcoat and hung it up.

'Yes, I rather thought she might,' said Coburg drily. 'Tea, anyone?'

Magnus showed him the glass of whiskey he was holding and said: 'There's some first-class Scotch in the cupboard.'

'I know,' said Coburg. 'And a really good Irish, which pleased Rosa. But at the moment it's just tea for me. I have to return to the Savoy later to talk to more possible suspects and witnesses about the latest murder.'

'The maid,' nodded Magnus. 'Dreadful business.'

'Tea for you?' Coburg asked Rosa.

'Yes please,' said Rosa. As Coburg put the kettle on, she

asked Magnus: 'So is this official? Us spying on possible enemies?'

'No,' said Magnus. 'It's very much a solo operation. Or, a duo now. Winston is suspicious of some in the Secret Service and where their loyalties might lie.'

'With Nazi Germany?' asked Rosa, surprised.

Magnus shook his head.

'Some of them are quite to the left of politics. There's a concern that those who are inclined that way and whose major loyalty is to the Reds might pass information to the Soviets. And, as the Soviets are currently in an alliance with Hitler . . .'

'It's all very tangled,' said Rosa. 'So, who do we report to?'

'I report direct to the Prime Minister, but in an unofficial capacity,' said Magnus. 'I might alert him to your involvement, just in case anything should happen to me and you can take over. Or not, depending on the circumstances.'

'When you say "if anything happens to you . . ."' put in Coburg, worried, pouring the boiling water into the teapot.

'We could be dealing with some dangerous people,' said Magnus. 'That's what Winston thinks. So, pooling our information, what do we know so far?'

Rosa told him about her conversation with Dotty Ravenwood.

'Yes, Julia Winship mentioned Mosley to me. Said it was a pity his close relationship with Hitler couldn't be put to good use.'

'But with Mosley currently under lock and key in Holloway prison, that's surely just a pipe dream,' said Coburg.

'Is it?' asked Magnus. 'Look at the people the Winships are cultivating. Politicians. Peers of the realm. Writers and artists.' He looked at Rosa. 'Celebrities.'

'I'm not a celebrity,' protested Rosa.

'You are in some people's eyes,' said Coburg, handing her a cup of tea. 'People listen to what you have to say because of who you are.'

'I'm just a jazz singer and pianist.'

'With a well-deserved reputation,' pointed out Magnus. 'You've appeared in major venues in capital cities across Europe. It wouldn't surprise me to find that Hitler himself has some of your records.' He smiled at her as he added: 'And I see the Savoy have put up a poster advertising you as their guest star for their afternoon tea spot this Sunday. I shall be there among your audience.'

'As will I,' said Coburg. 'I can see what you're getting at, Magnus, but most of the writers and artists and celebrities who were members of the BUF have been banned by the BBC, and no newspaper will give them space to air their views.'

'Those who were known members of the BUF,' pointed out Magnus. 'There are plenty out there who favour Hitler but haven't made their political views public yet.'

'So, you're suggesting that the Winships are trawling to bring in people of note who they feel share their views,' said Rosa.

'Yes,' said Magnus. 'And gradually build up a campaign to lobby for Mosley's freedom.'

'If that happened, he'd just get locked up again as a traitor,' said Coburg.

'Not necessarily,' said Magnus. 'It would depend on

who was in power.'

'Churchill, obviously,' said Coburg. 'He's not going anywhere until all this is over.'

'But say something happened to Churchill,' said Magnus.

Coburg and Rosa looked at him, alarmed.

'A plot to assassinate Churchill?' said Rosa, shocked.

'It makes sense,' said Magnus. 'It was a close-run thing for the leadership between Churchill and Halifax, and there are still many in the Tory party who'd prefer an appeaser to Churchill. If Churchill died it would create a vacuum at the heart of Government. Officially, the deputy Prime Minister is Attlee, but I can't see many Tories agreeing to serve under him as PM.'

'And if Mosley was free and stood for election to the vacancy,' mused Coburg thoughtfully.

'Exactly,' nodded Magnus.

'I don't really know much about Mosley,' admitted Rosa. 'I've read about him in the papers, of course. Leader of the British Fascists, friend of Hitler. Dotty Ravenswood told me he was a patriot. A hero who was wounded in the First War, which is why he walks with a limp.'

'He served,' said Magnus. 'And he was wounded, but not by the enemy. An observer plane he was flying crashed when he was showing off to his mother and sister.'

'So, he never actually fought?'

'He served in the trenches before he joined the Flying Corps, and he returned there after his flying accident, but the pain from his leg caused him to be returned to Britain after the Battle of Loos in 1915, so he spent the rest of the war behind a desk.'

'You sound like you don't have a lot of time for him,' said Rosa.

'For all his talk, he's a man with no real political loyalties, except to himself,' said Magnus. 'First, he was a member of the Conservative party, then he became an Independent MP, then he switched to Labour. Then there was the brief stint in his own outfit, which he called The New Party, before he started the British Union of Fascists.'

'Churchill did the same,' countered Coburg. 'One day a Conservative, the next a Liberal, and then a Tory again.'

'But not to the same extent,' said Magnus.

'I still can't get over the idea of someone wanting to assassinate Churchill,' said Rosa, horrified. 'Who would even contemplate doing that?'

'Plenty of people,' said Magnus. 'Some I could hazard a guess at, but there will be many more who we don't know about. And I feel that's why Winston asked me to do some digging. He knows his life's at stake.'

'And so, therefore, is yours if they find out what you're doing,' said Coburg grimly. 'And so is Rosa's' he added, looking at them, worried. 'I'm beginning to doubt the wisdom of this, as far as Rosa is concerned. You and I, Magnus, are old soldiers . . .'

'I'm doing it,' said Rosa firmly. 'This is too important not to.'

'I'll look after her, little brother,' Magnus promised Coburg. 'I'll make sure nothing happens to her.'

As Coburg and Magnus walked down the stairs to the street, Magnus commented: 'You've got a good one there, Edgar. She's a brave girl.'

'She is,' nodded Coburg. 'I just hope she's sensible with it.'

'Yes, she does seem to find herself in dangerous situations,' sighed Magnus. 'Although, by all accounts, her getting shot was really your fault.'

'Yes, it was,' admitted Coburg. 'I don't want to go through that experience again.'

'As I said, Edgar, I'll keep an eye on her. Keep her safe.'

They reached the car and Coburg unlocked it. 'The Savoy for you?' he asked.

'No. Drop me off at King Charles Street, if you don't mind.'

'The Cabinet War Rooms,' commented Coburg.

'I promised the PM I'd keep him apprised of whatever I found,' said Magnus, getting into the car. 'I think now is the time to do just that.'

CHAPTER THIRTY

Charles Tillesley had agreed that Coburg could use his office to talk to Dolly Wharton. Coburg had requested this for two reasons: the first was to ensure there would be no interruptions from maids with urgent questions for Dolly, and secondly, he hoped being in the manager's office would encourage her to answer his questions and not hide behind bland phrases such as 'I don't know anything about that'.

'Mrs Wharton, I know this is hard for you, but I do need to know all there is to know about Daisy Scott. Did you know she was pregnant?'

'I thought she might be,' said Dolly. 'But I never asked her. It wasn't my place.'

'I understand,' said Coburg sympathetically. 'I don't mean to put you in a difficult position, but one of your maids has been killed, and we need to find the killer urgently, before he or she strikes again.'

'She?' said Dolly, bewildered. 'You think it might be a woman?'

'We don't know,' said Coburg. 'We're keeping an open mind on it, but there is a possibility that it could be two people working together who did it. Possibly two women.'

She shook her head. 'No,' she said. 'That wouldn't be possible. None of my maids would do such a thing.'

'It doesn't have to be a maid,' said Coburg. 'It could be another member of staff. Who uses the sluice, for example, apart from the maids?

'Well, the cleaners,' said Dolly. 'That's where the mops and stuff are kept.'

'Kitchen staff?' asked Coburg.

'They've got their own services,' said Dolly.

'When anyone uses the sluice, do they have to fill in a time sheet for the time they're there?' asked Coburg.

'No,' said Dolly. 'If they had to do that they'd never do the work.'

'Tell me about Daisy Scott.'

'What about her?'

'As I said, she was pregnant. Do you know who the father might be?'

'No. I don't go poking my nose into other people's private business.'

'I understand, but in this case Daisy's private life may hold the reason why she was killed. We know she had relationships with some of the hotel guests, so it's possible that one of them is the father. But we also know she had relationships with other men. Do you know who?'

She shook her head. 'I don't listen to gossip,' she said firmly.

'But you're the chief maid,' said Coburg. 'It's your job to know what's going on, who might be suddenly off sick, who's not doing their work properly.'

'And I do,' she said. 'But that's not the same as poking into people's private lives.'

'We know that she had a relationship with the Earl of Lancaster, and he was killed here. Stabbed in the back, the same as Daisy. The key to these murders is Daisy's private life and I need to know about it if I'm to stop anyone else here being killed. Everyone here is a potential victim. That includes you and all your maids. I don't want another death on my conscience because I didn't get the information that could have stopped it. And whatever you say won't be held against you, I promise you. In fact, the exact opposite. Mr Tillesley has urged me to solve this case as a matter of urgency, to protect the Savoy's reputation and to make sure that no one falls victim to this murderer. I need to tell him that you gave me every piece of help.'

She hesitated, and Coburg saw that she was arguing with herself as to how much to say. Finally, she asked: 'Mr Tillesley won't be upset? Only he doesn't like gossip.'

'This isn't gossip, it's vital information. Even if it's unfounded and speculation, it may well have come from someone who might know, and we can look into it. Mr Tillesley is desperate to uncover everything to find this murderer. And so is Mr D'Oyly Carte. I need to be able to tell them both how vital you were. That you may well have saved this hotel, and lives.'

She nodded, then said: 'I'm only saying this for the hotel's sake. And for Mr Tillesley's and Mr D'Oyly Carte's, if that's what they want.'

'They do,' said Coburg. 'They're desperate. Anything. It doesn't have to be anything you know for sure; it could be something some of the women have said, even in passing. None of them seemed to like Daisy Scott, so I'm sure they must have said something to you about her. Not just her sexual adventures, but her attitude. People she'd upset.'

'There were plenty of them,' said Dolly disapprovingly. 'They didn't like the way she threw herself at the men here. Not just the guests, and there were plenty of them. You mentioned the Earl of Lancaster. He was just one.'

'We also know about the Honourable Gavin Pearce MP, Lord Winship and the Duke of Wexford,' said Coburg, to encourage her.

'Them and a dozen others,' said Dolly. And she gave the names of some of the other guests that Coburg and Lampson had already heard about; along with a few more that were new to them.

'What about other members of staff?'

'There was Harry Pickford. He works in the kitchens as a washer-up. I can't think why she set her sights low that time after all the lords and earls she'd been chasing. I guess she just got used to doing it with anyone, and Harry's quite a handsome bloke. A bit of a charmer, but not to be trusted. He's been in prison.'

'What for?'

'Fraud. That was before the war. His fiancée told me.'

'His fiancée? Does she work here?'

'Yes, but she's not one of the maids. She's a cleaner. Vera Bates. A bit thick, to be honest.' She shook her head. 'I say she's his fiancée, but I think he only did that so he could have his way with her. She wears a ring but I'm not even sure it's proper gold. There's no chance of him marrying her as far as I can see. He's just stringing her along.'

'I assume Vera found out about Harry and Daisy.'

'Yes. One of the other maids must have told her, because Daisy boasted about what she and Harry had done.'

'Do you know which maid told Vera?'

Dolly hesitated, then said: 'I do, actually, because I spoke to Vera. I'd heard that she was torn up about it. In fact she went off sick and I thought she might quit. So I had a word with her and told her she was too good for him, and she couldn't afford to give up a good job like the one she had just because of him. I didn't slag him off to her, though I wanted to, because she'd only have got angry with me. She's dotty about Harry.'

'Who was the maid who told Vera about Harry and Daisy?' prompted Coburg.

'Ella Kemble,' said Dolly. 'That's who Vera said told her.' She shook her head angrily. 'She's another nasty piece of work, Ella. A good worker, though. You can't fault her on that. Anyway, I had a word with Harry and told him he'd better get Vera back.'

'How did he react?'

'He started off by telling me to mind my own business, but he changed his tune when I told him that if Vera left I'd tell Mr Tillesley why. Not that I would have, but I wasn't going to have Vera forced out by that cow. I also told him that if Vera left she wouldn't be earning any more, and I knew for a fact that he was spending her money on betting, and he couldn't afford to lose that.'

'So, what happened?'

'Harry told Vera he was sorry, that it wasn't his fault, that Daisy had caught him at a bad moment when he was upset because he'd just learnt his brother who lived in Newcastle had died.' She gave a scornful laugh. 'I don't even think he had a brother, but it was what she wanted to hear. So, she forgave him, if he promised never to have anything to do with Daisy Scott again.'

'And did he keep that promise?'

'As far as I know, but it was nothing to do with him. Daisy didn't want anything more to do with him. She'd had her fun and that was it.'

'What sort of woman is Vera? Could she have killed Daisy in revenge for what she got up to with Harry?'

Dolly laughed. 'Vera? Never in a month of Sundays. For one thing she's a frail little creature, wouldn't say boo to a goose. If it had come to a fight between her and Daisy, Daisy would have wiped the floor with her. She was strong, Daisy. Tough. Streetwise.'

'What about Ella Kemble?'

'What about her?'

'She seems to have disappeared.'

'Yes, so I've heard. I know she didn't turn up for work,' she said disapprovingly.

'What sort of person was she?'

Dolly hesitated, then she said: 'Like I said, a nasty piece of work, but a good worker. If you ask me, her trouble was she was mad.'

'Mad?'

'About Giovanni, one of the waiters. When he was sent away I thought she was going to have a breakdown.'

'How did she get on with Daisy Scott?'

'Hated her.'

'Why?'

'I don't know. All I know is that whenever I saw Ella and Daisy together there was a look on Ella's face that could strip your skin off.'

'Did Ella have a boyfriend?'

'Only in her mind, and that was Giovanni.'

Magnus sat on the metal-framed chair in the corridor outside the Cabinet Office. The long narrow corridor ran the length of the underground Cabinet War Rooms, zig-zagging now and then, with occasionally a small corridor going off of it to side rooms.

Construction to turn the basement area of the large building that was the New Public Office, running from where Whitehall became Parliament Square to Horse Guards Parade, the side streets of King Charles Street and Great George Street marking its other borders, into the wartime seat of Government had begun in 1938 once predictions of war coming had become ever more convincing. There had been forecasts of two hundred thousand casualties a week in London when – not if – the bombing of the capital began. By August 1939 the War Rooms were operational, just a few days before the invasion of Poland by the Nazis led to Britain declaring war on Germany, and the evacuation of London's children, nearly a million of them sent away from their families to rural locations, each child carrying a gas mask and with a label hung around their neck with their name and age and home address.

During Chamberlain's time as Prime Minister the Cabinet War Rooms had seen little use, but once Churchill became prime minister he was determined to use them as the base from which to run the war. The two main rooms were the Map Room, which was manned by officers from the Navy, Army and Air Force round the clock, and the Cabinet Room. Further along the corridor were the Transatlantic Telephone Room, primarily for a telephone connection to President Roosevelt in America; and Churchill's office-bedroom, although Churchill rarely stayed overnight, preferring to sleep either at 10 Downing Street or the Number 10 Annexe, a flat in the New Public Offices located directly above the Cabinet Rooms.

There were also bedrooms for senior Cabinet ministers and military officers, along with rooms for the staff: typists, secretaries and telephone operators, the whole place bustling with activity twenty-four hours a day.

'Magnus!'

Magnus looked up and saw the heavyset figure of Churchill walking towards him along the corridor. Magnus rose to his feet and gave a slight bow as he said: 'Good evening, Prime Minister.'

'Sorry to have kept you waiting.'

'That's perfectly all right, Prime Minister. Thank you for making the time to see me.'

Churchill pushed open the door to the Cabinet War Room. 'Let's go in here. No one else'll be coming here for the next few minutes.'

Magnus followed Churchill into the large room and they settled themselves at the long table where the War Cabinet assembled.

'So, what have you got?' asked Churchill.

'You were right about the Winships. They want a peace deal at any price.'

'What's their plan?'

'Build up support for the release of Mosley among influential people whose opinions carry weight with the public. Writers, journalists, musicians, celebrities. Then, when he's free, despatch him to Germany to make a deal with Hitler.'

'Over my dead body,' Churchill growled.

'Yes, that's the other part of the plan.'

Churchill studied Magnus inquisitively, then gave a chuckle.

'Got any proof of the second part? Bumping me off?'

Magnus shook his head.

'Nothing that will hang them, it's all very much reading between the lines. But I'm fairly sure of it.'

'How far does it spread?'

'I'm not sure,' admitted Magnus. 'I've met some of their group, but most of them are pretty much second class. Hangers-on and aspirants. But I'm pretty sure there must be someone behind the Winships, someone more . . . serious.'

'No idea who?'

Magnus shook his head. 'You could always bring them in and quiz them.'

'We'd need something concrete to justify it if we're going to put the screws on them. And the screws will be needed, otherwise they'll just deny everything.' He lapsed into thoughtful silence, then said: 'There is one option. Kill Mosley and the conspiracy collapses.'

'No,' corrected Magnus. 'Kill Mosley and it changes direction. You still get assassinated and a new figurehead comes in Mosley's place. On the other hand, threaten to have Mosley killed if anything happens to you and that puts the freeze on the conspirators while they wonder what to do. And, as we know who most of them are, an eye can be kept on them.'

Churchill took a cigar from a box on the table, clipped off the end and lit it, then sat, thinking this over. Finally, he nodded.

'Makes sense,' he said. He got up and held out his hand. 'Thank you, Magnus. I knew I could trust you.'

'My pleasure, Prime Minister,' said Magnus. He shook Churchill's hand, gave a small bow, and left. Churchill walked across to the telephone on a side table.

'Prime Minister?' he heard the operator say.

'Tell Mr Bracken to come and see me in the Cabinet Room. I need to see him now.'

CHAPTER THIRTY-ONE

Saturday 21st September

As Coburg and Lampson headed for Ascot, with Lampson once again delighted to be doing the driving, Coburg related what he'd learned from Dolly Wharton. 'One interesting thing came up about Daisy Scott and Ella Kemble. It seems that as well as Daisy putting it about for the Savoy's guests, she also had a fling with one of the kitchen hands called Harry Pickford. This Harry Pickford was – possibly still is – engaged to one of the Savoy's cleaners, a woman called Vera. Daisy boasted to the other maids about getting off with this Harry Pickford, and Ella told Vera about it.'

'She grassed Daisy and this Pickford bloke up?'

'She did,' said Coburg.

'Why?'

'Apparently, Ella hated, despised and loathed Daisy Scott, according to Dolly Wharton. I'm guessing she hoped that Vera would go for Daisy and tear her eyes out.'

'Maybe she did,' said Lampson. 'Maybe this Vera was

the one who killed Daisy?'

'I suggested that to Dolly Wharton, but she laughed off the idea. Said Vera was a frail little thing and if it had come to a fight Daisy would have wiped the floor with her.'

'But if there were two of them involved, and the other was stronger,' said Lampson. 'Maybe this bloke Harry Pickford, having his own back on Daisy for dropping him in it by telling about him and her.'

'Yes, it's a possibility,' said Coburg thoughtfully. 'When we get back we'll talk to Vera and Harry and see what we think of them. The only drawback is that neither of them were on duty at the Savoy the night the Earl of Lancaster was killed.'

'So maybe they killed Daisy, and someone else did for the Earl. Maybe they just copied the way the Earl was done to put the blame on whoever did the first one.'

'In which case, who killed the Earl?' Coburg sighed. 'Sometimes I think we're no nearer to finding out.'

'Maybe we'll find out more today,' said Lampson as the high fence and the barbed wire and searchlights of Ascot prison camp came into view. 'See if Mr Piranesi's got anything new to add.'

They parked in the visitors' car park and, after showing their warrant cards, were taken to see John Whitehall.

'Good to see you both again,' smiled Whitehall. 'What can I do for you this time?'

'We'd like another word with Giovanni Piranesi, but, before we do, has he had any further visitors since we were last here?'

Whitehall took down the visitors' book and checked the

recent entries, then shook his head. 'No. At least, none who actually saw him. That woman who came before was here yesterday, Ella Kemble, but once again he refused to see her. Remember I told you she came here before, soon after he was interned. He refused to see her then.'

'What time did she come to see him yesterday?'

The man checked the book again. 'At 3 p.m.,' he told them. 'But she went away again.'

Coburg and Lampson exchanged glances. So, Ella was still very much alive. At least, she had been the previous afternoon. Then Coburg said: 'Can we see Mr Piranesi now?'

As they followed Whitehall across the square to the interview room, Lampson muttered: 'So, Ella's not dead after all. What's her game?'

'A very devious one, I'm beginning to think,' responded Coburg.

Oswald and Diana Mosley were in the living room of the small house they'd been allocated inside Holloway prison, reading – a magazine for him and a book for her – when there was a respectful tap at the door.

'Enter!' called Mosley. 'It's unlocked!'

The door opened and a uniformed prison warder entered.

'The governor wants you,' he said.

With an air of weary resignation, both the Mosleys put down their reading material and got to their feet.

'Just Sir Oswald,' said the warder.

Diana frowned. 'Why not me?' she asked.

'I don't know, ma'am,' said the warder. 'That's just my instructions.'

'Very well,' said Mosley. He smiled at his wife. 'You never know, it may be a pardon so we can get out of here.'

'If that were the case, why doesn't he want to see both of us?' snapped Diana, annoyed. 'You're not leaving here without me.'

'No, I am not,' Mosley reassured her.

He pulled on his coat and followed the warder out of the house and into the enclosed yard of the prison. They were heading towards the main building and the governor's office, when the warder pulled up outside another house. He opened the door and gestured for Mosley to go in.

'This isn't the governor's office,' said Mosley warily.

'The person who wants to talk to you is in here,' said the warder. 'With the governor's permission. First door on the right. I shall be here to escort you back.'

With that, the warden placed himself beside the front door.

Intrigued, Mosley stepped into the house and, after a few steps along the short passage, opened the first door on his right that he came to. He had presumed he would find a living room similar to the one in the house that he and Diana had, but instead he found himself in what was obviously an interrogation room. It was bare of all furniture except for a wooden table and three chairs. There was a fireplace, but no fire had been laid. Official posters decorated the walls, urging caution and alertness in all things, the largest poster bearing the well-known phrase: 'Careless talk costs lives'.

A tall, thin bespectacled man in his late thirties stood by the empty fireplace and he turned now to face Mosley, his curly red hair bouncing slightly as he moved towards the table.

Brendan Bracken, thought Mosley. Churchill's parliamentary private secretary, his lapdog or his attack dog, depending on whether you were viewed as friend or foe.

'Mr Mosley,' said Bracken, still with traces of his soft Irish accent, no matter how much he'd tried to distance himself from his County Tipperary roots.

'Sir Oswald,' Mosley corrected him primly.

'Not to me,' said Bracken. 'That implies a patriot with allegiance to the Crown.'

Mosley gave a scornful laugh. 'Those are fine words coming from a supporter of Irish Republican terrorism.'

'Another slander,' said Bracken. 'But then you have many such lies in your armoury.'

He sat down and gestured for Mosley to sit.

'You deny that your father was a founding member of the Irish Brotherhood, and you yourself were part of a group in Dublin with Michael Collins and Emmet Dalton?' said Mosley challengingly.

'My father's relationship with the IRB was nothing to do with me. He died when I was just three years old.' He gave Mosley a cold smile. 'And if you've done your digging properly, you know that most of my early life was spent in Australia. The stories about myself being with Collins and Dalton are just lies put about in an attempt to smear me in an attempt to harm Churchill.'

'Ah yes, of course, the hero of the hour,' said Mosley mockingly. 'I assume he is behind this visit?'

'We've uncovered a plan,' said Bracken.

'Just one?' said Mosley airily. 'I thought you people found plots and stratagems everywhere.'

'We do,' said Bracken. 'And we're good at foiling them. Take this one, for example. The plan is to mount a public lobby campaign by influential people to have you released.'

'That sounds a good plan,' said Mosley. 'I approve.'

'The idea behind it is that these people feel you are the one person who can come to an accommodation with Hitler and this war.'

'Again, that sounds to me very intelligent reasoning,' said Mosley. 'I believe I can come to such an accommodation, which would save thousands – possibly millions – of British lives and put an end to this dreadful bombing.'

'The only obstacle to this plan, as these people see it, is Churchill.'

'Churchill is a warmonger,' said Mosley. 'It doesn't bother him if millions die. Look at the disaster that was Gallipoli. Half a million dead. And yet here he is, twenty so years later, Prime Minister and doing the same again.'

'Would you rather this country was under the rule of the Nazis?' asked Bracken.

Mosley smiled. 'Nice try, Bracken, but you're not going to have me hanged for treason. I'm a patriot. Always have been.'

'As I was saying, the people behind this plan feel that the one flaw to it succeeding is Churchill. So their plan is to have him removed, thus leaving the way clear for you to begin negotiations with Herr Hitler on behalf of the Government.'

'Removed?' queried Mosley. He scoffed. 'Churchill won't resign. He's fought too hard to get what he has.'

'I didn't say he'd be asked to resign, I said he would be removed,' said Bracken. 'An assassination.'

Mosley's expression hardened.

'Any such plan is nothing to do with me,' he snapped. 'I could never sanction the assassination of this country's Prime Minister.'

'But you wouldn't object if it resulted in you being freed and negotiating the peace deal with Hitler. Which is why I'm here to warn you, and I would advise you to make sure this gets back to your supporters. First, you will not be freed. The only way you will gain your freedom is if Hitler should win this war. Secondly, if anything happens to Churchill, you will die within minutes of that happening. Orders have been put in place.'

Mosley glowered at Bracken.

'I'm pretty sure what you're suggesting is illegal and constitutes a crime.'

'At times of war the Government has special powers,' Bracken told him calmly. 'I would urge you, for your own sake, to make sure the people behind this plan are aware of this.'

Mosley regarded Bracken coldly, then asked: 'And Diana? Is she, too, to be sacrificed in the event of something happening to that warmonger?'

'That is up to you,' said Bracken. 'Personally, I agree

with Kipling: the female of the species is more deadly than the male.'

He stood up, walked to the door then stepped out into the passage and called: 'Warder! Your prisoner is ready to be returned to his quarters!'

CHAPTER THIRTY-TWO

Coburg and Lampson were once again in the interview room, facing Giovanni Piranesi, who regarded them sullenly.

'I have nothing more to say to you,' he told them haughtily.

'That's a pity,' said Coburg. 'Another person has been killed at the Savoy hotel and we're hoping you might be able to help us find the killer.'

'It was not me,' said Piranesi. 'I have been here all the time. Locked up, just for being Italian.'

'Tell us about Daisy Scott,' said Coburg.

Piranesi looked at them suspiciously. 'What about her?'

'You know her?'

He nodded. 'One of the maids.'

'Did you and she . . . ?' began Coburg, but he was cut off by Piranesi angrily smashing his fist down on the table.

'No! Whatever she said is not true!'

'Did she offer herself to you?'

'She did, and I said no. I knew what sort of woman she was. And even though my Maria was dead, I would not soil her memory with that whore.'

'It was Daisy Scott who was killed on Wednesday,' Coburg told him. 'The same way the Earl of Lancaster was murdered. A Savoy steak knife in the back.'

Piranesi looked back at him, his face a mask, but they could sense turmoil behind it as he took in this latest information. Eventually, he repeated: 'It was not me. I have been here the whole time.'

'Yes, we heard,' said Coburg. 'Can you think of anyone who might have wanted Daisy dead?'

Piranesi shook his head. 'No.'

'Ella Kemble was here again yesterday, asking to see you,' said Coburg. 'You refused to see her.'

'I did,' said Piranesi. 'And for the same reason as before. I blame her for Maria dying.'

'Why do you think she's obsessed with seeing you?'

Piranesi shrugged. 'I have no idea. Perhaps she is mad.'

'Did you ever have any sort of relationship with her?'

'Never!' bellowed Piranesi angrily.

'I don't mean a sexual relationship; I mean an amicable one. You know, a friendly word or two in passing.'

Piranesi hesitated, then he nodded. 'Perhaps at first,' he admitted. 'I talk to her. I talk to everyone. Nothing special. We smile, we say hello.' Then his face darkened. 'And then one day she come to me and try to kiss me, and I know what she is up to with all this smiling and chat. I tell her:

"No, I am engaged to Maria. Maria is the only one for me."' He scowled. 'She begin to cry. Asks me to hold her, just for comfort, but I know what she is doing. I tell her no. But still, she follows me. I go to the restaurant, she is there, waiting. I go to the kitchen, she is there. She doesn't say anything, but she looks at me like a little puppy wanting to be patted.'

'You weren't tempted?' asked Coburg.

Piranesi shook his head firmly. 'I know these sort of women. Once they get you – even just once – they dig into you, never leave you alone. They tear you to ribbons. Some men the same with some women.' He shook his head again and said sadly. 'Maria was not like that. She was special.'

As Coburg and Lampson walked into the main reception area at Scotland Yard they were hailed by the desk sergeant, who held out a piece of paper to Coburg.

'While you were out, there was a message for you from Sergeant Pelworth at Tottenham Court Road station. There's a woman's body been found on his patch and he thought you ought to know.'

'Did he say whose body?' asked Coburg, looking at the telephone number written on the piece of paper.

'No, sir, but he thought it might be someone you'd be interested in.'

Coburg and Lampson headed up the stairs to the office.

'Any bets it's Ella Kemble?' asked Lampson. 'We did put out an alert for her.'

'Yes, I was just wondering the same,' said Coburg. 'Yesterday afternoon she was at Ascot trying to see Piranesi, so when did she come back?'

Once inside their office, Coburg got the switchboard to get him the number of Tottenham Court Road station; and when he was through he asked for Sergeant Pelworth.

'DCI Coburg,' he said when Pelworth answered. 'I got your message.'

'Sorry to trouble you, sir, and it may be absolutely nothing, but we've had reports of a dead woman at a house on our patch in Goodge Street,' said Pelworth. 'It seems to have been an accident, she fell down the stairs, but it turns out that she works at the Savoy, and as I know you're looking into different incidents there . . .'

'You were quite right to get in touch, Sergeant. Do you have her name?'

'Yes, sir. Vera Bates. She's a cleaner at the Savoy.'

'Where's the body?'

'It's at Willis's, the undertakers in Warren Street. She was found by her fiancé, a Mr Harry Pickford, when he called to see her. The thing is, sir, the constable who went to the scene felt there was something not right. He reckoned it looked like she'd had a bang on the head. It could be that she hit her head when she fell down the stairs, or . . .'

'Give that constable my compliments, Sergeant, and contact Wallis's and tell them from me to do nothing to the body. I want an autopsy done first.'

'I've already told them not to proceed, sir, just in case.'

'Good. And if that constable's available, can you ask him to meet me and my sergeant at the house where she was found. He sounds a bright chap and I'd like to hear how things were when he found them right from the horse's mouth.'

He heard Sergeant Pelworth chuckle, and asked: 'Have I said something funny, Sergeant?'

'Not really, sir,' apologised Pelworth. 'It's just that the constable's name is Dobbin. Eric Dobbin. And when you said about the horse's mouth . . .'

'Yes, Sergeant,' said Coburg, and he also gave a small chuckle. 'I'm sorry if I sounded a bit short with you. If you'll give me the address of the house in Goodge Street where Vera Bates was found, tell PC Dobbin I'll meet him there shortly.'

PC Eric Dobbin was waiting for them in the street outside the terraced house where Vera Bates had lived. He was a very tall, earnest-looking thin young man in his early twenties and he saluted Coburg and Lampson as they approached.

'You're very prompt, Constable,' Coburg complimented him.

'I was at the station when you called, sir.' He gestured at the house. 'When I called before I told the landlady that I might have to return, so she lent me a key.' He unlocked the front door and they entered the house.

'There are three floors with two bedsitters each on the ground and top floors,' Dobbin explained. 'The other room is on the first floor, next to the toilet and bathroom. That was Vera Bates's room.' He gestured at the foot of the stairs. 'This is where she was found.'

'And Harry Pickford was here when you arrived?'

'He was, sir.' PC Dobbin took his notebook from the

breast pocket of his uniform and opened it. 'I took down his statement. He said he'd come to see his fiancée, Vera Bates, and that he let himself in with a key that Vera had given him.' Dobbin looked at Coburg and Lampson. 'The landlady, a Mrs North, said that she'd never authorised a key for the use of Mr Pickford and that if Miss Bates had given him one, or let him have one copied, it had been done without her permission. She asked me to get the key back from him, and I promised I would. I was on my way to see him when you telephoned Sergeant Pelworth.'

'That's all right, Constable. We'll be talking to Mr Pickford ourselves and we'll get the key off him and leave it for you at Tottenham Court Road station.'

'Thank you, sir. Mr Pickford said he found Miss Bates lying at the foot of the stairs. At first he thought she was unconscious, but then he realised she was dead. There's a telephone box not far from Goodge Street station and he called an ambulance from there. The ambulance crew contacted the station. I was at the station and was despatched here.'

'How did Mr Pickford seem? Upset?'

'He seemed shaken, but I'm not sure how upset he was. In fact, after he left and the body had been taken away, I went up to Miss Bates's room to see if there was any indication of what might have happened. Although she didn't smell of alcohol, I thought I'd check, because some alcohol doesn't have a strong smell. When I got in there I was fairly sure someone had been in there rummaging around in the chest of drawers and night table, because things inside both were a bit disorderly, whereas the room itself was neat and tidy, the bed made, and so on.'

'We'll go up and have a look,' said Coburg.

PC Dobbin held out a key ring containing two keys to the chief inspector. 'It's the smaller key, sir. The other opens the street door.'

'You come with us,' said Coburg. 'Lead the way.'

As they mounted the stairs, Coburg asked: 'Where did Harry Pickford go when he left, do you know?'

'To the Savoy hotel, sir. He works in the kitchens there and he said he had to get to work. He was the one who said she must have fallen down the stairs.'

They entered the room. As PC Dobbin had said, the room was neat and tidy, but when they opened the chest of drawers and the night table they saw what he meant: someone had been searching for something. But had they found it, whatever it was? Coburg wondered.

'Guv,' said Lampson, pointing towards the bed. He got down on his hands and knees, reached out, using a handkerchief to guard against his fingerprints contaminating the object, and carefully lifted out a wooden-handled knife with a serrated blade with what looked like dried blood on it.

'I didn't see that,' said Dobbin. 'But I didn't do a proper search in case I interfered with any evidence.'

Lampson held out the knife to Coburg.

'It's one of the Savoy's,' confirmed Coburg. 'Right, Constable. Tell the landlady that we'll be sealing the room so that we can examine it properly. In the meantime, I think our next step is to talk to Mr Pickford.'

As Coburg and Lampson made for the car, Lampson

asked: 'What d'you reckon to the knife, guv? A bit too obvious?'

'My thoughts exactly,' agreed Coburg. 'If Vera used it to kill someone she'd have hardly left it in her room, certainly not with blood on the blade.'

'So, someone dumped it there to frame her.'

Coburg nodded.

'It doesn't make sense for it to be Harry Pickford,' continued Lampson. 'If he was the one who killed her, he surely wouldn't have phoned the ambulance. He'd have known they might bring in the law.'

'Unless he was counting on people believing that she really had fallen down the stairs. I think our next call is at the undertakers to take a look at the body.'

CHAPTER THIRTY-THREE

Herbert Willis, the senior undertaker, stood with Coburg and Lampson beside the table in his back room on which the body of Vera Bates had been laid out.

'We got your message, Chief Inspector, so we haven't done anything yet except bring her in and lay her out.'

Vera Bates was indeed a small, thin frail-looking woman in her late twenties, just as Dolly Wharton had described her. Her skin was pale and Coburg expected it had always been pale, even before she died.

'Can we examine the back of her head?' asked Coburg.

'The injury,' nodded Willis. 'Yes, we noticed that when we brought her in.'

He half-lifted Vera's body so they could see the back of her head, where dried blood clotted her hair. Gently, Coburg pulled the strands of hair apart to reveal the injury beneath. It was a deep wound, about eight inches long.

'Thank you,' said Coburg as Willis let Vera's head down again. 'I'd like the body sent to Dr Welbourne at University College Hospital in the pathology department.'

'I'll arrange that,' Willis nodded.

'Would you mind telephoning UCH and letting them know the body is on its way for Dr Welbourne. Quote my name as reference.'

'Of course,' said Willis. He looked down at Vera. 'Do you think her death is suspicious?'

'It may be,' answered Coburg. 'We'll see what Dr Welbourne has to say. Before we go, do you have an ink pad?'

'Yes, in the office.'

'Would you bring it through, please.'

As Willis headed for this office, Lampson asked: 'Fingerprints?'

'Worth checking them against the handle of the knife,' said Coburg. 'But I'm pretty sure we'll find Vera's prints on it. Whoever killed her will have made sure of it.'

Lampson nodded. 'She never got that bang on the head from falling down the stairs. Not unless she cartwheeled down. Next move, guv?'

'The Savoy, to pick up Harry Pickford and find out what he's got to say for himself.'

Harry Pickford was at work in the kitchen when Coburg and Lampson returned to the Savoy and told him they'd like to talk to him.

'Is this urgent?' Pickford asked. 'Only Chef gets upset when people disappear.'

'It's about the death of your fiancée, Vera Bates,' said Coburg. 'We understand you found her body.'

'Yes,' said Pickford. He gave an unhappy sigh. 'Poor Vera. It was terrible finding her like that.'

'But you still came in to work.'

'It's what she would have wanted,' said Pickford. 'Vera had a strong sense of duty.' He looked towards the kitchen, then gestured to a side room. 'We can talk in there,' he said.

'Actually, we'd prefer it if we talked at Scotland Yard.'

Pickford stared at them. 'Scotland Yard? Why?'

'Because there are some disturbing indications that her death may not have been an accident.'

'What else could it have been?' demanded Pickford.

'That's what we're hoping you'll be able to help us discover,' said Coburg.

Pickford shook his head.

'I can't do it now,' he said. 'I can't upset Chef. How about tomorrow?'

'Leave Chef to us,' said Coburg. 'I'll explain to him that it's on police orders.'

'That'll only make him worry more,' said Pickford.

'Mr Pickford, your fiancée has died in what appear to be suspicious circumstances. Surely, if someone has harmed her, you want that person brought to justice.'

'Well, yeh, obviously, but . . .'

'In that case, you wait in the car with Sergeant Lampson while I go and talk to the chef.'

With that, Coburg headed into the kitchen, while Lampson took the unhappy Pickford by the elbow and steered him to the waiting car.

On their arrival at Scotland Yard, Coburg instructed Lampson to take Pickford to one of the basement interview rooms. 'I'll join you shortly, once I've called at the lab.'

Coburg took the knife to the forensic lab, along with the sheet of paper with Vera's fingerprints on it.

'I'd like you to check this knife for fingerprints. See if they match these, and if there are any others on it. If so, run them through records and see if any names come up. Also, I'd like to know what group the dried blood on the knife is.'

Once he'd got a promise from them that they'd look into it straight away, Coburg then made for the interview rooms. Lampson and Pickford were in Interview Room 2, along with a uniformed constable who stood behind Pickford who sat facing Lampson across the wooden table. Coburg took the empty chair next to Lampson and opened the questioning with: 'Let's start with how you discovered the body of your fiancée.'

'I went to the house to see her,' said Pickford. 'I let myself in. Vera let me have a copy of her key. When I saw her lying at the foot of the stairs I thought at first she was just knocked out, but when she didn't stir I knew it was something worse.'

'What did you do?'

'I called an ambulance. There's a phone box just round the corner from the house. I waited till the ambulance arrived, and they said she was dead. One of the ambulance men went to the phone box and called the police. I talked to the constable who came, then left.'

'Why?'

'I knew there was nothing I could do. She was dead, and I needed to get to work.'

'Your fiancée has just died and you went to work?' asked Coburg.

'What else was I supposed to do? If I don't work, I don't get paid.'

'Did you kill her?'

Pickford stared at Coburg, his mouth open in shock. 'Me? No, of course not! Why would I want to kill her?'

'We understand things hadn't been right between the two of you lately. After you had sex with Daisy Scott.'

'It was only once, and she got me at a bad time. I was vulnerable.'

'Vera ended your engagement?'

'No! All right, she did at first, but when I explained what had happened, how it had come about, how really sorry I was and it would never happen again . . .'

'Tell me about the bad time and you being vulnerable.'

'What do you mean?' asked Pickford warily.

'You said Daisy Scott got you at a bad time.'

'Yes, well, I heard that my sister is seriously ill.'

'What with?'

'Cancer.'

'Not your brother?'

Pickford looked at him, flustered. 'I don't get you.'

'We'd heard that you were upset because your brother in Newcastle had died.' As Pickford opened his mouth to respond, Coburg added: 'And, before you say anything, we can easily check if you actually had a brother in Newcastle. Or a sister, come to that. And, if she has cancer.'

Pickford's mouth shut and he sat looking at Coburg uncertainly.

'Just to clarify, whatever you tell us we'll check,' said Coburg. 'So the truth will be best.'

Pickford scowled. 'Yeh, all right. As far as I know both my brother and sister are all right.'

'So you lied about why you had sex with Daisy Scott to keep Vera sweet.'

'Well, wouldn't you?' demanded Pickford. 'It wasn't my fault, Daisy came on to me big time, throwing herself at me.'

'And you took the opportunity.'

'Yeh. But then that bitch Ella Kemble told Vera.'

'Why did she do that?'

'Who knows? Because she's a bitch.'

'So you came up with the story that Daisy took advantage of you feeling vulnerable because your brother had died.'

'She did take advantage of me!' burst out Pickford. 'It was Daisy who did the chasing, not me! And I had to protect myself.'

'From whom?'

'From Vera.'

Coburg looked at him, puzzled. 'Vera?'

'She may look all meek and mild and frail, but believe me she's got a temper on her. When she heard from Ella about me and Daisy she went berserk. Punched me in the face. Scratched me. Kicked me. If she'd had a weapon she would have been the one doing the killing. Of me!'

Coburg and Lampson exchanged looks at this new aspect of Vera Bates.

'Were Vera and Ella Kemble close?'

Pickford shook his head. 'They didn't used to be before. Then suddenly Vera's talking about Ella like she's her best friend. "She's the only one who's been properly honest with me," she said. That was because she'd told Vera about me and Daisy.'

'Did Vera and Ella see much of one another?'

'I suppose they must have. Vera was like that, if she thought you were her friend she'd cling to you like a limpet. That's how she was with me, except for the time she went for me. That's why I had that stupid thing with Daisy, because Vera was suffocating me.'

'But then she dumped you. Broke off the engagement.'

'Only for a bit. Then she said she wanted us to get back together.'

'After you apologised and said it would never happen again.'

'Yeh, well, I felt sorry for Vera.'

'You weren't worried she might beat you up again? Maybe kill you next time.'

'I promised her there wouldn't be a next time. I meant it.'

'Because you'd miss her money.'

Pickford looked at Coburg suspiciously. 'Who's been telling tales?' he demanded. 'That's all lies.'

'You're a gambler,' said Coburg. 'Worse, you're a gambler who loses, so you're always in need of money. Was that what you were looking for in Vera's room?'

'Who said I was in Vera's room?' demanded Pickford angrily.

'You were seen coming out of it. After you found Vera's body you went up to her room and had a rummage looking for money.' As Pickford stared at him, worried, Coburg added calmly: 'Or was it you who hit her on the back of the head before you threw her down the stairs?'

'No, never!' exclaimed Pickford. 'I told you already, I didn't kill her. On my life, I swear! I found her when I went in. Yes, I admit, I went up to her room and had a search. She'd promised me she was going to give me some money, that's why I went round there.'

'How much did you take?'

'She had ten quid in an envelope with my name on it in her drawer. A fiver and five oncers.' He reached into his inside pocket and drew out a crumpled envelope which he passed to Coburg. On it was scrawled in pencil 'Harry'.

'Where's the money?'

'I paid it to someone I owed,' said Pickford.

'Someone at the Savoy?'

'No, but this bloke knows I work there, so he said he was coming to collect it.'

'His name?' asked Coburg.

'I can't tell you that!' said Pickford, horrified.

'I would advise you to, otherwise it won't help your defence if we charge you with murder.'

Pickford leapt to his feet in alarm.

'Murder? I never murdered her!' he blustered. 'I never touched her!'

Coburg nodded at the constable, who pushed Pickford back down onto his chair.

'The name of the man you paid the money to,' repeated

Coburg. He took out a pencil and passed it to Pickford, along with a sheet of paper.

Reluctantly, Pickford wrote a name on it and passed it back to Coburg.

'Was it you who left the knife under Vera's bed?' asked Coburg, taking the paper.

Pickford looked at him, bewildered. 'What knife?'

Coburg looked at the constable.

'Take Mr Pickford to the custody block and have him remanded,' he said.

'What?' burst out Pickford. 'You can't do this!'

'You'll stay here while we check on the things you've told us,' Coburg told him. 'And if there's anything else you want to add, I'd advise you to do it, because if we find other things you've lied about, it'll be much worse for you.'

'What do you think?' asked Lampson. 'Did he do it?'

'It's possible,' said Coburg. 'If he killed Daisy out of revenge for her telling Ella, who in turn told Vera, and if Vera found out about it, he might kill her to stop her talking. But why kill Daisy and not Ella? And Pickford wasn't at the Savoy the night the Earl was killed, and I'm still sure they're connected.'

'That was interesting, what he said about Vera and her temper.'

'Yes, it was,' said Coburg thoughtfully.

'So what'll we do?' asked Lampson. 'Let him go?'

'We'll let him sweat for a bit. You never know, with the threat of a murder charge hanging over him he might suddenly start remembering things that might point us in

the right direction.' His phone rang and he picked it up.
'DCI Coburg.'

'Chief Inspector, it's Charles Tillesley at the Savoy.'

'Yes, Mr Tillesley.'

'I'm telephoning because Stella Wainwright, one of the
maids . . .'

'Yes, I remember her,' said Coburg.

'She says she's seen that young man again. The one she
mentioned to you who she thought was waiting for Ella
Kemble.'

'When?'

'Yesterday afternoon. She said he was meeting a man
who works in the kitchens.'

'Is she there at the moment?'

'Yes.'

'Tell her to stay there. I'm on my way.'

Coburg hung up.

'We may have a lead on the young man who might have
been waiting for Ella Kemble just before she disappeared,'
he told Lampson. 'The maid who saw him has told Tillesley
she saw him again, only this time he was meeting a man
who works in the kitchens.'

'We said there might be two of them involved,' said
Lampson as he got up and took his coat from the hook.
'One to hold her, one to kill her. Maybe we've finally struck
lucky.'

CHAPTER THIRTY-FOUR

Coburg and Lampson found Stella Wainwright was in the sluice at the Savoy, sorting bed linen into whites and coloured materials.

'Thank you so much for passing this information on to Mr Tillesley, Stella,' said Coburg. 'If more people were as aware of their duties to society as you, our job would be a whole lot easier.'

She smiled and blushed slightly. 'I was just doing what I thought was right,' she said, flattered.

'This young man you saw, you're sure it's the same one you saw waiting for Ella?'

'Oh yes,' she said. 'After what happened, this time I paid him closer attention to make sure it was the same man, and to see what he got up to. He was waiting outside, just like the day when Ella disappeared. In the same place, near by where the taxis arrive and put down. Only this time one of the cooks from the kitchen, Marcel his name is, I don't know his second name, came out and went up to him. It looked to me like the young man was waiting for Marcel, because he came towards him when Marcel appeared.'

'And what happened?'

'They said a few words to one another, then they walked off together.'

'How did they seem? Friendly? Worried? Angry?'

'Just ordinary,' she said. 'They didn't shake hands or anything. They just met up, said a few words, then walked off together.'

'In which direction?'

'Down towards the Embankment.'

'And then?'

'I don't know, I had to go and catch my bus.'

Coburg nodded and smiled appreciatively.

'Thank you, Stella. You've been enormously helpful.'

Their next call was to the kitchens, where Alphonse the chef demanded impatiently: 'Have you brought Pickford back?'

'I'm afraid we're keeping him because we still have some more questions to ask. Right now, we'd like to talk to another of your staff, a man called Marcel.'

'Marcel!' repeated the chef, angry. 'You come in here and disturb my staff, take them away . . .'

'We hope we won't have to take Marcel away,' Coburg told him.

'This interference is an outrage,' snapped Alphonse. 'How can I be expected to run a proper kitchen worthy of the name of the Savoy hotel with all these interruptions and comings and goings?'

'This is a murder investigation,' Coburg reminded him, politely but firmly. 'Two members of the hotel's staff have died recently in suspicious circumstances, as has a guest. Your job is to provide food – top quality food, I agree, having enjoyed it myself – and my job is to conduct an equally top-quality investigation into these deaths. That is what Mr D'Oyly Carte has told me he wants. If you like I'll arrange for him to come here and tell you so himself, so you'll know that I'm not doing these things just to be difficult.'

Alphonse glared at Coburg, tight-lipped, then spat out 'Take Marcel. Take all of them!' and spun on his heel and walked off.

'Just Marcel will do for the moment,' Coburg called pleasantly after him.

Alphonse strode to a short dark-haired moustached man wearing kitchen whites who was cutting meat into slices, muttered something to him, then gestured towards where Coburg and Lampson were standing. The man, obviously Marcel, looked towards the two policemen with a worried expression on his face. He wiped the knife he was holding, then put it into the wooden knife block, dried his hands on a towel, then walked warily towards Coburg and Lampson.

Coburg and Lampson both produced their warrant cards and showed them to him.

'Detective Chief Inspector Coburg and Detective Sergeant Lampson from Scotland Yard. Your name is Marcel?'

The man nodded.

'Your second name?'

'Leclerc.'

'Are you the only person called Marcel working in the kitchen?'

Marcel nodded, still wary.

'We need to ask you some questions.'

'What about?'

'If you come with us you'll find out,' said Coburg with what he hoped was a reassuring smile. The man was obviously very nervous and Coburg didn't want him suddenly making a run for it. They took Marcel to the small room where they'd quizzed the maids and found it empty.

'This'll do,' said Coburg.

He gestured for Marcel to sit at the small table and he took the chair opposite, while Lampson remained standing by the door.

'Yesterday, when you left work, you met a young man,' said Coburg.

Marcel looked at him warily, then shook his head. 'No,' he said.

'You were seen,' said Coburg. 'You came out of the hotel and walked towards this young man, who in turn walked to meet you. You talked briefly, then you went off together.'

'Whoever says this is lying,' said Marcel, but Coburg and Lampson noticed that even as he said the words he looked uneasy.

'In that case, I am taking you in for questioning at Scotland Yard,' said Coburg.

'No!' said Marcel, and leapt to his feet in sudden panic.

'Sergeant,' ordered Coburg, and Lampson moved

behind Marcel and took hold of one of his arms and forced him back down onto the chair. Marcel began shaking, his whole body vibrating, and his face crumpled and suddenly he began to cry, tears welling up in his eyes and running down his cheeks. Coburg caught the words 'We do nothing wrong' in between his sobs. He gestured for Coburg to release Marcel, but stood just behind the man, ready to move in if necessary.

'Tell me about the young man,' said Coburg.

'He my friend,' said Marcel.

'What's his name?'

'John.'

'His second name?'

'I don't know,' said Marcel, and he sniffled as he wiped his face with his hand.

'Tell us about Ella Kemble,' said Coburg.

Marcel looked at him, baffled. 'Who?'

'She's one of the maids here at the Savoy,' said Coburg.

Marcel shook his head. 'I don't know her.'

Coburg looked at him, weighing up Marcel's answer. Then he said: 'We need to talk to John. Where does he live?'

Marcel shook his head.

'I don't know.'

'Where does he work?'

Marcel shrugged and shook his head and said once more: 'I don't know.'

'When will you be seeing him again?' asked Coburg. 'Today, after work?'

Marcel hesitated, then hung his head down and mumbled: 'Maybe.'

Coburg gestured for Lampson to join him in the corridor outside the room, leaving Marcel momentarily alone.

'So, a couple of gay boys,' said Lampson.

'That's what it would appear to be,' nodded Coburg. 'But we need to check. Keep an eye on him while I arrange for a constable to come in and watch over him while we find this John and get confirmation.'

'How are we going to do that?'

'I'll have a word with Stella Wainwright.'

Coburg sought out Stella, who agreed to meet him in main reception in three quarters of an hour's time, at a quarter to five. He then phoned the nearest police station and arranged for a constable to come in and watch over Marcel. Once the constable had arrived and been installed outside the small room, Lampson asked: 'So, what's next for us?'

'We do what all coppers do, Sergeant. We wait.'

William Lancaster sat in his room trying to keep his attention on the book he was trying to read, Karl Marx's Das Kapital, but his attention kept wandering. His mind was filled with swirling images: Daisy Scott, Jenny Huxton, the night at the Savoy in their air raid shelter, the ruined streets all around. He put the book aside and ruefully reflected he'd have done better to try and lose himself in an Agatha Christie. Suddenly he heard a call from downstairs from his landlady.

'William! There's someone to see you!'

'Who is it?' he called back, thinking it's bound to be the police again trying to fit him up for murders at the Savoy.

As far as he knew no one had yet been arrested and there'd be pressure on them to charge someone, anyone.

'It's a lady!' called his landlady. 'With a big posh car!'

William frowned, puzzled. He didn't know any lady with a big posh car. At least, not in Stepney.

He went downstairs and was stunned to see his mother standing on the doorstep. Behind her, parked at the kerb, was the family's black Rolls Royce, with the chauffeur, James, in the driving seat.

'Mother!' exclaimed William. 'What are you doing here?'

'I've come to see you,' said Lady Lancaster. 'May I come in so we can talk?'

'You can use the living room if you'd like,' offered Mrs Mears.

'Thank you,' said Lady Lancaster, and she swept in, following Mrs Mears who led her to the living room, a neat, sparkling clean room smelling of polish, reserved for Christmas, birthdays and special guests. Her lodgers were not encouraged to use it.

Lady Lancaster took one of the high-backed armchairs whose fabric was embroidered with flowers, while William perched himself uneasily on a small wooden stool.

'Would you like some tea?' asked Mrs Mears.

'No. Thank you,' said Lady Lancaster politely.

'It won't take me long to put the kettle on,' said Mrs Mears.

'No, I just wish to talk to my son,' said Lady Lancaster. 'Thank you.'

It seemed to William that Mrs Mears almost gave a

curtsey before backing out of the living room. William also noted that although she pulled the door of the living room to, she didn't shut it completely, and William guessed she was outside listening. This kind of visit was worthy of precious gossip locally.

'I came because I'm leaving London tomorrow,' said Lady Lancaster. 'That's why I have the car. I sent for James to bring it to London to take me home.' She gave a small pause, then said: 'I'd like you to come with me.'

William stared at her, bewildered. 'Why?'

'For your safety. It'll be safer in Berkshire with all this bombing happening in London. With your father gone there's no reason for you to stay away.'

'Yes, there is,' said William. 'Jenny's here.'

Lady Lancaster hesitated, then she said softly: 'You can bring her with you.'

William stared at her.

'Do you mean that?'

'She obviously means a great deal to you, and if it will result in you coming home, then bring her with you.'

'I'll need to talk to her,' said William.

'Surely, if she loves you as much as you think, she won't hesitate.'

'There's her father to think about. She's all he has left.'

'Then, for God's sake, bring him as well. Whatever it takes to get you home.'

CHAPTER THIRTY-FIVE

Coburg and Lampson stood with Stella Wainwright just inside the entrance to the Savoy, looking out at where the taxis arrived.

'There he is,' she said. 'That's him.'

A thin young man had appeared and stationed himself by one of the pillars beside the taxi rank. He was doing his best to look inconspicuous, but Coburg noticed that he kept his eyes on the Savoy's doors.

'Thank you, Stella,' said Coburg. 'Come on, Sergeant. Act normal, we're just leaving, minding our own business.'

'Got you, guv,' nodded Lampson.

They left the hotel and walked towards the place where the taxis arrived. The young man ignored them; his attention was on the hotel entrance. Suddenly, at a nod from Coburg, Lampson and Coburg changed direction and moved in on either side of the young man.

'Good evening, John,' said Coburg. He produced his warrant card and showed it to the young man. 'DCI Coburg from Scotland Yard.'

The effect was immediate. The young man stared at them, then turned and began to run off like a frightened deer, but Lampson was too quick for him and grabbed him by the arm, gripping it firmly. Coburg took John's other arm and they made for the Savoy, walking the young man between them.

'Where are you taking me?' asked the young man, his voice high with panic.

'Initially, to the Savoy,' said Coburg. 'There, we'll ask you some questions. If your answers are satisfactory, that'll be the end of it and we'll let you see Marcel.'

At the mention of Marcel's name, John stopped and looked at them, now even more scared. Coburg jerked him forward and he and Lampson continued walking him towards the Savoy.

'This is not about what you and Marcel get up to,' said Coburg. 'It's about a murder.'

'I haven't murdered anyone!' squeaked the young man.

By now they'd reached the doors of the hotel. Coburg and Lampson, still holding on to the young man's arms to make sure he didn't suddenly make a run for it, walked him down the stairs to the basement and the room they'd seconded for questioning the staff. They sat John down at the table, then Lampson moved to stand a tall and imposing figure on guard at the closed door as Coburg took his seat opposite the young man. Coburg produced his notebook.

'Name?' he asked.

'John.'

'We already know that. Surname?'

John hesitated, then asked nervously: 'Will my parents have to find out?'

'That depends,' said Coburg. 'Name?'

'Preston.'

'Address?'

The young man hesitated, then gave an address in Camden Town.

'Yesterday about this time you were waiting outside the Savoy for someone. Who?'

John frowned, puzzled.

'But that's what all this is about, isn't it?'

'It is, but I need to hear you say it, otherwise I could be putting words in your mouth. Who were you waiting for?'

'Marcel.'

'And the day before?'

The young man nodded. 'Yes.'

'Marcel again?'

'Yes.'

'And the day before that, at about the same time?'

Again, he nodded.

'So, you were waiting for Marcel again.'

'Yes.'

'What about Ella Kemble?'

The young man frowned, puzzled, and asked: 'Who?'

'She worked here at the Savoy as one of the maids.'

John shook his head. 'I've never heard of her.'

'Or met her?'

'I've never met anyone who works here apart from Marcel.'

'When did you first meet Marcel?'

'It was about five days ago. I was in Charing Cross Road, where the bookshops are.'

'Who picked who up?'

The young man looked uncomfortable. 'It wasn't like that.'

'Who spoke to who first?'

'Marcel. He asked me if I had a light. I said I didn't smoke.'

'Why not? Everyone else seems to?'

John patted his chest. 'It's my lungs. I suffer with them. I've had bronchitis and pneumonia and pleurisy. My mum says I have to keep my chest warm and wear a scarf over my mouth when I go out to stop the damp air getting in.'

'And she's the one who stops you smoking?'

'Yes. She's a good mother. She watches over me.'

'What about your father?'

Suddenly John's wariness returned. 'What about him?' he asked.

'You asked me if your parents would have to know. Your mother sounds very caring, so I'm guessing it's your father you don't want to find out about you and Marcel. Does he know you're homosexual?'

'I'm not!'

'But you go with Marcel.'

'That doesn't make me homosexual,' said John defensively.

'Have you had girlfriends?'

'That's got nothing to do with it,' snapped John angrily.

'No, I guess it hasn't,' conceded Coburg. 'On Wednesday

night when you were waiting for Marcel, a young woman came out of the Savoy. She was carrying a large bag. Did you notice her?'

'No. Lots of people came out at that time. A lot of them were women. I didn't look carefully at them. I was watching out for Marcel.'

Coburg nodded thoughtfully and made a note on his pad.

'Very well,' he said. 'You can go. But I might need to see you again.'

After John had left, Lampson gave a sigh. 'So, nothing to do with waiting for Ella, just a couple of benders sneaking off to the Embankment for a hand job.'

With both Marcel and John dismissed from further investigation, Coburg told Lampson to go home, telling him he'd see him on Monday. 'Have a family day with Terry tomorrow, keep him on the straight and narrow.'

Coburg then headed back to the Yard where he found a report from the laboratory informing him that the fingerprints on the knife belonged to Vera Bates, and that there were no other fingerprints, confirming his suspicion that the knife had been wiped and Vera's fingers pressed against the handle, the knife then being left for the police to find, implicating Vera in the murders. The lab also told him that the blood type was O, which was the same blood type for Vera, and also for over half the population.

There was also a message for him from Dr Welbourne. Vera had been killed by the blow to the back of her head, which had been done by a heavy metal object, possibly a length of lead piping. Dr Welbourne also informed Coburg that Vera had been left-handed.

Coburg picked up the phone and asked the switchboard to connect him to the flat. When Rosa answered, he said: 'Just to let you know I'm on my way home. Is everything all right there?'

'Fortunately,' said Rosa. 'No word from Magnus.'

'Let's hope that means everything's fine,' said Coburg.

'You sound tired,' she said.

'I am,' admitted Coburg. 'But at least I have a day off tomorrow, so we can put murder and mayhem on the back-burner for a day and I can bathe in being one of your faithful audience when you appear at the Savoy tomorrow afternoon.'

'I think you'll have to share a table with Magnus,' said Rosa. 'Mr Tillesley tells me that every table is booked and they're turning people away.'

'Of course they are, my love. People recognise talent.'

'Or they're just curious to see how I do with a plaster cast on one arm. What do you fancy for food tonight?'

'Let's go out,' said Coburg. 'I fancy Italian.'

'Are there any Italian restaurants open any more?' asked Rosa. 'I thought they'd all been interned.'

'There's one I know. It's being run by a couple of Australians while their Italian relatives are inside. They do a superb lasagne.'

'Excellent idea,' said Rosa. 'Hurry home.'

CHAPTER THIRTY-SIX

Sunday 22nd September

In the Winships' suite at the Savoy, Julia Winship hung up the phone and looked at her husband, an expression of horror on her face.

'That was Dotty with the most dreadful news. Appalling!'

Winship looked at his wife, curious, wondering what had caused this upheaval. Usually, it was just some salacious tittle-tattle about one of her women friends, and he weighed up which one this was about, which was why he was as shocked as she was when she told him: 'They're going to kill Oswald.'

He stared at her, his face showing his bewilderment.

'Oswald? Oswald Mosley?'

'Of course Oswald Mosley!' she burst out angrily. 'How many Oswalds do we know?' She began to pace the room, agitatedly. 'Dotty went to see them this morning at Holloway and they told her.'

'But . . . why? Oswald's always been very careful in what he says.'

'Because someone hasn't been, and I'm worried it may be one of our group.'

'I don't understand,' said Winship, still bewildered.

'That dreadful man, Brendan Bracken, Churchill's puppet, called on Oswald at Holloway. He told him they knew of the plan to free Oswald so he could make a peace deal with Hitler, and they also knew that part of the plan was to get rid of Churchill. Bracken threatened Oswald. He told him that if anything happened to Churchill, then he – Oswald – would be dead within minutes of that happening.'

'It's that Dotty Ravenswood and her big mouth!' raged Winship. 'I said she should be reined in! Look at the way she went off at Rosa Coburg about Churchill and Oswald, and that was the first time she'd met her! My God! The woman's a liability.'

'But we've never shared the rest of the plan with her,' said Julia. 'We've only told her we supported the idea of Oswald being released to make a good deal to end the war. We've never said anything to her about killing Churchill. We've never said anything about that to any of them! Only to some of Oswald's inner circle, and I can't believe any of them would blab to the other side.'

Winship's face took on a worried expression, then he said awkwardly: 'Actually, I may have hinted at something like that needing to be done to someone.'

'Who?' demanded Julia.

'Magnus. He and I were talking, you know old soldier

to old soldier, and I was aware he knew that something had to be done about Churchill.'

'How? What did you say? What did he say?'

'Something along the lines of how would we handle Churchill in the event of Oswald negotiating a deal. He said that Churchill wouldn't stand aside for Mosley. He hadn't stood aside for Halifax. There was no way he was going to stand down as PM, and he certainly wouldn't let Mosley undertake any negotiations with Hitler or any of his people.'

'So, you told him that Churchill would have to be eliminated,' said Julia, outraged.

'Not in so many words,' defended Winship. 'I just said that Churchill was a problem that would need to be . . . dealt with. Removed to clear the way.'

Suddenly, Julia lashed out at him, slapping him hard around the face.

'You fool!'

'It was just old soldier talk,' appealed Winship. 'I thought he might know of someone who could help us in that way. A former comrade in arms.'

'I knew we should never have brought Magnus in,' hissed Julia. 'People said he was too close to Churchill. Old pals.'

'Yes, but the things he said about the war, about the country needing peace . . .' protested Winship.

'He was getting information out of you,' said Julia. 'I see it now!'

'It may not have been him,' said Winship in a desperate attempt to turn away his wife's anger. 'It could have been his new sister-in-law, Rosa Coburg.'

Julia shook her head.

'She only came to one meeting, and at that she was dominated by Dotty. No, it's Magnus. He was planted on us.'

'Who by? MI5?'

Julia shook her head. 'No, I've been cultivating a couple of people in MI5. If there'd been anything there, I'd have known about it. No, Magnus is acting on his own.'

'Who for?'

'Obviously Bracken, because it was Bracken who went to see Oswald. And Bracken does nothing without Churchill's say-so.'

'So, Magnus is working for Churchill.'

She nodded. 'Like I said, he and Churchill have always been close.'

'So, what do we do? Drop the plan?'

She stared at him, outraged by what he'd just said.

'Absolutely not! This country's future depends on the plan succeeding. The first thing we need to do is get Mosley out of jail so we can put him somewhere safe and out of harm's way.' Then she became thoughtful. 'No,' she corrected herself. 'The first thing to do is get rid of Magnus and break the link with Churchill. Without Magnus reporting back, I'm fairly sure we can create a smokescreen to obscure the plan. We'll deal with Churchill in good time, but first we need to get rid of Magnus.'

'But who will we get to do that?'

'The only people we can really trust,' said Julia firmly. 'Us. You and I.'

'No,' said Winship. 'Out of the question.'

'You killed people during the last war,' said Julia.

'That was different, that was war,' countered Winship. 'And they were the enemy.'

'Churchill is our enemy,' stated Julia. 'And so is Magnus. And a very dangerous enemy. With what he knows, he could have us sent to the Tower. You know what that means: you and I both sentenced to hang. Is that what you want?'

'Of course not,' said Winship.

'Then we have to get rid of Magnus.'

Winship looked worried. 'We can't,' he said.

'We can,' she insisted firmly. 'We'll do it in a way that keeps suspicion away from us. We'll stab him in the back, in his suite here at the Savoy. Everyone will think it's the same person who killed Lancaster and the maid. A serial killer on the loose.'

'But we can't just go to his room and stab him. He'll defend himself. Fight. Call for help. He isn't a feeble woman, like the maid who got killed, and he won't be fast asleep, like Lancaster. He's an old soldier, for God's sake.'

'It'll be simple. You grab hold of him, pull him to you, holding his arms tight. You're stronger than me. I'll stab him in the back. That's it. All over in seconds.'

'Are you sure you can do it?' asked Winship.

'Absolutely,' she assured him, her tone steely and determined. 'And we need to do it today. I remember he said he's leaving London tomorrow and heading back to Dawlish Hall. Phone him now while I go and get a steak knife from the restaurant. That's what the other two were killed with.'

Julia hurried out of the room. Winship looked at the telephone, feeling sick with apprehension at the thought of what they were going to do. Perhaps Magnus wasn't in his room. Perhaps he'd already left the Savoy and gone back to Dawlish Hall.

He picked up the phone and asked reception to connect him to Magnus's suite. He heard the phone ring, and then Magnus's voice saying: 'Magnus Saxe-Coburg.'

'Magnus, it's Eric Winship. Do you have a moment for myself and Julia to come and see you. Something's come up we need to talk to you about.'

'Certainly,' said Magnus. 'However, I've got to go out. In fact, I was on my way now. I have an important meeting, the last of my wretched boards.'

'On a Sunday?' queried Winship.

'International business doesn't take days off,' said Magnus. 'It won't take long. I'll be back by two o'clock.'

'Two o'clock,' confirmed Winship. 'And just us, old man. We don't want anyone else involved. What we've got to tell you is a bit hush-hush.'

'No problem,' said Magnus. 'I'll see you at two.'

Coburg looked at Rosa as she sat at the table, sorting through some of the sheet music she'd bought the day before.

'When we move into the new flat, the first thing we're doing is getting you a piano,' he said.

Rosa hadn't talked about it since the bomb had destroyed their flat in Hampstead, but he knew that the one thing she missed was her piano, destroyed and

313

disappeared beneath the wreckage along with all the rest of their possessions.

'That would be lovely,' she said. 'I've missed it, even though I'd only be able to play with one good hand. You're sure? A piano takes up room.'

'I'm sure.'

'We wouldn't be able to fit a grand into that flat,' said Rosa. She gave a rueful grin. 'I have to admit I thought about it when I was measuring up. An upright would go in nicely.'

'Then you and I shall go looking at uprights,' said Coburg. 'And we'll get a good one.'

'Good uprights can be expensive, too,' warned Rosa.

'It'll be a wedding present,' said Coburg.

'So, what shall I get you?'

'It'll be a wedding present for both of us,' Coburg clarified. 'Believe me, I get as much pleasure listening as you do playing.' He gestured at her plaster cast. 'Any idea when that could come off?'

'I'm due to see Mr Bailey on Tuesday,' she said. 'Hopefully he'll say it can come off straight away.'

The phone rang and Coburg picked it up. 'Coburg,' he said.

Superintendent Allison's voice could be heard.

'I'm sorry to trouble you on your day off,' he said, 'but I need to talk to you.'

'Yes, sir. What about?'

'I can't talk about it over the telephone. I'll tell you when I see you.'

Coburg frowned. This sounded ominous.

'At Scotland Yard?' he asked.

'If you would,' said Allison. 'Can you be here in an hour?'

'That was my boss,' said Coburg as he replaced the receiver. 'He wants to see me at Scotland Yard.'

'On a Sunday?' She gave a sigh. 'Oh well, I suppose crime never has a day off. What's happened?'

'He wouldn't tell me. Said it was something that he couldn't talk about over the phone.'

'Intriguing.'

Coburg gave her an unhappy frown. 'I'm betting it's one of the men we talked to about the murdered maid at the Savoy. They were a bit upper crust in the social order, and one of them in particular, a Member of Parliament, took exception to being questioned. I bet he's lodged a complaint.'

'About what?'

'About the fact he was having sex with the maid before she died. I think he's worried it might leak to the press, which won't be good for his image, or his marriage. But I could be wrong.' He pulled on his coat. 'I'll see you later. Hopefully I shouldn't be long, but if I'm held up I'll see you at the Savoy this afternoon. Are you all set?

She patted the plaster cast on her arm.

'So long as this doesn't get in the way. I have to keep reminding myself to make sure I don't hit the bass keys with it. And just in case you don't make it this afternoon . . .'

She leant in and kissed him. Coburg held her close and whispered. 'I'll be there.'

'You don't know what the Superintendent wants to see

you about,' she warned him. 'It could be something where he sends you off on some urgent assignment.'

'Not today,' Coburg assured her. 'This afternoon is for you.'

CHAPTER THIRTY-SEVEN

In the Huxtons' kitchen in Stepney, William Lancaster sipped at the mug of tea Tom Huxton had just put down in front of him, and inwardly thought of it as one of the rare benefits of rationing. Jenny had told him that her father liked five spoonfuls of sugar in his tea, but rationing had restricted that to one, and also meant that Mr Huxton had taken to making the tea weaker, for which William was grateful. Jenny and Mr Huxton watched him, waiting. This was a conversation that William hadn't been looking forward to, but one that he knew he had to have.

'My mother came to see me yesterday,' he told them.

'Yeh, we heard,' grunted Huxton. 'A big posh Rolls Royce parked outside Mrs Mears'. The whole street was talking about it.'

'What did she want?' asked Jenny.

'She said she's leaving London and going home to our

317

place in the country.' He took another sip of the tea, then said awkwardly: 'She wants me to go with her. And not just me, you as well. The three of us.'

Huxton didn't say anything, but the sour look on his face was expressive enough to let William know he disapproved.

'Where is it?' asked Jenny. 'Your place in the country?'

'It's just outside a small village called Binfield in Berkshire. Very peaceful. No bombing.'

'And we can all stay there? Me and Dad as well?'

'Yes,' nodded William. 'I would never have agreed to the idea if my father was still alive, but now he's dead there'll be just us there and my mother.'

'And servants?' put in Huxton, his tone aggressive.

'Well, yes,' said William awkwardly. 'It's quite a big place. It needs staff to maintain it. But they're well paid. Mother has always seen to that, despite protests from Father about how much it was costing him.' He gave a sour and scornful laugh. 'If he'd had his way he'd have had serfs working for him for nothing.'

'How big is it?' asked Huxton.

'Well, it's not as big as the manor house, but it's not far off it,' admitted William.

'Grounds?' asked Huxton. 'A lodge at the end of a drive? Stables? Courtyards? Outhouses?'

'Yes,' said William, forcing a nervous smile at the older man's sarcastic tone.

'Turrets?' demanded Huxton.

'One or two,' said William. 'But it's just a family home.'

'It sounds lovely,' said Jenny. 'Is it all countryside around it?'

'For miles,' said William, relieved to hear the warmth in Jenny's voice in contrast to her father's. 'Fields. And there's a large park attached to it. Henry VIII was said to have hunted there.'

'Henry VIII?' said Jenny, impressed. 'Did you hear that, Dad?'

'I did,' said Huxton flatly.

'The main thing is that it's somewhere safe,' said William. 'No bombing. And it'll only have to be for the duration of the war; though if you want to stay on I'm sure my mother will be happy for that. Imagine it. Far from the city, far from the war. There's a kitchen garden there. You've often said you wish you had a garden.'

'William's right, you said that, Dad, even when Mum was alive.' She looked earnestly at her dad. 'What do you think?'

'No,' said Huxton firmly. 'I've spent the whole of my adult life fighting for better rights for ordinary people and resisting the scum who look down on us. Those toffee-nosed gits who've only got what they've got – big lands and such – because they took it from the workers who created their wealth for them. You think I'm going to join that crowd after everything I've said and stood for?' He shook his head. 'Never!'

'It might save your life,' said William. 'And Jenny's.'

'And what would people round here say about me?' demanded Huxton. 'My name would be reviled. "Tom Huxton?" people would say. And they'd spit. "He was a traitor. Talked about the revolution and overthrowing the aristocracy, and now he's living like one, in a big mansion house out in Berkshire." A waster and a parasite, just like the people I've fought against all my life.'

'You wouldn't be a waster,' insisted William. 'Like I say, you can work in the garden if you like, growing food for local people. Local poor people.'

'Like one of these toffs who give out charity,' snorted Huxton.

'And you'd get paid.'

'So I'd be what . . . a servant?'

'No!' said William. 'Look, Mr Huxton, I love Jenny and I want us to be together. And I think she wants that, too.'

'I do,' said Jenny.

'Don't you want her to be safe?'

Huxton fell into an uncomfortable silence, obviously his emotions were in turmoil. Finally, he said: 'You two go.'

'Not without you, Dad,' said Jenny firmly.

'Please, Mr Huxton,' appealed William.

'No,' said Huxton, equally firmly. He turned to Jenny. 'But I'm giving you my blessing. You can go, with William. But after the war I want you to think about coming back. When it's safe.'

Jenny looked unhappy and undecided. 'I don't know, Dad.'

'I do,' said Mr Huxton. 'Like I said, once the war's over and the bombing's stopped, you can come back. I'd like that. It'll be no different to all our kids going away like they did last September to protect them.'

'But lots came home again. Like little Mo from round the corner.'

'Only a few came back. Most are still out there, in the

320

countryside, being safe. And that's where you're going. You and William.' He looked at William and held out his hand. 'What do you say, William? Will you look after my little girl?'

William reached out and took Huxton's hand in his and gripped it firmly. 'I will, sir,' he said. 'I promise.'

'And you'll bring her back afterwards?'

'I will,' said William.

Huxton released William's hand and turned to his daughter.

'Right, my girl. You'd better get upstairs and pack your stuff. You're going to need a few things while you're there, out in the sticks.'

'Thank you, Mr Huxton,' said William, getting to his feet. 'I'll go and pack and let Mrs Mears know what's happening. Then I'll phone Mother at the Savoy and arrange for her to come and pick us up.'

'In that big Rolls Royce?' said Huxton unhappily.

'It's just a car,' said William.

'It's more than just a car,' said Huxton. 'It's a symbol of the rich.'

'We could always get a bus to the Savoy,' said William. He looked at his watch. 'But the timetable's all over the place at the moment. And we'll have heavy cases to carry.'

'I could see if your uncle Charlie could pick you up in his fruit and veg van,' suggested Huxton. 'Although it'll smell a bit because he's been using it to move horse manure to his allotment.'

'No,' said Jenny, her tone suddenly firm. 'We're driving away from here in the Rolls Royce, and that's all about it.'

When Coburg entered Superintendent Allison's office he was aware immediately that something was seriously amiss. The superintendent rose to his feet, a grim and very unhappy expression on his face and gestured for Coburg to sit. Only once Coburg had sat down did he reseat himself.

'You wanted to see me, sir,' said Coburg.

'I did,' said Allison, and the look of serious intent he gave Coburg was one the chief inspector rarely saw from his boss. 'I regret to inform you that an official complaint has been made against you.'

Here it comes, thought Coburg grimly. The Right Honourable Gareth Pearce MP.

'May I enquire who from, sir?' he asked. 'And what it relates to.'

'At the moment I can't tell you the name of the complainant, only details of the allegations.'

'Allegations?' asked Coburg, disturbed at this introduction of the word.

'They concern allegation of improper conduct with – ah – a member of the public.'

Coburg looked at him, bewildered.

'Who?' he blurted out.

'Lady Lancaster,' said Allison.

Coburg stared at him, momentarily uncomprehending.

'I'm sorry, sir. I cannot imagine any way in which I've offended Lady Lancaster and why she should say I have.'

'She hasn't said anything, Coburg. This complaint has not come from her. It's about her. And you. Your relationship with her.'

'I don't have a relationship with her, sir,' protested

Coburg. 'I have spoken to her as part of the investigations into the murders at the Savoy, but no more than I spoke to many other people. What exactly is being alleged?'

'That you are having – or have had – an improper relationship with her. That allegation is based on the following: that after Inspector Lomax arrested William Lancaster as the chief suspect for the murder of his father, his mother, Lady Lancaster, appealed to Inspector Lomax that her son was innocent and asked for him to be released. He refused. Shortly after, you took over the case and Lady Lancaster offered you the use of her late husband's flat when she heard that your own flat had been bombed. She offered it free of charge to you. In return, you released her son.'

'That is an outrageous distortion of the facts, sir. I only authorised the release of William Lancaster when we had established without doubt that he could not have murdered his father.'

'There is also the matter of your staying at the Savoy without charge, after the Savoy were keen to get you to investigate the murder of the Earl of Lancaster.'

'If you recall, sir, when you first instructed me to take the case on, it was because pressure was being applied by the commissioner and other important figures in Government. I did warn you at the time that it was not a good idea, and I opposed being given the case. I did not want or seek the assignment. And, to clarify, I did not stay at the Savoy without charge, sir. I paid for the night myself and my wife stayed there.'

'Are you sure?'

'I am.' Coburg produced his cheque book from his inside

pocket and rifled through the stubs until he came to the one for the Savoy. He handed the cheque book to Allison. 'Here you are, sir.'

The superintendent took it, looked at it, then returned the cheque book to Coburg.

'Did the Savoy actually pay it in?' he asked.

Coburg looked puzzled, then he said: 'I assume so. I haven't checked my bank statement yet. It won't be sent to me for another month.'

'Would you mind checking?' asked Allison, and he gestured at the telephone.

'The banks will be closed on Sunday, sir,' Coburg pointed out.

'I meant the Savoy,' said Allison. 'They'll have a note of whether the account was paid.'

'It was,' said Coburg firmly.

'Then all I need to hear is that confirmation,' said Allison.

Coburg picked up the receiver and asked the switchboard to connect him to the Savoy hotel. When he got through he asked for Main Reception, and a few seconds later the voice of Arnold Hartz, one of the duty receptionists, was heard in his ear.

'Arnold,' said Coburg. 'This is DCI Coburg from Scotland Yard.'

'Yes, Mr Coburg,' said Arnold.

'I just want to check that when my wife and I stayed at the Savoy a few days ago for one night, that the cheque I paid for our stay has gone through your accounts.'

'If you'll hold on one moment, Mr Coburg, I'll check.'

There was pause, followed by the sounds of a drawer opening and the rustle of papers, and then Arnold was on the phone again.

'Yes, your cheque was handed in, but Mr Tillesley told me to mark your stay as gratis, on Mr D'Oyly Carte's instructions. Your cheque is in the hotel safe, waiting to be returned to you.'

Coburg stood, stunned, as the implication of this struck him. Then he said urgently. 'Please will you tell Mr Tillesley that his generosity is appreciated, but I did make clear that I would be paying for our stay. Please would you ensure that cheque is paid in at the earliest opportunity. Tomorrow, as soon as the banks open. I will explain to Mr Tillesley when I see him.'

'Yes, Mr Coburg. Certainly. I'll see to that.'

Coburg hung up and turned to Allison.

'For some reason they kept my cheque. Mr Tillesley, the manager, had apparently been told by Mr D'Oyly Carte that I be given the room gratis. As you have just heard, I've insisted that the cheque I gave them be paid into the bank tomorrow.'

'The problem is, Chief Inspector, that it will appear on the records as only having been paid in after this meeting between us.'

'But you heard yourself, sir. I paid the cheque. Look at the date, it was made out the morning after our stay.'

'But not paid in until after this meeting. I might believe you, Chief Inspector, but you can see how this could look to an independent investigator.'

'Surely, sir, any independent investigator will see that

325

I'm guilty of nothing here. The business of the hotel room at the Savoy was the result of miscommunication on the Savoy's part. Lady Lancaster offering myself and my wife the use of her late husband's flat was politely turned down by me, and had no bearing on whether nor not to release her son from custody. As you'll find if you talk to Lady Lancaster about it.'

Allison looked suddenly uncomfortable.

'If only that were possible, but there is a complication in regard to that. It has been suggested that you and Lady Lancaster were involved in an – ah – rather more than an inappropriate relationship involving releasing her son in exchange for the use of her London flat. It's been suggested that you and she have been . . . intimate.'

Coburg did his best to try to keep his anger under control as he snapped back, between clenched teeth: 'That is a despicable lie. There is absolutely no truth in it. For heaven's sake, sir, I'm just recently married!'

'Being married didn't seem to stop the Earl of Lancaster's inappropriate activities,' murmured the superintendent.

'I am not the Earl of Lancaster,' barked Coburg.

'You don't deny that you met with Lady Lancaster privately in her suite at the Savoy. Just the two of you.'

'At her request,' said Coburg. 'What she wanted to say was not something she wanted known. But I assure you, sir, that absolutely nothing of an intimate nature occurred between us, as I'm sure you will discover if you talk to Lady Lancaster yourself.'

'That is hardly likely, Chief Inspector,' said Allison

primly. 'That is not the sort of thing that one can raise with a lady, especially one of title.'

'How otherwise can I clear myself of this accusation?' demanded Coburg.

CHAPTER THIRTY-EIGHT

Rosa arrived at the Savoy and found Magnus and Charles Tillesley waiting for her in the reception area.

'Miss Weeks,' smiled Tillesley. 'As I thought would be the case, the tea room is full. We even have a list of people who are waiting for cancellations.'

'Which is why I'm going to head for our table,' said Magnus. 'I've left one of the waiters looking after it, making sure no one sneaks in and commandeers it.' He looked past Rosa towards the entrance and asked: 'Is Edgar with you?'

'He was summoned to Scotland Yard by his boss. He'll be joining us here.'

'Everyone's assembled,' said Tillesley, 'so, if you don't mind, I'll escort you to your dressing room.'

'And I'll wander in and take our table,' said Magnus. Then his face brightened. 'And here's Edgar, right on time.'

Rosa turned as Coburg entered.

'You made it!' She smiled.

'I said I would,' said Coburg.

'What did your boss want?' asked Rosa.

Coburg gave a sigh. 'As I thought, one of the guests at the Savoy had made a complaint about me, claiming harassment.'

'Will it lead to trouble?'

Coburg smiled and shook his head. 'No. I explained, and everything's all right. The trouble with some people is their self-importance makes them think the law doesn't apply to them.'

'Anyway, I'm on my way to my dressing room,' said Rosa. 'You and Magnus had better take your table. I'll see you after the show.'

She kissed him, then moved off with Tillesley, while Coburg and Magnus walked into the tea room and took their seats at their table, which was covered with a pristine white tablecloth like all the others.

'So what did your boss really want?' asked Magnus. 'Rosa told me your superintendent had summoned you.'

'Just some procedural stuff,' shrugged Coburg.

'Nothing to worry about, then?'

'Nothing at all,' said Coburg.

A waiter came and they ordered drinks, whiskies for both of them, along with a selection of sandwiches.

'I'm not sure if whisky and sandwiches constitutes Sunday afternoon tea,' commented Coburg.

'It's the Savoy,' said Magnus. 'Sunday tea is whatever you want it to be.'

Charles Tillesley walked into the performance space to

applause from the guests and took his place by the piano.

'Good afternoon. It gives me the greatest pleasure to introduce to you, on her first performance at the Savoy hotel, and one that we hope will be the first of many, that great pianist and vocalist, one of jazz's brightest and most talented performers, Rosa Weeks. You will notice that she has a plaster cast on her left arm, but she assures me that it will not impede her entertaining you. My lords, ladies and gentlemen, please give a warm welcome to . . . Miss Rosa Weeks.'

To a burst of rapturous applause, Rosa appeared from the back, wearing a long pale blue dress beneath a cream bolero jacket, the left sleeve of which almost hid the plaster cast. The applause continued as Rosa took her place at the piano. She smiled at the audience as she tapped at the plaster cast.

'Actually, it's really healed, but I thought I'd keep this thing on and play for the sympathy vote,' she joked.

As the audience laughed, she settled herself down at the piano and ran trills with her right hand on the keys, then two bass notes, and then she was into Hoagy Carmichael's 'Georgia on my Mind', and the plaster cast, the war outside, was forgotten as she strummed and toyed with the piano keys, her voice delivering the song with enough melancholy mixed with desire to bring lumps to throats and tears to the listeners' eyes.

'My God, she's good,' whispered Magnus.

After 'Georgia', Rosa segued into Gershwin's 'Summertime', and then lightened the mood with a slyly sexy version of Cole Porter's 'Let's Do It'.

'I think she remembered I mentioned about hearing her sing those two songs on the wireless,' smiled Magnus.

All too soon Rosa's first session was over, and as she rose from the piano to take her bow, the whole audience rose to its feet, hands clapping together along with cries of 'More! More!'

Charles Tillesley appeared, passing Rosa as she headed for her dressing room.

'Miss Weeks will be back in half an hour, after a well-deserved break,' he told them. 'So, please take the opportunity to relax, order refreshments and enjoy the second half.'

'I have to meet someone,' said Magnus, getting to his feet.

'Who?' asked Coburg.

Magnus hesitated, then whispered: 'I was told it's hush-hush and not to tell anyone, but it's the Winships.'

'What?' exclaimed Coburg.

'Sssh!' hissed Magnus. 'I'm only telling you because I think they're planning to entrap me in some way. Get me to say something that might be interpreted as treasonous so they can use it against me. I don't trust them.'

'I'll come with you,' said Coburg, starting to rise.

'No,' said Magnus, pushing his brother back down. 'You being there would only put them off. I want to see what they want.' He gave a thoughtful frown, then said: 'I thought I might ask Rosa to come and hide in my bathroom and listen.'

'You certainly won't!' snapped Coburg. 'If anything, it should be me.'

'No, she and I are supposed to be a team in this. She'd be furious if I chose you over her. And anyway, I need you to keep an eye on this table and make sure no one snaffles it.'

'You can't ask her!' hissed Coburg. 'She's in the middle of a performance.'

'She's on her break at the moment. It'll only take a minute.'

'No!' said Coburg firmly. 'She's concentrating. Preparing.'

Magnus sighed. 'I suppose you're right.' He looked at his watch. 'I'd better go and see the Winships, find out what they're up to. Keep guard on the table.'

With that, Magnus headed off.

In their room, the Winships were making last-minute preparations for their attack on Magnus.

'It's two o'clock,' said Julia Winship, looking at the clock. She showed her husband the steak knife she'd filched from the restaurant before putting it into her handbag.

'I'm not sure,' said Winship uncertainly.

'I am,' said Julia firmly. 'And I'll be the one with the knife. All you have to do is hold on to him.'

'Say someone comes in?'

'They won't. This is an ideal time. Everyone will be downstairs listening to Rosa Weeks in the tea room.'

She lifted the 'do not disturb' notice hanging from the handle of their door.

'We'll pop this on his door handle when we go in to Magnus's room. That'll stop any maids or casual callers interfering. Come on.'

'Perhaps he won't be there,' said Winship. 'He might be downstairs, listening to Rosa.'

'He'll be there,' said Julia, opening the door. 'He's an old soldier. Reliable and punctual. If he said he'd be there at two o'clock, he will.'

She led the way out of the room and along the corridor, her husband following. They took the stairs down to the floor below where Magnus's suite was located. When they reached Magnus's door, Julia Winship slipped the 'do not disturb' sign on the handle.

'Knock,' she whispered. 'And grab him as soon as we're in. Don't start chatting. We need to do this quickly.'

Winship gulped, then nodded and knocked at the door. The door opened and Magnus looked out. 'Ah, you're here,' he said. 'Good. Only I want to make sure I get back for Rosa Weeks' second session. She's taking her break at the moment.'

The Winships walked into the room.

'Her first session really was superb,' said Magnus, closing the door.

'Eric!' hissed Julia.

Winship hesitated, then suddenly launched himself at Magnus, enveloping him in his arms, pulling the startled Magnus close, face to face, belly to belly.

'What the hell . . . !' demanded Magnus.

'Hold him!' shouted Julia, and she took the knife from her bag, throwing the bag aside as she did so.

She pulled the knife back, ready to plunge it into Magnus's back with full force, but as she swung her arm forward she felt a violent and sickening pain in her knee which caused her to stumble and then fall to the carpet. Bewildered, she looked up, and saw Rosa recovering her balance after having kicked her. Suddenly, Rosa swung her foot again, this time smashing into Julia's head, and Julia slumped into an inert heap.

Eric Winship stared at his fallen wife, then at Rosa, stunned; and Magnus took the opportunity to pull his head back and then deliver a bone-crunching headbutt to Winship's face, breaking his nose and sending blood gushing out. Winship let Magnus go and staggered backward, and as he did Rosa swung her plaster-casted left arm at Winship, catching him on the side of the head, and he too crumpled to the carpeted floor.

'My God!' said Magnus. 'I didn't expect them to do that!'

Coburg looked at his watch. Where was Magnus? It had just gone five past two and Rosa was due to appear again in ten minutes. He was aware of someone appearing beside him and looked up, expecting it to be Magnus, but it was a waiter.

'Excuse me, Mr Coburg, but your brother has asked if you would go up to his suite,' the waiter whispered.

'Now?' queried Coburg.

'He said it was urgent.'

Coburg rose to his feet and said: 'I'll be back shortly. Please don't give this table away to anyone else.'

He hurried up the stairs to Magnus's floor. If Magnus said it was urgent, it would be, Magnus was not given to exaggeration. He knocked at the door and it was opened immediately, and Coburg found himself staring at his wife.

'Rosa?' he exclaimed.

'Magnus will explain,' said Rosa.

Coburg walked into the room, and saw Lord and Lady Winship sitting on the floor, propped against a wall. They had been tied up with the cord from the curtains and gagged by pillowcases tied around their mouths, the pillowcase around Winship's face was stained with blood. Magnus was just finishing tying their ankles with more curtain cord.

'What on earth . . . ?' demanded Coburg.

'They tried to kill me,' said Magnus getting to his feet. 'Stab me in the back. They'd have succeeded if Rosa hadn't been here.'

'But why were you here?' demanded Coburg of Rosa. He turned angrily on his brother. 'You said you wouldn't involve her! I told you . . .'

'Yes, I know, but I changed my mind,' said Magnus. 'And lucky I did.'

'I'd better get back,' said Rosa. 'I'm on in five minutes. Magnus will tell you all about it.'

'You're sure you're all right to appear?' asked Magnus, concerned.

'Of course,' said Rosa. 'I've had interruptions before to deal with. Nothing as weird as this, but some came close.' She headed for the door. 'I'll see you downstairs, Edgar.'

The angry Coburg turned to his brother as the door shut behind Rosa. 'Well?' he demanded.

'I'd arranged for the Winships to call here at two o'clock. I didn't know they were planning to kill me. As I told you, I thought they were just going to try and trap me into saying something they could use against me, make out that I was a traitor in order to protect themselves. I know what you said about not involving Rosa, but we're supposed to be in this together.'

'I told you . . .' grated Coburg, furious.

'I know you did, but as I walked away I thought about it and realised that if they made an allegation against me, it would just be my word against theirs.'

'So you went behind my back . . . !'

'It was a spur-of-the-moment decision!'

'Rubbish!'

'Can we forget about the recriminations. I admit I was wrong, but it was lucky I did what I did. In fact, Rosa said she'd be delighted to help out, and she agreed to hide in the bathroom. She kept the door ajar so she could hear what was going on. Lucky she did, because it meant she was able to peer out and when she saw Winship grab hold of me and Julia go to stab me in the back, she came out of there at a rate of knots and kicked Julia in the knee. Julia tumbled to the floor, and Rosa finished her off with a kick to the head.'

'Rosa might have killed her!' protested Coburg.

'Considering what she was planning to do to me, I can't see anyone would have objected to that,' put in Magnus, 'I certainly wouldn't. But, as you'll see, she was just knocked out for a bit.

'Meanwhile, Winship was still holding me tight with his arms wrapped round me. So I gave him a sharp headbutt, which sent him staggering back. At which dear Rosa bashed him in the head with that plaster cast of hers. Bang. Down he went like a felled ox. Magnificent.'

'You could have both been killed!' exploded Coburg angrily. 'You and Rosa. You should have involved me!'

'I keep telling you, I didn't know they were planning to kill me,' repeated Magnus impatiently. 'Also, I didn't want to lose the table. There are people in reception queuing in case a table comes free.'

'But . . .' Coburg began to protest, then words failed him.

'I called you up here after I remember you saying that you thought the maid who was killed here might have been killed by two people, one holding her and the other stabbing her in the back. That's just what these two were planning. I've phoned Bracken to come and pick them up and take them in, but I wondered if you might want to have a word with them first. You know, about the maid.'

There was a knock at the door, then a voice called out: 'It's me, Your Lordship!'

'Bracken,' said Magnus to Coburg. 'One moment!' he called. He turned back to his brother. 'He's turned up a lot quicker than I expected. I'm sure he'll have a couple of heavies with him.' He frowned, thoughtfully. 'On reflection, it might be better for Bracken and his people to have them first. Soften them up. What do you think?'

'I've got an idea that Bracken will insist on that being the correct procedure,' said Coburg sourly. 'National security having priority over murder.'

'Yes, I think you could be right,' said Magnus. 'I should have held off calling Bracken until you'd talked to them, but I wanted to make sure things were set in motion. Sorry about that.'

337

He made for the door. 'Still, it means you'll be able to get back to being in the audience for Rosa.' He smiled. 'What a kick that woman has! A pity women don't play rugby; she'd be an asset to any team.'

He opened the door and Brendan Bracken, accompanied by four large muscular grim-faced men wearing identical long dark overcoats and bowler hats, entered the room.

'Sorry to keep you waiting, Brendan,' said Magnus. He gestured at the bound Winships, who glared venomously at them. 'A present for you.'

CHAPTER THIRTY-NINE

In Lady Lancaster's Savoy suite, the ringing phone was answered by her maid, Jane.

'Lady Lancaster's suite,' she said.

'Is Lady Lancaster there?' asked a man's voice.

'I'll see. Who's calling?'

'It's her son.'

Jane held out the receiver towards Lady Lancaster as she approached her.

'It's William, Lady Lancaster,' said Jane.

Lady Lancaster took the phone.

'William?' she said.

'Yes, Mother. I'm phoning to tell you that we'll be coming with you to Binfield.'

'We?' she asked.

'Myself and Jenny. Just the two of us. We're packing now. Can you come to pick us up in Stepney when you're ready?'

'I'll be with you at your lodgings in an hour or so. I just have some final things to sort out and settle up the bill here at the Savoy.'

She hung up and looked at Jane.

'William and his fiancée will be coming with us to Binfield,' she told her. 'So, you'll ride in the front of the car next to James.'

'Very good, milady,' said Jane.

'Is all the packing finished?'

'Almost, milady.'

'Well hurry up and get it completed. I don't want to stay in London any longer than I have to. The sooner we get home to safety, the better.'

Coburg and Rosa relaxed on the sofa in the Eaton Square flat, each savouring a whiskey to celebrate a successful afternoon: Rosa's performance at the tea rooms to great acclaim from the enthusiastic audience, and saving Magnus's life from the murderous intent of the Winships.

'I still disapprove,' Coburg told her. 'You could have been killed.'

'As Magnus said, we hadn't anticipated they'd try anything as drastic as killing anyone. And, as it was, we handled it.' She patted the plaster cast on her arm. 'If anything, it let me know that my arm is fine. Which I'm sure Mr Bailey will confirm when he examines it.' She sipped at her whiskey, then asked: 'Are you sure everything's all right?'

'What do you mean?'

'I get the feeling there's something worrying you. Apart from the attempt on Magnus.'

Coburg hesitated, then sighed and said: 'Okay. Yes, there is.'

'I can always tell,' said Rosa. 'You may think you're being enigmatic and strong and silent, but I know when something's troubling you. So, out with it.'

'I was going to tell you anyway,' said Coburg. 'It was just a question of when.' He hesitated, then said ruefully: 'I need to tell you why the superintendent called me in.'

'So, it wasn't about some high-profile politician complaining about you?'

'No. It was a complaint, but not about that. I didn't want to tell you before because I thought it might put you off, just as you were about to perform.'

'Like I said, I had a hunch there was something,' said Rosa. 'What is it?'

'An allegation of corruption. Bribes.'

'Bribes?' said Rosa, derisively. 'You?'

'The allegations aren't true,' said Coburg. 'But there's a chance they might come to a tribunal. If that happens, everyone will know about it, so you need to know to be prepared.'

She went to him and put her arms around him.

'It's rubbish,' she said. 'Whatever it is, it's rubbish.'

'Yes, it is, but unfortunately, due to the generosity of Mr D'Oyly Carte at the Savoy, there's evidence that might be interpreted in an adverse way.' And he told her about the cheque that hadn't been paid in by the Savoy.

'But you've told them to pay it in now.'

'Yes I have. Just as I wanted them to pay it in when I wrote it.'

'So everything's all right then.'

'No, because if someone compares the date it was actually paid in, it will be shown to be after Superintendent Allison spoke to me about it. And there's another thing.' And he told her about the allegation that he'd released William Lancaster after Lady Lancaster had offered him her late husband's flat. 'A bribe,' he said.

'Nonsense,' she said. 'You released him because the evidence showed he didn't kill his father.'

'Yes,' said Coburg. 'And that charge will be straightforward to answer.' Then, awkwardly, he added: 'Unfortunately, that's not the same with the other allegation.'

'Which is?'

'That I had an inappropriate relationship with Lady Lancaster.'

Rosa stared at him. 'They mean, sex?'

'I didn't,' said Coburg firmly. 'Never! I have no interest in the woman that way. Or any other woman. There's only one woman for me and that's you.' He sighed. 'Unfortunately, it's just gossip and innuendo, and although it's based on absolutely nothing, that's the hardest kind of allegation to disprove. Especially as I challenged Allison to ask the lady herself, that she'd absolutely deny there had ever been anything between us. I am not interested in her.'

'No, but she is in you,' said Rosa wryly.

Coburg looked at her, puzzled.

'What do you mean?'

'Honey, that day when we met her at the Savoy, I saw the way she looked at you. Believe me, she had the hots for you.'

'Never!' denied Coburg.

'Edgar, you may be a whizz at reading criminals, but you've missed it when it comes to women. You're hot and a hunk. You're every woman's dream of what a man should be. Honest. True. Affectionate. Clever. Transparent. Also, good-looking and a great lover. Gossip comes from somewhere. She may deny it if asked, but her eyes said it when we met. And if anyone else close to her has noticed that . . .'

Coburg shook his head. 'No, this is wrong!' he protested.

'It is wrong,' agreed Rosa. 'And I believe you that nothing happened with her. But if things had been different and you and I weren't a couple and she'd come on to you . . .'

'I still wouldn't have done anything about it,' said Coburg. 'It would have prejudiced the investigation.'

'See what I mean?' said Rosa. 'Honest and true. That's you. How did all this start? Where did the complaint come from?'

'The superintendent wouldn't tell me, but I'm fairly sure it's come from Inspector Lomax.'

'The one you took over from after the first murder at the Savoy?'

'That's right. He's always been jealous of me, for some reason. My gut feeling is that he's done this to try to get at me.'

She shook her head and hugged him close.

'He's going to be disappointed. It won't happen. You want to know why?'

Coburg nodded.

'Because the superintendent has said he doesn't want to raise the matter with Lady Lancaster. So there'll be no evidence on that one. And the others can be answered, you said so yourself.'

'Yes, but they might still have to hold an inquiry, and if that happens I'll be suspended while they do it.'

'If that happens then we'll just go away on holiday until it's over and they come to the right conclusion.' She kissed him. 'And now, let's take this to bed.' She kissed him again and grinned. 'It's not only Lady Lancaster who's got the hots for you.'

Tom Huxton stood on the pavement and watched as the chauffeur put Jenny and William's bags in the boot of the Rolls Royce, then strode to the front of the car and got behind the steering wheel. Lady Lancaster's maid was in the passenger seat next to him, with Lady Lancaster sitting primly to attention in the back.

Jenny went to her father and put her arms around him.

'I'm sorry you aren't coming with us, Dad,' she said.

'I couldn't,' said Huxton. 'I just wouldn't feel right there.'

'But you could visit,' suggested Jenny. 'It'd be nice for you to see where I'm living.'

'Staying,' Huxton corrected her firmly. 'You live here. This is just a break you're taking to keep out of reach of the bombing.'

'Of course,' said Jenny.

'We have to go!' called Lady Lancaster from the rear of

344

the car. 'It'll be dusk soon and we need to be away from London before the bombing starts.'

'We're coming!' William called.

Jenny hugged her father again and kissed him.

'I'll be thinking of you, Dad,' she said.

'And I'll be thinking of you,' said Huxton. 'Every day.'

Jenny released him and climbed into the rear of the car and sat next to Lady Lancaster. William held out his hand to Huxton.

'I promise I'll take care of her, Mr Huxton,' he said.

'Make sure you do,' said Huxton gruffly.

He shook William's hand and watched him climb into the car and take his seat opposite Jenny, then pull the door shut.

The engine started and the car moved off. Huxton saw Jenny waving to him, and he waved back. He watched the car all the way until it reached the end of the street and then turned out of sight.

Huxton took a deep breath, then went indoors, shut the door and went into the kitchen. He sat at the wooden table and then, suddenly overcome with the grief of seeing his only daughter, who he'd cared for ever since she was born, being driven off out of his life, he put his head down on the table and wept.

CHAPTER FORTY

Monday 23rd September

Having told Rosa the real reason Allison had wanted to see him, Coburg felt better about telling Lampson.

His sergeant was already in the office when Coburg arrived, and once he'd hung up his coat, Coburg settled himself behind his desk and began to unburden himself.

'Ted, I've got to prepare you over something, in case you're called.'

'Called?' asked Lampson. 'About what?'

'A complaint of improper conduct has been made about me. I'm telling you in case you're summoned to give evidence if it comes to a tribunal of investigation.'

'A tribunal?' said Lampson, shocked. 'Whatever it is, it won't come to that, surely.'

'It may well happen, according to Superintendent Allison. He summoned me in yesterday to inform me. I think he's waiting while he decides what to do next. I don't think he wants to suspend me while this murder investigation's going on, but if the commissioner insists, he won't have any choice in the matter.'

'Who's made the complaint?'

'The superintendent didn't tell me. Apparently, at this stage, I'm not allowed to be informed.'

'So what is someone actually alleging?'

'Three things. One, that I accepted a free room at the Savoy in return for favours I'd done them. In other words, accepting a bribe. Second, that I released William Lancaster from custody in return for Lady Lancaster offering me her late husband's flat rent-free.'

'But your flat had been bombed. You had nowhere to stay.'

'True, but that's no excuse for taking bribes and presents. Apparently, the fact that I turned down the offer of the flat from Lady Lancaster isn't defence enough. Plus, the situation's made worse for me because although I paid for my room at the Savoy, the hotel didn't cash my cheque. The manager, Mr Tillesley, with the best of intentions, had apparently told the cashier to make the room free of charge to me and have kept my cheque, intending to return it to me. And even though I've told them to pay it in now, according to Superintendent Allison the fact it was paid in only after he spoke to me only goes to back up the claim of receiving expensive gifts.'

'It's nonsense, guv!' exploded Lampson. 'When they look into it, and especially when they hear from Lady Lancaster that you turned down the flat, and that we only released her son because we knew he couldn't have killed his father, they'll throw it out.'

'That's what I'd like to think, but it's doubtful if they'll actually speak to Lady Lancaster about it. At least, at this stage.'

'Why?'

Coburg hesitated, then said awkwardly: 'Because the other allegation is that Lady Lancaster and I have had a sexual relationship.'

'Rubbish!'

'Yes, it is. But someone found out that when I talked to Lady Lancaster I did it in her suite at the Savoy. That only happened because she requested it for privacy, but as no one else was in the suite at the time – she'd sent her maid away – someone has put that interpretation on it. And, according to the superintendent, because it's a delicate situation they feel they can't raise with the lady. Not at this stage, although if it came to a tribunal, they'd have to involve her. But at the moment, I get the impression they feel there's enough to suspend me pending a full investigation. And as the identity of the person making the complaint is at the moment being kept secret from me, I can't see what I can do to disprove the allegations.'

'It's that bastard Lomax who's behind this!' said Lampson angrily. 'He's determined to get his own back on you for you taking over the Savoy case.'

'I agree, but where did he get his information from?' asked Coburg. 'The fact that Lady Lancaster offered me her late husband's flat, and that the Savoy offered us our room free – even though I paid for it – can only have come from someone who heard our conversations at the Savoy.' He gave a heavy sigh, then said: 'Oh, and yesterday Lord and Lady Winship tried to kill my brother, Magnus. They called on him in his suite at the Savoy and Lord Winship grabbed him and held him, while Lady Winship pulled out a knife and was going to stab him in the back, when Rosa appeared from the bathroom where she was hiding and knocked her unconscious. She then knocked Lord Winship out as well, with her plaster cast.'

Lampson stared at him, open-mouthed. 'You're making this up!' he said.

'I wish I was,' said Coburg. He then proceeded to tell Lampson the background, the meetings of pro-Hitler people that Magnus had infiltrated, and to which Rosa had been invited; and that Magnus and Rosa had decided to work together to expose whatever treason was going on.

Lampson shook his head. 'Bloody hell, guv, Sundays are supposed to be a day of rest. It sounds like your day off was a nightmare.' Then he added thoughtfully: 'You say Lord Winship grabbed your brother and Lady Winship was going to stab him in the back.'

'Yes,' said Coburg. 'But, like I said, luckily for Magnus, Rosa stepped in.'

'My point is, guv, we said it's most likely that two people killed Daisy Scott using that exact same method.'

'Yes, my brother made the same point,' said Coburg.

'It makes sense. We know that Lord Winship was having it off with Daisy. Say she was blackmailing him, telling him he was the father of her baby.'

'I agree it's a possible motive for them murdering her, but I'm more convinced the murder of Daisy Scott is wrapped up with the murder of Vera Bates and the disappearance of

Ella Kemble. And I don't see the Winships as banging Vera on the head and pushing her down the stairs.'

'Why not? They're capable of it.'

'Motive,' said Coburg. 'Their motive for the attempt on Magnus was to stop him implicating them in a treasonous plot which could have led to them being hanged. I agree they had a motive for wanting Daisy dead, and they could have carried it out the way they were going to kill Magnus. But where do Vera and Ella fit into that scenario?'

'They wanted to shut them both up because they knew too much,' said Lampson.

'But they didn't shut Ella Kemble up because on Friday afternoon she was at Ascot,' said Coburg. Suddenly he struck himself on the forehead with his fist and let out an oath. Lampson looked at him in surprise. 'Guv?' he asked.

'I am such an idiot!' exclaimed Coburg. 'The answer's been staring me in the face!'

'What answer?'

'Ella Kemble and her obsession with Giovanni Piranesi. It's her!'

'What, the killer?'

'She was on duty the night that Lancaster was killed. She was at the Savoy when Daisy Scott was murdered. Two people did it, we said.'

'Ella Kemble and Vera Bates?'

'Exactly,' nodded Coburg. 'And she killed Vera because Vera was the weak link and liable to blab.'

'It's a bit of a leap of faith, guv,' said Lampson doubtfully.

'It's the only one that fits with what we know,' said Coburg.

'And now she's done a runner,' said Lampson ruefully.

'But not very far. Ascot. That's where we'll find her.'

'Ascot?'

'It's about her obsession with Giovanni. She keeps going back to Ascot in the hope he'll accept her declarations of love and tell her they'll be together. My guess is she'll have got herself a job somewhere there. Most likely as a maid at one of the hotels. There are plenty of hotels in Ascot because of the racecourse.' He got up. 'Right, I'm going to sort out an arrest warrant. Can you organise getting copies of the photograph we have of her. Then we'll head for Ascot and get the local police to trawl round the hotels with them.'

'Right, guv,' said Lampson. 'It might take me a while. You know what the copying department is like.'

'As soon as you can,' said Coburg.

Lampson waited until he was sure that Coburg had really gone, then he pulled out his notebook and flicked back through the notes he'd made, checking names. Then he took the file with the notes made by Inspector Lomax's team and checked them.

Yes, he said to himself with grim satisfaction. It was there.

Lampson found Effie Potteridge in the sluice at the Savoy, putting sheets and pillowcases in the big washing machines.

'Miss Potteridge,' he said. 'Sergeant Lampson. Remember we talked the other day.'

'Yes,' she said, her face showing both curiosity and a certain wariness.

'I've got a couple more questions I'm hoping you can help me with,' he said.

'I told you everything I know about Daisy, honest,' said Effie.

'I'm sure you did,' said Lampson. 'But it's about another matter. It seems that someone at the Savoy has been passing on information about DCI Coburg. Like the fact that Lady Lancaster offered him her late husband's flat after his own flat was bombed out. And that he was offered a room here at the Savoy on the house.'

Immediately, he noticed a look of fear in her eyes. Gently, he said: 'Joe Potteridge, the sergeant at the Strand police station, is a relative of yours, isn't he.'

'I didn't mean anything by it,' she defended herself, but with an agitation that showed she knew she was in trouble. 'He just asked me things, and I told him.'

'About Lady Lancaster offering DCI Coburg her late husband's flat.'

'He wanted to know!' exclaimed Effie. 'He kept pushing me about things.'

'Did you tell him that DCI Coburg and Lady Lancaster were having a relationship?' he asked.

'No!' she burst out, frightened. 'Absolutely not! That was Jane, her ladyship's personal maid.'

'You mean she told him?'

Effie hesitated, her mouth open and shutting, before finally she said: 'She told me and I told Joe. But I don't think they did. It was Jane who started it. I didn't want any part of it, even when Joe offered me money to get proof.'

'What sort of proof?'

'Anything. Soiled underwear.' She hesitated. 'He said I could make it up and it'd be all right, but I didn't. I didn't want anything to do with it.'

'So why was Joe going to pay you for all this? What was in it for him?'

'Not him . . . his boss. Joe said his boss was ready to pay good money to stitch Mr Coburg up. But I didn't want anything to do with it, so I didn't.'

Clutching the large buff envelope with the copies of the photograph of Ella Kemble, Lampson walked back into Scotland Yard, alert for any sign of DCI Coburg. There was no sign of him. Just in case the chief inspector might be with the superintendent, Lampson went to the reception desk and used their phone and got put through to Allison's office.

'Allison,' said the superintendent's crisp voice.

'It's DS Lampson, sir. Can I come and see you, sir? On a matter of great urgency.'

'What is this matter?' asked Allison.

'I need to tell you in the privacy of your office, sir. But it is extremely urgent.'

'Very well. I'll see you in my office.'

A few minutes later, Lampson was standing to attention facing the superintendent, who regarded him with interrogative wariness.

'You said it was extremely urgent,' he said.

'Yes, sir. It concerns the allegations being made against DCI Coburg.'

Allison bridled.

'I am not allowed to discuss the matter,' he said. 'How did you come to even know about it?'

'Internal gossip, sir.'

'Who from?'

'The Strand police station. And I've come with the evidence to prove it's a fabrication. And a deliberate one at that, instigated by Inspector Lomax.'

Allison glared at him. 'Be careful what you say, Sergeant. You're stepping over the line.'

'I am being careful, sir, but I feel it wrong for an honourable and honest man like DCI Coburg to be unjustly accused, and for false evidence to be deliberately manufactured, with bribes being offered to blacken his name.'

'Bribes?' echoed Allison, disturbed.

'Yes, sir. If I didn't speak up and the case against him went ahead, it would not only wrongly ruin his career, it would make a laughing stock of the force when the truth came out and raise serious doubts about the integrity of some senior officers.'

Lampson then told the superintendent what he'd learned.

'You're sure of this?' asked Allison.

'I am, sir. I got it all from Effie Potteridge, one of the maids at the Savoy who's a cousin of Joe Potteridge, Inspector Lomax's DS. Money was definitely offered for her to falsify evidence suggesting an improper relationship between the DCI and Lady Lancaster, even though no such relationship existed. I can bring Effie Potteridge in for you to talk to.'

'No, that's all right, Sergeant.' Allison lapsed into a thoughtful silence before saying: 'This is revenge for him having been taken off the Savoy case, I presume.'

'That's the way it looks to me, sir.'

'Very well.' Allison gave an unhappy sigh. 'When you return to your office, would you ask DCI Coburg to come and see me.'

Coburg's phone rang and he picked it up. 'DCI Coburg.'

'Chief Inspector Coburg, it's Charles Tillesley at the Savoy.'

'Yes, Mr Tillesley. What can I do for you?'

'I've got some bad news, I'm afraid. News I thought you ought to be made aware of.'

'News about what?'

'I'm afraid it's about Lady Lancaster and her son. They were both killed last night, along with a young lady, her ladyship's chauffeur and her maid.'

'Killed? How?'

'They left the Savoy yesterday as it was beginning to get dark. They were returning to the family home in Berkshire. As their car was leaving the outskirts of London, it was hit by a bomb. The air raid had just begun. I had suggested to Lady Lancaster that as it was getting late, she and her son stayed another night at the Savoy and departed this morning, but she was insistent. She wanted to get home.'

'A bomb, you say.'

'A direct hit. The local police found some papers with the Savoy-headed notepaper among the wreckage. There were the remains of five bodies in the car. It's so tragic. Lady Lancaster was so delighted. She told me her son would be moving back into the family home, along with his fiancée. I believe her name was Jenny.'

'You're sure it's them?'

'Sadly, yes. The police found the car's number plate. It was the same vehicle that was parked here on Saturday night. A Rolls Royce belonging to the Lancaster family. I thought you ought to know.'

'Indeed, Mr Tillesley. Thank you for letting me know.'

'After all that family had been through, with the Earl being killed, it seemed so tragically ironic.'

'It does indeed. Thank you again for informing me.'

'Have there been any developments on the investigation? The deaths of the Earl and the maid? Mr D'Oyly Carte was enquiring.'

'We're examining new evidence that's emerged,' said Coburg. 'I promise you I'll let you know as soon as we have any firm information.'

He hung up and stared at the phone. Lady Lancaster, William and Jenny wiped out, just as they were getting together as a family again.

The door opened and Lampson appeared with the large buff envelope.

'Those photos of Ella Kemble, sir,' he said. 'Sorry it took me so long, but you know what the photography department can be like.'

'I do indeed, sergeant,' said Coburg sympathetically.

'Oh, and Superintendent Allison asked if you would go and see him.'

Resignedly, Coburg got to his feet. 'I will indeed. I'm guessing this is it.'

'It may not be, sir,' said Lampson hopefully.

He was talking to an empty office. DCI Coburg had left the room.

CHAPTER FORTY-ONE

Once again, Lampson drove as they headed for Ascot.

'Don't think I'm not grateful, Ted, about you going to see the superintendent,' said Coburg, 'but you could have got yourself into serious trouble.'

'I knew it was a fit-up, guv,' said Lampson. 'And once I saw the name of that maid, I was sure she was the one. Potteridge isn't exactly a common name. And, just in case, I asked someone at the Savoy about her, and if she had a relative at Strand police station. And once they said she did, a detective sergeant, I knew what was going on. What will happen to him? And to Lomax?'

'Very little, I suspect,' said Coburg. 'Especially now Lady Lancaster's dead, no one will want to stir up a non-existent scandal. And it won't do the reputation of the police any good to publicise what Lomax and Potteridge were up to, especially as they'll both deny it.'

'Ironic, ennit,' said Lampson. 'Lady Lancaster and William being reunited, and him off to start a new life with Jenny Huxton, and bang – wiped out.' He gave a shudder. 'That could've been Terry. It could've been you and your missus if you hadn't decided to go out on the day they bombed your flats.'

'Sadly, it's all about luck when it comes to bombs falling. They come down from the sky and fall wherever. You've got much chance of being killed somewhere like London, or Liverpool or Birmingham, but you can also get killed on a country road if the air crew decide to get rid of their load so they can head home.'

Coburg had telephoned ahead to Ascot central police station, so they were welcomed on their arrival by Detective Chief Inspector Newsome. Newsome was small and clean-shaven, with the straight back and bearing that suggested a former military man. The fact that he had only one arm, the empty left sleeve of his jacket being pinned up adding to this conclusion.

'The result of the first lot,' he confirmed as he saw Coburg notice his pinned-up sleeve. 'I understand you were badly wounded during that as well, Chief Inspector.'

'I was,' said Coburg. 'I lost a lung.'

'My surgeon told me we can all get by with one of most things: arms, legs, lungs, kidneys, testicles,' said Newsome wryly.

'Mine said the same to me,' smiled Coburg ruefully. 'Either it's standard patter, or we both had the same man.'

'Your message said you were looking for a woman named Ella Kemble.'

Coburg took one of the photographs from the large envelope and handed it to Newsome. 'This is her. She's wanted for questioning over three murders in London, two stabbings and one woman beaten over the head.'

'She sounds dangerous,' said Newsome. 'What makes you think she's in Ascot?'

'She's obsessed with one of the Italian internees at the camp here. And she was here last Friday afternoon, so I'm guessing she's still here somewhere. She was working as a maid at the Savoy hotel until last Wednesday. It's possible that she may have got a job at one of the hotels here in Ascot.'

'I'll circulate these pictures among the beat officers. One of them might have seen her. I'll get them to take them round to all the hotels and large B&Bs,' said Newsome, holding out his hand for the envelope, which Coburg handed to him.

'Thanks,' said Coburg. 'Warn your officers, if they do encounter her, she might be dangerous. I believe she's unstable, so they're to take care.' He took two of the photographs back from Newsome. 'We'll also go round ourselves. Which is the best hotel here in Ascot? I'm thinking that after working at the Savoy, she'll aim for expensive, but I could be wrong.'

'The Royal,' said Newsome. 'It's in the High Street. You can't miss it, it's got a very ornate facade.'

'Thanks,' said Coburg. 'In the meantime, if any of your officers discover where she is, can I suggest they keep an eye on her but don't attempt to bring her in on their own. As I've said, I believe she's dangerous.'

PC George Wilkes frowned as he studied the photograph of Ella Kemble. 'I've seen her,' he said.

'When?' asked the desk sergeant, Sergeant Sims, who'd just handed him the photo.

'Yesterday. I took my girlfriend to Walters Hotel for Sunday lunch, and she was serving.'

'You sure it was her?'

'Pretty sure,' said Wilkes. He grinned. 'Eh, that'd be a bit of a coup, bringing in a murderer.'

Sergeant Sims shook his head. 'The orders are to proceed with caution. They say she's dangerous.'

Wilkes scoffed. 'A woman like that? Rubbish! I'll take Jerry Bean with me. What can she do against two of us?'

'They say she's stabbed two people and bashed another woman over the head.'

Wilkes gave a derisory laugh again. 'I'm in the Home Guard, military trained, and Jerry's a Berkshire boxing champion. Are you telling me the two of us can't overpower her if she gets difficult?'

'I'm telling you what the DCI said, and he was just passing that on from the two Scotland Yard blokes who are here.'

'Exactly, Scotland Yard,' said Wilkes scornfully. 'They think we're all yokels out here, with straw in our hair.'

Wilkes found Bean and they made for Walters Hotel and asked the woman at the reception desk for Ella Kemble.

'The new woman?' said the receptionist.

'If her name's Ella Kemble and she looks like this,' said Wilkes, and he produced the photo of Ella and showed it to her.

'That's her,' she said. 'She's in the kitchen at the moment. Shall I send for her?'

'No, that's all right,' said Wilkes. 'We'll find her.'

Ella Kemble was in the kitchen, chopping up carrots and parsnips when the two constables walked in. The cook, a large plump man, looked at them, affronted by this unannounced arrival.

'What's all this?' he demanded.

'We just want a word with your assistant,' said Wilkes.

He walked over to her and she stopped chopping the vegetables and looked at him warily.

'Ella Kemble?' said Wilkes. 'I'm going to have to ask you to come with us.'

'Why?' asked Ella.

'We believe you can help us in our enquiries into three deaths in London. Two senior officers from London have come to take you with them.' He took a pair of handcuffs from his belt. 'I must ask you to hold your hands out in front of you . . .'

He never finished the sentence. Suddenly Ella lashed out with the knife, the blade catching him on the side of the neck, and blood spurted out in a great gush. Wilkes gave a dreadful gurgling sound and then collapsed to the floor, writhing, his legs kicking as he held his hand to his neck in a desperate and futile attempt to stop the blood pouring out.

The cook stared in horror at this, and then bolted for the back double doors, rushing outside and pulling the doors shut behind him. He picked up a broom and rammed the shaft through the curved metal doors handles, preventing the doors being opened.

Inside the kitchen, PC Bean stared at the writhing body of PC Wilkes and the ferocious face of Ella Kemble as she advanced towards him, the bloodstained knife held menacingly in front of her.

Bean ran for the door, rushing out into the restaurant and pulling the door shut as he screamed: 'Help! Help!'

He felt the door crash against him as Ella threw herself at it and he managed to lean against it to stop it opening. As he turned to face the stunned guests in the restaurant, he shouted: 'Drag that big table over here!'

Three of the guests followed his frantic orders, bringing the heavy table, and he pushed it into place across the door with their help. He then told them to bring another to stack against the first table to hold it in place as, inside the kitchen, Ella threw herself at the door.

'Phone the police,' ordered Bean. '999. Tell them an officer has been killed and the woman who did it is trapped here, but I don't know how long we can keep her there.'

Coburg and Lampson left the Wellington Arms.

'Another dead end,' groaned Lampson. 'Maybe she's not in Ascot after all?'

'She is,' said Coburg. 'I can feel it. She wants to be where Giovanni Piranesi is.'

They turned a corner and immediately became aware that something was happening outside the Walters Hotel further along the street. A large crowd had gathered on the pavement in front of the hotel and six uniformed police officers were doing their best to hold them back and keep them calm.

Coburg and Lampson hurried forward and pushed their way through the crowd, only to be stopped by a constable. 'No entry,' he said firmly, holding up his hand.

'DCI Coburg!' exclaimed a relieved voice. The next moment DCI Newsome was with them. 'Let them through, Constable,' he barked, and the bewildered constable stepped aside and Coburg and Lampson followed the chief inspector towards the entrance to the hotel.

'I'd sent out constables to try and find you,' he said. 'Your suspect has barricaded herself in the kitchen of the Walters. Or, more correctly, she was locked in after she stabbed to death one of the two constables who went to bring her in. The other constable managed to get away and pushed some heavy tables across the door between the kitchen and the restaurant. There is a rear door, but the cook managed to escape that way and secured that door by means of a broom through the door handles. I've got men in the back courtyard guarding it.'

By now they were in the restaurant, where about a dozen uniformed officers were watching the door to the kitchen.

'The problem now is Miss Kemble has threatened to blow the place up if we don't let her go. She says she'll turn the gas on and wait until there's enough gas in the kitchen and then light a match. Is she capable of that, do you think? Even though it will mean her own death.'

'I'm afraid she's capable of anything,' said Coburg grimly. 'Killing your officer has signed her death warrant. She knows she'll hang for it.'

'Then what can we do? If we try to burst in and get hold

of her she's likely to kill more of my men. But we can't let her go.'

'No, we can't,' said Coburg.

He stepped forward towards the tables that barricaded the door to the kitchen. It had a small window in it.

'Ella Kemble!' he called. 'This is DCI Coburg from Scotland Yard. Come to the window and we can talk.'

There was a pause, then the face of Ella Kemble appeared at the window.

'Let me go!' she shouted. She held up a bloodied knife in one hand and a box of matches in the other hand and pressed them against the glass. 'Let me go or we all die!'

'Put down the knife and matches and I'll take you to see Giovanni,' said Coburg.

It was the only card he could play: her obsession with Giovanni Piranesi. The reason for the murders. The reason she was here.

There was a silence, then Ella said: 'You're lying!'

'No, I'm serious. That's why you're here in Ascot.'

'He won't see me.'

'He will. I'll make sure he does. I'm a detective chief inspector from Scotland Yard. I have the power to order it.'

'I don't believe you. As soon as I put down the knife and matches, you'll take me in.'

'I promise I won't.'

He couldn't take Ella to the internment camp while she still had the knife, but because she didn't trust him to take her to Giovanni, she wouldn't put it down. There was only one way out of this impasse.

'I'll go to the internment camp and bring Giovanni here,'

he said. 'You can look through the window in the door and see him come in with me. When you see him, I want you to put the knife and matches down and come out with your hands up.'

There was a longer pause, then she said: 'I'll only do it if I see Giovanni.'

'It'll take me a while to get him. I have to sign release forms for him. But I'll be back.'

Coburg turned to DCI Newsome. 'If I can take a couple of your constables, I'll go to the internment camp and fetch Giovanni. My sergeant will stay here with you.'

'Say he refuses to come?' asked Newsome.

'He'll come, either willingly or in chains,' said Coburg determinedly. Then he asked: 'Do you have a gun?'

Newsome nodded and patted his jacket pocket. 'I signed it out, but I'd rather not use it. Especially if she's turned the gas on in there.'

'There's no scent of gas yet,' said Coburg. 'If it comes to it, you might need to shoot her. Would you be able to hit her through that window?'

Newsome looked doubtful. 'I'm not that good a shot,' he said. 'We'd need to get her out from behind the door. And with no fear of gas.'

'I'll see what I can do,' said Coburg.

CHAPTER FORTY-TWO

At the internment camp, Coburg filled in John Whitehall on the situation, and Whitehall immediately sent two guards to bring Piranesi to his office. When Piranesi arrived, he looked at Coburg and the two constables warily.

'What is going on?' he demanded suspiciously.

'Mr Piranesi, I need you to come with me.'

'Where?'

'Ella Kemble has locked herself in the kitchen at the Walters Hotel in the town.'

Piranesi shook his head. 'That is nothing to do with me. She can stay there.'

'It is to do with you,' said Coburg. 'In fact, it's all about you. She's just killed a policeman. Before that she killed three other people: the Earl of Lancaster, Daisy Scott and a cleaner called Vera Bates. And all because of what she feels for you. We have to get her out of that kitchen without her killing anyone else, and the only way to do that is if she sees you.'

Piranesi shook his head.

'If what you say is true, she is mad. Next, she will kill me.'

'She won't kill you. I'll have police officers there to protect you. One of them will be armed with a gun. If she attempts anything, he'll shoot her if he has to. But I hope it won't come to that. All you have to do is walk with me into the restaurant. She'll see you and she'll put down the knife she's holding, and then she'll walk out of the kitchen and we'll arrest her.'

'I don't want to talk to her.'

'You don't have to. All you have to do is be there and let her see you.'

'She killed my Maria,' said Piranesi vengefully.

'And she killed the man who caused her to do it,' said Coburg. 'We can bring this to an end now.' As Piranesi hesitated, Coburg added: 'If you refuse, I shall take you there by force if necessary. Bound and gagged. I'm not going to have any more people killed by her.'

Piranesi hesitated again, then nodded. 'I come with you.'

Coburg walked into the restaurant, Piranesi beside him, the two constables flanking them.

'Any developments?' he asked Newsome.

The chief inspector shook his head. 'Everything seems to be quiet. I assume she's waiting to see if you turn up.'

Coburg took Piranesi by the elbow and led him to

the centre of the restaurant, in sight of the door but at a safe distance from it.

'Ella Kemble!' he shouted.

Ella's face appeared in the small window in the door to the kitchen. As soon as her eyes caught sight of Piranesi she began to push at the door, but the tables held firm.

'Stand back from the door!' shouted Coburg.

Ella's face vanished as she stepped back. Coburg gestured for the police officers to pull the tables to one side, freeing the door.

'Push the door open and throw the knife and matches out onto the floor!' he called. 'Then put your hands above your head and step out of the kitchen. Slowly!'

The door opened slightly and the knife and matches were tossed out, landing on the restaurant floor. Then Ella pushed the door open with her knee and edged forward, her hands held high above her head. Once she was out, Coburg shouted: 'Stop there! Stand still!'

She stopped and tears began to roll down her cheeks and she said, her voice beseeching: 'Giovanni! I love you! I did it for you! Everything!'

Piranesi stood looking at her, then he spat on the floor and sneered: 'Get away from me, bitch!'

'No!' screamed Ella, and began to run towards him, her arms outstretched. Immediately police officers ran to intercept her, rugby tackling her to the floor. Still sobbing, she began to kick and punch and claw at them, but gradually they managed to subdue her, rolling her onto her face and forcing a pair of handcuffs on to her wrists.

Coburg pulled a tablecloth from one of the tables and threw it to the officers. 'Bind her ankles with that,' he said. 'And tightly.'

Coburg and Lampson sat side by side at the table in the interview room. Opposite them, Ella Kemble sat on a heavy wooden chair, each wrist handcuffed to the arms of the chair. Her ankles were also shackled. Behind her stood two WPCs, along with two muscular male officers. Coburg was taking no chances.

'Ella Kemble, you are charged with the murders of the Earl of Lancaster, Daisy Scott, Vera Bates and Police Constable George Wilkes. You are not obliged to say anything, but anything you do say will be noted down and may be used in evidence against you.' He looked at her, his tone becoming less formal, gentler, as he said: 'So, would you like to tell us what happened, and why?'

Ella said nothing but fixed Coburg with a look of hate so intense that he rembered what Dolly Wharton had said about the venomous way she'd looked at Daisy Scott: 'There was a look on Ella's face that could strip your skin off.' She was giving him that same look now.

'Very well,' said Coburg. 'Then I'll tell you what we believe happened and you can correct me if I get anything wrong. First, the Earl of Lancaster. He raped Maria, Giovanni's fiancée, but you backed up the Earl's claim that Maria had consensual sex with him to make Giovanni doubt her. After Maria killed herself because of what had happened, Giovanni threatened the Earl. The Earl acted swiftly and had Giovanni moved to an internment camp.

'You were angry at this. More than angry, you were beside yourself with fury because the man you loved had been taken away from you and locked up, for which you blamed the Earl. You were determined to get Giovanni free, but first you took revenge on the Earl by killing him. You were on duty at the Savoy shelter that night.'

He looked at Ella, waiting for a response, but she said nothing, just looked back at him in defiant silence.

'So now we move to Daisy Scott. Daisy knew how you felt about Giovanni, and she tormented you by boasting to you that she'd had sex with him. You knew the sort of reputation she had so it was possible. She may have even added to it by telling you that she was pregnant, and the baby was Giovanni's. It was all a lie.'

At this, for the first time, there was a reaction from her as she stared at him, disturbed, and she opened her mouth as if she was about to say something, but then she clamped it shut again.

'At the same time you'd heard that Harry Pickford had been having sex with Daisy. In fact, I'm fairly sure it only happened between them once, but it gave you what you needed. Harry had told Vera Bates that it had only happened once and he'd never do it again. I think he meant it because Harry Pickford relied on Vera for money. But you told Vera it had happened between them again, and it was still going on. You persuaded her that Daisy had to die. Someone with more sense might not have been so easy to get caught up in your plan, but Vera wasn't the brightest penny in the box. And, frankly, you realised that if you were going to kill Daisy it would need two of you, one to hold her while the other stabbed her. But even then, you had doubts. Say Daisy struggled and got away? When she told people it would put you in the frame for killing the Earl. So, you had to make sure she was unconscious first, or incapacitated in some way. It would still take two of you, one to hold her while the other forced the poison down her throat. The poison you used was the stuff you use to get rid of the excess hair you suffer from. There's a warning on the label saying it's for external application only and is not to be taken internally.

'So, that was it. You and Vera caught Daisy one day when she was in the sluice. I'm guessing you locked the door so you wouldn't be interrupted. One of you held her while the other forced the poison down her throat.

'You then draped her over the edge of one of the sinks and Vera stabbed her in the back with a steak knife. We know this because you're right-handed and Vera was left-handed.

'The problem for you was Vera. You couldn't be sure she wouldn't say anything. As I said, she wasn't the brightest of people and was liable to say something that could give you away. So, you killed her. Went to her lodgings, bashed her over the head and pushed her down the stairs.

'After that, you moved here to Ascot so you could be near to Giovanni, hoping that when he came out you and he would be together.' He shook his head. 'It's never going to happen. You heard what he said. He doesn't want you, and you're going to hang for four murders.' He turned to Lampson. 'Have her remanded

372

into custody,' he said, getting to his feet.

'Yes, sir,' said Lampson. He nodded to the WPCs standing behind Ella. 'Bring her along, constables. But watch out for her feet. She kicks and bites.'

CHAPTER FORTY-THREE

Tuesday 24th September

Coburg got to his feet as Rosa appeared from the cubicles and walked into the outpatients' waiting area of St Thomas's hospital. She grinned and showed him her arm, which was now adorned with a support bandage, replacing the plaster cast.

'It's better,' she said.

'But Mr Bailey obviously thinks it's not better enough because he's put a strong bandage on it.'

'He says that's to remind me that I still need to be careful with it.'

'Did you tell him about hitting Lord Winship with it?'

She looked at him, shocked. 'No! Of course not! What sort of idiot do you think I am?' She put her arm through his and led the way towards the hospital exit. 'The main thing is it's an improvement. He said I have very strong bones and that I must have a high calcium count.' She smiled up at him. 'I'm so glad you took time off to come with me today.'

'I owe it to you,' said Coburg. 'I feel I've been neglecting you.'

'You were busy catching a murderer and stopping her killing even more people,' said Rosa. 'That's not being neglectful, that's doing your duty. But won't this get you into trouble, taking time off to take me to the hospital?'

'I think not,' Coburg reassured her. 'Frankly, Superintendent Allison owes me. Sergeant Lampson and I delivered a murderer to him. And he brought me in on my Sunday off to make totally false allegations against me. Which have now been proved false. The fact that Ella Kemble committed the murders shows I was right to think that William Lancaster was innocent. And I got Charles Tillesley at the Savoy to write a letter to the superintendent on Savoy hotel notepaper, which I delivered to him this morning, confirming that I had paid the cheque for our stay, and had been unaware that he and Mr D'Oyly Carte had not cashed it but decided to offer us the room free of charge without our knowledge, and that the situation had now been amended once I had been informed.

'Also, as a result of the murders being solved, Mr D'Oyly Carte, along with various other luminaries, not least the board of the Savoy, have expressed their gratitude to the commissioner.'

'So, you are the favourite son of the Yard again,' beamed Rosa. 'What about the Winships? What's going to happen to them?'

'Now the security services are involved, it's a bit up in the air. Are they treated as potential traitors, like Mosley and his wife, and kept under lock and key? Or will they be charged with attempted murder over the attack on Magnus? My guess is they'll be kept somewhere where they can be squeezed for information. Such as, who else was in the plot with them. The security services will want names, so it'll be a case of the carrot and the stick. Threats of what will happen to them if they don't co-operate, and offers of safe passage and clemency if they do. The aristocrats who are rounded up tend to be treated better than their compatriots lower down the social scale. You can get away with things if you're an aristo.'

'Lady Lancaster didn't get away with anything,' said Rosa sadly.

'Lady Lancaster wasn't guilty of any crime,' pointed out Coburg.

'No, but I guess being who she was, she thought she'd be safe if she made for her country retreat. Dreadful for her and for William Lancaster and his girlfriend.'

'Not to mention her maid and the family chauffeur,' added Coburg.

'Yes, but they were just starting a new life together.' Then she asked: 'Has there been any reaction from your nemesis, Inspector Lomax?'

'Not that I'm aware. My guess is he's gone to ground to sulk and lick his wounds. The fact that Ted Lampson and I brought the real murderer to justice will have upset him no end.'

'Good,' said Rosa. She looked at her watch. 'It's two o'clock. How long do you have before you need to get back to the Yard?'

'This afternoon, as the favourite son, the world is our

oyster. I thought we'd go and look at pianos.'

She put her arm around him and hugged her to him.

'You do say the most wonderful things.' she smiled. Suddenly she stopped and began to rummage in her bag. 'Oh yes, one more thing. This came this morning in the post. It's from Magnus.'

She produced an envelope and handed it to Coburg. He lifted the flap and took out a short note from his brother, along with a piece of card that bore the crest of 10 Downing Street. On the card had been scrawled 'Kipling was right. When I see her I'll tell her myself. She saved us both. W.'

Coburg looked at Rosa. 'High praise indeed, and from the highest. W, of course, is Winston, as in Churchill.'

'But Kipling was right about what?' she asked. 'The only Kipling I've read was The Jungle Book.'

'The female of the species is more deadly than the male,' said Coburg.

Rosa frowned. 'I'm not sure how much of a compliment that is. Attractive, yes. Talented, yes. Bubbly, perhaps. But deadly?'

'Trust me, in Churchill's eyes that's the highest praise he can give,' said Coburg. He gave her back the envelope and she returned it to her bag. 'Now,' he said, 'let's go in search of a piano, my attractive, talented, bubbly and wonderfully deadly wife.'

ACKNOWLEDGEMENTS

As I write this (July 2021) Britain, and the rest of the world, have endured over eighteen months of the Covid pandemic, with the resultant fears and restrictions. This has led to a mass fear of death and disease, resulting in levels of anxiety that in some have reached suicidal levels. To put this in context and to try to help people understand how people in Britain felt during the six years (1939–1945) of World War Two, add in a daily fear of being bombed by thousands of enemy aircraft, fears for the lives of relatives engaged in the war abroad, and with no way of making contact with them (the invention of the mobile phone was many decades away). Add in food shortages and rationing, the nightly blackouts, hospitals struggling to cope (there was no NHS at this time) and remember that this lasted for six years, four times longer than the current Covid crisis. Although this happened decades ago, for some of us, it was in our lifetime. I was born in central London in 1944, during the V2 blitz. In early 1945 my pram, being pushed by my elder sister, was blown up. My sister was aged six at the start of the war. My father was in a reserved occupation, so he volunteered as a fire fighter, nightly fighting the fires that raged through London as the bombs fell throughout the war. I grew up in a bombed-out area after the war because most of the buildings around us had collapsed, the streets destroyed. The area around Bayham Street/Plender Street in Camden Town is now mainly blocks of flats built during the 1950s as a result of the area being flattened by bombing.

For me, this book, and the rest of the hotel series, acknowledges and tries to empathise with what ordinary people experienced during the war. There is a talk of the stress on people's mental health of the last eighteen months of Covid. Read the above again, and this book, and become aware of the impact on people's mental health of living through the war.

JIM ELDRIDGE was born in central London in November 1944, on the same day as one of the deadliest V2 attacks on the city. He left school at sixteen and worked at a variety of jobs, including stoker at a blast furnace, before becoming a teacher. From 1975 to 1985 he taught in mostly disadvantaged areas of Luton. At the same time, he was writing comedy scripts for radio, and then television. As a scriptwriter he has had countless broadcast on television in the UK and internationally, as well as on the radio. Jim has also written over 100 children's books, before concentrating on historical crime fiction for adults.

Jimeldridge.com